D1232997

Also by M.T. Bass

My Brother's Keeper

Crossroads

Lodging

Somethin' for Nothin'

In the Black

By

M.T. Bass

An Electron Alley Publication
Mudcat Falls, U.S.A.

Electron Alley Corporation
14900 Detroit Ave.
Lakewood, OH 44107

Manufactured in the United States of America

Edited by Elizabeth Love (www.bee-edited.com)

ISBN 978-0-9833807-5-7
ISBN 978-0-9833807-1-9 (ebook)

www.MTBass.net

The characters and incidents contained herein are fictional. Any resemblance of persons, living or dead, may, in fact, be a violation of copyright statutes.

For My Dad

"Kids, dogs and airplanes."

"The business of America is business."
~Calvin Coolidge

"Things are more like they are now than they ever were before."
~Dwight D. Eisenhower

"The future will be better tomorrow."
~Dan Quayle

"That depends on what your definition of 'is' is."
~William Jefferson Clinton

In the Black

1965

The Memo

M E M O R A N D U M

January 4, 1965

TO: ALL DEPARTMENT HEADS
FM: Y.T. ERP, SR.

From this time forward, all right-handed people will be left-handed. Left-handed personnel will assume right-handedness.

Ambidextrous persons will be dealt with individually.

Sincerely,

Y.T. ERP, SR., PRESIDENT
ERP INDUSTRIES, INC.

YTE/www

~~~

"Good morning, Mr. Rangely."

"Hi, Dirk."

"Hello, Mr. Rangely."

"Good, er, ah..."

Like those born into the species *Homo politicus,* Dirk Rangely, Vice-President/Marketing, had come into this world with the innate understanding that the "Common Folk"—no matter how repulsive or disgusting they were—needed constant attention and frequent hand-holding, for they formed the true basis for power with a capital 'P'. On their broad and often sweaty shoulders were laid party platforms, legislative initiatives, foreign policies and economic reforms. At Erp Industries, Inc., the "Little Guys" ultimately did the real work that got product built and shipped, triggering the invoices that generated the company's income out of which Dirk Rangely drew his handsome salary and against which he filed his excessive expense reports. This concept of practical/materialistic/exploitive reverence for the "Little Guys" was by now so ingrained into Dirk Rangely that it had become encoded in his DNA molecules to curse future generations of Rangelys like other families were cursed with Huntington's Chorea or Dwarfism.

Dirk Rangely's peculiar genetic trait manifested itself as his tall, trim figure glided effortlessly—Dirk Rangely rarely engaged in any activity actually requiring effort—through the manufacturing plant on his self-appointed mission to greet every person he saw in his quick, New England accent with the phrase: 'Hi-there-how-are-you-today, [insert name here if known]'. He even encouraged the workers to call him by his first name, though many were reluctant to do so, more out of respect for his position than out of respect for Dirk Rangely himself. This canned phrase had evolved during his lifetime into a completely reflexive response to external stimuli, over which he could exercise no control and into which he could inject no feeling. It, too, was undoubtedly DNA encoded, and Dirk brimmed with pride each time he heard the first words out of his children's mouths: "Hi-there-how-are-you-today?"

In the Black

This particular January morning, though, Dirk Rangely seemed to walk through the plant in a daze, mumbling incoherently to himself, "H-the-ho-r-yo-toda…"

He was so curiously oblivious to the friendly, grass-roots hellos he so consciously cultivated that a buzz of whispered conversation followed in his wake like the wind through the dry, summer grass of Kansas prairies. Mort Mortenstein, Vice-President/Finance, noticed that those distant horizons upon which Dirk Rangely usually fixed his steely, Marketing gaze were evidently clouded. Mort Mortenstein clenched hard on his pipe, baring his teeth in a hungry grin.

"So, have you read the latest Memo?" Mort Mortenstein probed cautiously as he met Dirk Rangely halfway down the hall at the drinking fountain. Neither he nor Dirk Rangely noticed the young man bent over the drinking fountain sucking at the loop of cool water.

"Memo??!!" Dirk Rangely blurted out in anguished surprise, betraying the root of his sullen mood. Dirk Rangely had not actually read Y.T. Erp, Sr.'s latest memo, but he had eavesdropped on two people discussing its potential ramifications in the company cafeteria, and had quivered with horror at each of their envisioned scenarios. He carefully surveyed Mort Mortenstein's shorter, pudgier body and the three-piece suit that strained in places to contain it, momentarily awed at this self-inflated accountant's ability to detect another person's open psychological wound and stick his finger directly into it. "Oh, er, sure—of course. You, Mort?"

"I most certainly did," answered Mort Mortenstein earnestly. He pressed his advantage. "Do you think it will help our position in the marketplace?"

"Huh? Who the hell can tell, Mort?" Dirk Rangely said, gingerly passing his hand over the top of his head covered with thick, yet restrainedly curled, salt-and-pepper hair. "I'm beginning to worry about the Old Man and his cryptic memos."

"He works in mysterious ways, to be sure," Mort Mortenstein said, adjusting his ever-present, yet never lit pipe from the right side of his mouth to the left. "But let's not forget his New Year's Memo of 1957. He quite literally saved the company."

"Well, I'm not really *that* worried about the Old Man," hedged Dirk Rangely, suddenly sensing danger. After all, Mort Mortenstein's department was in charge of Payroll with a capital 'P'.

"A stroke of genius to sell size three-sixty O-rings as Hula Hoops after that Navy contract went down the tubes." Mort Mortenstein chuckled around the stem of his pipe, which added sinister overtones to his laugh. "The books never looked so good—as black as spades."

"Did I say worried? Actually, that was a poor choice of words," Dirk Rangely squirmed.

"Then, there was the Memo of 1958." Mort Mortenstein was relentless. He ground his teeth on the stem of his pipe, causing the hairs on the back of Dirk Rangely's neck to rise. "We called it the *Sputnik Memo.* Now, *that* was a memo."

"Of course, maybe the Old Man has been under a lot of pressure lately." Dirk Rangely glanced feverishly up and down the hall for escape from this conversation with Mort Mortenstein. He might have been able to bow out by taking a drink of water, but that idiot was there, apparently trying to drain the Missouri River single-handedly.

In the Black

"And then, the Memo of 1964," Mort Mortenstein intoned softly. He took the pipe from his mouth and pointed the stem directly at Dirk Rangely's heart like a deadly weapon. "I shed a bitter tear. We all did."

"I'll bet lawyers are behind all of this right-hand/left-hand stuff." Tiny beads of sweat began to form on Dirk Rangely's upper lip. "Or it *could* be Engineering."

"Well, Dirk, I'd love to stand here and shoot the breeze all day long with you, but I've got numbers to crunch." Mort Mortenstein stuffed his pipe back into his mouth and smiled savagely, pleased with himself at so unnerving a fellow executive. He walked past Dirk Rangely, giving him a hearty slap on the shoulder. Dirk Rangely thought he heard Mort Mortenstein chuckling to himself as he walked back to his office in Accounting. "And the Memo of 1960—what a sense of humor. What a sense of humor!"

"You know, the Company benefit plan does not cover accidental drownings in a God damned water fountain," Dirk Rangely barked at the youth still hunched over the drinking fountain. When the boy stood up and turned around, Dirk Rangely found himself face-to-face with Y.T. Erp, Jr. It was quickly becoming one of those days. "Christ Almighty—just joking, son—just joking. You know, a joke, eh? So, how about that Mort? What a character, eh? Of course, how much can you say about a man whose favorite Marx brother is Zeppo?"

Y.T., Jr. shrugged his shoulders.

"So, anyway, you're still around, eh?" Dirk Rangely put his arm around Y.T., Jr.'s shoulders and began walking down the hall, pulling the teenager along with him. "Are you down on the shipping dock still?"

"No, sir. I'm working maintenance with the Sugarman," Y.T., Jr. said respectfully, while at the same time eying Dirk Rangely with suspicion.

"Oh yes, that's right. That's right. I recall now, but, hey, shouldn't you be back at old Harry Truman High?"

"I took an early graduation so that I can start college sooner. Classes don't start until the twenty-fifth, so I'm putting in a few more weeks here at work for extra spending money."

"College, eh? Ah, yes." Dirk Rangely's eyes suddenly focused far down the hall at nothing in particular. Y.T., Jr. was amazed at how glassy Dirk Rangely's eyes had become on cue and wondered if this man had ever been allowed to attend any institute of higher education anywhere. "Well, believe me, the days you spend haunting those ivy-covered halls will be the best you'll ever know. So, which university will you be attending?"

"University of California at Berkeley."

Dirk Rangely stopped dead in his tracks, knowing that Y.T., Sr. had been a Harvard Man after which he had been a Navy Man (not Annapolis either?) before he became the Old Man, and wondered what to make of this apparent act of disrespect and rebellion on the part of the younger Erp. Dirk Rangely vaguely recalled news reports a few months back concerning students in California stirring up trouble over something typically inane like Civil Rights or Free Speech. If he wasn't careful, he could get sucked into the middle of an Erp family civil war right there and then. This day had certainly been fraught with danger—first the Memo, then Mort Mortenstein and now this. Dirk Rangely hoped that it was not portentous of the rest of the year to come. Rising to the occasion, he smiled down at Y.T., Jr. and said as sincerely as he could, "Well, I'd love to stand here and shoot the breeze all day long with you, but I've got numbers—I've got a million and one things to do. Remember what I said, college days will be the best days you'll ever have," Dirk Rangely smirked and gave Y.T., Jr. a hearty slap on the shoulder. As he began walking down the hall, he called back to Y.T., Jr., "Good luck to you." And then under his breath he muttered, "You'll need it."

"Good morning, Mr. Rangely," a secretary said as she passed Dirk Rangely in the hall.

"Hi-there-how-are-you-today, Margaret?" Dirk Rangely responded like one of Pavlov's dogs.

Y.T., Jr. watched Dirk Rangely say hello to everyone he passed in exactly the same way. He wondered if Berkeley, California, would be far enough from Kansas City and if January twenty-fifth would come soon enough to get him the hell away from the abundance of phlegm-brains surrounding him before they drove him crazy. Y.T., Jr. turned around and began walking in the direction opposite to the one in which Dirk Rangely had been leading him—in the direction he had been originally going—towards the Engineering Department.

"Damn!" Dirk Rangely exclaimed as he slammed the door to his office shut. "How could I have made such a mistake? How could I have let myself be so cornered—and by all people, cornered by Mort? And *then!* Then, getting ambushed by Little Erp like that!" Dirk Rangely paced furiously and began to soliloquize to the snarling Siberian tiger's head mounted on the wall behind his desk that he had gotten for a song at a church rummage sale to raise money for Christian Missionary work in Africa after bartering the poor priest insensible and embarrassing his wife into a severe case of hives. "What dark hours are these from which we must forge our days? What troubled waters are these we must navigate on our jour—"

"Excuse me, Mr. Rangely," said Jo Ann, Dirk Rangely's secretary, over the intercom into his office.

"Yes—yes, what is it?" Dirk Rangely exclaimed breathlessly, spinning around on his heels to face Jo Ann's voice as if she were actually in the room.

"Arthur Needleman on line three."

"I'm in a God damned meeting as far as Needleman is concerned," Dirk Rangely snapped at the little green box on his desk.

"Yes, sir," the box responded with Jo Ann's voice, then stopped hissing.

"This can't be happening to me—I can't let this happen to me. Am I losing my edge? I can't let this happen," Dirk Rangely muttered to himself. He began pacing his office again like a caged animal. He now ignored the tiger's head as he became absorbed in his favorite worry: that he was losing his 'edge'. Dirk Rangely loved to liken himself to a saber, the cutting edge of Erp Industries, Inc., and to keep himself sharp, he constantly ran himself over the whetstone of his past failures and indiscretions. "Imagine, talking to Mort—*to Mort!* That sniveling bean-counter! And then, on top of that, telling him what I was thinking, not what I wanted him to think that I was thinking. And about the Old Man no less! I can't let this happen. Jesus H. Christ, I'm getting senile like the Old Man. I can't let that happen until *I'm* the Old Man, and then it will be my unalienable right to get senile if I damn well see fit to do so. I will have earned it by then. But a senile Vice-President of Marketing, that won't do—no, that just will not do at all. It wouldn't be tolerated. Hmmm, but what if the Old Man really is getting senile? I might have to act senile to prove to the senile Old Man that I am capable of moving up into the Big Office. But at the same time, I can't really get senile, or I wouldn't be sane enough to run Erp Industries. Of course, if I did get senile accidentally, it would be the perfect excuse to cover anything up. I'll have to stay sharp and develop a sound stratagem for this."

Dirk Rangely began to feel a faint throbbing at his temples. The time arrived for decisive action. He checked his watch, but it was only nine-thirty in the morning, too early to head down to Dante's for some attitude lubrication with the usual 10W40 Tanqueray martinis. Dirk Rangely paced around behind his desk and sat down. He opened the top right-hand drawer to get out a packet of Alka-Seltzers. He broke two tablets in half. He worked up a mouth full of saliva and dissolved the halves one at a time in his mouth. The effervescent action against the roof of his mouth made him feel giddy. When he had finished, Dirk Rangely sat up and surveyed the fine oak grain of his desk top.

"What to do what to do what to do," Dirk Rangely sang to himself softly, feeling much relieved that he had banished a troublesome headache *and* the irksome memory of his conversation with Mort Mortenstein from his mind in one fell swoop. But soon he became distressed when he discovered his finger aimlessly circling a knot in the grain of his desk top. His desk was so neat, while everyone else's was cluttered with reports, recommendations, statistical charts, P & L Statements, Inventory Control Sheets, Production Run Projections, Production Run Summaries, Daily Totals, Weekly Totals, Monthly Totals, Year-to-date Totals, Supply Requisitions, Specifications, Drawings, Bills of Materials, Expense Vouchers, RFIs, RFPs, RFQs, Purchase Orders, Sales Orders, Document Change Notices, Document Documentation Notices, various memoranda, letters and who knows what else.

Anyone could look important and competent sitting at one of those desks, and Dirk Rangely wondered if, perhaps, for effect he should do something about the pathetically neat condition of his own desk top. It might not have been such a good idea to instruct Jo Ann to keep all that kind of—of—of *stuff* out of his office. He wondered what in the world she had done with it all. Maybe it was all crammed into the bottom drawer of that file cabinet out there by her desk that was always locked so that he could never open it up to see what she kept inside. Perhaps if he just asked her politely enough, Jo Ann would let him use some of that *stuff* to good effect whenever he needed a few props to enhance his aura of competence and efficiency—*but no!* Dirk Rangely pounded his desk top with his fist dramatically. He was no paper pusher. He was a top-level corporate strategist. Let all those other paper tigers wrestle with their reports and recommendations and whatevers, he had more important things to do.

"Right, Rudyard?" Dirk Rangely spun around and rhetorically asked the tiger's head on the wall behind him. Dirk Rangely had occasional bouts with alliteration that Alka-Seltzer did not seem to relieve. He turned back to his desk and took a deep breath. On the other hand, he wavered; it wouldn't be so bad to at least have a few pink telephone messages waiting for him that he could read with an exaggerated scowl on his face before crumpling them in his fist and tossing them into the nearest wastepaper basket in full view of everyone. Or even, if an occasional letter or Telex cable showed up in his in-basket—*but no!* Dirk Rangely shuddered at the dangerous tenor of his thoughts. He really was getting senile!

Letters and cables usually demanded responses and if there was anything worse than exposing one's thoughts in conversations with people like Mort Mortenstein, who existed only for the chance to inflict some mortal injury on a fellow worker's career, it was being irrevocably committed to some indefensibly stupid position or senile opinion *in writing*.

Dirk Rangely tried repeatedly to shrug off these troublesome thoughts, but his shoulders just got sore as he became more and more concerned about the nothing on his desk, and, considering how difficult it is to get nothing out of one's system, Dirk Rangely's stomach began construction again on an all-weather ulcer, despite the two Alka-Seltzers he had just taken. Dirk Rangely knew what he needed: a good, thorough leafing through a trade magazine, the only paper product he allowed into his office besides Kleenexes. Ah, there was something so magically relaxing about flipping each page and studying those soothing four-color vignettes of sleek jets, streaking sports cars and alluring females—the very stuff that full-blown daydreams are made of. But drat, no mail yet today. Dirk Rangely started drumming his fingers on his desk top faster and faster and faster, until they were literally galloping in place.

"What is the problem here? What is the problem what is the problem?" Dirk Rangely sang softly. Suddenly, he reined in his stampeding fingers. "That's it! Of course! I'm spending too much time in the plant! What am I doing here anyway? I should be out on the road." Dirk Rangely jumped up and ran over to the door. He pulled it open enthusiastically and called out to his secretary, "Jo Ann, book me on the early morning flight out to the coast. Drop everything and get it done right away."

"Which coast?"

Dirk Rangely immediately slammed the door closed. "Damn insolent secretary! Why do they always have to be second guessing you?" He thought for a moment, then opened the door again. "Los

Angeles. And call Needleman out there and tell him I'll be out to discuss his forecast."

"Yes, sir." Jo Ann smiled.

Dirk Rangely could not be sure, but he thought he saw Jo Ann smile and wondered what it might have meant. No matter. He confidently slammed the door closed, taking comfort in the knowledge that decisive action had been taken and that a business trip was in the works. His spirits could not be dampened now, not even by the fact that he thoroughly despised Arthur Needleman, the West Coast Sales Manager, and often wondered seriously whether Needleman was not, in fact, an agent for the KGB, especially after that night he had gotten Dirk Rangely lost in Los Angeles' heart of darkness with some dubious directions written out on a cocktail napkin.

Dirk Rangely went back to his desk and sat down to pause reflectively. There was no time like 'estimated time en route', he reflected. Dirk Rangely always felt "five miles closer to heaven" every time he sat strapped into a Boeing 707 window seat with a line of midget Tanqueray bottles at parade rest, an in-flight magazine filled with glossy daydreams, and a pair of headsets pouring out the insipid kind of music that so moved his very soul every time he rode an elevator. If only he could be a pilot himself, then his whole job would be to fly from one place to another. As it was now, whenever he got to wherever he was going, Dirk Rangely had to go to work. When he became the Old Man, he would certainly do something about that. Leaning back in his chair and crossing his feet up on top of his desk, he closed his eyes to muse about how things would be when he, Dirk Rangely, became the Old Man.

Suddenly, Dirk Rangely put his feet down and sat up straight. He searched through his desk drawers until he finally found an old, forgotten pad of blank paper. He took his Cross pen from his shirt pocket and, fingers trembling, slowly turned it so the point was exposed. He took a deep, deliberate breath. Dirk Rangely began writing his name, slowly and awkwardly, over and over and over again with his left hand. When he had filled the first page, he flipped it over and began again. It was no use, though. By the fifth page, his hand ached and Dirk Rangely still could not even decipher the twisted and tortured scribbles of his own name. He tossed down his Cross pen in disgust.

"Why can't I just be right-handed, like I always have been?"

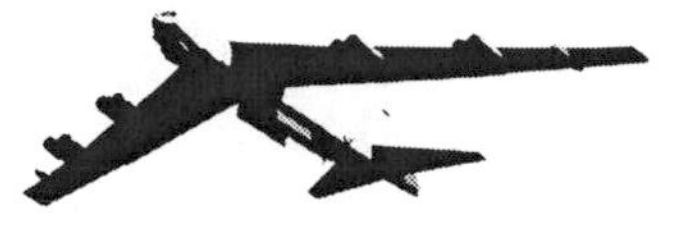

Frik and Frak

That Smile! At once it repelled and absorbed him. It sent a chill through his body like the cold blade of a knife laid flat against the base of his spine.

Y.T., Jr. quickly averted his eyes and in his desperation latched his gaze upon Wanda W. Willet, his father's secretary, which sent a shiver of an entirely different nature through his body that eventually lodged in his stomach and threatened to dislodge his breakfast.

Wanda W. Willet was a bony, emaciated woman of forty-five who prided herself on her trim figure, yet had, before she left, stirred scarecrows to unionize for job protection in the small farming community from which she hailed. Her entire face came to a point at the end of her nose, giving her a rodent-esque countenance. Her skin was pulled back painfully taut over her cheek bones and her lips were so pursed and puckered that her mouth resembled another, less pleasant bodily orifice. She had a habit of sticking pencils into the nest of hair on top of her head and forgetting about them that added to the illusion that her hairdo had actually been assembled by a pair of mating magpies.

Wanda W. Willet was born and raised in a town called Digby in Finikie County, Kansas, which was so far off of U.S. 283 that the only road through town was a hardened artery of dirt that to this day is unnamed and unnumbered. She was the only child of a farm implement sales and service man, who was quite popular in Finikie

County, and his weary, wind-blown wife. Wanda W. Willet's upbringing was an intensely uneventful one, reaching its zenith when she graduated with a degree in Education from the Kansas State University Extension Center in the relative metropolis of Hays, Kansas. Much to her parents' dismay, the day after she received her diploma she scurried right on back to Digby and moved right back into the same upstairs bedroom that had always been hers. She eventually took over Miss Pyle's position as school teacher after Miss Pyle had been discovered dead in her home three weeks after she died. It seemed that none of her students felt motivated enough to report her as missing, so it was left to the Finikie County Fuller Brush salesman to inadvertently discover her body beneath a toppled stack of class essays, stiff as a board.

Wanda W. Willet taught kindergarten, elementary grades, junior high school and senior high school, all in a one-room, red-brick school house just west of Digby proper. Her students were the nepotistic farm hands of the rugged individuals who tilled the high plains of southern Finikie County. Wanda W. Willet found complete fulfillment teaching in a school that had no principals, no other teachers, no Parent Teachers Association and especially no football and basketball coaches who ineptly tried to teach driver's education and typing classes—that had no marching band, no drama club, no chess club, no biology club—that had no proms, no homecomings, no sock hops and no cheerleaders to counsel about teenage pregnancies Teaching school in Digby was a pure, unadulterated experience of education, unfettered by any extra-curricular nonsense that would require Wanda W. Willet to interact with another human being on a purely social level. The school board was made up of three farmers named Joe who met once a year at Joe Number Three's farm house during the winter when farm duties were at a lull. Sometime during their judicious consumption of alcoholic beverages and the endless hands of five card draw poker, nothing wild, Wanda W. Willet was given a four and one-half percent pay increase if the past year's crop yields had been good or a two and one-half percent increase if the moisture content was high or the test weights had been low.

All went well for a dozen years or so until that fateful October in 1957 when the Russians played with the thermostat connected to the Cold War by launching *Sputnik I* into orbit. The farmers all knew, of course, that this was a malicious communist plot aimed specifically at them to ruin their crops of newly planted winter wheat by some kind of insidious manipulation of the weather from outer space. Co-incidentally, it was also in that very same October of 1957 that the son of Joe Number Two on the school board, Joe Number Two, Junior, came home with a reading assignment of *War and Peace* by Leo Tolstoy, who was widely mistaken not only in Digby, but all of Finikie County, for Leon Trotsky, and suddenly the collusionary threat of the Red Menace was right there in their own north forties, just like good old Senator Joe "Tail Gunner" McCarthy had tried to warn them. With her own father voicing the loudest denunciations—sales of plows and discs had fallen off dramatically in 1957—"Red Army Colonel" Wanda W. Willetski was forced to leave Digby. She went to Kansas City, Missouri, and there, Y.T., Sr. recognized the vast, untapped potential of her fascist, dictatorial talents acquired over the twelve years spent in the one-room, red-brick school house.

"My door is always open for you to come to me with your problems and suggestions," Y.T., Sr. would tell his workers during impromptu speeches made on the Machine Shop floor or in the course of informal discussions held with the key punch operators in the Accounting Department. Of course, it was Wanda W. Willet's task to see that not one of them ever passed over the threshold to Y.T., Sr.'s office, and in this task, her well-honed perversion of the Socratic method served her well.

"Ex-excuse m-me, Miss W-Willet," murmured Horace Cooley, supervisor of the Drafting Department, where Y.T., Sr. had most recently been giving impromptu speeches. Horace Cooley was a tall, frail man whose posture had been irrevocably curved by twenty years bent over a drafting board. He wore thick, frameless glasses. His hands shook visibly as if he were afflicted with palsy. He was so soft-spoken that he had not once called attention to any of the occasional shortages in his paycheck that had occurred over the past twenty years. For Horace Cooley to have left the Drafting Department and to have presented himself before Mr. Erp's secretary required that he draw upon reservoirs of courage that were unimaginable even to himself in his wildest dreams. "Ex-excuse me, b-but I would like to s-speak to M-Mr. Erp, please."

Slowly and deliberately, Wanda W. Willet looked up from her desk. Years of inhaling chalk dust had made her voice hoarse and scratchy like the old seventy-eight RPM Victrola records she sang along with in her apartment, making a sustained conversation with her impossible for anyone with normal hearing. "Of course. And you would have an appointment, would you not?" she asked, as always with full knowledge that the petitioner did not.

"A-A-Appointment?" Horace Cooley stuttered, unnerved at first by Wanda W. Willet's appearance and then even more so by the tone of her voice.

"Yes, of course, Mr. Cooley, an appointment. You did make one, did you not?"

In the Black

"B-But Mr. Er-Er-Er-Erp said…" Horace Cooley trailed off, noticing for the first time that directly behind Wanda W. Willet, Y.T., Sr.'s office door was closed as it always was during the hours of eight to five.

At this point, with an exaggerated sigh of exasperation, Wanda W. Willet would always take off her white rhinestone glasses with the sharply pointed wings and let them dangle from a chain around her neck. She did just that and squinted her brown, rat-like eyes at Horace Cooley.

"Bu-But it—but, this Me-memo," Horace Cooley stammered on bravely. "Th-This is going to s-seriously e-effect the e-efficiency of the D-D-D-Drafting D-Department. I ju-just don't see how we w-will be able to g-get all of our wa-wa-wa-wa-wa-wa-wa-work done. We are behind as it is n-now."

"And you wish to speak directly to Mr. Erp concerning this matter?"

"He s-said we could c-come to him with p-p-problems and s-s-suggestions. He said his d-door is—"

"But you have no appointment?" Wanda W. Willet turned her head and looked sideways at the trembling twig of a man before her.

"W-well n-no. But he s-said his door w-would always—"

"Mr. Cooley." Wanda W. Willet shook her head. "Mr. Cooley, would you not suppose Mr. Erp to be quite a busy man?"

"Well, y-yes, I would suppose—"

"And just how many people would you suppose Mr. Erp has working for him here at Erp Industries, Incorporated?"

"Oh, g-gosh, I don't know. M-Maybe three hun-or n-no, four—or —"

"Six hundred, sixty-two in this facility, which does not include the warehouse personnel in Lee's Summit. And now, what if each and every employee here wanted to see Mr. Erp today? *Hmm?* How much time would you suppose he would have to speak with each and every one of them?"

Horace Cooley rolled his eyes skyward as he went through the calculations in his head to cipher the answer for Wanda W. Willet. "I-I don't know off the t-top of my head M-Maybe, oh, a minute or—"

"If Mr. Erp worked one hour overtime in the morning and one hour overtime at night and worked straight through his lunch hour as well, he would be able to spend exactly one minute with each employee, less an average of ten seconds for each person to enter into and egress from Mr. Erp's office, leaving a scant fifty seconds to actually conduct their meeting Now, Mr. Cooley, as Mr. Erp's secretary, I am required to take down the minutes of all of Mr. Erp's meetings. You have heard of taking the minutes of a meeting, have you not, Mr. Cooley?"

"Ye-yes."

"Well, certainly in all my years, I have never taken the seconds of any meeting. Have you ever heard of such a thing Mr. Cooley?"

"Er, no, I—"

"Now, if I let you into Mr. Erp's office for only fifty seconds, you and he could not very well have a meeting if there are no minutes for me to take, now could you Mr. Cooley?"

"I-I su-suppose not."

"And if you do not have a meeting with Mr. Erp, then how do you suppose that you and he could have any meaningful discussion about your concerns over this particular memo and its impact on your Drafting Department?"

"If I-I d-d-didn't—"

"And if you do not discuss this situation with Mr. Erp, then you will not have accomplished the task you set out to accomplish when you came here, which would mean that you would have to come here tomorrow and again the next day and the next and the next. Now, Mr. Cooley, if you were Mr. Erp, could you afford to spend all your days having six hundred sixty-two non-meetings which did not allow you to discuss or resolve any of the issues and challenges facing you and your loyal and trusted employees?"

"Bu-but—"

"You see, then, that if Mr. Erp spends all of his time not solving problems, Erp Industries, Incorporated, would more than likely not be the successful and profitable enterprise that it is, would it not?"

"No—I mean yes—I, er, ah," Horace Cooley thought about all of this for a moment, rubbing his chin with his visibly shaking hand. "Very w-well, th-then, c-could I m-make an appointment to s-see—"

"Now *really*, Mr. Cooley." Wanda W. Willet sighed a very loud sigh that evidenced the great magnitude of her patience. "Mr. Cooley, if Mr. Erp wanted to see you, would you not come to his office immediately?"

"Y-Yes. Of c-course I w-would."

"So you understand, then, that Mr. Erp can see anyone of the people who work for him whenever he so desires?"

"Y-Yes, I s-suppose that—"

"Then why would Mr. Erp ever make an appointment to see any one of his employees? Would that not be redundant with the authority that is clearly within his rights to exercise?"

Horace Cooley shook his head as if to clear his thoughts.

"Thank you ever so much for coming by the office today, Mr. Cooley. It was so nice to see you again. And rest assured that we will be sure to call upon you when the need arises to discuss Mr. Erp's Memo with you. Good day."

Wanda W. Willet put her glasses back on and turned her attention to the work on her desk once again. It was as if Mr. Cooley had simply evaporated into thin air and no longer existed.

"Bu-bu-bu-bu-bu-bu-bu-bu-" Horace Cooley stammered on in a state of highly agitated despair. He searched about the reception area for some just umpire or referee to cry foul and to penalize Wanda W. Willet for her infractions upon his sensibilities. Instead, he saw the two gentlemen sitting on either side of the door to Y.T., Sr.'s office like a matched set of bookends, identically dressed in light blue shirts, red ties, dark blue blazers, and gray polyester slacks. Then he saw *That Smile!* It cut through him to the very core of his trembling being like the cold January wind howling outside, and just as if he were naught but a frail, brittle leaf, blew him out of the door through which he had come, right past Y.T., Jr. and all the way back to the Drafting Department where he spent the balance of the day aimlessly tracing French curves from a template, tip-toeing at the very boundary of a nervous breakdown.

That Smile! belonged to the younger of the two Erp Industries, Inc., company pilots, who, when they were not plying the jetways across North and South America or on the airport apron with their heads stuck into one of the hellholes of the Erp Industries, Inc.'s Learjet or in the office of the Fixed Base Operator trying to get laid by the buxom, blonde receptionist, were usually posted behind Wanda W. Willet on either side of the door to Y.T., Sr.'s office.

No one, with the possible exception of Y.T., Sr., knew what their names were. The older man was an ex-Colonel of the Air

Force (ours); the younger, a Navy ex-Commander (ours too). Dirk Rangely had once overheard Y.T., Sr. refer to them as 'Frik and Frak' and wasted no time in tirelessly spreading such an important piece of G-2 around the plant on his regular rounds of spreading his own friendliness. No one dared to call them Frik and Frak to their faces, though, for the ex-Colonel and the ex-Commander were second only to Y.T., Sr. in intimidating people simply by their presence.

The ex-Colonel usually hid his face behind a *Playboy Magazine,* which he hid behind a *Life Magazine,* while he sat next to the door to Y.T., Sr.'s office. A growing gray-blue cumulonimbus cloud of cigar smoke inevitably towered from behind the magazines, always threatening but never raining on the ex-Colonel's rumpled silver hair. His hair had an innate, wiry resistance to combing and brushing—which is not to imply that a comb or brush ever got near his head. His clothes were always just as rumpled as his hair, having an acquired resistance to ironings and wire hangers. His red tie served double duty as an ashtray for his cigars and was often seen to cough up a fine silvery dust as it flapped on breezy days. Since taking his twenty-year retirement from the Air Force, the ex-Colonel had—like an old baseball that has lost its tightly-laced horsehide cover—become a bit unraveled.

Rumor around the plant—feverishly nurtured and fertilized by Dirk Rangely—had it that the ex-Colonel was the bombardier on the *Enola Gay,* the one who had actually pushed the button to drop *Little Boy,* the very first atomic bomb, on Hiroshima, the one who had killed 68,000 and injured 76,000 Japanese with just the slightest single movement of his thumb. The rumor helped intimidate people and sweep them out of the way as the ex-Colonel walked with the ex-Commander through the plant, making cracks about the different female employees like, "I'd sure like to redline that bitch," or, "I've got a heat-seeking missile for her six."

The truth of the matter about his service record was that the ex-Colonel had been the co-pilot of *Bockscar,* the B-29 that had dropped *Fat Man,* the first plutonium bomb (as opposed to the first uranium bomb), on Nagasaki, killing 38,000 and injuring 21,000 Japanese. After Berlin, Dresden, Frankfurt and "those fucking marble factories in Schweinfurt," after long months of training in the Utah desert and then Osaka, Yokohama, Amagaski, Kokura, and Tokyo, Nagasaki was just another day in a long, long war. The ex-Colonel flew the Nagasaki mission with the exact same grit, determination and precision with which he had flown every mission of his career. And when he was done, he did what he always did when he was not flying: he ran a series of low-level, sperm-strafing missions on the naked bodies of whatever willing nurses and/or natives he could find on Tinian or any of the other Mariana Islands. In fact, on the co-pilot side of his B-29, instead of miniature Rising Sun flags, he had painted miniature Betty Grable gambs to mark each of his scores. No one knew how or why, but the ex-Colonel—even though he was only a Captain at the time—had the most impressive record in the Pacific Theater of Operations.

After a tour of flying fighters up the Yalu River to Mig Alley in Korea and a stint in West Germany that entailed many more sexual dogfights than aerial, the ex-Colonel ended up at Area 51 in Nevada as a test pilot on the U-2 spy plane development program. It was there that he first met Y.T., Sr., who was personally supervising the trouble-shooting of the electronic black-box payloads that the then fledgling Erp Industries, Inc. was under contract to design and build. The ex-Colonel was amazed at Y.T., Sr.'s voracious sexual appetite that appeared to surpass even his own record during World War II. In fact, it did, but Y.T., Sr. was not stationed in the Pacific Theater of Operations, but rather spent the war in the Navy Bureau of Aeronautics in Washington, D.C. It was not long before the ex-Colonel was loading himself and Y.T., Sr. into whatever could fly to escape the hot, lonely Nevada desert for anywhere to knock-up anything that moved or simply breathed. Even long after the two men had parted ways after the U-2 program, the ex-Colonel often showed up without notice at the Kansas City airport in a twin-seated F-106 or F-4 to whisk Y.T., Sr. away at MACH 2 to grab a quick piece of ass. After the ex-Colonel took his twenty-year retirement from the Air Force, Y.T., Sr. immediately recognized the need for a man of such caliber in his organization and hired him on as a corporate pilot, even though Erp Industries, Inc., had no corporate aircraft at the time.

That Smile! belonged to the ex-Commander. It was the kind of smile that shifting continental shelves rip in the earth during earth quakes—that lions snarl over a dying antelope as they wait for their prey to expire—that mature cumulonimbus clouds flash in bolts of lightning. *That Smile!* betrayed a wildness, a savage uncontrollableness and unpredictability of the sort that make up the very essence of tornadoes and hurricanes. But there was something more, a human element—the twinkle in the eye of a linebacker charging the blind side of frail split end carrying the football—the chortlings of used car salesmen upon spotting a female senior citizen walking onto the lot—the smile of a fighter pilot on an unfriendly's six with his AIM-9 *Sidewinder* missiles armed and growling in his headset.

"So, a Navy man," Y.T., Sr. said, looking over the ex-Commander's resume on that fateful day the ex-Commander had mysteriously come in off the streets to apply for a job. A series of rented single-engine Cessnas, Pipers, and Beechcrafts had been used by Y.T., Sr. and the ex-Colonel to execute "missions" to St. Louis or Memphis or Little Rock, until Erp Industries, Inc., was able to afford a used cabin-class twin. Success in the sixties afforded a move up to a Learjet, but it also meant that a co-pilot had to be found for the ex-Colonel, as required by the F.A.A. "Why did you scuttle out of the service?"

"Scorched the wrong gooks." *That Smile!*

Y.T., Sr. knew immediately that this was his man. "How's that?"

"In Vietnam. Ruff-Puffs were about to be overrun. Dropped dead on target, but some of the napalm splashed the wrong way. Guess it looked bad to Bar-B-Q a few of the Allies." *That Smile!* "Besides, I never learned the stall recovery procedures for a desk. If you get my drift."

"Hmmmm. I see. And what about this Air America thing?"

"CIA operation. Didn't like me flying their precious new 727s fifty feet off the deck through Cambodia and Laos. Claimed I kept getting vegetation stains on the leading edges of the wings." *That Smile!* "But I think that Company flight Engineers kept getting shit in their pants."

"Uh-huh. But what about this here? Getting kicked out of the Missouri National Guard?"

"One CAVU Sunday afternoon searching for targets of opportunity in an F-4. Rolled over and dived on a tug pushing three barges. On pull-out, the fuel drop tanks released. Scared the piss out of the tug crew. They abandoned ship. The runaway tug and barges took out a bridge just down river from Hannibal. Radio Intercept Officer got a good chuckle out of it. The Guard didn't." *That Smile!*

"And TWA doesn't want you to fly for them?"

"Suppose not." *That Smile!* "You?"

"Absolutely."

The ex-Commander sat erect on the right hand side of the door to Y.T., Sr.'s office and watched the world of Erp Industries, Inc., go by from behind his green, teardrop sunglasses. His clothes were always impeccably neat and pressed. There was not a single speck of dandruff on his shoulders nor a stray water spot on his high-gloss Oxford wing tips. His arms were folded with precision across his chest. His head was always cocked at a forty-five degree angle to his shoulders, a habit long ingrained to broaden his field of view while scanning for unfriendlies. Instead of a cigar, a slender, wooden toothpick rolled methodically from one side of *That Smile!* to the other.

"I am an executive of this company and I am entitled to the privileges normally accorded such a position," demanded P. Peckerfelt, Vice-President/Manufacturing, of Y.T., Sr. shortly after the ex-Commander had been hired. "I should be able to have access to the corporate aircraft for business travel if it is available."

"Why I could not agree with you more," agreed Y.T., Sr.

"You couldn't?" P. Peckerfelt was almost disappointed. He had rigorously prepared himself for this confrontation with an entire stack of index cards full of arguments that bulged his suit coat pocket.

"Certainly," smiled Y.T., Sr.

"Then I can use the Learjet to go out to Lockheed tomorrow?"

"Well, I am afraid that is going to be a bit of a problem."

"But you said—"

"Yes, of course, but you see the problem is that the right engine is getting a hot section and the plane is down at the moment." Y.T., Sr. appeared to ponder for a moment. "Tell you what, though, just meet the pilots at the airport in the morning. We'll make arrangements for another plane."

"Why thank you." P. Peckerfelt positively flushed with the thrill of victory.

"Have a nice flight," Y.T., Sr. said through the gritted teeth of his smile.

P. Peckerfelt was met at the airport the next morning by *That Smile!* Instead of a business jet, the ex-Commander loaded P. Peckerfelt and his luggage into a ragged T-6 *Harvard,* an old, prop service trainer, and they took off. No turn was made at less than a sixty degree bank. Every maneuver pulled at least two Gs, which made the air frame creak and groan in protest—exhilarating to the ex-Commander, but an unpleasant reminder to P. Peckerfelt that he was but a frail captive of the laws of physics and that should they crash, his body would be torn to bits by the forces of the impact without mercy. The ex-Commander flew under power lines and so close to roads that he read over the intercom the posted population of each town they passed to his passenger who was too busy trying not to become ill to pay any attention. He flew so low over the desolate farming regions of Western Kansas that he chaffed the amber waves of grain with the tips of his propeller, sending kernels of wheat up to beat against the belly of the airplane like a hail storm. While in Denver for a fuel stop, P. Peckerfelt quietly slipped away from the ex-Commander and got on a commercial flight to California. He never again asked to use the company Learjet and all Y.T., Sr. had to pay was an extra clean up charge for the inside of the T-6. He never regretted hiring the ex-Commander.

The ex-Commander caught a glimpse of Y.T., Jr. outside in the hallway and smiled a little broader. He unfolded his right arm and gave a slight, crisp snap of a salute. Y.T., Jr. smiled back. He liked Frik and Frak, especially after they had flown him out to Berkeley last October to look over the university. They had taken him to Fu Loin's Bar, Grill, Gift Shop, Curio Emporium, Taoist Book Store, Camera Shop, Photo Development Center, Buddhist Reading Room, Fireworks Factory, Chopstick Warehouse and Whorehouse down in San Francisco's Chinatown. Frik and Frak had put it to the Asians again and again from airplanes and still loved to put it to Asian women again and again in bed—such is the love/hate turmoil that brews in a soldier's soul.

Y.T., Jr. returned the salute and headed on to the Engineering Department, wondering if on the twenty-fifth they would take him back to Fu Loin's for more miscegenational mischief. If nothing else, Y.T., Jr. had inherited his father's insatiable taste for women.

Of course, from his vantage point behind the shrubbery outside the windows to Y.T., Sr.'s office, Wanda W. Willet's shadow, Private Investigator Parmakianski, shivered and watched everything that happened inside, making the appropriate entries in a greasy, grimy notebook.

The Hall of Science

"The workers you saw out on the factory floor make money for me…and these learned bastards in here spend it all," Y.T., Sr. would always say as he passed through the Engineering Department when hosting a plant tour for a representative of that hallowed stalwart of capitalism known as THE CUSTOMER. "I am also of the firm conviction that there comes a time when all engineers should be shot in the head so that production can actually begin."

Y.T., Sr. would always be sure to make this last comment loud enough for Vasili Ivanovich Dzhugashili, Vice-President/Research and Development, to hear, then would wait and watch as the color drained from his face and his eyes squinted shut in a painful grimace behind his tiny, round, wire-rimmed glasses. Outside of adding more than a few pounds to his short, stocky frame, Vasili Ivanovich had changed very little in the years since Y.T., Sr. had met him in a Washington, D.C., radio repair shop in 1946. His hair still thrust straight up into a high plateau of a flattop and his eyebrows were still so bushy that they formed a veritable hedgerow across the bottom of his forehead. His chubby, round face had been lined and gutted by years of oppression under the Stalin regime and then by years of trying unsuccessfully to adjust to the new and very different way of life in America, which had become his home after World War II through the shady arrangements of one ex-Luftwaffe Corporal named Rolf Guderian.

Rolf Guderian had been a guard at the P.O.W. work camp where Vasili Ivanovich endured World War II in its entirety, having been captured on the very first day of the war when Hitler unleashed his Blitzkrieg against Russia. Four years later when the end neared and the outcome appeared obvious, Rolf Guderian, through deft manipulation of what was left of the Nazi Bureaucracy, got Vasili Ivanovich and himself out of Germany. Then, through quite immodest exaggeration of Vasili Ivanovich's credentials as a physicist from the Academy of Sciences in Moscow, he got them to the United States where the State Department promptly misplaced them and forgot about them in the excitement of laying claim to Werner Van Braun and his cadre via Operation Paperclip, while the Russians got stuck with Poland. With their fates forever interwoven by the exploits of their escape, Vasili Ivanovich and Rolf Guderian opened a radio repair shop in an attempt to stave off poverty. Unfortunately, business was less than mediocre and they were forced to live in near destitution, sleeping on cots and eating from a hot plate in the repair shop itself.

In the autumn of 1946, Y.T., Sr. brought his RCA Console 6000 into Vasili Ivanovich and Rolf Guderian for service. When he returned to pick his radio up, Y.T., Sr. discovered that Vasili Ivanovich had replaced all the vacuum tubes inside with small metal buttons. Business being what it was, Vasili Ivanovich had a good deal of time to tinker around in his workshop and, occasionally, he came up with inventions like those small electric buttons. Y.T., Sr. spent the balance of the day at the little radio shop talking with the bashful Russian scientist. Rolf Guderian silently hung back with suspicion until Y.T., Sr. offered to buy the two hungry foreigners dinner. By dessert, they had agreed to become the first two employees of Erp Industries, Inc. The little metal buttons that

Vasili Ivanovich had put into Y.T., Sr.'s radio would, two years later, be re-invented by Bell Laboratories and would be called transistors.

Correctly reading the ill congressional winds that were beginning to stir with regards to un-American activities and recognizing the imminent danger of employing an ex-Soviet engineer, Y.T., Sr. decided the time was right to leave Washington, D.C., and relocate his company in America's heartland. Erp Industries, Inc., came to occupy the second floor of a shoppette above a Rexall Drug Store, Lucky Pierre's Beauty Salon and Vernon's Bait and Tackle Shop, in Raytown, Missouri, a sleepy little hamlet just east of his mother's hometown of Kansas City. In those early days, Y.T., Sr. was Vice-President/Manufacturing, Vice-President/Sales, Vice-President/Finance, Vice-President/Procurement, Vice-President/Personnel—in fact, he was Vice-President/Everything except Engineering. That role was Vasili Ivanovich's by virtue of being the only engineer employed by the company. In its infancy, growth came painfully slow for Erp Industries, Inc. Each day brought fresh battle against deteriorating odds, as Y.T., Sr. struggled to keep his young company solvent.

"Alright you sons-of-bitches!" Y.T., Sr. screamed as he burst into the back corner of the second floor that served as the Engineering Department. The acrid odor of women getting permanents and the faint rumblings of hair dryers drifted up from Lucky Pierre's Beauty Salon downstairs. "Up against the fucking wall! Everybody! *NOW!*"

Vasili Ivanovich heard the commotion outside the closet that had been converted into an office for him—quite commodious accommodations compared to those he had as an underling at the Academy of Sciences. He got up to investigate and when he stepped out into the "Engineering Lab", still clutching his slide rule, he found Horace Cooley, his draftsman, and Rolf Guderian, his technician, with their backs against the wall and their hands on top of their heads. Pacing back and forth in front of them was Y.T., Sr., waving a forty-five caliber pistol and, apparently, frothing at the mouth like a mad dog.

"You! Get over here!" Y.T., Sr. screamed upon spotting Vasili Ivanovich's portly figure in the door to the closet. He aimed his pistol at his one and only engineer. "You—get your ass over here you red-souled, Russian son-of-a-bitch!"

Vasili Ivanovich set down his slide rule and obediently joined the rest of the Erp Industries, Inc., Engineering Department against the wall with his hands on his head. He had been threatened with execution once before. Outraged that the natural sciences seemed to be straying from the tenants of socialist theory, Stalin ordered a purge of the Academy of Sciences. Vasili Ivanovich, without any knowledge of the crime with which he had been charged—he was being held accountable for the fact that the universe was not conforming to Marxist doctrine—stood silent for four and a half hours as a panel of Communist Party members discussed the seriousness of his unidentified political infidelities and whether or not he should be stood up against a wall and shot. The majority of the panel favored immediate execution, but they acquiesced to the astute Party member who noted that Dzhugashili was also Stalin's true surname. It was agreed that the Party Chairman might take a dim view of the execution of a family member with dire results ensuing for members of the panel. At the same time, though, they could not undermine the effectiveness of the purge by acquitting Vasili Ivanovich completely, so they decided to accept compulsory military service as atonement for his transgressions. Instead of staring back at a firing squad, the bewildered physicist found himself staring at Polish border guards patrolling the other side of the barbed wire fence that demarcated their respective countries. From there, Vasili Ivanovich found his way onto the roll call list of Luftwaffe Corporal Rolf Guderian.

Vasili Ivanovich looked down at Rolf Guderian standing against the wall next to him. Rolf Guderian looked back with an expression that read, 'I told you so, you stupid *scheisskopf*'.

Vasili Ivanovich nodded with resignation at the greasy little ex-Nazi with the head four sizes too big for his body.

"Did those Skunkworks prototypes ship yet?" Y.T., Sr. demanded of Vasili Ivanovich.

"Comrade Erp—" Old habits as well as Vasili Ivanovich's thick Slavic accent were hard to break. "I mean, *Mister* Erp, we seem to have had problems with random voltage spikes in the output signal."

"I don't want to hear about random voltage spikes in output signals or about EMI or about RF leakage or about dithering or about mismatched impedances or about channel crosstalk or about root mean squared amplitude modulated oscillations or about any other lame-brained engineering mumbo-jumbo!" Y.T., Sr. screamed, waving the pistol directly under Vasili Ivanovich's nose. "You are already five and a half months late in shipping those God damned things. And need I remind you, you maladjusted Muscovite, that this is not the Soviet Union. Here in America, we have THE CUSTOMER. And if we do not ship parts to THE CUSTOMER, we cannot invoice THE CUSTOMER. And if we do not invoice THE CUSTOMER, THE CUSTOMER does not pay us. And if we do not get paid, we do not make payroll. And if we do not make payroll, we shut our doors. And if we shut our doors, I am going to ride you like a mule the hard way, all the way back to Red Square and string you up by your toes."

"I believe if we can just be allowed time to isolate—"

"I am going to isolate the left lobe of your brain from the right lobe if those units do not ship by five o'clock today!" Y.T., Sr. cocked the hammer of his pistol and pressed the muzzle against Vasili Ivanovich's forehead.

"But sir!" Vasili Ivanovich exclaimed. He looked up nervously at the round clock on the wall. "I just do not see how that could be poss—"

Y.T., Sr. aimed, fired and hit the dead center of the clock, stopping the hands. All at once, every pore on Vasili Ivanovich's body opened up and poured forth a steady flow of perspiration. At the discharge, Horace Cooley began trembling spastically and murmuring Hail Marys under his breath. Rolf Guderian smiled in admiration at the efficient manner in which Y.T., Sr. was dealing with the recalcitrant Russian.

"Very well. As you wish." Vasili Ivanovich sighed heavily. He took off his glasses to wipe the sweat from the lenses, then went to work.

Horace Cooley and Rolf Guderian spent the rest of the day against the wall at gunpoint while Vasili Ivanovich tinkered and tested, tested and tinkered, tinkered and tested, tested and tinkered with the four black boxes stuffed with electronics that the United States Air Force had been anxiously awaiting at Area 51 in Nevada for almost a year. At four-fifty that afternoon, when the problem had been finally isolated, identified and rectified, Y.T., Sr. marched Vasili Ivanovich, Horace Cooley and Rolf Guderian with the four black boxes down the hall to the shipping department at gunpoint. After seeing the prototypes packed up and sent off on a truck, Y.T., Sr. put on his pistol's safety and, without a word, went back to his office. Horace Cooley fell to his knees and gave thanks to God.

"The Fuhrer would not have let you get off so easy," Rolf Guderian muttered maliciously behind Vasili Ivanovich's back.

"Yes. Yes, you are right. Nor would Stalin." Vasili Ivanovich mopped the sweat from his brow and recalled memories of his short, clumsy, brooding and aloof second cousin as a child in the Georgia region of the Soviet Union. Then, with a heavy sigh, he said, "But we must remember that this is America."

"America—Shamerica. You *scheisskopf*, I told you that those resistor values were not right, but you never listen to me," Rolf Guderian sneered. "Next time I hope he blows your God damned brains out all over the wall."

"Yes. Next time," Vasili Ivanovich agreed without paying attention, rather thinking that—contrary to Rolf Guderian's usual inept opinion—he should have been able to predict the unexpected capacitance between the solder joints on the number three circuit board and the metal cover can that caused the random voltage spikes in the output signal.

Much to Rolf Guderian's undying dismay, Vasili Ivanovich never did get his brains blown out all over the wall, for Vasili Ivanovich was never again late with a prototype shipment to THE CUSTOMER. Above and beyond that, never did a prototype that he shipped ever fail to meet THE CUSTOMER'S specifications. Such was the enduring strength of the impression that Y.T., Sr. had made that day with his pistol. And it was largely due to the inspired performance of the Engineering Department that Erp Industries, Inc., began to gather in more contracts and bigger contracts from THE CUSTOMER. As the company prospered, though, Y.T., Sr. saw that Vasili Ivanovich had less and less time to invent the new and better electronic mousetraps which were at the very foundation of the company's continuing success. So Y.T., Sr. kept pushing

Vasili Ivanovich to hire more and more engineers until he found himself responsible for supervising nine engineers and a dozen technicians. But Vasili Ivanovich loathed being the head of the Engineering Department and the responsibilities that were thrust upon him. He did not want to one day become the Old Man like Rolf Guderian or Dirk Rangely or that troublesome head of manufacturing who was always plotting and scheming against Y.T., Sr. as if he had a personal vendetta to settle with the Erp family—that P. Peckerfelt fellow. All that Vasili Ivanovich wanted to do was tinker and experiment in his laboratory. His joy came from the modest inventions (like the transistor) that inevitably found their way into Erp Industries, Inc.'s products.

Rolf Guderian, on the other hand, lusted after power. Before World War II, he found himself in the backwaters of the Nazi Bureaucracy as a tender of meticulous duties that everyone else eschewed. He was physically not front line Aryan Army material, so when the hostilities broke out in earnest, he found himself in an ill-fitting Luftwaffe uniform guarding Russian prisoners of war near Dresden. The life and death power he held over those Slavs infected him with a terminal quest for authority. At Erp Industries, Inc., Rolf Guderian was and always had been utterly worthless as a technician, but he gleefully shouldered the managerial and administrative duties that Vasili Ivanovich disdained and often ignored completely. At first, he immersed himself in such controversies as whether white or canary, legal or letter sized writing pads should be used uniformly throughout the Engineering Department, and the subtle intricacies of properly matching color coded tabs to the subject material for the engineering files, not to mention overseeing the expenditures and the operation of the departmental coffee pot. In the one thousand and one decisions about pencils, paper clips, staples, rubber bands, typewriter ribbons and note pads, Rolf Guderian found personal expression as well as the opportunity to sharpen his skills as an administrator to a ruthless degree. As the years passed, he came to assume more and more responsibilities until he was in charge of furniture acquisitions, the department operating budget, and even the hiring and firing of staff personnel, though engineers and technicians were still hired by Vasili Ivanovich. Rolf Guderian eventually assumed the title of Chief Engineer, even though he had never taken a degree and had no technical experience beyond being Vasili Ivanovich's inept personal technician. Rolf Guderian officially reported to Vasili Ivanovich, but he had slowly and steadily been building up an empire for himself and in private moments envisioned himself as the competent Prime Minister to an old, feeble-minded President—much in the fashion that Hitler had come to take control of all Germany while serving under Hindenburg.

Like all good bureaucratic kingpins, Rolf Guderian measured the success of his organizational imperialism by the number of people reporting to him. Vasili Ivanovich had nine engineers, twelve technicians, and a new secretary for a total of twenty-two. After deft maneuvering over the past two years that brought Horace Cooley's entire Drafting Department under his direct supervisory control, Rolf Guderian out-numbered Vasili Ivanovich fifty-three to twenty-two. Unfortunately, the majority of people in his ranks were file clerks, administrative assistants, technical writers and secretaries who accomplished little of value, but, of course, this mattered not to Rolf Guderian. What did matter were results as measured on the five-foot by six-foot organizational chart of Erp Industries, Inc., on the wall of his office that he consulted at least as often as Hitler had consulted a map of Europe.

Rolf Guderian had a secret plan for a future Business Reich that he kept under lock and key. He shared these blueprints for a new order only with the two Program Managers who were his closest advisors and blindly obedient henchmen. Co-incidentally, both Adolf Himmlerlicht and Herman Eichmanhoff were uniquely qualified—outside of the roots of their family trees—to be Program Managers by virtue of being graduate engineers who had put themselves through state universities by selling used cars. Everyone who sat in on a meeting with them was spellbound at their dazzling presentations and at the glowing optimism contained in progress reports that might as well have begun, 'Once upon a time…' and ended, '…lived happily ever after'. Vasili Ivanovich and his engineers had little use for Himmlerlicht and Eichmanhoff and avoided them at all costs. As such these two brown-shirted, corporate fascists had little knowledge of what the Engineering Department was working on. Yet no one had ever noticed that instead of actually managing the new development programs that Erp Industries, Inc., had undertaken, Himmlerlicht and Eichmanhoff had deftly begun reporting on the reports that they were giving until they reached the ultimate efficiency of reporting on the work that they were not doing. Of course, this is not to say that they were not busy men. Quite the contrary, Himmlerlicht and Eichmanhoff were continually on their way from one meeting to the next, briefing Sub-Contract Administrators, Buyers, Manufacturing Managers, Quality Control Supervisors, Marketing Representatives, Source Inspectors, government auditors and, of course, THE CUSTOMER, with their legendary purple prose. When they had no one to meet with, they met with each other and Rolf Guderian to review the Master Plan. Fortunately for them all, Vasili Ivanovich never forgot the day that—quite literally—he had been under the gun to complete a project.

One overwhelming obstacle stood in the way of Rolf Guderian's ambitious plans: neither he, Himmlerlicht nor Eichmanhoff had the slightest idea of what it was that Erp Industries, Inc., manufactured and sold, and try as they might, they could not get their hands on that precious information. One might have thought that the people who designed and engineered the products would be intimately familiar with their ultimate functions, but Vasili Ivanovich and his engineers were all quiet, serious men who were interested above all else in the advancement of science and technology. They viewed the products they developed for THE CUSTOMER as merely catalysts for their research and cared not at all to learn about the mundane day-to-day tasks performed by the odd-shaped boxes—usually painted flat black with white stenciled part numbers—they invented. Considering the absurd production schedules that never coincided with reality, let alone the Gregorian Calendar, P. Peckerfelt and his manufacturing people never had the luxury of time to investigate and contemplate whatever became of the conglomerate of sub-assemblies that were frantically put together to get shipped before the month's end. To Mort Mortenstein, the boxes were all just abstract part numbers that his department breathed life into by converting them into dollars and cents via the mysterious, algebraic-like functions of accounting. Perhaps Dirk Rangely came closest when he would say, "Erp Industries, Inc., designs, develops, manufactures and markets sophisticated electronic products—so-called 'Black Boxes'—for use in the Aerospace and Defense Industries." When pressed to tell what exactly it was that these "Black Boxes" did when installed in the bellies of aircraft or deep in the bowels of Navy destroyers,

Dirk Rangely would always hold up his hands and explain that he was not at liberty to divulge that information as it pertained to United States Department of Defense programs that were classified. Fortunately for the concealment of Dirk Rangely's ignorance, what he said was true.

Y.T., Jr. did not know what Erp Industries, Inc., manufactured and, quite frankly, he did not care. At the moment, he was much more interested in loitering outside the door to the Engineering Department where, unnoticed, he could watch Vasili Ivanovich's new secretary as she sat at her desk typing a letter. True to her name, Scarlett Angelina Brookings was a flaming red head with gray eyes and a liberal splattering of light freckles on her cheeks and arms that Y.T., Jr. would later learn extended over a good portion of her body. Even though Rolf Guderian scoffed at Scarlett Angelina Brookings and never failed to comment upon her shortcomings in comparison with a blonde-haired, blue-eyed Aryan ideal, she was quite beautiful.

Ever since Y.T., Jr. had been ten years old, he had spent portions of his weekends and school vacations working at his father's company. He cut the grass, raked the leaves, trimmed the shrubbery, and swept the sidewalks clean—or shoveled them clear of snow in the winter. He even repainted the yellow lines on the blacktop of the parking lot. It was not until the summer Y.T., Jr. turned sixteen that his father gave him his first job working inside the plant in the Shipping Department with Orley Bovine.

Orley Bovine was a hillbilly from the Ozark Mountains whose teeth seemed to shoot out of his gums in every different direction, a trait that he used to great advantage in prodigious feats of flinging tobacco laden spittle from his mouth. Legend had it that he could even spit around corners. Indeed, during his tenure in the Shipping

Department, Y.T., Jr. became a respectable spitter himself. He also learned how a mere shipping clerk could afford to buy expensive watches, diamond rings, and a new Cadillac every September when the new models came out of Detroit. Beneath Orley Bovine's uncut, unpolished backwoods exterior beat the heart of a slick marketing representative working for a number of independent distillers so far back in the hills of southwest Missouri that only he could find them. On Mondays, envelopes with numbers on the outside and ten dollar bills on the inside began showing up in the Shipping Department. On Friday afternoons, mason jars of white lightning found their way onto the floors of the cars with license plates corresponding to the numbers on the envelopes. It was not as if Y.T., Sr. was blind to the enterprising ways of Orley Bovine. In fact, he thought it most beneficial to have his son get a gut-level lesson in *Laissez-Faire* capitalism and he never questioned the extra money that Y.T., Jr. got from helping Orley Bovine on Friday afternoons.

The next summer, instead of packing, labeling and shipping out cardboard boxes filled with "Black Boxes" and, during idle hours, lounging on the loading dock out back with Orley Bovine refining his spitting techniques, Y.T., Jr. was assigned to work in the Machine Shop as a machinist's apprentice. Y.T., Jr. had never before been in the Machine Shop and was only vaguely aware of its presence. From the Shipping Department he could hear the dull, steady thump-thump-thump-thump-thump that sounded like the very heartbeat of the building and could feel the faint synchronized pulsations in the floor. But like all the other regular workers, he learned to tune the noise and vibrations out after his first week there. The Machine Shop occupied the entire basement level of the Erp Industries, Inc., building and on the first day his father took him there, Y.T., Jr. hesitated as an animal-like fear welled up inside of him at the sight of the dark hole of a doorway at the bottom of the stairs. As he descended to the basement level, the full orchestration of the Machine Shop—the monotonous, thumping rhythm of the punch presses, the whir of the grinders, the whines of the drill presses, the groans of the screw machines, lathes, gear cutters, and milling machines—rose to a deafening crescendo. Pausing to allow his eyes to adjust to the dim artificial light enough to follow the lanes outlined with yellow lines on the floor, Y.T., Jr. was taken back by the rows and rows of massive, dark machines tended by shuffling men with missing fingers and measurable hearing loss dressed in heavy boots and oil-stained smocks. The men looked up as Y.T., Jr. and his father passed by, but said nothing and made no gestures. The air felt hot and appeared hazy with a mist of oil. After only five minutes, Y.T., Jr.'s skin felt greasy. He could not hear when his father introduced him to the expressionless man in safety glasses who would be his supervisor for the summer.

As a boy of seventeen, Y.T., Jr. found himself on the very bottom rung of the sacred ladder of seniority by which everything and everyone in the Machine Shop was measured. Beyond that, everyone in the Shop knew who he was and knew that his stay there would be short. As his father's surrogate, he bore the brunt of any beef or grudge that was held against the Old Man, which is not to say that anyone openly persecuted or abused the boss's son. But Y.T., Jr. worked harder than he had ever worked in his life and worked harder than anyone else in the Machine Shop had ever worked. For that matter, he worked harder than anyone in any machine shop anywhere had ever worked since the outbreak of the Industrial Revolution.

As their apprentice, he learned little about the function and operation of the machine tools. Rather, he fetched the bar stock, rolled steel and castings to feed the machines and keep them running throughout the day. He gathered and carried away their scrap. He cleaned floors, walls, ceilings and the uncleanable machines themselves, often working overtime to finish what had been demanded of him. By the end of the summer, Y.T., Jr. was a bone-weary teenager whose hands were scabbed and scarred from handling unforgiving metals. His skin was pale from days of working from seven in the morning until eight-thirty or nine at night under the artificial light of the dungeonous basement. His ears rang and he never again put Brylcreem on his hair. He was genuinely grateful for the school year to begin for the first time in his life and vowed never again to be subjected to that kind of labor. Y.T., Sr. was pleased, but for good measure, he had his son work in the Machine Shop again over Christmas break and spring vacation.

The summer of 1964, when Y.T., Jr. was eighteen, his father had him work with the Sugarman, the crusty, old Negro who was charged with maintenance of the Old O'Reilly Candy Factory Building that now housed Erp Industries, Inc. Y.T., Sr. had acquired the building in Meadowlawns just outside Kansas City in 1958, when his company had outgrown the second floor above the Rexall Drug Store, Lucky Pierre's Beauty Salon and Vernon's Bait and Tackle Shop in Raytown. The Sugarman had come to Y.T., Sr. with the property. He had been a fixture at the Old O'Reilly Candy Factory Building ever since 1925 when he first started looking after the building and the equipment that poured out tons and tons of chocolate confections. The Sugarman had grown old with the building. Together their facades had become lined with the passing of time. Their joints creaked and their respective plumbing often got clogged up. Even so, the Sugarman still brimmed with vigor and life, and from his workshop located at the very center of the building, he kept his protégé of so many years up to the task of serving Erp Industries, Inc.

On quiet days, when all was well with the Old O'Reilly Candy Factory Building, the Sugarman would receive visitors in his workshop for idle conversation and, perhaps if they so desired, for a sip from his hip flask, which was always filled with the crystal clear liquid that Orley Bovine supplied him free of charge. Besides Orley Bovine, Vasili Ivanovich was known to stop by late in the afternoons when the burden of responsibilities oppressed him. When Arthur Needleman came into the plant from the West Coast, he always made sure to stop in at the Sugarman's workshop for a shot of moonshine and a few laughs before he went to the Marketing Department, which, of course, made Dirk Rangely doubly suspicious of that night in Los Angeles and of those dubious directions on that cocktail napkin that lead him into the very heart of urban darkness. Horace Cooley occasionally sought out a moment of peace and quiet there to calm his nerves and to find the strength to finish out another day's shift. Frik and Frak came so that Frik could barter trinkets from Fu Loin's in return for the right to borrow another issue from the Sugarman's complete and up to date collection of *Playboys*. Even Y.T., Sr., himself was known to pass a few idle hours in the Sugarman's workshop, which was a source of agonizing annoyance for people like Dirk Rangely, Rolf Guderian and Simon Salisbury who would not lower themselves to call upon a mere janitor and could imagine no reasonable explanation for such behavior in others.

In the Black

"You don' keep them feet together, boy, you gonna be walkin' all over you balls. Then you be sorry, fo' sho'," the Sugarman scolded Y.T., Jr as together they picked up a desk to move it to the opposite side of the Marketing Department offices. For the New Year, Dirk Rangely had embarked upon a major re-alignment of Erp Industries, Inc.'s corporate marketing strategy, beginning with a bold re-arrangement of all the desks and file cabinets under his command. As a result, Y.T., Jr. found himself at work on a Saturday moving furniture with the surprisingly spry Sugarman. After they set the desk down in its proper new space, Y.T., Jr. and the Sugarman sat down side-by-side on the desk top to catch their breath. "Who the hell taught you how to lift, boy?"

"There isn't anybody that has to teach me how to lift," Y.T., Jr. responded with good-natured rebellion, knowing that he was sure to get a lecture on the subject for his own good.

"You better learn to use those legs and learn 'em good, cause that back of yours ain't gonna stay young forever. Fo' damn sho'."

"Get out of here."

"Boy, I know that one day you gonna wake up with a crick in your back sos you can' never stand up straight."

"Oh, go on." Y.T., Jr. laughed.

"You go on you self, boy, and you be bent over looking down the rest of you life—in fact, you be looking down at you balls on the floor, oozing up twixt you toes, ifen you don' learn a thing or two from your old Sugarman. Fo' damn sho'." The Sugarman pulled out his hip flask and took a short pull. "Ah, now ain't that as sweet as rain on them daisies in the graveyard."

"Did Orley come through with a good batch?"

"That man is a saint of a sinner. Fo' damn sho'."

"Say, let me have a taste, huh?"'

With his eyes widened to show a broad band of white all around his irises, the Sugarman gave Y.T., Jr. an exaggerated look of shock and dismay at his request. He held the flask away on the other side of his body.

"Please?" Y.T., Jr. asked with a sweet and polite voice. "Come on, it's Saturday."

The Sugarman narrowed his eyes down to slits and scrutinized Y.T., Jr. carefully.

"So what's the big deal? There's no one around."

"I don' rightly know ifen you can handle it, boy." The Sugarman exaggerated his concern.

"Come on. I worked with Orley on the dock. I helped him every Friday and he sometimes let me have the leftovers for the weekend."

The Sugarman knew that already. "Well, I tell you one thing, you ain't no desk and you ain't no file cabinet neither. And ifen you fall down dead drunk, I ain't picking you up and moving you, too. Fo' damn sho'. No, sir."

"I'm not going to fall down dead drunk from *one* sip." The Sugarman reluctantly handed Y.T., Jr. the flask. When he took a healthy gulp, the Sugarman poked him hard in the ribs with his elbow. Y.T., Jr. choked and began coughing. He tried to speak, his voice only a hoarse whisper.

"Sheee-it damn, boy." The Sugarman grabbed back his flask and shook his head in disgust. "You don' know how to lift and you don' know how to sip—what is the Sugarman to do with you, boy? Ain't you never gonna learn nothin' a'tall?"

Y.T., Jr. could only cough and laugh at the same time.

"So you tell me, slick, I just wants you all to tell me one thing here." The Sugarman took another drink, then capped and returned the flask to his back pocket.

"What's that?" Y.T., Jr. asked, his voice still hoarse and broken up.

"How come you be going back to that there Engineerin' Department every time I turn around?"

"To, you know, to adjust the heat back there," Y.T., Jr. said softly—almost under his breath. He coughed again and tried to clear his throat.

"Uh-huh. Uh-huh—boy, ain't no heat that needs to be ad-justed five, six times a day. Uh-uh. Fo' sho'." The Sugarman shook his head slowly from side to side.

"And, ah, I had to change light bulbs that were starting to flicker and stuff."

"Twenty-three times? Sheee-it damn, boy, ain't but twelve lights back there and I *know* they all didn' take no powder all at the same times." The Sugarman gave Y.T., Jr. a stern, fatherly look. He shook his finger at the boy. "Now don' you go a lyin' to your Sugarman man, boy."

"Well, I…" Y.T., Jr. trailed off and looked away.

"Well you—well you—well you what, boy?"

"I, ah…"

"Come on, boy, come on—sheee-it damn, you don' even have to tell me. It's written all over you face like this mornin's headlines." The Sugarman laughed from deep within his belly. "Fo' sho'—that's fo' damn sho'. I can read you like this week's scratch sheet, boy. You been goin' down to make time with Miz Carrot Top, huh? Little Missie Red—tell me now, boy. And don' you go lyin' to your Sugarman."

Y.T., Jr. looked away to try to hide his wry, half-smile.

"Ha-ha. I knowed it." The Sugarman laughed and slapped his thigh. "I knowed it—I knowed it. I got you collared, boy."

Y.T., Jr. looked down at his feet dangling just off the floor and shrugged his shoulders.

"So tell me, boy, are you in the funk, yet? Hmmm?"

"In the funk?" Y.T., Jr. asked, looking up at the Sugarman, who smiled broadly and flared his nostrils.

"Sheee-it damn, boy!" The Sugarman groaned and slapped his forehead. "In the funk! Laid some pipe—don' you tell me that you don' know nothin' about chippies neither. What in tarnation is the Sugarman gonna do with you, boy?"

"Hey, I know about girls," Y.T., Jr. protested.

"Uh-huh, uh-huh. You know about chickie-poo, now do ya? Well what do you know, boy? And don' tell me they tuck you in at night and bring you breakfast in the mornin'. That ain't no chippie, that's you mama. What do you know, boy?"

"I know enough to get sent off to school 'cause I got one pregnant," Y.T., Jr. blurted out defiantly.

"Ha-ha! Sheee-it damn, I knowed you was alright, just like you old man." The Sugarman took out his flask and offered it to Y.T., Jr. "So, tell me now, boy, we gonna have a God damned little red-headed Erp diggin' round and round?"

"No. That was a different girl—from school. This past summer, she, er, she went away." Y.T., Jr. took a drink and passed the flask back to the Sugarman. He watched him take a pair of huge gulps and put the flask away. "I don't even know that red-head's name."

"Well, why don' you ask her, boy? It ain't as if you ain't had no damn opportunity. You probably done wore out them valves on the radiators in that damn Engineerin' Department."

Y.T., Jr. sighed heavily. "I don't know. She's different. She's not like anyone else. Not like that—that cheerleader that, you know, went away. She's—she's different somehow. I can't explain it."

"Uh-oh. Uh-oh, boy, that sounds like love." The Sugarman shook his head slowly. "She's got you by the short hairs, boy, and she's draggin' you to a bed full of rattler snakes."

Y.T., Jr. looked down at the floor and nodded.

"Hi-there-how-are-you-today, men?" Dirk Rangely blurped out as he walked by the desk where Y.T., Jr. and the Sugarman sat. The smell of white lightning in the air slowed Dirk Rangely down. He stopped, turned and looked back at the pair staring blankly back at him, until they slowly got down off the desk and started moving furniture again. Dirk Rangely hurried back to his office to check on their progress as compared with the special blueprints he had coerced Horace Cooley into secretly preparing for him.

From his very first day back to work over Christmas Break, Y.T., Jr. found himself gravitating towards the Engineering Department more and more. He had, indeed, adjusted the heat so often that the room was a perfectly constant seventy-two degrees. He had replaced all the light bulbs—even the ones that were not flickering—had caulked every window, had oiled every squeaky chair, had spackled and retouched every mar on the walls, and had even planed down the door on the back storage room that had been sticking for the past thirty years. But Y.T., Jr.'s over-powering attraction for Scarlett Brookings had an almost equal and opposite reaction that held him suspended in an orbit around her. He could not stop thinking about her, yet at the same time, he could not bring himself to approach her any closer—not even simply to say 'hello'. When January twenty-fifth came, he found himself, his steamer trunk and his suitcases on the company Learjet streaking down J-80 on his way to college in California and he had not spoken one word to Scarlett Angelina Brookings. Frik and Frak tried to cheer him up with a dinner on Fisherman's Wharf and, of course, a visit to Fu Loin's.

"Ah, Flick and Flak, you come again. So good to see you," said the short, balding Fu Loin as he shuffled up to the drunken trio. He bowed deeply and peered over a pair of eye glasses with lenses as thick as Coke bottles. "Ah, good to see you. And so good to see Little Whitey again."

"No, no—not Whitey. Y.T. It's Y.T. Y-period. T-period," Y.T., Jr. tried in vain to correct the grinning Fu Loin.

The ex-Commander smiled *That Smile!* at all the young, scantily clad Asian prostitutes lounging around the "Reading Room" portion of Fu Loin's establishment. The ex-Colonel's excitement was betrayed by his doubly-widened eyes and the large, hot, bulbous red glow at the end of his cigar.

"Ah, Flik and Flak, I have many good sclews for you. Many good sclews for you and you little fliend."

~~~

The Car Pool

"The man was truly one of the great unsung geniuses of our time," Mort Mortenstein pontificated to his two companions. They were seated at their usual Wednesday noontime table in a dark, quiet corner of Dante's.

"Come on, Mort, the guy's a twit," said Hugh Betcha, Vice-President/Materiel, through a mouthful of spaghetti. Another forkful circled in a holding pattern in his right hand, while in his left, a thick slice of garlic bread made a final approach to his gaping mouth.

"He had those chiseled good looks. He could sing. He could dance." Mort Mortenstein waved his unlit pipe around in the air as if he were trying to conduct the conversation like a maestro might conduct an orchestra. "The man did the undisputed best Chevalier impression of them all. No contest."

"A twit, Mort," Hugh Betcha said with a dozen threads of spaghetti dangling from his mouth like worms.

"It is a shame that so few can appreciate and respect such a truly superb talent. It is an art. An art, you understand." Mort Mortenstein bit hard on the stem of his pipe and threw his head back to focus on the ceiling. "There are so few who can lay claim to that unique blend of timing, poise, grace, intuition, humility and talent—not to mention the ability to think quickly on one's feet—required to be a bona fide genius at such a craft. Look at George Burns. Now here we have another outstanding straight man, but he only had to carry his wife. He could not hold a candle to Zeppo Marx, though. After all, Old Zep was supporting three comedians with his performances, not just one."

"A twit."

"Sure, the others got the laughs, but where would they be without *him?* I'll tell you where, flat on their faces. Zeppo was the one that laid the groundwork, built up the background, provided the context, to give their punch lines meaning and relevance. Do you think that is easy?" Mort Mortenstein shook his head. "Simpletons. Groucho, Chico, Harpo—*buffoons,* all of them. And they got the recognition. But, of course, Old Zep got all the girls. And I understand the man made a fortune in California real estate."

"A flaming, bug-eyed twit."

"A genius of the first order—a man decades ahead of his time!"

"A God damned, mother-fucking T-W-I-T, *TWIT!*"

The third man at the table, Simon Salisbury, Vice-President/Personnel, sat between Mort Mortenstein and Hugh Betcha, silently enduring the argument that was as regular as their Wednesday lunchtime meetings. He methodically picked out the clam bits from his linguine and washed them down with measured sips from a glass of Chablis. Simon Salisbury was a slight, scholarly man who wrote memorandums to himself and often seriously considered whether or not they might warrant some sort of reply. He refused to squander his mental energies on the trivial matters, such as movies, baseball, television or the weather that Mort Mortenstein and Hugh Betcha always disagreed about. The two seemed to argue for no apparent reason other than to argue, for certainly their debates showed absolutely no great depth of understanding or keenness of vision on either man's part. Every week, Simon Salisbury quietly ignored their inane banter until the argument would begin to boil over from the verbal to the physical. Mort Mortenstein would begin brandishing his pipe as if he had pulled it from a sheath and Hugh Betcha would begin stabbing and slashing at his food with a murderous look in his whiskey-filmed eyes. At the very moment that an eruption appeared imminent, Simon Salisbury would bring the table conversation back to the matters at hand. His voice was soft, but of such clarity that no one failed to hear what he said. Wiping a stray drop of wine from the corner of his mouth, Simon Salisbury interjected, "So, gentlemen, now that Erp the Younger has embarked upon his collegiate career, do you believe that our little dilemma in the Hallowed Hall of Science can be rectified such that we may begin collecting from Mr. Dzhugashili?"

"Huh? Oh, sure." Mort Mortenstein broke off his glare at the hulking Hugh Betcha, who shoveled the last of his spaghetti into his mouth and gnashed his teeth down hard upon it. "Actually, though, I'd be more pleased if we could place a few more secretaries with his engineers. If we lose a bit with the red head in return for more business, eh, it will have been worth the investment."

"You know what I heard? I heard that the Old Man gave the jail bait that Little Erp knocked up an all-expense paid trip to Sweden—if you know what I mean." Hugh Betcha wiped the splatters of tomato sauce from his ruddy-complected face. He signaled the waitress over to order a second helping of spaghetti. "Hey, you know what they call an abortion in Prague? *A canceled Czech.*"

The accounting overtones of Hugh Betcha's joke shook loose a chuckle from Mort Mortenstein. Simon Salisbury grimaced at his partner's poor taste, but politely took a sip of wine to mask his expression.

"A canceled check," Mort Mortenstein said, taking out his black, hard-covered journal and making a note in it. "I like that. A canceled check. That's very good."

"Yes. Well," Simon Salisbury winced. He pulled a memo he had written to himself from a file folder and glanced over it. "I met with Rolf Guderian Friday. He asked if there might not be a more appropriate job title for an Administrative Assistant's Assistant."

"What did you tell him?" Mort Mortenstein asked with interest.

"I told him that, yes, there was a more appropriate title, 'Secretary'. Of course, he protested, claiming that there was a clear need for another class of administrative worker to help bridge the gaps in his organization that are hampering the efforts of his people to be able to effectively perform the functions expected of them. He is obviously scheming to hire more people."

"And? So?"

"I told him that I would have my staff work up a job title and issue a job description for him to review. I did make it clear, though, that this new position would have to be filled exclusively with women."

"Very good," said Mort Mortenstein, smiling and making a note in his journal.

"Of course, that did not entirely displease Mr. Guderian," smirked Simon Salisbury. He re-filed his memo in the folder.

"I'll bet not—the horny little kraut," Hugh Betcha noted with contempt. He blew his large, bloated nose into his napkin with a series of loud, juicy snorts.

"He also inquired into the number of salesmen that Dirk Rangely has working for him," Simon Salisbury added with a measure of concern in his voice. "I checked with our people. It appears that Mr. Guderian is concocting a plan to change the job title of all salesmen to 'Sales Engineer" and then have them transferred to his department's payroll."

"That guy has a real talent for being an asshole," Hugh Betcha said as he carefully watched the waitress set down another plate of pasta in front of him. "He'd make somebody a hell of a straight man, eh Mort?"

Mort Mortenstein ignored Hugh Betcha's backhanded slap. "Well, the Assistant's Assistant thing is good, especially since Rolf is always willing to pay a premium for his blonde-haired, blue-eyed beauties. But this move to get hold of Dirk's department, I don't like it. Dirk's a good client, too. If Guderian gets his hands on the Marketing Department, that will upset the *status quo* and the balance of power. There might be no stopping him then, which might very well mean trouble for us."

"Mr. Guderian cannot do anything without going through me," said Simon Salisbury with Chamberlain-like certainty. "I think we can keep the situation under control and hold Mr. Guderian's ambition's in check."

"Very good," Mort Mortenstein said, making another note in his journal. "Now, what about commodities?"

"How about 'em?" Hugh Betcha shot back.

"What do our positions look like?"

"Warehouse is running about seventy-seven percent capacity. No sweat. Stock turnover is running seven to ten weeks, a bit longer on some of the strategic metals, but everything is copacetic." Hugh Betcha took a big gulp of Jim Beam whiskey, then attacked his spaghetti again.

"I saw in the *Wall Street Journal* where magnesium prices are quite depressed," Simon Salisbury said, implying impending doom with the tone of his voice.

"Magnesium's down?" Mort Mortenstein asked with concern. He looked at Simon Salisbury, then at Hugh Betcha. "Do we have magnesium?"

"Yeah, Mort, we have magnesium. But that's just spot market fluctuations," Hugh Betcha dismissed with a wave of his fork. "*No sweat.*"

"Yes. Right. Well then, what about this Asian thing?" asked Mort Mortenstein. "Any chance of a favorable situation developing for us?"

"Nah, I'm telling you we'll just roll over the slant-eyed bastards like we did on Guadalcanal—or drop the Big One on them and be done with it," Hugh Betcha said into his plate, punctuating his opinion with a slurp of noodles.

"I have done a good deal of research into the current situation and into historical precedents that are likely to forecast future trends," Simon Salisbury said with a look of disdain aimed at Hugh Betcha. He pulled another memo to himself from his file. "Contrary to our learned colleague's views, I believe that this conflict is likely to escalate soon and continue on for a number of years. Besides one another, the Vietnamese have been fighting the Chinese, the Japanese, the French—for nearly ten years after World War II as De Gaulle tried to save this little pearl of their empire—and now, vicariously, the United States as our government tries to shore up the Huong regime in the South. Historically the place is a tar pit and has been so for thousands of years. Once a foreign power steps into a conflict there, it cannot get itself extricated from it. The way which I envision events, first the advisers, then the off shore ship activity and the aircraft sorties all lead to an inevitable conclusion. With the passage of the *Tonkin Gulf Resolution,* it will not be long before President Johnson commits ground troops."

"Confidence factor?" asked Mort Mortenstein.

"Eighty percent within the next twelve months. Ninety percent within the next eighteen months," Simon Salisbury read matter-of-factly from his memo.

"Alright, then, I think we should get moving and see what we can do. Hugh, I want you to start looking at copper, samarium, magnets and, of course, ball bearings. Let's see what we can do to lock up deliveries at least as far out as the end of this year and perhaps into 1966 if possible."

"We could get massacred if we actually have to take delivery of what we commit to Mort," Hugh Betcha warned.

"But, if they start shooting up hardware in a big way over there, we'll be sitting in the cat-bird seat when lead times start pushing out." Mort Mortenstein said with a growing grin as he clenched his teeth down hard on the stem of his pipe. "Especially ball bearings. Everyone will be screaming for ball bearings. See what you can do to get them locked up all to ourselves. Especially ball bearings."

"Might take some up-front money," Hugh Betcha said. "And we could run into a bit of a warehouse crunch in the short term."

"Let me take care of all that. You just let me know what you need. I think Simon here is right that this Vietnam thing will go big." Mort Mortenstein made a note in his black journal. "That's all I have. Fellows? Anything else?"

Simon Salisbury shook his head and put away his folder of memos.

"Did you hear what happened down in manufacturing?" Hugh Betcha asked with a tomato sauce-stained grin. "That stupid son-of-a-bitch Peckerfelt. Somehow his people sent four ship sets of completely empty boxes to the Navy—absolutely nothing inside, not even solder droppings. Just empty tin cans. Boy, the Navy really blew their bilge at that one."

"You mean, the units went all the way through Quality Control testing and nobody detected the omission?" Simon Salisbury asked with astonishment.

"You mean old 'One Hundred Percent Test' Tillman?" Hugh Betcha laughed out loud. "That idiot tries to watch *I Love Lucy* on his oscilloscopes."

"Is the Navy going to come down hard on us?" asked Mort Mortenstein. "A team of auditors is the last things we need right now if we are going to move on this Asian opportunity."

"Nah, the Old Man smoothed it all out," said Hugh Betcha. "I think he got Orley Bovine to take the rap and sweet talked the Navy into believing it was a mix-up with another spares order in Shipping. But I'll bet a dollar to a dime that Peckerfelt's ass is in the Old Man's sling."

"I wonder what the Old Man's got on Orley Bovine," Mort Mortenstein said, thinking out loud. He made a note in his journal, then snapped the cover shut.

"Empty boxes? Unbelievable." Simon Salisbury shook his head.

"Well, believe it. Obviously, Peckerfelt is running a class act down there in Manufacturing." Hugh Betcha let out a thunderous belch. "And you know what else I heard? You know why Dirk Rangely doesn't have any Negroes working for him?"

"No, why is that?" asked Simon Salisbury with special interest, being in charge of personnel.

In the Black

"Because he doesn't want any *black marketeers* in his department." Hugh Betcha laughed heartily, but his joke drew only icy stares from his car pool companions.

The Freshman from Ukiah, California

Y.T., Jr. owed it all to a seventeen year old, auburn-haired cheerleader named Rebecca Sue Simmons.

On the home team hash mark at the south forty-seven yard line, Y.T., Jr. did what every male pupil, teacher, administrator and janitor—*especially* the janitors—at Harry S. Truman High School dreamed and only dreamed of doing. Rebecca Sue Simmons, who represented the widely acknowledged pinnacle of beauty in Meadowlawns, Missouri, the affluent suburb of Kansas City where Y.T., Jr. and his classmates lived, did what she had never ever done before, not even with Barry Boswagger, her steady boyfriend since sophomore year who was the Truman *Fighting Eagles'* alleged "triple threat" football team captain.

Three months later, upon the death of a laboratory rabbit labeled 'AZ-776', Rebecca Sue Simmons began a list of *if onlys* that, like arithmetical *pi,* continued on *ad infinitum* and can only be approximated by rounding off. *If only* she and Barry Boswagger had not argued at the Fourth of July fireworks display. *If only* she had not left her purse in his car when, furious with Barry Boswagger after their tiff, she decided to ride home with sister cheerleaders Donna, Denise and Robin. *If only* they had not stopped at Steak and Shake for French fries on the way home. *If only* Y.T., Jr. had not come in just at the very moment when she was alone, penniless and embarrassed at the cash register. If only she had not, in her anger, foolishly hit upon a scheme to make Barry

Boswagger insanely jealous by letting Y.T., Jr. buy her French fries, sit with her and even drive her home. *If only* she had not been so completely disarmed by Y.T., Jr.'s sly, infectious smile and his alpine-lake blue eyes. *If only* she had known the evil exhilaration of racing a motorcycle through the night on winding country roads at speeds well in excess of all posted limits. *If only* she had not drunk any of that strange, clear liquid out of the mason jar that Y.T., Jr. had with him. *If only…*

Rebecca Sue Simmons was destined to spend the rest of her days factoring out her life through formulae that would never equate with reality. Yet in all her calculations, there was one variable that she blindly refused to admit or allow: *If only* she had not been secretly and inexplicably attracted to the handsome, aloof teenager who seemed to be the very antithesis of all the holy tribal hierarchies and sacred social rituals of life at Harry S. Truman High School that were as real to her as hard wooden desks and bland cafeteria food.

In the Harry S. Truman High School yearbook, the *Eagletarian,* Rebecca Sue Simmons' picture seemed to be on every other page, year after year. Y.T., Jr., on the other hand, was nowhere to be found, even though his thick, wavy blonde hair and his strong, ruggedly cut features would have made a striking portrait. Though perhaps a bit lean for five-foot, eleven inches, he was tall enough and athletic enough—as tall and almost as athletic as Barry Boswagger—to be a football quarterback or a basketball guard or a baseball pitcher, but Y.T., Jr. never tried out for any sport. Rebecca Sue Simmons had never-ever seen him at a football game or a pep rally assembly or a Friday evening bonfire or a homecoming dance, such was the depth of his atheistic rejection of school spirit. Instead, Y.T., Jr. wore a weathered, leather Naval aviator's jacket, assumed a studied, irreverent slouch and chain-smoked cigarettes in the boy's room with the likes of Marty Keegan and Billy Saul Sawyer, in open defiance of the school rules and the authority vested in Vice-Principal Snyder by the Board of Education.

Marty Keegan, Billy Saul Sawyer and Y.T., Jr. had been best friends since the fourth grade, long before Rebecca Sue Simmons or Barry Boswagger or William McBeezers, the Senior Class President, or Suzie Meanderdil, the *Eagletarian* Editor-in-Chief, or Mindy Covers, the Pep Club President, or any of the socially conscious others had come to the rolling farm country that would eventually become incorporated as Meadowlawns. In Rebecca Sue Simmons' eyes, a more unlikely trio could hardly be found. Y.T., Jr. was the handsome son of a wealthy businessman with the biggest house in Meadowlawns, who should have been one of *them,* but, inexplicably, was not. Marty Keegan's father was dead and he himself was a short, skinny loudmouth who was always getting into trouble. He did not look like a football player and did not act like a football player, but he was the leading receiver of Barry Boswagger passes, much to the dismay of Barry Boswagger and Head Coach Sox who both concurred that he was unfit to wear the uniform of the Truman *Fighting Eagles.* If a fight broke out on the football field, Marty Keegan was sure to be in the middle of it. He would have won a junior varsity letter, but he was caught bringing beer on the team bus heading home from the last game of the season. Marty Keegan made a poor representative of Harry S. Truman High School's best.

Billy Saul Sawyer was one of the few country hicks bussed in from his father's hog farm in some God-forsaken corner of the school district. He was big-boned with a broad, open face that

Rebecca Sue Simmons thought looked moronic. His head was inevitably stuck under the hood of some car and his hands were always black and grimy. It was one thing to be a moron, but totally inexcusable to be a filthy moron. Billy Saul Sawyer was an untutored mechanical genius who kept Y.T., Jr.'s Harley Davidson running at peak performance. All too often, Rebecca Sue Simmons had noticed the three of them driving off in Billy Saul Sawyer's loud, growling, red Chevy pick-up truck, leaving their assigned seats in Mrs. Newcomb's third hour English class empty. She just could not understand what Y.T., Jr. saw in those two when Harry S. Truman High School had so much more to offer.

The worst of all Y.T., Jr.'s transgressions was his outright betrayal of Harry S. Truman High School. Vague rumors circulated of some sort of scandalous affair between him and a girl from rival Valley View High School in the next district over, a decidedly middle class institution compared to Harry S. Truman High School. Y.T., Jr. made no effort whatsoever to even try to date any respectable girl of a recognized social standing even approaching Rebecca Sue Simmons' status as Head Cheerleader and odds-on favorite for Senior Homecoming Queen. In fact, until that Fourth of July in the Steak and Shake, she was not entirely sure that Y.T., Jr. knew just who and what she was, which left a painful wound to her own vanity. With a blindness akin to that of a fervent religious fanatic, Rebecca Sue Simmons could not understand nor openly tolerate Y.T., Jr.'s wholesale rejection of her values. Yet, this seeming societal prince of darkness secretly intrigued and infatuated her. Often, upon passing him in the hall between classes or spotting him across the crowded school cafeteria at lunch, she privately speculated and frequently fantasized on what might have happened to that girl from Valley View High School.

In the Black

"Holy shit! I can't believe it!" Marty Keegan exclaimed as, dressed in gray sweats, he trotted around the running track that encircled the Harry S. Truman High School football field. Y.T., Jr., with Billy Saul Sawyer behind him, rode his Harley 74 motorcycle around the track, pacing Marty Keegan and keeping him company as he ran. It was the October after that momentous Fourth of July in 1964. The changing and falling autumn leaves were symbolic of other changes and falls. Barry Boswagger had fumbled four times and had thrown five interceptions in an embarrassing 49-3 loss to the Valley View *Stallions*. Rebecca Sue Simmons had been absent from school all week, spoiling her perfect attendance record of the past three years and abdicating her homecoming crown. "So that's why she kept puking at football games instead of leading cheers. Nobody could figure it out."

"I think he's yanking us, Keeg old buddy," Billy Saul Sawyer drawled behind Y.T., Jr.'s back. "Ain't nobody gonna mount the queen bee, 'cepting that worthless drone Boswagger."

Y.T., Jr. just smiled and stared at the front tire of his Harley as he made slow even S-turns on the cinders to stay abreast of Marty Keegan as he jogged.

"This is the biggest scandal to rock Harry S. High since old Coach Sox exposed himself to the fourth hour Home Ec class," said Marty Keegan. "Come on Erp, spill your guts. Who-what-when-where-how?"

"Aw Keeg, why don't you just put all that hot shot reporter shit out to pasture," moaned Billy Saul Sawyer.

"When it's in your blood, it's in your blood, and I can smell a front page story brewing for the *Meadowlawns Citizen Journal!* Banner headlines, seven columns long! 'SLEEPY SUBURB EXPLODES IN TURMOIL!' 'CHEERLEADER FUMBLES VIRGINITY!'

'EAGLE TEAM CAPTAIN LOSES WHAT LITTLE MIND HE HAD!' 'HEIR TO ERP EMPIRE KILLED IN CRIME OF PASSION!'"

"You couldn't smell pussy if it was sitting on your face," said Billy Saul Sawyer.

"Up yours, farm-boy. Forget him, Erp baby. Just tell me all about it."

"Not much to tell, really," said Y.T., Jr.

"He must have raped her," Billy Saul Sawyer said to himself as if he were thinking out loud. "That's it. That must be it."

"No, she was what you might call a 'Target of Opportunity' at the Steak and Shake." Y.T., Jr. smiled at his use of one of the ex-Commander's favorite phrases. "And I had had enough of Orley Bovine's best to decide, what the hell, so I engaged the enemy. A little white lightning, a little ride in the country on the old Harley D. and a little scrimmage out there at about the forty-five yard line." He pointed to the middle of the football field. "Like I said, not much to tell."

"Holy shit! Here? Right here on the very turf of Barry Boswagger's greatest triumphs?" Marty Keegan cackled out loud. "You bastard! You son-of-a-bitch! You will go down in history! I can see the sports page headlines now! 'BOSWAGGER BENCHED AS ERP GOES *IN* FOR THE SCORE!' I can't believe it! You of all people! That's great! That's positively great! I am in awe!"

"Some aspire to greatness. Other have it thrust upon them." Y.T., Jr. shrugged his shoulders modestly.

"So, how was she?" asked Billy Saul Sawyer. "Better than self-abuse and farm animals?"

"I hate to say it, but—"

"Oh no! Don't, please don't!" Marty Keegan pleaded. "Don't ruin the best fantasy I ever beheld in my wretched, miserable life!"

"Erp old buddy, we want the truth." Billy Saul Sawyer patted Y.T., Jr. on the shoulder. "Give it to us straight. We'll take it like men."

"Eh, her body might be seventeen going on twenty-four, but her brain is seventeen going on twelve." Y.T., Jr. watched Marty Keegan put his fingers in his ears and start singing the Harry S. Truman High School fight song. "She got a couple of shots of moonshine in her and she wouldn't shut up. Her hips were on vacation, but her lips were working overtime. It was like screwing a ventriloquist dummy for Christ's sake."

"You ain't gonna have to get hitched to her, are you?" asked Billy Saul Sawyer.

Y.T., Jr. turned around and looked back at Billy Saul Sawyer as if the farm boy had lost his mind. "Hell no! Barry can have her. They deserve one another."

"No? Did I hear you say no?" Marty Keegan asked, taking his fingers out of his ears. "You mean there's still a chance for me and her?"

"Well, I don't know about that. She's gone to live with an aunt and uncle in Chicago to finish school at some private institution that my dad's picking up the tab for."

"And Harry S. High loses a Homecoming Queen," sighed Billy Saul Sawyer, as if he were broken-hearted at that prospect.

"You know, I'll just bet that Barry Boswagger is one hurting turkey. He must be a completely broken man," said Marty Keegan. "Can you imagine? He's got three years invested in the biggest soc bitch in the whole school and Erp here comes along like some migrant farm worker and plucks the cherry right off his tree."

"What happens to you?" asked Billy Saul Sawyer. "Old man Simmons doesn't get your balls to mount in his trophy room, does he?"

"Nope." Y.T., Jr. smiled. "I just get to get out of this hole."

"How's that?"

"They're graduating me in December and shipping me off to college in the *promised land.*"

"Holy shit! Not California!"

"The one and only."

"Do you think Becky Sue would let me get her pregnant so I could go to college, too?" asked Billy Saul Sawyer.

"God Damn you, Erp!" After running eleven laps, Marty Keegan broke into a sprint. Y.T., Jr. accelerated to keep up with him and called out how fast he was running from his speedometer. Marty Keegan sprinted two hundred twenty yards around to the back stretch, then veered onto the infield and collapsed on the grass. He rolled onto his back, panting heavily. Y.T., Jr. circled back on his Harley, pulled up next to Marty Keegan and shut down the engine. He lit a cigarette, then leaned over to put it into his friend's mouth. After the first drag, Marty Keegan began coughing and hacking. "Thanks, Erp."

"What in tarnation do you do this to yourself for?" asked Billy Saul Sawyer getting off Y.T., Jr.'s motorcycle.

"Got to keep in shape. Or he'll screw me over," said Marty Keegan breathlessly. "Coach Sox hates my guts. But he can't cut me. 'Cause I'm the fastest guy on the team. So I got to stay in shape."

"But why play at all? Or is it your secret ambition to be Barry Boswagger's best friend."

"No, it is my secret ambition to see my by-line one day grace the pages of the *New York Times,*" said Marty Keegan loftily.

"Columbia University looks for that outgoing, extra-curricular bullshit and if that's what I gotta do to get in, then I'll play the game. Besides, it's more fun than fucking Spanish Club."

"Bullshit."

"Bullshit?"

"Yeah, bullshit."

"Well, also 'cause I like to hit people, see? There's nothing like getting up a full head of steam on a kick-off or a punt and then just plowing into somebody. That's really why Coach Chick won't let Coach Sox cut me. He thinks I'm pisser, 'cause I hit like a son-of-a-bitch."

"I say fuck all that Barry Boswagger country club bullshit."

"Yeah." Marty Keegan took a drag off the cigarette and exhaled loudly. "But I like to hit people."

"Do me a favor," said Y.T., Jr. "Hit Barry Boswagger a good one at practice for me."

"My pleasure, Mr. Erp."

Y.T., Jr. sat on the steps of Bashford Hall Dormitory, thinking how he owed it all to Rebecca Sue Simmons that just when he had finally found a truly worthy reason to go to work every day at Erp Industries, Inc.—*i.e.,* red-haired, gray-eyed Scarlett Angelina Brookings—there he was, two thousand miles from home at the University of California in Berkeley. As Y.T., Jr. meditated on the capricious and willingly malicious nature of fate, he noticed a large irregular stain on the sidewalk where someone must have spilled a can of maroonish-brownish paint. Even though the spot had obviously dried long ago, students on their way to and from classes took great pains to avoid stepping on the spill. Y.T., Jr. spent the afternoon studying the splotch as one might lie on his back to stare at the billowing shapes of cumulus clouds float across the sky. He sat there until the sun set. The spill's shape became vague and tenuous as it merged with the darkness. Even in the dim of the campus street lights, people stepped around that spot. Y.T., Jr. got up and walked to downtown Berkeley where he caught the Bay Area Rapid Transit to San Francisco. From the downtown Transbay Terminal, he walked to Fu Loin's and asked for Penelope Xing.

The unexpected turn of events during the autumn of 1964 caused Rebecca Sue Simmons' scheme to use Y.T., Jr. against Barry Boswagger to backfire with tragic results for her. Y.T., Jr. improvised on the situation and from the ashes of her ruin, he intended to rise up and take control of his life. His enrollment at Berkeley was to be his ticket to freedom, freedom from the staid, stagnant world of Meadowlawns and escape from that factory known as Harry S. Truman High School that produced mindless cogs for society much like the Machine Shop in the basement of the Old O'Reilly Candy Factory Building spat out metal part after metal part for consumption by Erp Industries, Inc. Most of all, though, he wanted to derail the *Y.T., Jr. Career Express* that had seemed unstoppable as it whisked him through high school on his way to Harvard and, after Harvard, to a place beside his father at Erp Industries, Inc., where he would be groomed to become the Old Man one day himself. Y.T., Jr. won the battle to attend the University of California instead of Harvard with surprisingly little objection from his father, but his ascent soon encountered turbulence.

Y.T., Jr. began to sense trouble from the moment he first pushed open the door to his dorm room on the eighth floor of Bashford Hall. The right side of the double-sized room was a scene that might have been staged for the University of California college catalog photographs. The right side of the room was bright, cheerful, and impeccably neat, with the floor swept, the bureaus dusted and the bunk beds made up smartly with matching bedspreads. At each of the two desks was a neatly dressed student sitting erect with an open text, a pair of sharpened #2 pencils and a stack of 3 x 5 note cards in front of him. They studied intently, even though classes were not scheduled to begin until the next day. The left side of the room was cordoned off by a pair of blankets hung from the ceiling. A bedspread draped over the window, making the left half of the room dark. The Dark Side looked as if a Search and Seizure Warrant had been issued and executed by zealous Treasury Department Agents wielding axes and sledge hammers. On the bottom bunk, a sleeping bag undulated as the unseen occupant tossed and turned, even though it was almost eleven o'clock in the morning. On the top bunk sat a bare mattress that would be Y.T., Jr.'s. He would be an occupant of the Dark Side.

When Y.T., Jr. first came in, the two students at the desks on the right side ignored him, apparently too engrossed in their studies to be bothered with the stranger who entered into their room without knocking. But as Y.T., Jr. began bringing in his suitcases, wading through the papers, text books, record albums, Marvel comic books, and dirty laundry that littered the left side of the room, they stole glances up from their texts and secretly exchanged concerned looks over the blonde-haired stranger in the leather aviator's jacket. After communicating silently behind Y.T., Jr.'s back through subdued gestures, exaggerated facial expressions and mouthed words, they stood up simultaneously, as if on cue, and slowly approached the imaginary boundary between the left side and the right side of the room. They silently watched Y.T., Jr. unpack, as close to the precipice of the Dark Side as they dared to venture.

Y.T., Jr. heard someone clear his throat behind him. He looked over his shoulder at the two occupants of the right side of the room. They were a pair of average students of average height, of average build with average looks. Since they did not dare to enter the forbidden zone of the Dark Side, Y.T., Jr. went over to meet them. For an awkward, silent minute, the two parties regarded one another. The two average students searched Y.T., Jr. for some sign or clue as to whether he might be friend or foe. Y.T., Jr. decided that these two were so horrendously average that they would not be able to pick themselves out of a group photograph.

"Ahem, we did not mean to disturb you, but we thought we would introduce ourselves. I am Nelson Fullman," said average student number one. He reluctantly stretched out his hand across the boundary to the Dark Side. "From Eugene."

Y.T., Jr. looked at Nelson Fullman's outstretched hand for a moment, then shook it firmly. It was like grabbing a damp washcloth. "Y.T., Erp, Junior."

"Erp?" Nelson Fullman asked himself as he withdrew his hand.

"I'm Fellows, Norman Fellows. From Eugene—Eugene, Oregon," said Nelson Fullman's companion. "Pleased to meet you. Pleased to meet you."

"Right," Y.T., Jr. said, wiping his hand dry on his pant leg after shaking hands with Norman Fellows. He pointed at the churning sleeping bag on the lower bunk on the Dark Side. "Who's he?"

Nelson Fullman and Norman Fellows looked at each other. Nelson Fullman admitted sheepishly, "We, um, do not know."

"Don't know," echoed Norman Fellows softly, shrugging his shoulders.

"Did he just get in, too?" asked Y.T., Jr.

"Well, no." Nelson Fullman frowned. "Actually, he has been here since the very start of last semester."

"Last semester," Norman Fellows mumbled.

"He's been here five months and you guys don't know who he is?" Y.T., Jr. watched Nelson Fullman and Norman Fellows sheepishly shrug their shoulders and shuffle their feet uncomfortably.

"He's always sleeping," protested Norman Fellows. "He's always sleeping during the day and stays out all night—if he even decides to come back to the room at all. And when he comes and goes, he sneaks in and out when we're gone at classes or meals or when we're sleeping."

"I tried once to stay up all night to try to catch him when he came in," Nelson Fullman sighed loudly, "but I guess I dozed off. We do not know, really, even what he looks like."

"We've never seen him, except for his hair." Norman Fellows pointed at the top of the sleeping bag where all that could be seen was a mass of matted, stringy brown hair. "Not terribly sociable. He's just not terribly sociable."

"A real mystery man, eh?" Y.T., Jr. asked with a measure of disbelief. He looked back at the bunk on the Dark Side and smiled to himself. He was already beginning to prefer the company of the roommate he had yet to meet.

"Yes, so it seems."

"So it seems."

"So, you would be from…" Nelson Fullman ventured tentatively.

"Kansas City."

"We're from Eugene—Eugene, Oregon," said Norman Fellows.

"Yeah, you said."

"Oh."

"Oh."

"I didn't miss anything, did I?" Y.T., Jr. pointed to the desks where Nelson Fullman and Norman Fellows had been studying before he came in. "I thought classes didn't start until tomorrow."

"They do, but we registered early this morning and stopped at the bookstore on our way back, so we are all ready to go," Nelson Fullman smiled proudly. "We are just getting a little head start on everyone else. After all, it is a dog-eat-dog world out there."

"A dog-eat-dog world," echoed Norman Fellows.

"Out there?" Y.T., Jr. pointed out the window with his thumb.

"Well, you know, in the real world," explained Nelson Fullman.

"What real world?"

"The competition is fierce, very fierce," blurted out Norman Fellows impatiently. "If you want to succeed, you can't let up for a minute—not for a minute."

"Succeed? At what?"

Nelson Fullman and Norman Fellows looked at one another, perplexed at the sudden and unexpected breakdown in communications.

"Why, at life, of course," Nelson Fullman said, astonished at Y.T., Jr.'s failure to grasp the obvious. "To get a job. To win promotions. To climb to the top."

"To the top of what?"

"Well, you know, top, um, top management," Nelson Fullman said.

"You know, top management. To become business leaders, the captains of industry, so to speak," Norman Fellows said with enthusiasm. "Nelson here is good with people and I've got a knack for numbers and figures that—"

Y.T., Jr. suddenly burst out in a hearty laugh as if he had finally gotten the sense of the punch line that they were trying to explain to him. "You mean that you want to be an executive, like a Vice-President of Finance and that Nelson here wants to be a corporate Vice-President of, say, Marketing?"

"Exactly," smiled Nelson Fullman, relieved that they spoke the same language after all. "Now you have got it."

"Now you've got it."

Y.T., Jr. doubled over with laughter at the two queer fellows from Oregon who actually aspired to become phlegm brains like Mort Mortenstein and Dirk Rangely and were apparently prepared to devote their lives to that end.

"And just what is it that you hope to become?" asked Nelson Fullman indignantly, perturbed at the impertinence of this person from Kansas City.

"Yeah, what do you want to be?"

"A nigger janitor." Y.T., Jr. laughed.

With obvious horror in their eyes, Nelson Fullman and Norman Fellows backed away from Y.T., Jr. A madness inhabited the Dark Side and in the short time since their new roommate had entered, the darkness had already infected him. Y.T., Jr. was still laughing out loud as they sat back down at their desks, being careful not to turn their backs on the raving lunatic in the leather jacket. They pretended to study, but they really remained on guard for any violent outburst that might endanger their persons. Y.T., Jr. lit a cigarette and stared at the two tragically average students from Eugene, Oregon. Nelson Fullman and Norman Fellows really wanted to ask him to stop smoking, but they were simply too afraid.

As the days and weeks passed, Y.T., Jr. became convinced that Nelson Fullman and Norman Fellows were once Siamese twins that had been separated physically, but not spiritually or emotionally. From the moment their alarm clocks simultaneously went off at precisely seven AM, their lives were synchronized and they marched through the day with an excruciatingly annoying togetherness. They dressed alike, acted alike, spoke alike and even thought alike, as evidenced by their mindless propounding of veritable Xerox copies of each other's opinions on world events as reported in *TIME Magazine* and the *Wall Street Journal,* the two journalistic beacons that guided their way. Worst of all was that every Friday evening after dinner, Nelson Fullman and Norman Fellows would spread out four Monopoly game boards on the floor and combine the pieces of four game sets to engage in a ruthless marathon of buying, selling, and going directly to jail, do not pass go, do not collect two hundred dollars, until they would collapse from financial fatigue in the wee hours of Sunday morning.

After three months at Berkeley, Y.T., Jr. still had not met the mystery man who occupied the bunk below his. The only time anyone saw him, he was completely cocooned in his sleeping bag. He slept during the day while they were all at classes, slipping in and out when no one else was around or awake. Frequently he disappeared for two or three days at a time. All in all, though, Y.T., Jr. still preferred his company to the company of Nelson Fullman and Norman Fellows, so he spent as little time as possible in the dorm room. And since it seemed to Y.T., Jr. that his classes were populated by Barry Boswagger-types and Rebecca Sue Simmons-types, on weekends he spent as little time as possible on campus.

"What are you doing out there?" asked Penelope Xing. Y.T., Jr. answered, but due to the fact that he was outside the dingy little room on the fire escape, she could not hear what he said. Frik and Frak always preferred women of pure Asian extraction. Y.T., Jr.

found their types more curious than attractive, though. Penelope Xing was Chinese-American. Y.T., Jr. found her oriental features overlaid on a Caucasian face beautifully erotic. Besides that, he could understand her when she spoke, since her accent was very slight. Penelope Xing wrapped the wool, U.S. Army surplus blanket from the bed around her slight, doll-like body and went over to the open window. She looked outside and saw Y.T., Jr.'s profile silhouetted against the glow of Saturday night in San Francisco. "Hey you."

"Hey me what?"

"Hey you, what are you doing out there?"

"Nothing." Y.T., Jr. flipped the butt of a cigarette out over the rail and watched it fall into the dark void of the alley five stories below.

"I don't know if Fu likes people out back there like that."

"Come on out."

"Me? What for?" asked Penelope Xing.

"For a look-see."

"To look and see what?"

"Come on out and see for yourself."

"But Fu—"

"Hey, forget him. Just come on out and see."

Penelope Xing could just barely see Y.T., Jr.'s boyish grin through the darkness. She climbed out through the window, trying not to fall and trying to keep the blanket wrapped around her naked body. Chilled by the cold April night air, she sat down close to Y.T., Jr. and pressed against his body. "Cold out here."

"It's not so bad."

"Chilly." Penelope Xing shivered.

"Look." Y.T., Jr. pointed out to the east, towards the panoramic view of the Embarcadero, San Francisco Bay, and the lights of

Oakland beyond, that could be seen from the fifth floor fire escape on the back of Fu Loin's establishment.

"It's a beautiful view," Penelope Xing whispered. "I never noticed before."

Y.T., Jr. lit a cigarette. He held it up to her lips so she could take a drag. "You fell asleep."

"I'm sorry. I have mid-terms next week," Penelope Xing said, looking down in shame.

"Mid-terms?"

"I go to San Francisco State College."

"Oh yeah? What are you studying?"

"History."

"History? Whatever for?"

"Because I like it." Penelope Xing gazed out across San Francisco Bay. "Sometimes it's nice to think about what it would be like to live in another place, in another time."

"Instead of being who you are now?"

"Maybe."

"Is it really so bad?"

"Sometimes." Penelope Xing bit her lip and nodded slightly. She began to shiver visibly from the cold. Y.T., Jr. put his arm around her shoulders. "I'm sorry—you know, you should have woken me up."

"That's okay. I just came out for air." Y.T., Jr. smiled at Penelope Xing.

"I'll give you your money back."

"No problem." He offered her the last drag of the cigarette. "Don't worry about it."

"How come you always ask for me? I'm not very good."

"I wouldn't say that."

In the Black

"I know I'm not as good as the other girls. And most of Fu's regulars don't want me because I'm not Chinese enough if they're American and I'm not American enough if they're Chinese, so usually I only get walk-ins. You are the only one who ever asks for me."

"I think you are just fine."

"I thought maybe I should take up yoga. I think it helps some of the other girls. I just can't figure out how, though."

Y.T., Jr. laughed.

"Don't laugh at me." Penelope Xing pouted. "I'm serious."

"Are you done for the night?" Y.T., Jr. asked.

"Well, business usually falls off after two-thirty or so, maybe because everyone is too drunk to get it up by then. If it's slow, Fu lets me go home"

"What time is it now?"

"About two."

"Do you mind if I stay for a bit?"

"Go again?"

"No." Y.T., Jr. smiled.

"On me? I feel bad that I fell asleep."

"I have something for you." Y.T., Jr. winked at Penelope Xing.

"What is it?"

"Close your eyes."

"Why?"

"Come on, just close your eyes. And no peeking—get it?"

"Get what?" asked Penelope Xing.

"No peeking. You know, no Peking."

"Very funny. You are a regular Bob Hope."

"Just doing my bit to keep the troops happy. Now, close your eyes," Y.T., Jr. ordered sternly. He waved his hand in front of

Penelope Xing's face to make sure she was not peeking. "Okay, now open your mouth.

"Oh no. Oh no. I know what—"

"You are peeking." Y.T., Jr. shook his finger at her.

"But—"

"Trust me." Y.T., Jr. smiled the disarming smile that had been Rebecca Sue Simmons' undoing. Infected, Penelope Xing smiled back. She closed her eyes and opened her mouth. "Come on, open up. Wider."

"It's not that big," Penelope Xing chuckled without opening her eyes.

"Come on. Open up real big." Y.T., Jr. rustled around in a large grocery sack that was beside him on the fire escape. He pulled something out of the bag and quickly pushed it into Penelope Xing's mouth. "Bite down hard."

"Twinkies!" Penelope Xing tried to say around a mouthful of cream-filled golden snacking cake. Y.T., Jr. picked up the grocery sack full of Twinkies and dumped it over her head. She giggled with glee as twin packs of the Hostess treats bounced all about her. A few fell from the fire escape to the dark alley below. "My favorite."

"I know."

"Thank you." Penelope Xing kissed Y.T., Jr. on the cheek and wrapped her arms around his neck to hug him. From inside the room came a powerful pounding on the door and a shrill voice screaming in Chinese. Penelope Xing leaned over Y.T., Jr. to scream back into the room in Chinese. After a fierce sounding exchange, she sat down next to him again, adjusted the blanket around her body and reached for a twin pack of Twinkies.

"Trouble?"

"No, just Fu. A bunch of sailors came in, but I told him you go again." She smiled and took a bite of Twinkie.

Y.T., Jr. got back to Berkeley from Fu Loin's at about four-thirty Sunday morning. A heavy fog shrouded the campus. He decided to have one last cigarette before going up to his room, so he sat down on the steps of Bashford Hall to smoke by the maroonish-brownish splotch that everyone superstitiously avoided. Out of the mist along South Strawberry Creek, a tall, lanky figure appeared. Y.T., Jr. watched what appeared to be a skinny, unkempt co-ed come directly towards him. The figure jogged up the stairs past him without a word, look or a nod to acknowledge the presence of the only other human being awake on campus at that hour of the morning. Y.T., Jr. realized that this person was really a male with very long, brown hair. He was dressed in a suede, frontier-fringed jacket, blue jeans, bright red tennis shoes and—*bright red tennis shoes!*

"Hey you, hold it!" Y.T., Jr. exclaimed, recognizing the red Keds sneakers that, co-incidentally, always happened to be parked on the floor next to his bunk whenever the sleeping bag on the lower bed was occupied. He hopped up and pointed at what must have been his co-inhabitant on the Dark Side. "You're Clinton Owsley, aren't you?"

The tall, long-haired stranger in red sneakers froze and slowly turned around. "Who are you, man, a cop?"

"No. I'm your roommate."

Clinton A. Owsley III stepped down three steps next to Y.T., Jr. so that the two roommates could scrutinize one another for the first time in almost four months. Clinton A. Owsley III had a lean, narrow face with tiny dark eyes, a large nose and thin drawn lips. His long, uncombed, brown hair parted in the middle and fell below his shoulders. Even on the same step as Y.T., Jr., he looked down at him. "You must be the new guy, huh?"

"Yeah, I—"

"Hey, man, how did you know who I was?"

"Those tennis shoes. They practically glow in the dark."

"Hmmm. And how did you know my name?"

"From your mail. I read it off an envelope that was sitting out on the desk."

"Wild, man, you are a cop aren't you—a cop at heart."

"What's with you? You got your picture hanging in a post office somewhere? Is that what makes you the original phantom of Bashford Hall?"

Clinton A. Owsley III smiled a crooked smile. "Dig it. So, what's your name, man?"

"Erp, Y.—"

"Erp? Far out. Are you one of the gun slinging Earps, like Wyatt Earp of Wild West fame? You know he lived in Frisco after he gave up his gun slinging ways, you know."

"Different Erps." Y.T., Jr. shook his head. "Spelled with an 'A'."

"Too bad, man, you got the cool eye of a slinger." Clinton A. Owsley III grinned and sat down on the steps of Bashford Hall. "Step into my office and have a seat, Slinger. Tell me, what brings you out to roam our lovely campus in the early morning dew?"

"I was just getting back from Frisco," Y.T., Jr. said as he sat down on the steps next to his roommate. He watched as Clinton A. Owsley III took out a thirty-five millimeter film canister filled with marijuana and a packet of Zig-Zag rolling papers and began to roll a joint.

"Far out. I don't ever remember seeing you on Pine Street or down in the Haight," Clinton A. Owsley III said as he worked quickly with practiced skill.

"I was down in Chinatown."

"What were you doing down in Chinatown, man?"

"I know some people."

"Heavy. That is a serious scene down there. Got some truly heavy hitters in that district." Clinton A. Owsley III sighted down the completed cigarette for straightness, rolled it between his thumb and forefinger to check the pack, wet the rolling paper by drawing it through his lips and finally lit it. He took a long draw and passed it to Y.T., Jr. "Toke up, Slinger, some of the best Gold on the Bay."

Y.T., Jr. took the hand-rolled cigarette and did exactly as Clinton A. Owsley III had done. He had never smoked marijuana before, but he recognized the odor from Fu Loin's where it often drifted out from the back rooms mixed with the smell of incense, cheap perfumes and hair spray. As he exhaled, Y.T., Jr. felt a dizzy, light-headedness begin to affect him that was better and quicker than Orley Bovine's best.

"So, Erp, what brings a cool slinger like you to town?" Clinton A. Owsley III asked. They passed the joint back and forth as they spoke.

Y.T., Jr. laughed, thinking about Rebecca Sue Simmons. His thoughts suddenly shifted gears. He stopped laughing. "I fell for a fairy tale."

"A fairy tale? I don't dig, man."

"The so-called promised land. All those stories in the papers and the magazines about the revolution taking place out here."

"You mean the Free Speech Movement?"

"Yeah, I thought something was happening out here—something different, a revolution. Something new, not the same old thing that I left K.C. to get away from."

"I'm hip."

"So what happened? Was it all just hype? Nothing but headlines to sell papers?"

"I'll tell you, man, those demonstrations were right on, man. It was the real thing. Like I was just standing there watching what was going on with like a thousand other dudes. And we were all just milling around like and all of the sudden everyone—all at once, all one thousand of us—everybody was on the same trip at exactly the same time, feeding off the same electricity with the same wavelength going through every one of us and it just, you know, happened. A real happening just spontaneously broke out, and I was a part of it. Like, I didn't even know what it was all about until I read about it the next day. But it was real. And it was righteous. It was far out."

"So what happened? Where's the revolution?"

"Like I said, man, it was just one of those spontaneous things that just happened. I don't have anything to do with any of those Free Speech Spooks or any of that other political bullshit, but I just got swept away with the whole thing, a thousand dudes standing up and saying fuck this shit all at once on the same wavelength, but I think that all those tedious motor mouths making speeches and writing position papers and making demands just made the whole thing too tedious, if you know what I mean."

"Yeah, I guess." Y.T., Jr. thoughtfully smoked the marijuana cigarette.

"So how do you get on with Mr. Dow and Mr. Jones?" Clinton A. Owsley III asked, pointing up to the eighth floor of Bashford Hall behind them.

In the Black

"You mean Fullman and Fellows?" asked Y.T., Jr.

"Man, did you notice that in their closet they hang their shirts and jackets and even their pants with the flies facing east? They do it in reverence to the New York Stock Exchange and the Wall Street Financial District. That truly blew my mind, man."

Y.T., Jr. laughed out loud. "They always struck me like a pair of phlegm-brained Siamese twins."

"*Ex-actly,* man. You know, I had a Psyche class with them last semester and they didn't even know I was in it. They defy classification as a human species, man." Clinton A. Owsley III sucked on the joint. "Vicious, too. Those dudes are vicious, man."

"Huh? They seem harmless enough."

"Well dig it, there used to be another dude in the room, some kid from Ukiah, California, or some damn place, and they all used to be buddy-buddy—a regular Siamese trio, man. Only this dude from Ukiah didn't know the score. He swallowed their dog-eat-dog Zen hook, line and sinker. By the end of October, he was a basket case, man, just asking to crack. He was positively hyperventilating about succeeding before he had ever even started. Then, he flunked some damn English Comp mid-term or something."

"So what happened? Did he drop out?"

"Drop out?" Clinton A. Owsley III smiled wryly. "Yeah man, in a way he did. See, once Mr. Dow and Mr. Jones figured out that this dude had screwed up and flushed his future by flunking an English Comp mid-term, they started acting like he didn't even exist. They didn't talk to him, wouldn't let him read their *TIME* magazines and their *Wall Street Journal,* man, and didn't let him play in their Monopoly games every weekend. Mr. Dow and Mr. Jones came down hard on the kid, and the kid came down hard on himself and he jumped out the window and came down real hard on the sidewalk."

"Come on. You are yanking me. He jumped out the window because he flunked a test? A stupid fucking test? Give me a break already."

Clinton A. Owsley III crushed out the joint and put the butt into a second film canister full of roaches. "True, man. The gospel truth. The Wiz don't lie, man."

"Come on, that's ridiculous."

"See, I was grooving on back to hit the rack and I found him." Clinton A. Owsley III pointed to the maroonish-brownish stain on the sidewalk. "Right there, man. A real bummer. What a bring down."

"Shit." Y.T., Jr. felt the good feeling generated by smoking the marijuana vanish, leaving a desolate aridity of thought within him. He stared at the splotch with new insight into why everyone took such pains not to step on it.

"I got to crash, man," Clinton A. Owsley III stood up. "You're alright, Erp. Next time you're making tracks back from Chinatown in the wee small ones and are too wired to crash, just stop on by the chemistry lab in Latimer Hall. Just tell the guard the Wiz sent you."

"The Wiz?"

"Of Oz—as in Owsley. We all need a stage name, Slinger." Clinton A. Owsley III headed up the stairs. He called back over his shoulder, "You're alright, Slinger. Just watch out for Mr. Dow and Mr. Jones, man."

"Right." Y.T., Jr. nodded slowly at the new portent of Clinton A. Owsley III's warning. His mind laced with *delta-9-tetrahydrocannabinol,* he stared at the stain left by the freshman from Ukiah, California, as if it were a Rorschach Test. After thirty-five years, another maroonish-brownish stain had faded from another sidewalk square three thousand miles away on the other side of the country, but not from the collective psyche of the Erps. That stain was where Y.T., Jr.'s grandfather had landed when he went out the window of his Wall Street office building on that fateful day in October of 1929, when his margin calls came in.

Afterwards, Y.T., Jr.'s grandmother, Anna Elise, watched her entire life get dismantled by lawyers in the most meticulous and tedious manner under the auspices of the New York State Probate Court. The effect of all the legal proceedings, arguments, appeals, petitions, affidavits, testimonies, etc., was downright novacainic on Anna Elise's sensibilities. She shed tears over the loss of her jewels and furs. Later, she only winced when the furniture and art collection were lost. She was numb by the time the Packards and Deusenburgs had gone and was nearly comatose when the estate on Long Island, the apartment in Manhattan, and the summer house in Cape Cod were all neatly and legally disposed of. After justice had been served, the bulk of what remained of the estate paid for the lawyers and Anna Elise Erp was left with just enough money to return to her childhood home of Kansas City with her fourteen year old son, Y.T., Sr., who was the sole-surviving male Erp.

Anna Elise's maiden name was Cassidy. The Cassidy family lived in Kansas City since before there was a Kansas City. Fueled by tales of the 1848 California Gold Rush, Wesley Cassidy quit the Philadelphia butcher shop where he apprenticed to march west in 1854 in search of fame and fortune. Three years later, he had made it only as far as the juncture of the Kansas and Missouri Rivers where he traded his dreams of gold for two cows and a meat cleaver to begin a business supplying cured meats to pioneers traveling west on the Oregon and Santa Fe Trails.

Wesley begot Wilbert, who begot Willis, Wallace, Wiley and Anna Elise. All except Willis, who succumbed to mustard gas poisoning in the Argonne Forest during World War I, and Anna Elise, who was unfortunate enough to be born into the Cassidy Clan a female, joined Wesley Cassidy in the family business. Through hard work and good fortune, the business grew steadily. When cattle came to the end of the Chisholm Trail, Cassidy men were there waiting with sledge hammers and cleavers. The Cassidy Stockyards became the biggest in Kansas City, making the family one of the wealthiest of the growing frontier town. The business grew even more as they acquired great tracts of land in eastern Kansas for ranches and feedlots. Wallace Cassidy fathered no sons to get involved in the business. Wiley Cassidy had two sons, William and Wilson. William Cassidy opened a restaurant specializing in Kansas City Strip Steaks, further expanding and vertically integrating the family's beef monopoly. Wilson Cassidy took the reins of the family empire when his father Wiley Cassidy was ruled legally incompetent after a crippling stroke.

The Cassidy family business was death, and the Cassidies took their business quite seriously. Anna Elise wanted to live life to its fullest and to enjoy every moment without restraint. She was not interested in becoming a quiet, proper matriarch of the Cassidy Clan. She pursued fun in every manner and means available, often scandalizing the good Cassidy name in the process. In desperation, Wilbert Cassidy finally sent his wayward daughter to a finishing school in New York that had come highly recommended by concerned business associates back east. There, in short order, Anna Elise managed to lose her heart, her virginity and her hand in marriage to the dashing young heir of the Erp Fortune. She also lost the family of her birth, as her marriage to the son of a man who had amassed his fortune by rum-running and God-only-knew-what other illegal activities and immoral means was abhorrent to the stoic, mid-western values of the Cassidies. After much soul searching, Wilbert Cassidy finally decreed that his only daughter would be cut loose from the herd and left to find her own way in life. Anna Elise hardly even noticed, though. She was young, beautiful and, most important, finally free of the stench and death that was the Cassidy stock in trade—free to enjoy the wild society life of New York City in the decade known as the *Roaring Twenties.*

In the eyes of her brother Wiley Cassidy, events had come full circle upon Anna Elise's return to Kansas City in 1931. She had forsaken the Cassidies for the Erps and now she was getting her just desserts. Wiley Cassidy saw to it that when the Last Will and Testament of their father was probated she remained exiled from the Cassidy family, the Cassidy estate, the Cassidy family business, the Cassidy fortune and the measured Cassidy charity. Nearly penniless at the depths of the Great Depression, Anna Elise was forced to look for work for the first time in her life. She finally found a job at the O'Reilly Candy Factory, boxing confections. It was hard work for anyone, but doubly hard for Anna Elise, who as a Cassidy and as an Erp had been immune from manual labors. Twelve-hour shifts of handling cardboard dried and split her hands. The smell of chocolate, which had once been such a delight, now turned her stomach. Anna Elise rented a cheap flat close to downtown Kansas City, downwind from the stench of the Cassidy Family Stockyards.

Anna Elise Erp bore up under her trials and travails. She found the strength to carry on by concentrating her love and attention on her son. She found joy and fulfillment in his life rather than her own. Together, they saw the Great Depression through, both working at the O'Reilly Candy Factory. She tutored him in school subjects and, though bereft of his natural father, saw him learn the ways of men and the world from the Negro janitor at the O'Reilly Candy Factory who was called the Sugarman. She saw Y.T., Sr. go off to attend Harvard University using the trust fund that his father had established, which had—miraculously—survived the liquidation of the Erp fortune. She watched him join the United States Navy and survive World War II, when so many others perished. She saw him go into business for himself and prosper, regaining some of the lost family wealth and enabling her to finally quit the O'Reilly Candy Factory and move from her tiny apartment into his huge, beautiful home in the suburbs. And though he never married, she saw him have a son to carry on the Erp family name. This pleased her most of all, in spite of the unsavory details of the entire affair.

"So, is this what you do here in the chemistry lab while the rest of the world sleeps?" Y.T., Jr. asked Clinton A. Owsley III. He had come to Latimer Hall at 1 AM Saturday morning after an uneventful Friday evening spent aimlessly roaming the Berkeley campus. Y.T., Jr. picked up a Pyrex beaker of blue liquid and a plastic laundry detergent bottle. "You spend your time searching for the secret formula for New, Improved *Whisk?*"

Clinton A. Owsley III shook his head and smiled a crooked smile. "Oh, man, I do not believe this."

"Believe what?"

"Believe you, man. New, improved *Whisk?*"

"What is it then?"

"Here, suck on this." Clinton A. Owsley III tossed a light blue sugar cube to Y.T., Jr.

"What for?" Y.T., Jr. caught the sugar cube and held it up between his thumb and forefinger to look at it.

"Try it, man, you'll like it. I guarantee it."

"How come it's blue?"

"Cause it's got New Improved *Whisk* on it, man. Now stop being a cop about all this and do what I say." Clinton A. Owsley III grinned from ear-to-ear when Y.T., Jr. popped the sugar cube into his mouth. "It will get rid of that ring around your mind, man, and you'll find out why they call me the Wizard of Oz."

"The *Wizard* of Oz? You know, I thought they called you the Wizzer of Oz, 'cause you're always pissing into the wind."

"I like you, Slinger, you're alright," Clinton A. Owsley III laughed. He lit a Bunsen burner and pulled a stool up next to the lab table. "Now, tell you what, man, you just sit here nice and quiet like and watch this here Bunsen burner for a minute or two while I tidy up a few things around here."

"What for?"

"Humor me, man. Just humor me."

Y.T., Jr. shrugged his shoulders and sat down on the stool. He leaned on the table with his chin in his hands and stared at the sharp blue methane flame. Slowly the crystalline compound C15H15N2CON(C2H5)2 that Clinton A. Owsley III manufactured in the Latimer Hall chemistry labs in the middle of the night began to take effect. The LSD unraveled and rewove Y.T., Jr.'s thought patterns over and over with steadily increasing frequency. The Bunsen burner became a sensory anchor as the psychedelic drug unleashed a tempest of perceptions and hallucinations, until in his mind he felt the many-colored, wax-like impressions that life had deposited on his memory melt and run together in a swirling vortex, a kaleidoscopic tornado that cut a wide swath through his psyche.

From all outward appearances, Y.T., Jr. sat perfectly still on the lab stool, quietly concentrating on the Bunsen burner flame. Two and a half hours later, Clinton A. Owsley III awoke him as if from a state of suspended animation.

"Is this stuff illegal?" Y.T., Jr. asked, realizing that he was suddenly capable of such leaps of imagination and insight that they could only be accurately measured in light years.

"Always the cop," Clinton A. Owsley III laughed. "No, man, not yet. But it will be one day."

"How come?"

"Cause it's too damn much fun."

"Yeah…" Y.T., Jr., stoned out of his mind, slowly nodded his head. "Yeah, it is."

"Well, Slinger, shall we be off?"

"Off? Off where?"

"On our trip." Clinton A. Owsley III popped a blue sugar cube into his mouth.

With that, Y.T., Jr. and Clinton A. Owsley III began an odyssey that led them from Berkeley, across the dark, expansive void of the cold waters of San Francisco Bay, to the far galaxy of lights on the slender peninsula of California beyond. The drug-induced intensity of each moment made the most common events and objects—the whoosh of the rapid transit doors closing, the changing of traffic lights at a deserted downtown intersection at 4 am., a sunrise just like every other sunrise in Golden Gate Park, black coffee and glazed donuts at the House of Do-Nuts, the ornate and excessive lines of the Victorian architecture in the Haight-Ashbury District, lounging in the Panhandle reading comic books, riding cable cars up and down the hills, passing out blue sugar cubes Johnny Appleseed-style to the wildly dressed people on Pine Street—take on epic proportions. Their journey ended early Sunday morning when Y.T., Jr. went to Chinatown to seek out the embrace of Penelope Xing. Clinton A. Owsley III tagged along and was overwhelmed by the pleasures to be had at Fu Loin's. It was there, that night, that he lost his virginity.

As the school semester wore on, Nelson Fullman and Norman Fellows noticed, with dismay and disgust, certain changes in Y.T., Jr. His hair began to get longer and his dress became more and more casual, bordering on the unorthodox in comparison to their average attire. He kept later and later hours, often disappearing altogether on the weekends. When he was in the room, he listened to loud, electric rock and roll music imported from England and seemed to take an inordinate interest in comic books. Through their average eyes, they saw only that the Dark Side corrupted another victim.

On January twenty-sixth, the day that Y.T., Jr. began classes at the University of California at Berkeley, Rebecca Sue Simmons miscarried at a suburban Chicago hospital. Upon hearing this news, Y.T., Sr. quietly abandoned his efforts to gain legal custody of the child.

P.I. Parmakianski

"The right man in the right job," was one of the guiding philosophies of Y.T., Sr. And in his own opinion, Y.T., Sr.'s ability to execute that philosophy was the principle factor contributing to his success.

It had not been so easy, though, for Y.T., Sr. to find a man quite the caliber of Private Investigator Parmakianski. A man was needed who was unwavering in his resolve and dogged in his determination; who was loyal, obedient and housebroken, knowing when he was wanted and when he should make himself scarce; who was blessed with a stunted ambition and a hormonally inactive initiative; and who, above all else, was pervasively inept and embraced a skewed set of moral sensibilities. Private Investigator Parmakianski was all of this, and more.

Private Investigator Parmakianski detested his own name. A private eye's moniker should be hard-hitting like 'Spade' or 'Hammer' or 'Gunn'. Instead, his name floundered aurally like a beached mackerel. To add insult to injury, his first name was not Sam or Mike, but Julius. There was simply no salvaging Julius in any way, shape or form to post on the frosted glass of an office door or to have emblazoned on a business card. But this handicap had not wavered his resolve. He simply answered only to Private Investigator Parmakianski, thus avoiding ridicule by giving clients, suspects and witnesses such a mouthful of syllables to spit out that they were usually left breathless.

Private Investigator Parmakianski had been treated like a pariah by the other boys in the upstate New York orphanage where he was raised. Much to the chagrin of the nuns, he filled the blank slate of his past with the stories and the stylings of Dashiell Hammett, Mickey Spillane, and the like. By the time he was fourteen, Private Investigator Parmakianski was sneaking away from the orphanage to New York City where he gawkily followed buxom, long-legged women and dapperly dressed men, pretending they were all suspects in the unsolved murder cases festering in his imagination, until the police collared him and sent him back to the stiff hickory switches and the stern chastenings of the nuns. Needless to say, there were no prospective foster parents for a gangly adolescent who acted like a hard-boiled, yet pint-sized, Mike Hammer. At eighteen, Private Investigator Parmakianski was discharged from the orphanage directly into the Army, where he was as unpopular with his G.I. barracks mates as he was with his orphan bunk mates. The sole saving grace of his tour of duty at Ft. Dix was that he at least got the chance to fire a pistol, making him somewhat less of a menace to himself and the general public once he found himself a civilian again, free to roam the streets of New York City with a large caliber semi-automatic pistol bulging beneath his left armpit.

The gangly-gawky orphan Parmakianski grew up into a gangly-gawky Private Investigator Parmakianski, who usually towered over the crowd by at least a head—a distinct advantage when tailing a suspect, but hard on the knees when trying to look inconspicuous. His greatest asset was his trench coat, which concealed a body upon which clothes absolutely refused to hang properly. Belts never lined up straight across his waist. Shirt buttons zig-zagged up his chest. Neck ties always slanted off at inappropriate angles, at times almost parallel to his ribs. His shoulders sloped downhill, sometimes to the left, sometimes to the right, but always with the effect of causing one shirt sleeve to appear shorter than the other. If one sock stayed up on his leg, the other flopped pathetically about his ankle—and it was always the sock exposed by the pant leg which, co-incidentally, was that day shorter than the other. Private Investigator Parmakianski's second best asset was a gray felt hat, which covered a part that meandered across his scalp, at places running perpendicular to his ears, and a cowlick that stood at an aggravating attention.

After his discharge from the Army, Private Investigator Parmakianski fulfilled his ambitions by servicing lonely widows and desperate old maids on Social Security or modest pensions who beseeched him to retrieve their runaway pets and/or to track down long lost lovers. Most times, it did not matter if he succeeded, just so long as he would visit with his client once a week to have a cup of tea and report on the progress of the case. Such was not the life he had constantly read, dreamed and fantasized about as a youth in diametrical opposition to the prayers of the nuns for his soul, but it sufficed money-wise while he waited for that one day when a beautiful, blonde broad would chassé into his office with her heart on her sleeve, hurt in her eyes and hundreds in her fist.

Unfortunately, during a dog day afternoon, while hot on the trail of a missing beloved canine, Private Investigator Parmakianski accosted the French Ambassador to the United Nations and his miniature poodle. During the altercation, he discharged the entire magazine of his semi-automatic pistol, killing the Ambassador's dog and shooting out a display window at Bloomingdale's. The Ambassador lodged an official protest with the State Department. The dog was cremated. The beautiful, blonde broad never came.

Bloomingdale's rejected his application for a charge account and Private Investigator Parmakianski found himself bounced out of New York City. He drifted west, through Albany, Buffalo, Cleveland, Gary and Chicago, until he was finally found in Milwaukee living out of a 1956 Rambler parked next to a pay phone—the number of which he had listed in the Yellow Pages under 'Detectives'—by the private investigators hired by Y.T., Sr.

"She's at it again, J.P.," Y.T., Sr. would whisper conspiratorially over lunch at the West Side Grill where they always held their clandestine meetings in full view of the Erp Industries, Inc., production line workers who crowded the bar on breaks, during lunch hours and after their shifts. If Y.T., Sr. really wanted to learn about the sexual exploits of any of his employees, he needed only to stop by the Sugarman's workshop, have a shot of white lightning and ask. The Sugarman knew everything that happened in his building. Usually, though, Y.T., Sr. would sic Private Investigator Parmakianski on the trail of some wayward middle manager to get blurry, grainy photographs and unintelligible tape recordings of telephone conversations, knowing full well that the middle manager would know full well he was being watched and followed, and would adjust his conduct accordingly. The real beauty of it, though, was that other employees, out of the fear of being watched and followed themselves, often toed the line without ever actually being watched and followed. When Y.T., Sr. had nothing for Private Investigator Parmakianski to do, he put him to the absurd task of discovering just who Wanda W. Willet's secret lover was.

"Don't worry, Mr. E. It'll be Jake," Private Investigator Parmakianski would answer in grand gumshoe fashion, taking the suspect cigarette butt or gum wrapper or handkerchief or telephone number or whatever piece of evidence Y.T., Sr. provided to keep him occupied while his services were not required. Only Y.T., Sr., who paid him a healthy retainer, was allowed to address him as anything other than Private Investigator Parmakianski.

"I knew I could count on you." Y.T., Sr. had to smile, for he found the antics of his personal private eye amusing and entertaining.

It was quite amazing, then, that Private Investigator Parmakianski ever learned certain secrets—secrets that would rock Erp Industries, Inc., to its very foundation. He wrote them all down in the greasy, grimy notebook that had become his most faithful companion ever since he was forced to begin stuffing his shoulder holster with tissue paper to make it bulge beneath his left armpit after that unfortunate afternoon at Bloomingdale's.

Leon Debs

In the Sugarman's workshop at the very heart of the Old O'Reilly Candy Factory Building, Y.T., Jr. paced. Sufficiently distracted by the youth's restlessness, the Sugarman lowered the June, 1965, issue of *Playboy* just enough to peer over the top with his bulging yellow-white eyes. He followed Y.T., Jr. back and forth and back and forth without moving his head.

"Shee-it damn, boy, I'ma gonna nail you foot to the damned floor," the Sugarman finally growled in exasperation.

Y.T., Jr. stopped pacing. He looked down at his feet, then directly at the Sugarman. "I guess then I'd end up pacing around in circles."

"Then I be nailin' both you damned foots down." The Sugarman tossed aside the magazine and reached for his hip flask. He muttered to himself between sips, "Shee-it damn. 'Nough to drive a man to drink. Been stompin' 'round this here *es-ta-blish-ment* like he got some damned bug upen his ass that don' know which way be out. No talkin'. Jest walkin' like a damned fool. What is it boy? Talk to me."

"I don't think you'd understand," Y.T., Jr. said gravely, shaking his head.

"Understand? Understand what, boy?"

"Oh, nothing." Y.T., Jr. shoved his hands deep into his pants pockets and took a step to begin pacing again.

"You been back here two weeks an' alls you does is pace back an' fore liken a dog at the gate when thems bitches be in heat. Now, you sits youself down an' 'splain to your Sugarman what be on you mind."

"I told you. It's nothing."

"I is gonna find me a sufficient two-by-four and crack you upside the head, ifen you don' sit you ass down an' talk to you Sugarman."

Y.T., Jr. sat down on the stool next to the workbench. He looked around at everything in the workshop but the Sugarman.

"Boy!" The Sugarman squinted his eyes down tight and bared his teeth.

"Alright. Alright. It's that redhead. In Engineering."

"Uh-huh. Uh-huh. I done noticed you ain't been *ren-o-vatin'* the Engineerin' Department liken you was a'fore. What's she done, boy? She done tie you pipe in a knot?"

Y.T., Jr. shrugged his shoulders and shook his head.

"Then what, boy?"

"I can't explain it. Every time I get ready to make a move, I get this feeling, like something's not quite right."

"Shee-it damn, boy, you ain't even talked to that girl yet, have you."

"I ain't afraid. Something's just not straight up about her. I look in her eyes and there's like a cold hard chill inside and I start thinking I've got to really watch my step and say the right thing at the right time and do the right thing at the right time, or else—I don't know. It's strange. This has never happened to me before."

"Damn. How you folks spends so much money to get so smart and still be so stone dumb."

"How's that?"

"Just what them per-fessers be teachin' you at that damned *u-nee-var-city* any ways?"

"What's that got to do—"

"Boy, a lady ain't out lookin' fo' business—that's the games us mens play—an' ifen she is, she ain't no lady. Chippies, sweet-pea chippies, they be lookin' fo' what it is they don' even knows 'bout yet."

"I don't follow you."

"You jest listen to you Sugarman. Ain't no fine struttin' lady worth the salt in you sweat who gonna put out by appointment. She be a woman, boy, not no damned doctor an' not no damned *au-to-mo-bile* mechanic. Love don' keep no appointment book and happiness don' pay no mind to no calendars. So, boy, you can reckon an' figure 'til you can't reckon an' figure no more, but there ain't no plan in the world no man can devise to make a lady fall in love."

Y.T., Jr. thought about what the Sugarman said and slowly nodded his head. "But, then, how do I—"

"How? How? Shee-it damn, boy. You don' go an' make plans on how to breathe an' how to make you heart to beat all day long, now do you? Huh?"

"No."

"There you go. There you go. As natural as raindrops fallin' on flowers. That's how it gots to be or it ain't love."

"But—"

"You and you old man—two peas in a pod." The Sugarman laughed and slapped his thigh. "I swears, you goes off to them fancy schools an' learn so much 'til yous can't even think no mo'. Boy, you be lucky you Sugarman be here to set you old man straight years ago 'bout you mama."

"My mother?"

"Sho' 'nough. There'd be no you here to be moanin' 'bout redheads ifen you old man didn' take no notion to listen to you Sugarman."

"About my mother?"

"Sho' 'nough. Sho' 'nough."

"Tell me about her."

"She be gorgeous, boy. She be a shining ray of mother sunshine herself—an angel to behold from 'bove."

"I never even got to see her."

"I knowed it. I knowed it."

"I want to know."

"Now, boy, I—I don' rightly knows ifen it be my place here to—"

"Dad never talks about her."

"Reckon not. No, I reckon not."

"Tell me about her and dad."

"It be a long story, boy."

"I've got time. I've got all summer."

The Sugarman let out a long, loud sigh. He reached for his hip flask, took a long pull and passed it to Y.T., Jr. In a low and gentle tone of voice he began to tell the boy about the tragically short and tempestuous affair between Helen Troyer and Y.T., Sr.

Despite Y.T., Jr.'s collegiate and romantic frustrations, 1965 was beginning to look like a very good year for others. On March 2, *Operation Rolling Thunder,* the sustained bombing of North Vietnam by U.S. air forces commenced. On March 8, the First Marine Battalion arrived at Da Nang. On May 3, the U.S. Army's 173rd Airborne Brigade began landing in Vietnam. On June 18, U.S. Air Force B-52 *Stratofortresses* based in Guam made their first strike of the conflict against targets in South Vietnam.

Every Wednesday at noon, in a back corner booth at Dante's, Mort Mortenstein lapsed into giddy spasms of greedy delight as he listened to updates by his two colleagues. Over triple helpings of pasta, Hugh Betcha told how lead times on strategic commodities were beginning to push out further and further, generating inflationary pressures on prices and how, by exercising contract options, they were becoming an increasingly influential presence in the samarium, magnesium, copper and magnet markets. They had, in fact, locked up sixty percent of the Free World's ball bearing production for the next three and a half years, so that this nefarious triumvirate possessed the power—on paper, at least—to bring the machinery of the Western World to a grinding halt. Simon Salisbury, allowing himself salubrious smiles and sipping at unprecedented second glasses of Chablis, read from his tautological memos, citing figures representing the latest sortie rates and the forecast attrition rates for U.S. Armed Forces aircraft, as well as the increased ground troop commitments being requested by General William Westmoreland from President Lyndon Johnson for use in South Vietnam. 1965 was, indeed, going to be a very good year.

The *piece de resistance* for the car pool came on April 1, 1965, when, in a bold and inspired stroke of genius, Simon Salisbury hatched a scheme which not only resolved the dilemma of *The Memo*, but turned a tidy profit in the process. For a nominal per-employee charge back out of each department's operating budget, which was arranged through Mort Mortenstein's department, Simon Salisbury's department made a dexterous modification to an employee's file, in one fell swoop of white-out turning a lifetime of right-handedness into left-handedness or vise versa as circumstances so dictated. Then, to each file was added an official Certificate of Attendance from a front called the B. F. Skinner Institute of Applied Psychological Technology for a training course that purportedly employed the very latest in behavior modification techniques to undo in two weeks what Simon Salisbury's clerks had done in two minutes, thereby legitimizing what genetics had wrought after untold generations of procreation.

Seizing the initiative, Department Managers used *The Memo* as an excuse to cut much of the deadwood from their organizations, making Erp Industries, Inc., a leaner, more efficient operation. The sole exception was, of course, Rolf Guderian, who gleefully bloated his empire with every laid-off ne'er-do-well he could get his hands on at generously reduced wages. He hired so many discarded personnel, in fact, that the B.F. Skinner Institute was forced to negotiate a volume discount with the ex-Luftwaffe Corporal. Nearly everyone at the company enthusiastically embraced the aptly named *Operation April Fools,* though, to be rid of the perplexing problems inherent in Y.T., Sr.'s executive directive as stated in his New Year's Memo of 1965, and employees, who no longer feared for their futures, soon settled back into their familiar routines, getting back to the business of doing—and not doing—their jobs.

For such meritorious service, above and beyond the call of duty, Simon Salisbury sent himself a memorandum suggesting that, as Director of Personnel, he should, in light of the stunning success of *Operation April Fools* and the huge profits thereby generated, reward himself with a salary merit increase, which he immediately approved and, in turn, promptly notified himself of said raise in a congratulatory memorandum back to himself.

But beneath the complacent placidity that by summer had settled over Erp Industries, Inc., after the deft resolution of *The Memo* dilemma, there welled up a gaseous, noxiously boiling pool of discontent. This simmering lava of rage usually vented itself in the person of Leon Debs, a steaming geyser of profanity who haunted the warehouses and stock rooms of the company. Leon Debs was a five foot, four inch flyweight, who hung up his gloves with a record of 0-32-2, having spent his pugilistic career as a stepping stone for rising young fighters with the one thing that he lacked: boxing talent. Leon Debs was obviously tenacious to the point of self-destruction. He also possessed a stunning punch, but he telegraphed his every move, so much so that he was nicknamed 'The Wire' in boxing circles. His chin was punched with upper cuts so often and with such force that his mouth had been battered into a permanent, crooked smile, which was a cruel mask, indeed, for a man who was filled to the very brim of his soul with bile and venomous spite for every animate as well as inanimate object he set his jaundiced eye upon. Of course, Leon Debs had an opinion on everything and never hesitated to express that opinion by means of a curse, an obscene gesture, a phlegm-laden glob of spit, or even a well-directed stream of urine, which he especially preferred when showing his contempt for the U.S. Postal Service and the telephone company at their unattended facilities.

As lead warehouseman, Leon Debs was assisted by two Czechoslovakian brothers whose surname he could not pronounce because it had no vowels in it, so he called them Doug and Ike. Having served a two-year hitch in the Army as a buck private in Korea, Leon Debs took immeasurable pleasure in directing a verbal tirade every now and then against the Supreme Commander of the Allied Powers and the Commander-In-Chief of the United States Armed Forces for their incredible ineptitude and gross stupidity. Doug and Ike had jumped ship in Newark harbor three years prior, intending to make their way to Cleveland to find their Uncle Malachek Walsplat, a well-known haberdasher and drapery cleaner in suburban Parma. Their plan, unfortunately, depended upon being stopped by Ohio Border Guards, at which time they would ask for directions to Uncle Malachek's home. Unable to read any English, they breezed through Ohio without ever knowing it. A wrong turn in Des Moines, Iowa, took them to Kansas City where they finally ran out of Korunas and were forced to find work.

As well-indoctrinated proletariat, Doug and Ike found their greatest joy in their labors. And, of course, their "most, best-est comrade" was Leon Debs. They were totally devoted to the wiry, foul-mouthed, spiteful little man and greeted the triple-*forte* abuse he heaped upon them with bellowing laughter that infuriated Leon Debs to the very brink of insanity, inspiring him to redouble his efforts until the tirade reached gale force proportions. Even though Doug and Ike both stood well over six feet tall and together tipped the scales in excess of five hundred pounds, Leon Debs had little to fear from them. They were gentle, good-natured souls who followed him around like two St. Bernard's might trot happily after a snarling, yappy terrier.

It was a sunny June afternoon three weeks after Y.T., Jr. returned from Berkeley for summer vacation when Leon Debs finally erupted in earnest and became, instead of a perverse pariah, a leader of men.

"Jesus H. Christ, Mrs. McGurdy, just what in the hell are those God damn turds doing on that God damn plate?" Leon Debs exclaimed vehemently as he pushed his tray down the cafeteria line at Erp Industries, Inc., with Doug and Ike in tow close behind.

"Ho-ho-ho. Why, Mr. Debs, that is our Luncheon Special for today," replied Arlotta McGurdy, who was the heart and soul of the cafeteria kitchen. Mrs. McGurdy was at least six weight classes above Leon Debs. Years of stirring batter and kneading dough developed her fore arms and biceps into powerful muscular masses. She could whip, grate, and puree far bigger men than Leon Debs rather handily, but Mrs. McGurdy was also one of those terminally cheerful-by-nature persons who would not hurt a cockroach if it were not for health regulations. She had spent a decade and a half of her culinary career preparing three meals a day at the Missouri State Hospital for the Criminally Insane in Jefferson City and came to accept abuse from her customers as par for the course. On the whole, Mrs. McGurdy rather enjoyed such cafeteria line banter, but was disappointed to discover that the inmates at Erp Industries, Inc., were far less imaginative and creative in their verbal skills than the inmates in Jefferson City. Leon Debs, though, was a refreshing exception. "Today's Special is Salisbury Steak."

"YYYLLLEEEEEECCCKKK!!!" Leon Debs spat on the floor to further punctuate his disgust.

Doug and Ike looked at each other, smiled their dull, novacainic, Eastern European smiles and bobbed their heads in agreement with Leon Debs. They joined in together with their Slavic accents, "Yleckta! Yleckta! Yleckta!"

"Ho-ho-ho. Mr. Debs, I'll tell you that *all* the boys from the Schizophrenic Ward *always* came back for second helpings—and some came back for thirds and fourths of *my* Salisbury Steaks," Mrs. McGurdy announced proudly.

"God damn it, Mrs. McGurdy, those are the ugliest, vilest, most disgusting looking, shit-shaped excuses for an entree that I have ever seen in my entire God damn life!" Leon Debs declared. By now, the line behind him was beginning to congest and clot with the lunch hour rush of workers. "No self-respecting fly would set foot upon those ludicrous lumps!"

"Ho-ho-ho. Mr. Debs, you certainly know how to sweet talk a girl, now don't you."

"Listen Typhoid McGurdy, I am sick of this *shit!* Every God damn day we pay for the outrageous indignity of eating your salmonellosis sensations that, by international agreement, have been banned as a kind of biological weapon too insidious, too cruel, and too inhuman to be used by civilized nations in time of war! Your bacteriological nightmares make a mockery of the Geneva Convention! Your anthraxious artistry rapes and violates the Hippocratic Oath, three of the ten amendments comprising the Bill of Rights and at least one of the Ten Commandments! You are a pestilence that has swept across our land! You are a plague visited upon us! I am sick of this *shit,* you botulistic bitch!"

"Ho-ho-ho."

"Monday it was God damn meat loaf! Tuesday it was God damn Swiss steak! And Wednesday it was some God damn awful shit that must have been left over from a God damn nuclear bomb test in the God damn Nevada desert—nobody knew what in the hell it was!"

"Ho-ho-ho. Why, Mr. Debs, that was shepherd's pie."

"God damn it, it was the fucking black death, Mrs. McGurdy!"

"Oh Mr. Debs, *really,"* blushed Mrs. McGurdy, who truly believed that hamburger was God's gift to the food service industry.

"THE FUCKING BLACK DEATH!" Leon Debs screamed at the top of his lungs.

What ensued was not pleasant. Leon Debs went through a series of obscene motions that implied a certain biological causality between Mrs. McGurdy's Salisbury Steaks and his own digestive tract, to the general enjoyment of Doug, Ike and the strange, brooding men in oily smocks from the Machine Shop. Immediately thereafter, all pandemonium suddenly broke loose as traditionally inert food groups took flight. The summer air overflowed with the sights, smells, sounds, and the very substance of stewed tomatoes, succotash, powdered mashed potatoes, lime flavored gelatin, lumpy tapioca, and, of course, Mrs. McGurdy's Salisbury Steaks, which amazed everyone when they miraculously defied gravity by tenaciously clinging to the walls in spite of their weight.

By the time the security guards arrived to quell the riot, the eruption began subsiding of its own accord. There were only two casualties. Ike got a lump on his noggin from a nuclear-hardened biscuit that had actually been launched in a preemptive strike by Orley

Bovine. Ike and his brother laughed it off as just being a part of the fun of being an American. After all, their papa never had such fun at the munitions plant in Prague, under the Germans or under the Russians. Normally, Dirk Rangely never set foot within the domain of Arlotta McGurdy. He knew better and, besides, he had a company credit card to buy lunch at Dante's. But the commotion that arose when the cafeteria became a free-fire zone got the better of his curiosity and he sustained the other wound. His camel hair sports jacket was mortally stained by a glop of Mrs. McGurdy's mushroom gravy and eventually had to be put out of its misery. It was euthanasia by incineration.

The Erp Industries, Inc., Cafeteria Riots of 1965 received very little coverage in the news media: the *Meadowlawns Citizen Journal* published Mrs. McGurdy's Salisbury Steaks recipe. Many who were close to these events, though, would later recall that lunchtime of unrest as they watched the Six O'clock News and saw riots erupt in the ghettos of Los Angeles, Cleveland, Detroit, Newark, *et al;* as they saw political protest spread like a cancer from far-flung college campuses to the very capital of their great nation; as they saw, repeatedly, the violence of American taking arms against American. Though few realized it at the time, they had glimpsed the dark side of life in the United States. The monsters of the American nightmare reared their ugly heads and shown themselves. Not only were the times changing right before their very eyes, they were a part of it.

As is usually the case with great watershed events in history, the majority of the people in the immediate vicinity of the Erp Industries, Inc., Cafeteria Riots of 1965 were not involved in the action by their own volition and were, in fact, more interested in simply getting out of the way than in protesting the injustices of Mrs. McGurdy's oppressive culinary practices. When the food fight began,

Scarlett Angelina Brookings abandoned her cottage cheese and peaches to join in with the frantic exodus of innocents from the lunchroom. In her dash to safety, she ran right into the arms of a handsome, blond-haired young man, who, once he got over his surprise, asked her out for that Saturday night. Overcome by the rush of events and the emotions of the moment, she accepted.

Y.T., Jr. decided that 1965 might not turn out so badly for him after all.

~~~

Harvest Moon

They thought he had lost his mind. They thought he had crossed that thread-thin line God had drawn so precariously between genius and insanity. In the evenings after the day's work was done and others were home eating dinner or watching television, he sat in a sagging lawn chair set up in the middle of the parking lot adjacent to the Old O'Reilly Candy Factory Building. Even as others slept through the night, he sat alone, sipping Orley Bovine's moonshine and silently watching the moon itself migrate across the sky. No one said anything. No one dared—not even when morning came and the parking lot filled up around him as he slouched in the lawn chair and slept. But Rolf Guderian kept his own vigil, watching Vasili Ivanovich through the Venetian blinds in his office, sensing that the time might soon be right for a corporate *anschluss*.

"Full moon? Shit, I've got your full moon right here, farm boy," Marty Keegan snickered. He jumped up on top of the tombstone of Wilbert Cassidy, "Loving Husband and Beloved Father (1863-1912)," and, balancing carefully, pulled down his pants to expose his ass to Billy Saul Sawyer.

Y.T., Jr. shook up a can of beer and opened it, aiming at the pale white target that shined in the light of the moon.

"Holy shit! A Budweiser enema!" Marty Keegan exclaimed as cold beer splashed on his buttocks. In spite of swinging his arms wildly, he fell on top of the grave of Wilbert Cassidy, and broke out in hearty laughter.

"Sinful. A damn sinful waste of beer," Billy Saul Sawyer slurred in between chuckles. He sat next to a pyramid of beer cans on top of the memorial to Willis Cassidy, "Democracy's Brave Defender (1899-1919)," whose body still lay somewhere in France.

"Sometimes sacrifices must be made," Y.T., Jr. said, smiling and raising the half-empty Budweiser can to his lips.

"You realize that this is it, don't you?" Marty Keegan said, pulling up his pants. He buckled his belt and helped himself to another beer. "This is it. The end—the end of an era, boys."

The smile slipped off of Billy Saul Sawyer's face. He looked down into his beer.

"Yeah, I'm going to miss desecrating these hallowed grounds with you degenerates," Y.T., Jr. said. He sat on the tombstone of Wesley Cassidy, "R.I.P. (1835-1889)." His feet dangled off the ground and he kicked the gravestone with his heels as he swung his legs in a steady, even rhythm.

Billy Saul Sawyer nodded in agreement. "Remember all them secret clubs we started and all them oaths unto the death we took in this here graveyard by the light of the moon at midnight when we were just kids?"

"Hell yes—that was during my Mark Twain period, if I recall correctly," Marty Keegan said, pacing up and down the orderly row of Cassidy graves.

"What splendid little suburban pirates and grave robbers we were," said Y.T., Jr., shaking his head. "Always plotting and planning to murder Gus at the Texaco station for his belt changer or to kidnap housewives from the A & P for ransoms of gold and silver."

"We sure wasted an awful lot of time plotting and planning," said Billy Saul Sawyer.

In the Black

"Hey, what the hell else could we do? We were just kids and when you're kids that's all you can do. Besides, it wasn't the gold that was important. It was the brotherhood. You know, blood brothers through thick and thin like we were."

"Bound together by ties stronger than real brothers," Billy Saul Sawyer sighed. He looked up at Marty Keegan, then at Y.T., Jr. He frowned and peered back into his beer can. "They were good times."

"Shit yeah, they were good times," said Marty Keegan. "But hell, remember the time we greased up that baby pig from your dad's farm and let it loose in Newcomb's third hour English class? I was sure I herniated myself from laughing so hard at Vice-Principal Snyder chasing that pig up and down the halls."

Billy Saul Sawyer smiled weakly and chuckled quietly.

"Snyder was seriously pissed at us after that," said Y.T., Jr. "You'd have thought he was on a mission from God to get us thrown out of Harry S. High."

"Never did, though," said Marty Keegan. "As hard as that son-of-a-bitch tried, he never got us. We were always one step ahead of that bastard."

"Yeah, that bastard," agreed Billy Saul Sawyer. "But, you know, the all-time best was the junior varsity homecoming game against Valley View."

"Holy shit! That was the Pulitzer Prize of our pranking career," exclaimed Marty Keegan. He held his beer can up to his mouth as if it was a microphone. "Yes, ladies and sports fans, it is a heck of an afternoon for a football game and this has been a heck of a football game. We have thirteen seconds left on the game clock and the Valley View *Stallions* have just scored a dramatic touchdown to tie the score at seventeen all. The *Eagles* are back to receive the kick-off. The *Stallions* line up and kick it deep. Number eighty-one, Keegan, takes the ball at the two yard line and sprints to his left. he's at the five, the ten—no, now he cuts back to his right, heading straight towards the *Eagles* side line with the entire Valley View team in pursuit and—what's this? What's this? Ladies and germs, this is highly irregular. Yes, highly irregular. *Eagles* number double zero—that would be an H. Davidson by my roster—has just sped out from under the stands on a—on a—yes, ladies and genitalmen, on a motorcycle! And he's heading onto the field! Keegan cuts back and, without missing a step, jumps on behind double zero! The Valley View *Stallions* are perplexed! They are dazed and confused, frozen in their footsteps by this clever ploy! Now, Keegan and Davidson cut up field, parting the *Stallions* special team tacklers as if they were the Red Sea! They cross midfield and shift into third gear! And now both the *Eagles* and the *Stallions* team benches empty onto the field in hot pursuit of Keegan and Davidson! They're at the twenty—the ten—the five—Touchdown! Keegan scores! And the fans go crazy! The gun goes off! The *Eagles* win and the crowd pours out onto the field! It is pandemonium here, ladies and gentlemen! What a spectacular victory for the Harry S. High *Fighting Eagles!*"

"I thought Boswagger was going to chase us all the way to Topeka," said Y.T., Jr. "He just wouldn't give up."

"Yeah, too bad you guys couldn't stick around. It was like a riot or something," said Billy Saul Sawyer. "It was great. They tore down the goal posts and everything."

"Well, I didn't figure that we were due for any back slapping from Coach Sox—even though we did win the game for him," said Marty Keegan. He stopped pacing and lifted himself up to sit on the gravestone of Wilbert Cassidy. "It was one for the record books, that's for sure. We had some great times, eh? It's the end of an era."

They all quietly drank their beers in the still of the cemetery at one AM. The moon dodged in and out of a broken layer of clouds.

"But what I want to know once and for all," Marty Keegan suddenly spoke up, "is just how thin is a red C-hair—or haven't you found out yet?"

Y.T, Jr. looked up and smiled.

"I think I recognize that smile," said Billy Saul Sawyer, furrowing his brow.

"Erp?" asked Marty Keegan.

"Not quite as thin as the margin by which you got into Columbia University," said Y.T., Jr.

"Don't yank me, Erp," warned Marty Keegan.

Y.T., Jr. smiled.

"God damn you! God damn you, Erp," Marty Keegan exclaimed.

"How does he do it, Keeg?" asked Billy Saul Sawyer, shaking his head in disbelief. "How does he do it?"

Marty Keegan threw his beer can at Y.T., Jr. It sailed over his head and into the darkness, trailing a comet-like tail of foam. "God damn you, Erp. First, it was that Annette chick from Valley View who was built like a brick shit house. Then it was my beloved Becky Sue, and now this mysterious little red riding hood who could send Ann-Margaret skulking off to the dog house."

"How does he do it, Keeg?"

"He's the luckiest son-of-a-bitch alive. That's how."

"No luck. No luck involved at all." Y.T., Jr. shook his head.

"God damn you, Erp. What does that red head see in you, anyway?"

Y.T., Jr. shrugged his shoulders and smiled.

"Maybe it's that his old man owns the company," said Billy Saul Sawyer.

"Do you mean to imply that such a perfect vision of beauty would prostitute herself to this frigging pervert here just to get at his old man's dough?" Marty Keegan asked indignantly. "No way, farm boy. No way. No woman that beautiful could possibly be a whore. It'd make me lose all faith in the opposing sex. I'd have to become a Jesuit monk or some damn thing."

"Oh yeah, sure," said Billy Saul Sawyer. "You wouldn't last two weeks as a priest, Keeg. You'd get kicked out for looking up the nun's dresses."

"Heavens! What a nasty habit that would be," Y.T., Jr. said.

"ARRRRRRRGGGGGGG!" Marty Keegan slapped his forehead and fell over backwards behind Wilbert Cassidy's gravestone.

Billy Saul Sawyer hid his face in his hands.

"Something I said, fellows?" Y.T., Jr. asked innocently.

"It's the end of a fucking era!" Marty Keegan shouted from out of sight behind Wilbert Cassidy's gravestone.

As Wilson Cassidy chomped on his illegally imported Havana cigar and gazed out the window of his office over the complex of buildings, the sprawling expanse of holding pens and the maze of chutes and gates that all inevitably led to the Cassidy slaughter houses, the thought of Budweiser beer cans littering the family grave sites was an irksome aggravation masked by problems that could—and would—impact the course of future history.

Wilson Cassidy was a hard driving businessman whose gift was the ability to see through the stench, the bloodshed, and the mutilation that surrounded him to that most immutable of business truths: The Bottom Line. Under his direction, the Cassidy Beef Packing Company had become a monolith that dominated the market and he himself was revered as the veritable pope of the beef processing industry. He had negotiated and won exclusive government contracts resulting in massive orders from school lunch programs across the country and for military bases around the world. After threatening to start his own chain of hamburger stand franchises, a sole source agreement was forthcoming ensuring that each and every one of the "billions and billions served" would always and forever be Cassidy Grade A Prime. Commodities brokers tracked Wilson Cassidy's every word, gesture and fidget to divine cattle futures as if he were, puffing on his ever present cigars, the smoldering Oracle of Delphi. In top secret laboratories and think tanks, teams of veterinarians, biologists, chemists, geneticists—even philosophers, psychics and clergymen—who all swore personal allegiance to Wilson Cassidy, toiled day in and day out to discover and to harness the secrets of life in order not only to yield more burgers, more briskets, more roasts and more steaks per head, but to do so according to schedules greatly accelerated from the normal and natural maturation cycle of the species. The results of their endless experiments with food additives, vitamin supplements, steroids, artificial insemination and test tube fertilization would one day find its way into the stomachs of Americans everywhere, contributing to the very bone and fiber of the nation. Wilson Cassidy felt himself pushing at frontiers, just as his great grandfather Wesley Cassidy had done when he first came to Kansas City in 1857.

Yet standing at his office window riding the crest of his accomplishments and, at the very pinnacle of his power, surveying all that he ruled, impending doom cast its cool shadow upon him.

At fifty-eight, the Bottom Line for Wilson Cassidy was that, after three failed marriages and scores of perfunctory affairs, he was childless. The great empire that stood as a monument to over a century of spent Cassidy blood, Cassidy sweat, and Cassidy tears was without an heir. As if by divine right, the family beef packing dynasty had always been ruled by a hand through which coursed Cassidy blood and Wilson Cassidy would sooner see it all destroyed than to have the business go public, becoming a bureaucracy run by a committee chosen by ignorant, voting stockholders whose only virtue was enough cash to buy shares of stock.

As time passed, Wilson Cassidy's options slowly and steadily dwindled. His brother, Wallace Cassidy, adopted children. They carried the Cassidy name, but no Cassidy blood, showing a marked propensity to aspire to become no more than dishwashers, waitresses, and busboys in his steakhouse restaurant. None of them would have anymore business sitting at the head of the Cassidy table than a Hindu priest. Wilson Cassidy was left with only one solution—and a radical solution it was, one sure to spread dissent and unrest to the far corners of the Cassidy clan: The Cassidy decree handed down by his father had to be reversed and peace had to be made with Anna Elise Erp. Although the thought of reconciliation aggravated his heartburn and pushed his dangerously high blood pressure that much higher, Wilson Cassidy nonetheless followed events closely and believed that the success of Erp Industries, Inc., was Cassidy blood made manifest, albeit, out of frustration, in a totally alien field of endeavor. And though Y.T., Sr. was too old to take the helm of the Cassidy Beef Packing Company, his son was coming of the age when he might be taken in, groomed and prepared to carry on the grand Cassidy family heritage—bridging the gap, at least, until the scientists working night and day in Wilson Cassidy's clandestine laboratories could unlock the secrets of life, unfreeze the bank full of his cryogenically preserved sperm and create a genuine, pure-blooded Cassidy to ascend to his rightful place on the throne.

As the autumnal equinox approached, Clinton A. Owsley III found himself hitchhiking west on a lonely Nevada Highway. Tucked into his boot was an ivory-handled derringer that, like a sea shell collected at the beach, was a souvenir of a most memorable summer vacation. Lured by rumors and tales told on the street of a group of people actually living out a Wild West fantasy, he headed for the Comstock Lode country in search of the "Red Dog Project" as soon as school let out in June. He eventually met up with Murph, the red-haired, pot-bellied, Zen-and-John-Wayne-dialog-spouting loudmouth who had rustled a group of turned-on people off of Pine Street in San Francisco and led them to Virginia City, convincing them along the way to trade in their Edwardian ruffles, top hats and canes for chaps, Stetsons and six-guns.

"Now listen and listen good, pilgrim, when your feet hit the floor in the morning, you are alive as you have never been alive before," Murph bellowed at Clinton A. Owsley III soon after his arrival as they sat at Murph's table in the Red Dog Saloon, the focal point of the group's activities. "Because this isn't real! It's better than real—it's the second reel of the Hollywood Zen of happy trails, of head 'em off at the pass, of hi-yo Silver! This is the *reel* reality without cars and smog and telephones and all that concrete bullshit of the Twentieth Century. Look around you, pilgrim, there's no folding, no spindling, no mutilating here! Look around you! This is *Rawhide!* This is *Gunsmoke!* This is the *Lone Fucking Ranger* right here for you and me and everybody, so just kick the dust off your mind and toss back some red-eye and you are here—you are there! Just relax and let your thoughts click by at twenty-four frames per second and life becomes a double feature at matinée prices! Do it! Be it! Live it! Remember, the West was won and we are one with the West. And don't you forget it, pilgrim!"

Clinton A. Owsley III immediately endeared himself to Murph and the Red Dog Project with handouts of the LSD sugar cubes he had cooked up in the Latimer Hall chemistry labs. After a week of haunting the dusty streets of Virginia City, the dark, smoky interior of the Red Dog Saloon and the wide open ranges of the Red Dog Ranch just outside of town, walking, talking, riding, shooting and thinking like a cowboy, he began feeling like a cowboy and, just like Murph said, each day became another episode in the ever unfolding story of how the West was won—again. Of course, the illusion was aided immeasurably by the generous portions of marijuana, amphetamines, barbiturates, peyote buttons and Owsley's LSD consumed by all. No one but the townsfolk seemed to mind that the sound track for this group celluloid hallucination was a hybrid of folk music and rock 'n roll that was played at 120 decibels. In the minds of the Red Dog cowpokes, it was just right.

As Clinton A. Owsley III hitchhiked, thoughts skidded around the hairpin turns in the folds of his gray matter at the speed of light, supercharged with prototypes of a *new and improved* recipe for LSD that he had developed while in Virginia City. He felt himself in tune with the same primordial urges and instincts that drive great herds of caribou down from the tundra into the forests or, perhaps more appropriately, frantic clutches of meandering Monarch butterflies from the Great Lakes across the North American continent to Mexico. An occasional semi erupted out of the darkness and Clinton A. Owsley III stood hypnotized by the glare of angry headlights, gripped by the growl of grinding gears, mesmerized by the music of crescendoing cylinders, enthralled by the storm of hot, turbulent air humid with spent diesel fuel that embraced and caressed him—so much so that he usually forgot to stick out his thumb for a ride.

On the fifth floor fire escape on the back of Fu Loin's establishment, Penelope Xing sat, alternately sipping a glass of wine, eating Twinkies and chain-smoking cigarettes as she knitted. At three in the morning, all her suitors had retired for the evening. An insistent siren from a distant quarter of the city cut through the quiet. Moments later, stillness returned and snores from the alley below could be heard again. The summer seemed intolerably long to Penelope Xing, but the flow of the American Educational System would soon be peaking and those tidal pools called campuses would be teaming with life once again. She watched the glowing half-moon rise over Oakland to shine on San Francisco Bay. She did not know what it was she knitted, but whatever it turned out to be, she hoped Y.T., Jr. would like it.

"Hand me that wrench, will ya?" Billy Saul Sawyer stuck out his plump, greasy left hand. His right hand was still stuck in amidst the engine of Y.T., Jr.'s Harley-Davidson. "You're back off to Berkeley and Keeg's packing off to New York, so what am I supposed to do?"

Y.T., Jr. shook his head gravely. He hopped down off of the work bench in the barn on the Sawyer family hog farm. He grabbed a wrench out of the tool box. "This one?"

"Uh-uh. Half inch."

Y.T., Jr. handed Billy Saul Sawyer the wrench he needed, then leaned against the Sawyer family pick-up truck. He took a long, thoughtful drag off his cigarette and carefully studied Billy Saul

Sawyer giving his motorcycle one last tune up before taking it back to Berkeley with him on the Erp Industries, Inc., Learjet. "You sure about this?"

"What am I supposed to do? Sit here all my life smelling them stinking hogs?"

"Yeah, but Billy Saul—"

"Besides, I don't really got no choice."

"Why's that?"

"I ain't going to college like you and Keeg. Draft Board's done gone and made me one-A. They're going to have my ass one way or another."

Y.T., Jr. nodded. "But the Marines?"

"Why not?" Billy Saul Sawyer looked up from the motorcycle engine. "They're the best, ain't they? I've never been the best at anything in all my life."

Y.T., Jr. smiled at Billy Saul Sawyer.

"And, I'll be in San Diego for boot camp. It's not that far, is it? So, maybe you could cruise down on the ol' Harley to see me sometime."

"Sure, Billy Saul. Sure."

Billy Saul Sawyer set down his tools and stood up. He looked at Y.T., Jr. "You think I'm doing the right thing?"

Y.T., Jr. looked back at Billy Saul Sawyer. He nodded slowly as he crushed out his cigarette butt and exhaled the last of the smoke. "Yeah. Be the best. Be the best Billy Saul."

Billy Saul Sawyer grinned. "They got nice uniforms, huh? You ever seen them fancy dress blues? Maybe I'll finally get me a girl. You know what they say about women going for a man in uniform."

"Aw, you don't need a uniform to get—"

"You don't need it, but I sure do. I can use all the help I can get." Billy Saul Sawyer noticed a worried expression on Y.T., Jr.'s face. "It'll be okay. Everything will work out fine. I know what I'm doing."

Y.T., Jr. just nodded, but he knew that Erp Industries, Inc., had recently added a second shift to handle the steadily increasing orders in support of the efforts of the Air Force, the Army, the Navy, and the Marines to execute United States foreign policy in Southeast Asia.

As people ebbed and flowed about him, Vasili Ivanovich sat in his lawn chair night after night through the summer. Late one October evening, Rolf Guderian saw the distinguished silhouette of Y.T., Sr. cross the parking lot, walking towards the lawn chair and the ridiculous Russian. This was it, he thought. With a dry mouth and moist palms, he watched with agitated anticipation.

Y.T., Sr. softly stepped up behind the lawn chair and gently put his hands on Vasili Ivanovich's shoulders.

Vasili Ivanovich turned and looked up at Y.T., Sr.

Y.T., Sr. nodded. "All systems go."

"The moon!" Vasili Ivanovich whispered in a gasp of awe.

"Yes, my friend, the moon."

Together, they toasted the earth's ancient satellite and the enormous task before them with Orley Bovine's best, while inside Rolf Guderian stormed about the Engineering Department, stomping his feet, kicking the file cabinets and tearing out his hair in frustration.

~~~

The Emerald City

"ERP!" Rear Admiral Hemmings bellowed.

"Yes, sir," Y.T., Sr. snapped back as he reported for duty at the Navy Department building in Washington, D.C., four short months after the Japanese attack on Pearl Harbor.

"At ease!"

Y.T., Sr. spread apart his feet, clasped his hands behind his back and relaxed imperceptibly.

The Admiral growled audibly and moved his lips visibly as he looked over Y.T., Sr.'s orders, the precious paperwork by which Y.T., Sr. lived, breathed and—at least in Navy eyes—would certainly cease to exist if lost or destroyed.

Y.T., Sr. carefully, yet discreetly, surveyed the artifacts of a life-long naval career and the myriad icons symbolizing those prized intangibles of courage, bravery, loyalty, leadership, honor and sacrifice that made the Admiral's office half a temple to power and half a personal Hemmings museum. Curiously, a wooden airplane propeller sat propped up in a corner behind the desk.

The Admiral tossed Y.T., Sr.'s orders aside and catapulted himself out of his chair. The orders balanced on the edge of the desk, then fell to the floor. At fifty-six, the Admiral's body had lost much of its fighting trim. Yet despite the passing tides of time and an ill-fitting white uniform, his stature and bearing alone projected an authority felt in the room like heat from a roaring fire. His head sat nearly on his shoulders with only the shortest, stoutest and stiffest of necks fully concealed by the collar of his uniform. His face looked weathered as if he had spent the entire thirty-six years of his naval career standing on the forecastle of a destroyer staring into a raging typhoon with one eye audaciously squinted at the gale's fury. His voice boomed with enough volume to be heard over the firing of a battleship's sixteen inch guns. When he stood in one spot, as he did then, The Admiral inevitably began swaying to and fro, back and forth as if his legs were firmly planted on the deck of a ship riding out the sea's pulsating swells. Few were the men who could look him directly in the eye without becoming sea sick.

"ERP!" The Admiral suddenly began pacing behind the massive oak desk that had become his bridge, seeing that Y.T., Sr.'s gills were not turning green. "I am a son-of-a-bitch! Everybody knows it! Now you do, too!"

"Yes, sir."

The Admiral squinted at Y.T., Sr. His answer had come quickly, perhaps too quickly. "Do I detect disappointment at your posting here?"

"I chose the Navy to serve at sea, not to sail a desk."

"Ha! Wars are fought from the decks of carriers, battleships and destroyers, but are won and lost in battles between sons-of-bitches like me and that ornery peanut farmer with sea gull shit for brains who buys enough votes every six years in Georgia to sit in the U.S. Senate! Congress giveth and Congress taketh away, Erp! Your duty will be to see that when Congress giveth, it giveth to the Navy—more to the point, to the Bureau of Aeronautics!"

Y.T., Sr. said nothing.

"Remember, Erp, any numb nuts can point a rifle and squeeze the trigger! It is not so simple a task to get that weapon system funded, designed, built, tested and delivered into that numb nuts' grubby little fists at the right time with sufficient ammunition to point it and squeeze the trigger—and not blow up in his face—such that the desired effect is achieved, namely to kick the enemy's ass! This billet will be no backwater liberty for you, mister! Understood?"

"Understood, sir."

The Admiral stopped pacing. He stared at Y.T., Sr., swaying to and fro to the rhythm of the ocean currents submerged deep within his psyche. "I take care of my men! I will take care of you! Do your duty and we will be square! First: get yourself lieutenant bars! I will have no Ensigns on my staff!"

"Yes, sir." That past Thursday, Y.T., Sr. had graduated Officer Candidate School and earned the rank of Ensign. In less than a week, he was promoted for simply reporting for duty.

"See my adjutant as to your office quarters! I will be sending over reports, background materials and a few essential supplies." The Admiral momentarily flashed the craggiest of smiles, then scowled again. "Brief yourself thoroughly."

"Yes, sir."

"And Erp, if you think those yellow Jap bastards are sneaky, inscrutable SOBs," the Admiral growled, "you just wait until you go up against the Hill—and don't look for help from anyone around here just because they have stripes on their sleeves! The Navy did not pick you for this job! I did! You will be on your own!"

"Yes, sir."

"Dismissed!"

The Admiral's adjutant led Y.T., Sr. down the hall, out the Navy Department Building, across the Potomac River and through what seemed to be at least seventeen of the seventeen and a half miles of corridors at the construction site that, when completed in 1943, would be the largest office building in the world, the Pentagon. Unofficially, Y.T., Sr. was its very first occupant. His office had no lights, no electricity, no heat, no furniture or even walls, only boxes upon boxes upon boxes stacked up all around him, some containing files and reports and others, oddly, filled with cigarettes, imported liquors and nylon stockings. The newly promoted Lieutenant appropriated two saw horses, an unmounted door, a sturdy crate, a Marine Corps issue Coleman lantern and got to work. Day after day, night after night, he read Top Secret OSS reports on Nazi, Japanese, Soviet, French, and British aircraft capabilities and weapons research; analyzed defense contractor proposals that promised destructive power in the same fashion Madison Avenue promised powerful new laundry detergents for whiter sheets; poured over classified Navy battle reports, technical specifications, engineering feasibility studies, qualification test reports, flight test reports, maintenance logs, milestone charts, bubble charts, cost analyses, and, of course, the slow and painful progress of World War II as reported in the *Washington Post, TIME* and *Life*.

One sunny April morning, when the cherry blossoms were blooming, the Admiral ordered Y.T., Sr. to Florida, where in a few short weeks he earned a set of golden aviator wings to wear on his chest at the Naval Air Station, Pensacola. Upon his return to Washington, he shadowed the Admiral on his rounds from one Navy program office to another, as he gave audience to parade after parade of Program Officers, Administrative Support Officers, Technical Staff Advisers, Contracting Officers and their innumerable assistants to weave their tangled webs while the Admiral either dozed or stared out the window at the nearest body of water, no matter how small or how shallow it was. Y.T., Sr. was just beginning to have that weary sense of *déjà vu*—as if he had heard it all before—when the Admiral sent him to the Naval Air Station, Patuxent River, to experience firsthand the latest experimental fruits of aeronautical research that had survived the practical as well as political pitfalls on the journey from drawing board to flight line. With wartime rationing pinching the country, the Admiral's supplies of cigarettes and liquor were invaluable in winning friends among the test pilots and maintenance officers and in getting them to talk freely about things seen and unseen, reported and unreported, hardware fact and paperwork fantasy.

On the Admiral's orders, Y.T., Sr. was assigned his own Chance-Vought F4U *Corsair* prototype. He immediately began flying the fighter back and forth across the country, stopping to tour U.S. Naval Bases. He interviewed everyone from the Wing Commanders down to the white caps who topped the tanks, checked the oil, kicked the tires, washed the windshields and armed the bombs before take-off. He also toured the manufacturers of ships, air frames, engines, radios, avionics, electronics, bombs, machine guns, cannons and torpedoes, until he felt as though he had walked every inch of the very bowels of America's Arsenal of Democracy and knew every rivet, bolt and wire of the Navy's war machine. Upon his return to Washington, The Admiral deemed Y.T., Sr. battle-worthy, having absorbed a career's worth of knowledge in four and a half months.

August 7, 1942, the United States engaged in their first offensive action of World War II. As Marines lined the decks of troop transport ships and bobbed in flat bottomed landing craft, listening to the pre-dawn naval bombardment of Guadalcanal, Y.T., Sr. sat outside the office of Senator Thurman Troyer, intellectually and emotionally armed to the teeth to promote and fight for naval aviation, on his first offensive action of the war.

The Senator, though, refused to see him. He made an appointment for the next day and, again, sat idly outside the Capital Hill office of the honorable senator from Georgia. Day after day, Y.T., Sr. was stood up until he began to feel himself naught but a pawn in the game between the Admiral and the Senator, stationary at King's Five while the Bishops, the Knights and the Rooks of government crisscrossed before his very eyes, working their political gambits.

It was at the Senator's office where Y.T., Sr. first saw the woman who would one day be Y.T., Jr.'s mother. She was a cool blonde even more beautiful than the pictures of her that graced the society pages of the *Washington Post,* the *Washington Times Herald* and the *Washington Evening Star*. The moment their eyes met was less a moment when love bloomed triumphant as it was an instant when two people confronted their own immutable, mortal destinies. Helen Troyer and Y.T., Sr. briefly and wordlessly regarded one another, then the daughter of the Admiral's arch enemy quickly slipped past and went into the Senator's office.

"Daddy, whoever in the world is that man outside your office?" Helen Troyer asked. Her words dripped sweetly with soft musical slurs of the deep south.

"I take you to mean that sailor boy, there, who has been loitering repeatedly and—I dare hope not—endlessly outside my door. I swear, he appears to possess the tireless tenacity of a Georgia bulldog," the Senator boomed as if he held the Senate floor. "He is, my dear, merely some lackey sent over by that insufferable Admiral Hemmings to aggravate me and annoy my being with the notion that the Navy might fly more aeroplanes when it should be sailing ships."

"But I thought General Arnold—"

"Yes, my dear, yes, that Hap Arnold has his head screwed on proper about a united and independent Air Force, while unfortunately the collective Navy brain trust has apparently and regrettably become rather waterlogged. What can you do about a band of mutineers rabid enough to sabotage a great patriot like Billy Mitchell? But you shouldn't tire your pretty head over such doings, my dear. Pay that sailor boy no mind. He'll be gone in another week or two."

"Mmmm." Helen Troyer floated over to the window and gazed out across the Mall. She hummed softly to herself.

"Unless, of course, this uncouth Yankee swabbie has made improper advances towards you. I do believe he is sweet talking Madeline. She is not discouraging his appointments with the appropriate enthusiasm. If that boy is out of line with you, I will see to it personally that he is sent to Alaska straightaway to cool himself off."

"No Daddy. Just something about his eyes," Helen Troyer mused softly. "And his smile."

"Damn Navy—pardon my language, darling, but I do declare there are times I get the notion that we might, indeed, have been better off if *all* the Navy's ships were at the bottom of Pearl Harbor, especially those damn—those *darn* carriers. Where were those Navy planes when we needed them? If the admirals are afraid to fly them, then, dad burn it, give them to Hap Arnold. He'll make righteous use of them."

Helen Troyer hummed the melody of "Bewitched, Bothered and Bewildered" softly to herself at the window.

"She be—she be a—she be a—she be a—a—a—a vision, boy. A vision from God hisself. Blonde and saucy, she be. Blonde and saucy. And a—and a—and a—and a—a—a—a—a—" The

Sugarman stuttered himself out of breath. He sighed and pulled a white handkerchief from his back pocket. He wiped the sweat from his brow. It was late into the swing shift. All he could say was, "Blonde and saucy. Blonde and saucy, she be. Blonde and saucy."

"Beautiful, huh?" asked Y.T., Jr., sitting at the Sugarman's workbench, playing with a pair of pliers and paging through a *Playboy.*

"Boy, she maked the hair stand up as straight as Kansas wheat on the back of many a man's neck. Sho 'nough. Maked a man ready to take on the whole damned world hisself."

"Y.T., Jr. smiled. "Yeah, sure."

"I be serious, boy. She be the queen of Washington *so-ci-e-ty.* Fo' sho. Done maked every man jump right ups and snaps to attention like a parade full of generals through a shanty town of buck privates. And she done had them smarts, too. She played them po' Washin'ton boys like an angel plucks on the strings of her harp."

"Yeah? And how did dad ever meet such a queen of *so-ci-e-ty?"* Y.T., Jr. asked skeptically.

"Ha-ha! Yeah! You old man, he done sat outside her daddy's office every day all day long waiting to see him, tho', course, he never did—not a once, not during the whole damned war."

"He was supposed to be some kind of congressman, huh?"

"Yes, sir. You grandpappy done be a United States Senator. He be big, boy, a big and powerful man."

"And whatever did she see in my dad when she could have had anyone in Washington?"

"Boy…" there was a hint of warning in the Sugarman's voice that Y.T., Jr. missed.

"After all, he was in the Navy three and a half years and during the whole war never set foot on a ship. The closest he ever got to a beachhead was a golf course sand tr—"

The Sugarman reached out and cuffed Y.T., Jr.'s left ear so hard the boy fell off his stool.

"God damn it!" Y.T., Jr. stood up, cupping his hand over his ear.

The Sugarman shook his finger in front of Y.T., Jr.'s face. "I be damned proud of that boy o' mine. You best be proud, too. Fo' sho."

"For Christ's sake, that's what even he says about himself."

"Franklin Delano Roosevelt didn' shoot no rifle at no Nazis, but he done seen us through the worst of it. Don' you forget it. Nuh-uh. No how."

"Yeah, but what did she see in him?"

"You daddy weren' no dollar-a-year man, no sir. I'll allow you that, but he be something special any hows. He be the Admiral's eyes and ears, bein' everywhere an admiral can' rightly go and hearin' things an admiral don' never hear. And when the Admiral done stood 'fore Congress and done stood 'fore the President of these United States, you daddy be right there behind him with the answer the Admiral needs."

"The President?"

"But looky here boy, you gots to unnerstand all that glitters don' be gold and don' be diamonds neither. See, the Senator be a big important man, uh-huh. He thought he had the whole wide world on a string like some God damned yo-yo and it made no matter who you be neither, he yanked you ups and downs, ups and downs. You mamma, now, she be a songbird in a golden cage what that the Senator put her out for everybody to see and give a listen to, but he never let her fly and flyin' free be more important than playing *so-ci-e-ty* games. And I'll tell you, boy, it take no small man to stand up to the Senator and take the one thing he loved even more than he loved his power."

Y.T., Jr. lit a cigarette and smoked thoughtfully. His left ear was still ringing.

The Sugarman peered through the swirling blue smoke, studying Y.T., Jr.'s face.

"What, boy? You gots a question on you tongue. What is it? I can sees it, but I can' reads it."

"Why did she die?"

The Sugarman shifted uneasily in his chair. "Complications, boy. I believe it be complications."

"Cause of me?"

"I—I ain't no doctor, boy, I—I—" The Sugarman got up and began pacing.

"She died when I was born, huh?"

The Sugarman nodded. He stared down at his feet.

"I killed her, then. Is that why he hates me?"

The Sugarman stopped pacing. He looked up at Y.T., Jr. "He don' hate you none, boy. He—"

"He loved her didn't he?"

"I believe he did. Fo' sho. That be the gospel truth."

"Then I guess I can't really blame him."

"But—but boy, I, ah…I…"

Two weeks after Y.T., Sr. first saw Helen Troyer outside the Senator's office, he woke up at four AM thinking of her. He sat up and smoked a cigarette in the darkness, turning and regarding her image from every possible angle in his mind. He had yet to speak a single word to her but knew he suddenly had a personal stake in the Admiral's struggle with the Senator. Y.T., Sr. quietly rose and dressed without waking Darla Sue Somebody-Or-Other, one of the thousands and thousands of girls in sweaters, skirts, and saddle shoes from Somewhere Else, USA, who followed the yellow brick road to Washington, D.C., only to end up working twelve hours a day, seven days a week at the War Department. Y.T., Sr. came to know quite a few of these women during his time in Washington. Darla Sue happened to work for the Army Air Corps typing contracts, and she helped him keep tabs on the aircraft procurements of the Navy's rival service. He left a pair of nylons for her, then hurried to the airport to joyride the junior Senator from Massachusetts in a new Navy fighter plane—Georgia was not the only state in the union, nor Thurman Troyer the only man who wielded power in Washington, D.C.—before going back to the Hill to continue his one man siege of the Senator's office.

Washington, D.C., had not changed much, really, in the twenty-three years since Y.T., Sr. had first arrived as a ninety day wonder. Behind the marble monuments chiseled with immortal words, within the labyrinthine halls humid with History, beneath the faceless facade of an apparently impermeable bureaucracy were people, and people made government work in all the often irrational and logically perverted ways that humans themselves work, manifesting in that small, concentrated geographic area all the variant modes of chaos endemic to the species. Y.T., Sr. fought World War II on the links of the Chevy Chase Country Club, over bean soup at the Capital Building, at the bars of the Carlton and Mayflower hotels where defense contractors gathered and in the midst of Georgetown cocktail parties. He learned exactly who stood behind the curtains of government and industry with their hands on the levers of power and what made these men, who were dwarfed back down to human proportions only by the smoke and fire of their machines, tick.

Ilium, Georgia, had changed even less than Washington, D.C., It was still the quiet agricultural town west of Georgia Highway 19 that the Senator remembered from his youth just after the turn of the century. In 1956, he retired from Congress and returned to spend his reclining years as Ilium's most distinguished citizen. His days were spent at Cal's Barber Shop, the Ilium Feed and Grain Store and the Wayside Diner, engaged in campaigning and politicizing for the sheer joy of it—except when the sound of the familiar red and white Cessna 180 was heard circling overhead. Ilium had no airport, but still the single-engine tail-dragger dropped from the sky to land at the unplanted end of a peanut field on the family farm owned by the Senator's in-laws. The sound of the plane could only mean that Y.T., Sr. had come to town again—just as he had done nearly every month of every year since 1946—to visit the family cemetery and to place fresh flowers on the grave of Helen Troyer.

At the very first sounds of the plane, the Senator politely, but abruptly, disengaged from conversation and made his way to Holly's Bar and Grill. He sat alone at the far end of the bar, drinking boiler makers and cursing the day—August 7, 1942, to be exact—that a young blond-haired, blue-eyed Navy Lieutenant first appeared outside his office on Capitol Hill. After an hour or two, when the airplane rose again from the peanut field, The Senator watched until it disappeared, then went home to grieve over his lost daughter and to despair over the secret deal he had struck so many years ago with Anna Elise Erp.

~~~

In the Black

1966

The Medium is the Message

"Paper is our most important product," Dirk Rangely often snickered ironically. He was not a complete fool and he had spent nearly his entire adult life as an infinitesimal cog in the great machine of what President Eisenhower labeled the Military-Industrial Complex. He knew the rules: no cannon roared, no airplane flew, no aircraft carrier sailed, and no Erp Industries, Inc., black box did whatever Erp Industries, Inc., black boxes do, until the associated paperwork equaled that cannon's, that airplane's, that aircraft carrier's, that black box's own weight. But rules are made to be broken and, of course, to a self-styled man of action such as Dirk Rangely, paperwork was an arthritis that cramped mobility, a cancer that sapped strength, a heinous manifestation of collective corporate senility to be avoided at all costs. "After all, which would you rather do, pal, screw Bridget Bardot's brains out or read reviews of her movies?"

The only time Dirk Rangely committed anything to paper was in a toilet stall and he applied an aesthetic of scatological utilitarianism to the literary efforts of all others, from James Joyce ("whoever the hell *he* is") to Simon Salisbury ("that limp-cock little pimp"). His hatred for paperwork was grounded in a hybrid metaphysics based upon a peculiar skew of Judeo-Christian values and beliefs that accommodated an irreverent idolatry for Alexander Graham Bell, Thomas Edison, and Vince Lombardi, in spite of the First and Second Commandments. Dirk Rangely theorized long ago that the secret to solving the universal problem of the spontaneous appearance of that ever-troublesome wood by-product was to keep it in perpetual motion. It was an elegant hypothesis, which he felt aptly suited his own dynamic personality. He, therefore, ingeniously devised the most intricate and most circuitous routing maze known to bureaucratic mankind, insuring that any and all of what Dirk Rangely viewed as the slings and arrows of white-collar warfare aimed in his direction were deftly deflected back into the mail to ricochet repeatedly between the in-baskets of others around the world, until—as unlikely as the prospect was—they might re-appear, perhaps decades later, dog-eared, brittle and yellowed, to be swallowed up by the cold, dank darkness of the bottom drawer of Jo Ann's file cabinet.

Y.T., Sr. wrote one and only one memo a year. Dirk Rangely found this admirable, but still, in the end, one too many. If only *he* were the Old Man. But for a man whose hair on the back of his neck bristled like a cornered dog at the chatter of typewriters, the occasion of Y.T., Sr.'s annual New Year's Memo was as important to Dirk Rangely as the second coming of Christ. Make no mistake, he never cast his eyes upon the memo itself. Rather, his concern was only that he received a copy, for Y.T., Sr.'s annual New Year's Memo was sent exclusively to Erp Industries, Inc., Department Heads and, therefore, was a concrete re-affirmation of Dirk Rangely's very being and his continued existence as Vice-President/Marketing. *The Memo* also provided a clear and complete roll call of the competition vying to become the Old Man. Alas, Dirk Rangely did not know who Marshal McLuhan was. In fact, he often mistook him for R. Buckminster Fuller, believing 'The Global Village' to be a California housing development consisting entirely of "those geodesic dome things."

Until Y.T., Sr.'s New Year's Memo of 1966, Dirk Rangely was haunted by only one nightmare horrific enough to wrench him from his sleep in a cold sweat: on a business trip, entertaining THE CUSTOMER at an expensive Los Angeles restaurant, eating and drinking and drinking and drinking, until at the evening's end, upon leaving the restaurant, Dirk Rangely suddenly realizes, keys in hand, that he cannot recall the make or model or color of his Hertz rental car, generating a moment of sheer unadulterated terror as he is confronted with a parking lot full of nondescript, late-model cars—hell enough to drive back to the motel through Watts following Arthur Needleman's hopeless directions, earnestly, anxiously searching for a bridal boutique, a golf pro shop, a Mercedes-Benz dealership or any sign of affluent suburban civilization as he knew it, but to walk through Watts!—"Ahhh! Valet parking! Why didn't I use valet parking?" Dirk Rangely would wake up screaming, which his wife thought sounded suspiciously like "Valerie Parker! Why did I screw Valerie Parker," but she could not be sure.

"Melvin Vapors? Who the hell is Melvin Vapors?" Dirk Rangely asked himself as he frantically paced about his office. He searched for an answer in the frozen snarl of Rudyard's—the stuffed Siberian tiger's head mounted on his wall—face, but to no avail. Certain vicious rumors had started circulating through the halls of Erp Industries, Inc., concerning a top management shake-up shortly after the beginning of 1966. With his copy of Y.T., Sr.'s New Year's Memo of 1966 decomposing in some unknown person's in-basket, probably in Bangkok for all he knew, Dirk Rangely was forced to go to extreme and perilous lengths to see with his own eyes what everyone else seemed to know for fact. In the middle of the night, he broke into Vasili Ivanovich's office to Xerox the mad Russian's copy of Y.T., Sr.'s New Year's Memo of 1966. Bleary eyed, he skipped the text entirely and went directly to the distribution list: Betcha…Dzugashili…Guderian…Mortenstein…Peckerfelt…Rangely *(thank God!)*…Salisbury…Tilman…and…and…and…Melvin Vapors!?

"Who the hell is Melvin Vapors? God damn it, does he have an office? A secretary? A personalized parking spot?"

Dirk Rangely felt despondent when he learned that no one—not even his own secretary—had seen him, met him, spoke with him or knew what department he headed. The more that Dirk Rangely could not learn about Melvin Vapors, the more he found to admire in Melvin Vapors' management style and the more he feared for the failure of his own planning, scheming and strategizing to become the Old Man. He sulked in his office for weeks. In desperation, he booked a business trip to California to vent his frustration on Arthur Needleman. On the flight, Dirk Rangely slipped into a gin-sodden slumber and dreamed of being forever banished to an infinitely large parking lot purgatory in an endless search for a Hertz rental car by a gaseously visaged grim reaper named Melvin Vapors.

An account of Dirk Rangely's three AM visit to ransack the engineering files in Vasili Ivanovich's office as well as a vignette of his thoroughly inept and comical attempts to use so simple a machine as a Xerox copier—he nearly blinded himself by forgetting to close the lid—were carefully recorded in the greasy, grimy notebook of Private Investigator Parmakianski.

~~~

Do Not Fold, Spindle or Mutilate

"Ah, tellible. This vely, vely tellible," Fu Loin muttered over and over and over again as he paced back and forth in the lobby of the fixed base operator at the San Francisco Airport. Fu Loin clutched a Chinese language copy of *The Analects of Confucius,* which was the only possession he had been able to carry with him out of mainland China when he fled Mao Tse-tung's advancing communist forces in 1949. That volume of dog-eared pages never left his side, and he often used it to slap the buttocks of his nearly naked charges to hustle them off to their suitors. Now, he clung to those pearls of humanistic wisdom like a nun to a rosary as he anxiously searched the approach path of runway 28 for some sign of the Erp Industries, Inc., Learjet carrying Y.T., Sr.

It was not surprising that Fu Loin was the first to learn what had happened to Y.T., Jr. He could feel every tremor on the streets of San Francisco like a spider feels the tugs of prey on his web, and many were the customers Fu Loin had collected from the lace work of concrete veiling that moguled peninsula of Northern California. On the other hand, no one had ever imagined that in the swell of pride and cultural gratification Fu Loin felt at seeing the son of his very first and most honorable customer also patronize his establishment—for a man who worshiped alone at his ancestral shrine, that his business should span generations was a measure of success far more sublime than even the healthy profits that always danced across his abacus—he had appointed himself as Y.T., Jr.'s unofficial godfather, to look after and to help the boy in any way he could.

As Fu Loin incessantly paced and frantically massaged his prized, leather-bound tome, Penelope Xing sat quietly in the dim corner of the waiting room at San Francisco General Hospital. She had done and undone and re-done and re-undone the same square yard of knitting so many times that her fingers trembled as if from arthritis. The rosy-fingered dawn of Sunday morning had been upon the city for so long now that she had begun to dread the moment the doctor would come to her with news of Y.T., Jr.'s condition. She looked for comfort from Clinton A. Owsley III across the room, but saw in his eyes that his mind was still filled with drug-induced pandemonium from the night before. She closed her eyes with the hope of release from the strain and the stress of this tragic ordeal. She wanted her mind to drift freely, like a Freudian derelict, if only for a moment, but the same thoughts and images kept coming back again and again like incessant waves against her bow. Her lips silently formed the same words over and over.

"I am the wind!" Penelope Xing would shriek as she and Y.T., Jr. raced down the Pacific Coast Highway every Sunday morning at dawn after he had returned from his nomadic Saturday night wanderings in the Haight and Filmore Districts to make love to her, then take her away from Fu Loin's.

Penelope Xing had never ridden on a motorcycle and had no desire nor intention whatsoever to do so. In her mind, motorcycles were barbaric metal steeds of death for brutal gangs like the Hell's Angels, those modern day furies of anarchy who pursued their own unique brand of apparently nihilistic revenge on the highways and byways of California. So, when Y.T., Jr. brought his Harley-

Davidson back to Berkeley on the Erp Industries, Inc., Learjet for the new school year, Penelope Xing confronted a direct threat to her primordial, *a priori* sense of order and to civilization as she knew it. She wanted nothing to do with Y.T., Jr.'s vehicular demon and she told him so.

"What if it rains?" she asked, trying to be polite at first, but Y.T., Jr. just stared at the ground and shook his head.

"But my hair will get mussed and my clothes will get all wind blown," she whined. Y.T., Jr. rolled his eyes back and lit another Marlboro.

"I am not going to sit on top of a raw, unhoused engine with thousands and thousands of angry little gasoline explosions going off between my thighs," she insisted. This excuse was Y.T., Jr.'s favorite. It was original. He laughed out loud.

"Look, you don't even have any helmets. If we fell off, we would be hurt. We could get killed," she explained rationally, prophetically.

Y.T., Jr. listened patiently, then called her bluff with his morphinically persuasive smile. Penelope Xing folded like a bad poker hand and reluctantly got on the Harley behind Y.T., Jr.

At first, it was worse than she or even Alfred Hitchcock could have ever imagined. Penelope Xing was terrified to near excretion by Y.T., Jr.'s bizarre and perverted twist on running the bulls at Pamplona through downtown San Francisco rush hour traffic. Whenever her right leg twitched with the life-preserving urge to save herself by slamming on the brakes, Y.T., Jr. inevitably twisted the throttle up a notch or two until the city passed by as a blur of concrete, metal, brick and asphalt reaching out to grab her and flay her skin off as they banked to pass each car or truck and to whip around each corner. The forces of acceleration, deceleration and the centrifugal force of each turn groped and clawed at her body like the bad lovers who came to Fu Loin's every weekend with crumpled twenty dollar bills in their fists and anger in their eyes. The queasy feeling of motion haunted her intestines even while stopped at traffic lights. She did not know if her tears were more from fear or from the wind relentlessly whipping her face.

Then, a funny thing happened. Traffic thinned out. The tunnel-like streets of downtown San Francisco emerged on bright, sunny, open road, and instead of enduring the blender-like blur of the city, with a little squinting, Penelope Xing's eyes were able to focus again—on far away hilltops, on freely floating puffs of cumulus, on ocean white caps driving relentlessly towards the shore. Carbon monoxide no longer burned her throat. The salted ocean air cleared her mind like breathing pure oxygen. The speed didn't seem to bother her any more, except when she looked over Y.T., Jr.'s shoulder at the speedometer or when a pickup truck towing a fish-tailing Airstream trailer suddenly blossomed out from around the next corner. But after a moment or two, the fear rippling her bodily fluids calmed again and the balance of the Harley no longer felt so precarious, so that her mind passed on to thoughts other than her imminent and medievally painful death.

Penelope Xing first imagined, then began to see the sharply drawn line on each curve of the Pacific Coast Highway, beyond which lay uncontrolled flight over a cliff into the ocean or a point blank kiss with the face of a rock wall at eighty miles per hour. At first, she thought Y.T., Jr. to be flirting with that line, but soon realized it was more than just a playful teasing. Y.T., Jr. chased that line and Penelope Xing began to feel its nearness like wind blowing across a high Sierra lake, imagining how the plunge beyond it might be like the bracing chill of a dive into mountain waters. There was no retreat, only victory, then the next battle, the next chance to lay your life on the line or beyond it. She held tight to Y.T., Jr.'s rib cage as he hunted that line, chewing on the Pacific Coast Highway like she had learned from assigned history texts how Patton and Rommel had chewed on Africa and Europe with their armies—only to Penelope Xing, this was not academic history, this was real.

Penelope Xing closed her eyes. She listened to the Harley's deep throated engine respond to every twist of the throttle and shift of the gears. She felt the pistons beating through her flesh, her blood, her soul. The slip stream no longer raped her, but caressed and embraced every inch of her body all at once. It was like being on the peak of the highest mountain on earth, with no place to run, nowhere to hide, breathless from the climb and exposed to the splendorous wrath of some Zeus blowing against her soul. Suddenly, the walls of her claustrophobic, four-cornered life—the peeling plaster of her tiny apartment in the Haight, the dusty chalkboards of San Francisco State classrooms, the cramped study desk buried in the musty stacks of the library, and dingy, depressing room number five-sixteen at Fu Loin's establishment—crumbled and fell away from about her.

"I am the wind!" Penelope Xing would shriek, suddenly feeling completely untethered.

"So blow me," Y.T., Jr. would reply back over his shoulder. And when they stopped at Monterey or Carmel or Big Sur or just some secluded spot along the coast for their Sunday afternoon picnic, she did so with a smile on her face and joy in her heart. Penelope Xing was falling in love.

A vision of Y.T., Jr. crossing that sharply drawn line in a twist on the Pacific Coast Highway and hurling off into the oblivion of the ocean's entrails abruptly brought Penelope Xing gasping back to the cold reality of the hospital waiting room. She looked to Clinton A. Owsley III, but kept to herself, wiping a tear from her eye and picking up her knitting to begin again.

Being that the accident happened at two AM at Seventh and Market Streets in downtown San Francisco, the police had only two witnesses, both indigent fanciers of muscatel, white port and, that particular night, MD20/20, who vigorously disagreed whether it had been an Ernest and Julio Gallo or a Mogen David delivery truck—in reality, it had been a peach truck—that had clipped the back wheel of Y.T., Jr.'s Harley-Davidson and disappeared into the night. Both witnesses did agree, though, that rider and bike promptly parted ways with the motorcycle skidding across the pavement on its side, showering sparks until it finally burst into flames so bright that their eyes were pained. Y.T., Jr. tumbled into his coma amidst a brief flurry of IBM punch cards that the University of California at Berkeley used for student registration.

"Bummer, man, bummer. He looks like the back of the Grateful Dead's PA equipment!" Clinton A. Owsley III gasped when he and Penelope Xing came into the Intensive Care Unit and saw all of the IV, respirator, catheter and monitor tubes and probes attached to Y.T., Jr.'s motionless body beyond the glass partition. He began to panic. "Look at him! He is wired for fucking sound, man! Who's been working on him? Dr. Frankenstein? Somebody do something! Get him out of there! Calling Dr. Howard! Dr. Fine! Dr. Howard! Somebody do something for Christ's sake!"

"You shush your mouth or I will suture it shut," warned the head nurse, shaking an angry, black finger at Clinton A. Owsley III. "We've got *sick* people here. You understand? And we certainly don't need…" As the nurse relentlessly continued to read out the riot act to the two intruders in *her* Intensive Care Unit, Clinton A. Owsley III's mind became unstuck and whirled off on a new and remarkably unpredictable tangent. In the chemically scrambled signals his brain received from his sensory organs, the nurses eyes flared with pointed, blow torch flames that flushed and warmed his cheeks. Her Afro became a writhing nest of water moccasins. Her skin began to melt into a black, tar-like puddle on the spotless, white-tiled hospital floor and her gullish screeching suddenly became intelligible to him and only him: "I'm melting! Merciful heavens, I'm melting!"

Just as the 'Hail Dorothys' began to ring in his ears, Penelope Xing stepped up, took Clinton A. Owsley III by the arm and quickly led him away, amused, bemused and slightly embarrassed as he sang 'ding-dong the witch is dead' in a wavering falsetto voice the whole way back to the waiting room.

Metaphysical and pharmaceutical considerations aside, Clinton A. Owsley III and reality had never been on the best of terms. The son of an MGM studio accounting executive and an ex-blonde ex-starlet whose on-screen attributes had little to do with acting, his childhood can be described most charitably as celluloidally Walter Middy-ish. He was never able to neither separate himself from the fictions of translucent thermoplastic polymers nor fully integrate himself mentally with the empirical world surrounding him. Clinton A. Owsley III sat always the lone spectator in the darkness of his own mind, watching the cinema-scope images projected on his retinas. His mother and father might have realized something was wrong when they caught him preparing to flay the family poodle alive shortly after seeing Walt Disney's *Davy Crockett,* claiming he had just "kilt me a bar"—or when he blew up the swimming pool diving board after watching *Bridge on the River Kwai.*

Instead, they laughed at his antics and fueled his fantasies further with coon skin caps, Roy Rogers costumes, and, perhaps most regrettably, a chemistry set frightfully soon after he saw Spencer Tracy in *Jekyll and Hyde* on the late show. Clinton A. Owsley III learned quickly and easily as a rich teenager in that mythical kingdom called Hollywood that if drugs did not make coherent the plot mechanics of life, they at least generated dazzling special effects and omnisciently transcending thematic insights that were as intense as they were transitory. By the time Mr. and Mrs. Clinton A. Owsley II suspected that their son's mind might be lost in a manic maze of organic chemistry formulae, it was too late. A string of expeditions by several world-renowned psychiatrists all returned empty handed and, thus, they had no choice but to have young Clinton III institutionally committed three hundred miles away at the University of California at Berkeley.

When Y.T., Jr. came back to Berkeley in September of 1965 for the new school year, Clinton A. Owsley III waited in the empty apartment they had leased on Telegraph Avenue, still dusty and residually stoned from his days on the Red Dog Ranch with Murph. After only a few near-coherent syllables, Y.T., Jr. quickly surmised that either Nevada's clean, clear air or Clinton A. Owsley III's own clean, clear LSD had corroded vital synapses in his roommate's nervous system so that his brain was like a neglected car battery: the cables were connected, but the juice just wasn't getting through. Y.T., Jr. knew that if he didn't take matters into his own hands—and quickly, too—his roommate would be dead before the second semester.

The very first thing Y.T., Jr. did was convince Clinton A. Owsley III to stop giving his LSD away for free. LSD was *the* fuel driving the Bay Area social machine that churned out new music, new art, new ideals, new beliefs and new values. It was a movement that was gaining momentum and, from a marketing viewpoint, enhanced demographics, a fact that was even noted by that eternal entrepreneur, Fu Loin. Y.T., Jr. realized that he had his hands on the spigot for the best source of high octane LSD-25 in California, if not the entire United States. Drawing upon his days on the Erp Industries, Inc., loading dock with Orley Bovine, Y.T., Jr. began working to make Clinton A. Owsley III's name synonymous with top shelf quality among the 'Better Living Through Chemistry' crowd. Soon everyone wanted hits of his White Lightning, Owsley Blue Dots or Pink Owsleys or Purple Owsleys or sheets of genuine Owsley Microdots—so many people, in fact, that within two months after Y.T., Jr. took charge of the distribution of Clinton A. Owsley III's legendary molecular magic, they filled their apartment with nearly every material possession two American college students could possibly covet from a capitalistic society. Clinton A. Owsley III was excessively happy. But for Y.T., Jr., it was not enough.

"I'm bored," Y.T., Jr. sighed out loud.

"Bored? How can you be bored?" asked Clinton A. Owsley III. "This is my best batch yet."

Murph, who had, himself, become bored with the Red Dog Ranch in Nevada, homesick for the patented Bay Area brand of madness, and overly fond of Purple Owsleys, lay sprawled out on a bean bag chair in the corner of the apartment on Telegraph Avenue, mentally turned inside out by the now infamous Owsley LSD.

"I'm bored," Y.T., Jr. said louder, gazing distractedly about the apartment and deciding that Murph looked like a starfish devouring a bean bag oyster.

"For someone who is supposed to be having a religious experience, Slinger, I'd say you've got a pretty piss-poor attitude."

"Fuck all that Timothy Leary bull shit."

"You simply have no respect whatsoever for any authority, do you?"

"Timothy Leary is a bore."

At this, a little red warning light went off in Murph's head, telling him that something important—possibly historic, though he was too stoned to be sure—was happening elsewhere in the room.

"Relax, Slinger. You're always so wired. Sit back and groove on it. Let it take you away."

"This trip is going nowhere fast."

"Well, maybe if we got out and did something. We could go catch the late show of *Fantasia.*"

"Always the spectator, huh, Wiz."

"Bad vibes, Slinger. Bad vibes."

"Not bad vibes. Not good vibes. Just no vibes." Y.T., Jr. stood up and began to pace about the apartment. "I feel like a fucking house plant, Wiz—a very stoned house plant, for sure, like a demented Mr. Green Jeans watered me with a God damned rainbow of different food colorings—but still, just a house plant. A fucking dieffenbachia or something."

Murph's brain began operating like a Dick Tracy comic strip, labeling everything in the room using little white signs with arrows pointing at objects and saying 'Stereo', 'Television', 'Refrigerator', and, even though it was just his Timex, 'Two-way Wrist Radio'. The sign above Clinton A. Owsley III said, 'Thesis'. The sign above Y.T., Jr. said, 'Antithesis'. This was it, a living breathing Hegelian Dialectic breaking water and thrashing about like a large mouth bass hooked on ten pound test line right before his very eyes. "Hey…Pilgrim…you make the best God damned acid in the whole God damned galaxy. I am mentally Osterized."

"Thanks, Murph."

"You know what really bugs the living shit right out of me?" Y.T., Jr. asked, ignoring the exchange of social pleasantries between Clinton A. Owsley III and Murph.

"What? What's that?" asked Murph, excited that he was ringside for a philosophical slug fest made manifest.

"Those two phlegm brains from last year."

"Who? Fullman and Fellows?"

"Yeah," grumbled Y.T., Jr. "Those two shit-for-brains."

"Who's that?" asked Murph.

"Our roommates in the dorm last year," explained Clinton A. Owsley III. "Why in the hell are you thinking about those assholes? You're not going to bum out on us, are you, Slinger? You can't do that to me. You just can't. You're my anchor. Without you, I'm done for."

"Why should they get away with that shit, huh? What right did they have to push that kid out the window?"

"What shit? What kid?" asked Murph breathlessly. "What window?"

"Oh man, you're not going to start bitching that there's no justice in the world, are you?" moaned Clinton A. Owsley III. "Oh, Slinger, you aren't turning radical on me? I've got enough guilt in my life already. I don't need you making like Mario Salvo and giving speeches around the apartment all day and all night."

"To hell with the rads and all their hot air. You know, back in Meadowlawns, Keeg and Billy Saul and me, we didn't ever take it. And we didn't just talk about it either. We dished it out."

"Take what? Dished what out?" asked Murph, frantically trying to make sense of the dialectic.

"Those guys deserve to get pimped good," said Y.T., Jr.

"Pimped?" asked Murph.

"What do you mean pimped?" asked Clinton A. Owsley III.

"What would be their worst fucking nightmare come true?"

"The collapse of the Federal Reserve System," offered Clinton A. Owsley III.

"No good. They've probably got gold stockpiled somewhere."

"A surprise SAT audit?"

"Nah. They probably studied for twelve years and passed legit."

"Some Purple Owsleys in their Flintstones Vitamins," offered Murph out of the blue.

"Murph!" That dangerous Erp smile slowly spread across Y.T., Jr.'s face. "Murph! My man!"

"Oh no. Oh no. Murph, he's got that look, that smile," protested Clinton A. Owsley III. "The last time he smiled that smile, I…I…"

"You got laid," said Y.T., Jr.

Clinton A. Owsley III smiled. "Yeah. I got laid."

"Can you get me laid?" asked Murph, finally sensing the full potential of the dialectic.

"Sure," smiled Y.T., Jr.

And so the *Triumvirate* was born. Y.T., Jr. didn't really care one way or another, but Murph insisted they should have a name and insisted on that particular one, because his lawyer-father had told him repeatedly while trying to influence his high school language elective choice that Latin is a powerful tool for making people feel uneasy, which is why doctors and lawyers use it with such reckless abandon. Once they had a name, Clinton A. Owsley III became adamant that they should have an emblem that would be their signature and designed one that was an eyeball inside a triangle inside a circle, which was suspiciously identical to the pyramid peak on the back of a one dollar bill—evidence of the profound power that a positive cash flow had to cut through fantasy and hallucinations to succeed in changing his life where so many others had failed.

Y.T., Jr., Clinton A. Owsley III and Murph never did put Purple Owsleys into the Flintstones Vitamins of their two blatantly bland ex-roommates from Eugene, Oregon. Instead—and far more severe—they ordered Nelson Fullman a three year, pre-paid subscription to *Pravda* and made Norman Fellows an official member-in-good-standing of the Students for a Democratic Society. As the two committed capitalists puzzled over the strangely familiar emblem that had been affixed to their door shortly thereafter, their self-confidence began to corrode audibly and soon they were bickering like pathetically paranoid Siamese twins who didn't know if they could even trust themselves any more, let alone their inseparable partner.

No one in San Francisco knew exactly who or what or why the *Triumvirate* was, because they took such pains to keep their identities a secret, but the group became a major source of entertainment throughout the Bay Area by pulling pranks and staging practical jokes whenever an opportunity presented itself. The *Triumvirate* was rumored to be who had baked Ex-Lax into brownies and passed them out to innocently unsuspecting Hell's Angels gang members at Ken Kesey's La Honda ranch during a weekend acid test. At the Fillmore Auditorium one night, all of the Grateful Dead's guitar and amplifier chords were mischievously switched around moments before show time, causing forty-five minutes of high decibel dissonance while band members were stricken with a drug induced laugh-attack and Bill Graham climbed the walls in a self-induced anxiety attack. The appearance of Clinton A. Owsley III's art work on the Audioptics' light show screen behind the stage left no doubt who was responsible for the mayhem, appreciation of which was shown by a standing ovation. A protest rally held in the eucalyptus grove near the Life Sciences building of the University of California at Berkeley drew thousands demanding the immediate release of the Nairobi Trio, supposedly the vanguard of a new extremist splinter group spun off from the Black Panthers. An afternoon of eloquent and impassioned speeches finally convinced school officials to turn over the three laboratory chimpanzees to radical leaders, who stood dumbfounded as the apes began scratching, biting and pissing all over them in their wild attempts to break free of their leashes. A flag hoisted below Old Glory with the tell-tale triangle-eyeball emblem, told the crowd who could claim victory.

No one was safe. Nothing was sacred. No chain dangled unpulled and no cage remained unrattled. On the night Y.T., Jr.'s motorcycle was struck by the peach truck, he was heading to Fu Loin's with thousands of IBM cards to be re-programmed by Fu Loin's basement sweat-shop key punch operation in a wickedly inspired plan to turn spring semester registration into utter computerized chaos.

It didn't take Y.T., Sr. long to realize that the medi-babble being administered to him by the staff doctors about his son's condition amounted to a benign overdose of verbal placebos. No one knew if Y.T., Jr. would ever come out of the coma and, if he did, just what his condition would be. As he stood flanked in tight formation by Frik and Frak, listening to gravely visaged physicians speak in muted, hopeful tones about medical statistics, Y.T., Sr. was struck with a chilling sense of *déjà vu* as his mind hearkened back many, many years ago to the image of Helen Troyer's lifeless body lying in a Bethesda Naval Hospital bed.

Between his fruitless meetings with representatives of Neurology, Cardiology, Radiology, Hematology, Endocrinology, Gastrology, *ad nauseam,* Y.T., Sr. carefully surveyed the entourage that gathered at his son's bedside. Every night after classes, Penelope Xing sat and read out loud to Y.T., Jr. from her assigned history texts until she fell asleep in the hard, wooden rocking chair. Clinton A. Owsley III planted himself alone in a far corner, so still at times that he himself might have been diagnosed as comatose were it not for a respectable rendition of "Somewhere Over the Rainbow" sung softly under his breath over and over and over and over. Murph had recently taken to wearing ski goggles and a day-glow green jump suit, specially modified with aluminum foil, plastic wrap and a *Triumvirate* emblem patch over his heart. He insistently lectured anyone who would and would not listen that he was not from outer space, but from "another space." Y.T., Sr., Frik and Frak all watched curiously as day in and day out a parade of Barnum and Bailey-like characters—including the likes of Ken Kesey and his Merry Pranksters, Sonny Barger and his Oakland Hell's Angels, Jerry Garcia and his Grateful Dead, Grace Slick and her Great Society, Marty Balin and his Jefferson Airplane, Jimi Hendrix and his Experience, among countless others— meandered through the Intensive Care Unit at San Francisco General Hospital to pay tribute to the heroic fallen half of the dynamic duo of recreational chemistry.

As soon as the doctors told Y.T., Sr. that his son was stable enough, he had the Erp Industries, Inc., Learjet equipped and staffed as a flying hospital room and took his son back to Missouri. Y.T., Jr. was admitted to Kansas City Memorial Hospital and placed not three doors down from Wilson Cassidy, who had blown a gasket in his heart upon hearing the news of the tragedy that had befallen the only unfrozen, breathing heir to his family's beef empire.

After three weeks in a coma in Kansas City Memorial Hospital, Y.T., Jr. awoke hearing echoes of Penelope Xing's soft voice reading about Charlemagne in his ears, but the first thing he saw when he opened his eyes was Scarlett Brookings. Her red hair and tight midnight blue dress a stark contrast to the severe hospital whites, she sat close by the bed with her hand beneath the blankets, gently and playfully fondling Y.T., Jr.'s testicles.

"My, what big eyes you have," Scarlett Brookings purred.

"The—aaaahhhhh—the better to see you with," Y.T., Jr. sighed. The light hurt his eyes, but he fought his reflexes to gaze upon Scarlett Brookings glowing, red-lipped smile.

"And what big strong hands you have."

"The better to caress you with, my dear." He reached out and weakly stroked her freckled cheeks.

"And *my, my, my,* what a *big, stiff,* magic wand you have."

"The better to screw you silly with, my dove."

And they did just that, after which the nurses were at a loss to explain the sudden and fleeting elevation in Y.T., Jr.'s vital signs.

~~~

No Man is an Island

P. Peckerfelt, VP/Manufacturing, was a lonely, somewhat disturbed bachelor who, during his evening and weekend hours away from Erp Industries, Inc., often found himself hovering dangerously, exhilaratingly close to the Junior/Misses Lingerie Department at the Meadowlawns Sears, Roebuck and Company store, alarmed at the power of his own inexplicable attraction to that precipice over which lay a briar patch of scandal and shame amidst the tender, pastel blossoms of young girls' panties. It was never very long before P. Peckerfelt's particularly simian appearance—the bald, sloping forehead; the spinnaker-gutted abdomen; the short, bandy bow legs; the longer than normal arms; the hairy knuckles; and, if one stood close enough, the continuous grunting-belching of his ulcers at work—began to alarm young, nubile shoppers and their mothers. Since store detectives and security guards gathered like flies to a wildebeest carcass at the slightest disturbance in usually idyllic suburbia, P. Peckerfelt, would, at the very first, nasal-sounding, "Code-13-to-Junior/Misses-please" request over the store paging system, hurriedly trot back to the relative safety of Craftsman power tools with a palpitating heart and a rising lump of fear in his throat at the mysterious, forbidden urges that so often welled up out of the dark murky pool of his psyche during visits to Sears, Roebuck and Company.

No one, not Y.T., Sr., not Simon Salisbury, not his own mother, not even P. Peckerfelt himself, knew what his father, the late Peter

Peckerfelt, had in mind when he placed the singular initial 'P' on his son's birth certificate for a first name so long ago. All opinions of the few who might have even bothered to ponder this particular secret the elder Peckerfelt took to his grave tragically soon after his son's birth when he choked to death on a prune pit would have been unanimous, though: 'P' stood for paranoid. P. Peckerfelt was motivated by fear just as surely and predictably as Mort Mortenstein was motivated by the love of money and Dirk Rangely was motivated by the ravenous appetite of an already morbidly obese ego.

There were so many things in life for P. Peckerfelt to fear, not the least of which was incurring the *Dreaded Chair Treatment,* during which Y.T., Sr. stood on a chair in his office directly beside P. Peckerfelt, haranguing down at him at the top of his voice for what seemed like hours concerning the latest of his transgressions, until a thoroughly intimidated P. Peckerfelt wished Y.T., Sr. would simply be done with it by standing him up against the wall and shooting him in the head. Of course, P. Peckerfelt had never discussed that possibility with Vasili Ivanovich. There was also his recently acquired fear of flying which caused his molars to grind from take-off to baggage claim and found him desperately exercising his intimate knowledge of the labyrinthine corridors of the Old O'Reilly Candy Factory Building to avoid Frik and Frak whenever he heard that grizzled Air Force drawl up ahead in the hall making some loud, lewd comment, such as, "My pickle is hot for that cunt." In high school, P. Peckerfelt watched varsity football from the bench as a third string offensive guard in a near paralyzing panic that he might actually be called upon to play, thereby sustaining a crippling knee injury. He slipped and fell in the locker room shower after his Senior-year homecoming game, side-lining himself from the big dance with a compound fracture of the arm and a sprained ankle. Nazi Panzer tanks absolutely petrified him during World War II, but it was frostbite that wounded his feet as he carried a bazooka—which was never fired due to a lack of available targets—across Europe during the winter of 1944. At Erp Industries, Inc., P. Peckerfelt faced the end of each and every month with abject terror, scrambling madly in an adrenalin induced frenzy to ship every possible unit of product in the desperate hope that a favorable P & L Statement might be bestowed upon his department by Mort Mortenstein's department, thus sparing him another humiliating episode of the *Dreaded Chair Treatment.*

Some—in fact, most of P. Peckerfelt's co-workers used his fears like Gestapo instruments of torture. With lunation precision, every twenty-nine days, twelve hours, forty-four minutes and 2.7+ seconds an apocalyptic memorandum from Simon Salisbury inevitably appeared in P. Peckerfelt's in-basket to promise inevitable doom from pending Congressional labor legislation, an upcoming worker safety survey and audit or, worst of all, possible union organizing activities—a recurring nightmare the mere mention of which during daylight hours caused P. Peckerfelt to break out instantaneously into a cold sweat and shivers. Hugh Betcha pursued his own personal inquisition by continually harping on inventory levels: too high and profits would be eroded by carrying charges; too low and production lines might shut down from a lack of parts. P. Peckerfelt could never seem to win. Rolf Guderian often cornered P. Peckerfelt in the men's room to cackle with maniacal glee as he described some improbable sounding contraption that the Engineering Department was inventing and the severity of migraine headaches it was certain to cause for P. Peckerfelt when he tried to actually manufacture the Rube Goldberg inspired design.

A dramatic, gin-sodden scowl from Dirk Rangely or a severely arched eyebrow from Mort Mortenstein, especially just after the end of the month, were enough to give P. Peckerfelt ample food for paranoid thought as he found himself staring at his alarm clock at 3:47 in the morning. It was psychological warfare even North Koreans might have taken pride in.

Others—in fact, precious few—in reality, none of P. Peckerfelt's co-workers could be counted as genuine friends. Perhaps he came closest when he traded short sips of moonshine and long, late afternoon sighs with Vasili Ivanovich in the Swiss-like neutrality of the Sugarman's workshop. P. Peckerfelt would stew over his latest session of Y.T., Sr.'s peculiar brand of motivation therapy. Vasili Ivanovich would absent-mindedly try to rub the indelible memory of the forty-five caliber muzzle impression from the middle of his forehead. A chasm of silence gaped between them, unbridged by conversation in spite of their common bond of fifteen years' worth of suffering at the hands of the Erps, Guderians, Salisburys, Rangelys, and Mortensteins, of this world. The seeds of friendship, sown upon rocks, failed to ever sprout.

The only business associate with which P. Peckerfelt was able to maintain some semblance of a near normal relationship was Arthur Needleman—and that was facilitated by the fact that the two men lived nearly two thousand miles apart. Arthur Needleman somehow always came through with a big order just when P. Peckerfelt's production backlog was slipping; or a new program when Congress canceled a long running cash cow; or a need to visit THE CUSTOMER in California when the pollen count in Kansas City became unbearably high or General Accounting Office auditors were scheduled to arrive at Erp Industries, Inc.; or a fresh, new joke that simply made P. Peckerfelt laugh out loud. In spite of the certainty that Arthur Needleman was involved in some vicious, secret conspiracy against him, P. Peckerfelt was always glad to take his calls or to join him for a semi-relaxed, almost enjoyable dinner at Dante's when he came to visit the plant from California. For his part, Arthur Needleman played upon the strings of P. Peckerfelt's paranoia like a psychiatric Isaac Stern. With the subtle, lyrical touch of a true virtuoso, he channeled the latent energy of those myriad fears into the melodies of commerce known as purchase orders, blanket agreements and multi-year production contracts, thereby becoming the most successful salesman in the history of Erp Industries, Inc., much to the chagrin and envy of Dirk Rangely.

Arthur Needleman recognized something that all the others (except Y.T., Sr.) missed or, perhaps, refused to admit: P. Peckerfelt was the second most powerful man at Erp Industries, Inc. There were as many theories of ascension to the Big Office as there were pretenders to Y.T., Sr.'s throne. There was the Rangely Doctrine: "The key to the Big Office is having your finger on the pulse of the marketplace—after all, THE CUSTOMER pays the freight." There was Guderian's First Law of Primacy: "The key to the Big Office is having your finger on the pulse of technology—after all, without technology, THE CUSTOMER would never come knocking at our door." There was the Salisbury Hypothesis: "The key to the Big Office is having your finger on the pulse of personnel—after all, people invent technology and people manufacture products from that technology, thereby forming the cement-like bond between Erp Industries, Inc., and THE CUSTOMER." Finally, there was Mortenstein's Constant: "The key to the Big Office is having your finger on the pulse of company finances—after all, you cannot deposit THE CUSTOMER, technology, or people in a bank account. P. Peckerfelt did not have a theory, but he did what none of the others could do: P. Peckerfelt made profits for the Erp Industries, Inc., and handsome profits they were.

The power of profitability afforded P. Peckerfelt allowances for a great deal of aberrant behavior with respect to what were commonly accepted business practices and business etiquette. In fact, the several interested observers of the Manufacturing Department's operations were at a total loss to understand how anything got accomplished in manufacturing—and that was just the way P. Peckerfelt wanted it. In spite of the voluminous epistles of Simon Salisbury extolling the virtues and the positive benefits of maintaining open and regular inter-departmental communications, P. Peckerfelt's desk was a veritable compost heap of unanswered letters, ignored memoranda, unfinished budget forecasts, uncompleted employee evaluation forms, *etc.* P. Peckerfelt knew that his job was not "to communicate". His job was to take raw materials and alchemize them into the black magic of classified military electronics and, in doing so, to spend less money (at least 20% less or else endure the *Dreaded Chair Treatment)* than THE CUSTOMER had agreed to pay for those black boxes. Attending meetings was not his job either.

"If I have to go to a God damned meeting to find out what the hell is going on around here, then just take me down to the pound and put me out of my misery," P. Peckerfelt would grunt-belch under his breath as he sent one of his supervisors off as his surrogate to a meeting or a conference or a seminar he was supposed to attend. If the meeting was called by Rolf Guderian or either of his brown-shirted henchmen, Eichmanhoff or Himmlerlicht, he always sent the foul-mouthed Leon Debs, who would insure that the meeting disintegrated into profane pandemonium inside of ten minutes. Dirk Rangely would have been horrified to learn that in 1960, P. Peckerfelt used one of the telephone lines into his office to call himself on his other telephone line and then put himself on hold for the next five and a half years. He simply could not be convinced that talking on the telephone was part of his job description.

There were only two exceptions to P. Peckerfelt's hard and fast rule *never, ever* to attend Erp Industries, Inc., social functions: the annual Fourth of July company picnic and the annual company Christmas party. Attendance was mandatory for all company executives, though Y.T., Sr. rarely stayed longer than fifteen minutes himself. P. Peckerfelt always endeavored to find a remote hickory tree in a far corner of Meadowlawns Memorial Park or a dim corner in the ballroom near the kitchen of the I-70 Hilton Hotel where he could peaceably drink himself into a Buddha-like stupor that left him with a five-and-a-half-month long hangover. Something strange happened after the 1965 Erp Industries, Inc., Annual Christmas party, though. When P. Peckerfelt woke up at 3:47 am, as was his regular nightly habit, he was not in the dim corner of the I70 Hilton Hotel rented ball room or at home in bed or even behind his desk at the Old O'Reilly Candy Factory Building, as was sometimes known to mysteriously happen. He was naked and lying next to the naked body of Prunella Spoons in a fifth floor room at the I-70 Hilton Hotel.

Prunella Spoons was a pert, bubbly and painfully cheerful widow ten years younger than P. Peckerfelt, who spent her time with a transistor radio earphone plugged into her ear canal and a microscope pressed into her eye sockets as she stuffed miniature electronic components into printed circuit boards and soldered them into place. Everyone hated her. She annoyed the gaggle of gossiping women she worked with not only by being the most beautiful production line worker at Erp Industries, Inc.—which was not difficult considering that on a scale of one to ten, the aggregate beauty of the gaggle of gossiping women was still an imaginary number—but also by singing, humming, whistling, laughing and generally carrying on as if her 7-3:30 shift at the Old O'Reilly Candy Factory Building was the social event of the century. The truth was that Prunella Spoons was terminally happy everywhere she went, whether it was to the Meadowlawns A & P, Bob's Big Laundromat or even Dr. De Sade's Dental Clinic. Conventional wisdom dictated that after receiving a huge settlement from the Missouri State Highway Department because her husband had been accidentally crushed by a steam roller, Prunella Spoons was obliged never to work another day in her life. Yet, in spite of her good fortune and the beckoning of daytime TV soap operas, she and she alone boasted a perfect attendance record on the production line.

For nearly ten years, Prunella Spoons had been stirring up P. Peckerfelt's murky, psychic gumbo of desires whenever she breezed by him in the corridors of the Old O'Reilly Candy Factory Building. She was always quick with a cheerful, heartfelt "Hello Mr. Peckerfelt" and smiled so sweetly that his breath was sucked right out of his lungs by the close proximity of her presence. A lingering gaze upon her graceful form bent over her microscope as if in prayer broke P. Peckerfelt loose from his mental moorings, setting him off on brief, sometimes but not always lurid day dreams until reality inevitably brought him up short like a dog running at full speed to the end of his chain. He always found himself nodding absently in agreement whenever Frik commented to Frak on her beauty and sensuality ("I'd sure like to go Popeye in her pussy"). He even inexplicably appeared at the Meadowlawns Bowl-O-Rama on several Tuesday evenings—the same evenings that the Erp Industries, Inc., woman's league bowling team consisting of Wanda W. Willet, Arlotta McGurdy, Dirk Rangely's Secretary Jo Ann, Scarlett Brookings, and Prunella Spoons bowled—with the same mystifying and foreboding feelings which often over powered him at the Sears, Roebuck and Company store.

When P. Peckerfelt woke up beside a naked Prunella Spoons at 3:47 in the morning, he was mortified, but not because of the suspect urges welling up from within. And not because he could not remember any of the events of the evening before that brought him to be in bed with her. And not because the only two times in his life he had slept with a woman—once in France during World War II and once at Fu Loin's through the thoughtful arrangements of Arthur Needleman—his penis burned like a three alarm fire for months. Of course, P. Peckerfelt knew for fact that an affair with another Erp Industries, Inc., employee was the kiss of death for his career. After all, the only reason he became VP/Manufacturing was that his ex-boss had gotten caught red-handed screwing the woman who worked three stations to the left of Prunella Spoons in a pile of packing material in the shipping department after hours and refused to pay Orley Bovine the blackmail money demanded of him. But he was not mortified over the future of his career. For the over twenty years since World War II, P. Peckerfelt continued to psychologically shoulder his unfired, U.S. Army issue bazooka. Whatever else had happened the night of the 1965 Erp Industries, Inc., Annual Christmas Party, P. Peckerfelt vented that twenty years of frustration. He had finally gotten off a clean shot with his bazooka and, from his survey of the battle scene at 3:47 AM in the

I-70 Hilton Inn Hotel room, he had hit his target. But at that moment, he was mortified because he realized that, for the very first time in his life, he was in love.

Y.T., Sr. immediately suspected as much when the very first application of the *Dreaded Chair Treatment* for 1966 did not seem to have its usual stool loosening effect on P. Peckerfelt. Y.T., Sr. could not afford to have his number two man moping around the plant pie-eyed in love when there were profits to be made, so straight away he met with Private Investigator Parmakianski at the West Side Grill to put the matter into the gangly detective's predictably incompetent hand. Shortly thereafter, Y.T., Sr.'s interest in the investigation was diverted by his son's motorcycle accident and he rarely thought of it except on those several occasions when he had to go down to the Meadowlawns Police Department to bail out a confused and embarrassed P.I. Parmakianski after his arrest for loitering in the Junior/Misses Lingerie Department at the Meadowlawns Sears, Roebuck and Company store.

"I am nothing if I am not one of those damned crotchety old bags who would argue pigs could fly just for the hell of it," Anna Elise Erp stated after telling the Sugarman about the latest episode involving bruised peaches and a particularly surly grocery clerk at the Meadowlawns IGA store. Anna Elise and the Sugarman dined together at Dante's every third Thursday of the month, much to the consternation of the less enlightened citizens of lily white suburbia. As a direct result, every third Thursday was inevitably the lowest grossing night of the week. "Even this pasta is overcooked. Just where is that greasy little waiter of ours?"

"A soul be needin' to be needed, fo' sho'," the Sugarman noted aloud with his uncanny ability to see through into the shadows of people's hearts.

In the Black

"At the moment, I *be needin'* a waiter, *fo' sho'*—you old black fool."

"Who you be callin' fool, woman?"

"Pass the Parmesan, please." The Sugarman did. He mumbled unintelligibly in, around and through a churning mouthful of cannelloni, much to Anna Elise's aggravation. Unable to stand it any longer, she blurted out, *"Peaches! Bruised peaches!"*

"Say *what?"*

"Is this all my life has come to? Bruised peaches?"

"Woman—"

"I suppose it's because I have no more battles to fight." Anna Elise's voice was weighted with sorrow. "No more victories to win. I am old and worthless."

"Jesus H. Christ. 'Scuse me, Antonio! *An-tone-nee-yo!* Here. Over here." The Sugarman flagged down their waiter and, tugging at the sleeve of Antonio's red jacket with one hand while he pointed at the floor with his other, told him, "Some poo' fool sho' to be slippin' and slidin' in this here pool of self pity and fallin' down on her lily white honky ass. You best be moppin' it up right away. Don' you be lookin' at me like a coon froze in a flashlight, boy, hep to it."

Antonio continued to give the Sugarman a puzzled look. He looked to Anna Elise for guidance, but she only shrugged her shoulders, so he fetched a pitcher of water and filled their glasses. Anna Elise watched with annoyance. When he finally left, she whispered across the table, "I'm dying, Homer."

"Right this fuckin' minute? With a gob fulla *spa-get-tee* in yo' mouth? Can' it wait? *Pul-leeze,* woman, I be digestin'. Can' you see that? Damn. I neve'. Damnation."

"Homer McKinley Morganfield, you son of a bitch!"

He smiled a broad and friendly grin, as if to agree with her assessment, then laughed out loud.

She smiled back and shook her head. "No, I suppose that would be rather rude of me to die right this *fucking* minute. Forget about it." And so, she didn't tell him about the doctor, the lump or the biopsy. She hadn't told anyone, not even her son.

He asked quietly, cautiously after a few bites in silence, "Tonight?"

"Oh, I don't know. I just don't know if I am up for it."

"He needs you."

"No one needs me."

"He needs you."

She sighed. "It brings back too many memories of darker times."

"Yo' little boy be in the hospital. He be needin' you."

"They say he should be okay. He's getting better, right? How does he look?"

"I seen him. He be better. Bit by bit, but he needs you, woman. He needs you now."

Anna shrugged her shoulders and skated a piece of veal across her plate with her fork.

"Been two weeks since junior had his accident and done come back to home."

"I know. I know." Her eyes moistened. "Remember? Remember Bethesda?"

"I do. I do, fo' sho'."

"I don't think I could go through it all again. What if—" Anna Elise wiped a tear from her cheek.

"You can. You will. He be needin' you."

"Well, maybe. Maybe after a few stiff belts," she sniffed bravely.

"And 'member how we stole you brother's bran' spankin' new *Cad-de-lac?*"

"Wilson was madder than a wet hornet."

"That was one stone fine *aut-to-mo-bile.*"

"Too bad it ended up in the Chesapeake bay."

"Oh, yes ma'am, a damn shame. I shed me a bitter tear or two over tha' m'self."

"Poor, poor Wilson."

They laughed and commanded Antonio to fetch another bottle of Chianti straightaway. The Sugarman entertained Anna Elise with tales from their cross-country trek to Washington, D.C., shortly after World War II had ended in the Cadillac *El Dorado* misappropriated from her brother: how she sat in the back so he could play chauffeur through downtown St. Louis, Indianapolis, and suburban Washington; how sometimes he huddled on the floor boards as she drove through gales of unfriendly stares in small towns along the Mason-Dixon line; how they laughed for hours, giddy from exhaustion after driving through the night, in a toy store while shopping for gifts for her brand new grandbaby; how with grim determination on their faces they parked their long black sedan of a Trojan horse in front of the Capitol Building to battle and conquer Senator Thurman Troyer.

Had Thurman J.D. Troyer not become a politician, he surely would have withered and died like an unwatered plant. From the instant of conception, the chromosomes of his mother and father meshed like fine gears, putting into motion the most efficient political machine the state of Georgia would ever see. He was blessed with the legendary striking good looks of his mother's family, as well as their oozing, oily charm and, of course, the in-bred infra-structure of tradition peculiar to the deep South of the United States. Paternally, he was equipped with towering physical strength, seemingly endless reservoirs of stamina, a true filibuster's gift of gab and the ability to read people like thirty point newspaper headlines. Environment conspired with heredity to pump his conscience down to a near perfect vacuum and to instill a system of moral values as simple as tallying votes or totaling left over campaign funds. His entire life had been one long political campaign—literally, in that four days after his birth, against doctors' explicit orders, the swaddled Troyer babe was carried from one end of Georgia to the other in his mother's arms to press the flesh (mostly cheeks and lips) in support of the first in the life-long string of his father's unsuccessful bids for the governorship. Jefferson Davis Troyer was a far better peanut farmer than a politician, but his son avenged his many losses and "done his kin proud" by ascending that Mount Olympus of American government, Washington, D.C.

Thurman Troyer was at his level-best horse trading with his peers in the Senate cloak room. It mattered little whether he was garnering votes for passage of a bill or swapping livestock from his Ilium, Georgia, peanut farm with other landed gentry members of the World's Greatest Deliberative Body. He loved to feel the heat of face-to-face, toe-to-toe negotiations flush his cheeks and swore he could actually hear the snap of backbone when the nearly imperceptible relaxation of muscles about the eyes and mouth signaled the breaking of his opponent's will. For leisure, he sipped Jack Daniel's sour mash whiskey and charmed doting flocks of wealthy matrons at various society functions about town with juicy gossip about the inner workings of government and his own indelible marks made in shaping mankind's future recorded history, all the while gauging in the back of his mind whether his audience of the moment might mark an 'X' by his name on a voting ballot.

In the Black

Katherine "Cissy" McClean found Thurman Troyer to be an intolerable bore who took himself far too seriously, yet she nodded and smiled approvingly as the guest of honor at her dinner party droned on and on and on. It was the spring of 1943. The war dragged on and small wonder why, she thought, with interminable wind bags like the Senator running things. Although the war took its toll on Washington, D.C.'s second largest industry, what with food and gasoline rationing as well as a continuous stream of downbeat news reports about the fighting and killing overseas, Cissy McClean had been able to maintain her position of preeminence as the capitol's premier party thrower. The secret of her success on the society pages was that she knew a hostess could not ignore the public's insatiable taste for conflict, drama and intrigue. It took more than fine food and famous faces to get newspaper cameras clicking and Washington whispers wafting. Cissy McClean nodded and smiled approvingly at the man she had secretly selected to provide the entertainment for that evening.

As Cissy McClean well knew, Thurman Troyer never missed a ritualistic gathering of the rich and powerful of Washington society, lest his absence be noticed less than his presence, and to insure due notice of his attendance at such functions, he never failed to parade about with the most valuable social asset he possessed on his arm, his famously beautiful and infamously eligible daughter, Helen, for all the world—or at least all the world's ambassadors—to see, to admire and to envy. Cissy McClean was also keenly aware that the feud between Senator Troyer and Admiral Hemmings had attracted wide public interest, having been fought openly and bitterly in Washington, D.C. newspapers during the first dark days of World War II when everyone was looking for someone else to take the blame for the embarrassing debacle of Pearl Harbor. Even though the Army eventually got their own war in Europe while the Navy got a war all to themselves in the South Pacific, the military's internecine acrimony was never more than a few degrees short of a full boil, and Cissy McClean could feel the temperature rising as she stood with Senator Troyer watching her guests being seated for dinner. She smiled with a touch of Machiavellian malice as the Senator's eyes narrowed to near slits and his ears flushed bright red at the sight of Helen Troyer being seated, exactly as Cissy McClean planned, next to a handsome young Naval officer, notorious in his own right for his prodigious womanizing as well as for his effectiveness as a member of Admiral Hemmings' staff. The young Naval officer was Y.T., Sr.

Helen Troyer tried valiantly to ignore Y.T., Sr. by attempting to sustain a conversation with an impossibly droll little man from the U.S. Department of Agriculture on her left. Her efforts were in vain as the dullard had been scrupulously screened and selected by Cissy McClean to block her only possible avenue of retreat.

Cissy McClean had also deftly positioned on Y.T., Sr.'s right "The Countess", an elderly Yugoslavian refugee with some extremely obscure lineage to Slovenian royalty who was renowned for her indecipherable English as well as her audible dozing between dinner courses. He ignored her snoring and stared overtly at Helen's delicate profile as she nodded in agreement with agrarian history slowly unfolding in a painful monotone.

Senator Troyer steamed at the sight of his daughter being visually mauled by a Yankee infidel. Already the canapés he hungrily devoured before dinner were beginning to march through his intestinal tract like Sherman had marched through Georgia.

Delighted, Cissy McClean scanned her other guests for any inkling of recognition of the drama beginning to unfold in their midst.

In the Black

Helen Troyer's mind began to drift from the lecture detailing the precise genealogy of the Morovian 5 strain of wheat being recited by the bureaucratic troll at her side. She imagined herself looking down on the Mall from her father's office window, watching pigeons gather on sidewalk grates for warmth, thinking of the flocking mentality of Washingtonites, being suddenly startled at the realization that a young Naval officer was staring directly back up at her from below. She began to feel Y.T., Sr.'s present stare like a heat upon her neck. An instinctive surge of adrenalin mainlined into her blood stream as if she were a quarry alarmed at the nearby presence of a predator. She began to coldly calculate her strategy to deal with Y.T., Sr. as, inevitably, she knew she would have to do sometime during the course of dinner.

Heading back to Navy Bachelor Officer's Quarters after a long day of idle waiting at the Capitol, Y.T., Sr. often paused on the Mall to catch a glimpse of Helen Troyer's alluring silhouette framed in her father's office window like a bird in a gilded cage. He would try to imagine what it would be like to sit as close to her as he was there at Cissy McClean's dinner party and what they might talk about. As Helen Troyer struggled to ignore him, Y.T., Sr. mentally inventoried her charms, counting among them the few very minor flaws in her beauty, knowing, as Leonardo Da Vinci must have, that the regularity of perfection can be boring and bland. An arousing Spanish fragrance teased him. Other women trolled with stink bait as if angling for carp, he mused, but this one was probably one hell of a fly fisherman. Having been taught by her father, one of the best fly fishermen in all of Congress, Y.T., Sr. was correct, but it was one of the few things he had not yet found out for sure about her through his many Capitol Hill connections.

Helen Troyer had endeavored to learn much about Y.T., Sr. as well. From Army C.I.D. reports requested by her father, she learned everything from his hat size (7 7/8) on down to his shoe size (9D). She read about his father's suicide on Wall Street, his mother's family exile and menial job at the O'Reilly Candy Factory, his school days at Harvard University and his numerous amorous exploits since coming to Washington, D.C. In a paragraph which made Senator Troyer swear out loud when he read it, she discovered that, unlike most Washington-brand warriors, the battle ribbons worn on the breast of his uniform were genuine. Y.T., Sr. had shot down four Japanese Zeros flying off the U.S.S. Hornet aircraft carrier when he was unexpectedly caught in the midst of the Battle of Midway during a fleet inspection tour for Admiral Hemmings. But all of the typically turgid prose of government reports told Helen Troyer too much about events and too little about the kind of man Y.T., Sr. really was. That information she gleaned by gossiping with her father's secretary, Madeline, who had inexplicably put her job in jeopardy by clandestinely dating the young Naval officer so despised by Senator Troyer.

He had known for sometime now how bored she was with the stilted society role defined by her father and thrust upon her.

From all accounts—but most vividly and graphically from Madeline—she knew how he fed on Washington society like a hungry predator.

He knew from the society pages that endless rumors of her pending engagement to the son of this southern governor or that western senator, this Texan rancher or that Midwestern business leader circulated freely and frequently. He knew from Madeline that she had begun to resent her father's on-going matrimonial negotiations as if she were merely one more blue ribbon heifer to trade away off the farm in the Senate Cloak Room.

She knew, just by looking across the room at the fear, anger and frustration in her father's eyes and the gleaming smile on Cissy McClean's make-up caked face that Y.T., Sr. was the one man in all of Washington who could take the Senator on and, perhaps, prevail.

"And enough already about wheat," she whispered to herself. She turned to look at Y.T., Sr.

He stared back, giving no quarter. He would not make it easy for her. He knew that would be the wrong approach.

"Ahem." She cleared her throat and offered a small, coy smile.

He smiled the morphinic Erp smile. He said nothing.

With the arrival of the fruit cup, Helen Troyer elected to seize the initiative. She said with a gusty sigh, "If I have one more meal of chicken, I do believe I shall positively die."

A moment of silence. A long moment of silence.

"Actually, I do not believe we have ever been properly introduced," Y.T., Sr. said softly and politely.

Damn, that was my line, she thought to herself. She bowed her head and blushed ever so slightly.

"I am Navy Lieutenant Erp, Y.T. Erp, and I am very pleased to meet you," he said in a crisp whisper that made her instinctively lean towards him to hear.

Across the room, Senator Troyer stoked his temper like a steamship's boiler.

"Helen Troyer of the Ilium Troyers." She looked over at her father, who was too far away to hear them speak. "My father is the senior Senator from the grand state of Georgia," she said mechanically.

"Yes, of course. I know of him."

They both smiled.

It seemed to Senator Troyer to be the longest dinner he had ever endured—and he had endured plenty in his life time of politics—watching helplessly from across the room as the flower of his life was sniffed, fingered and tossed in the blustery breeze of Lieutenant Erp's line of Navy bullshit that he blew her way throughout the meal. As each course was served then later taken away from him untouched, Thurman Troyer's discomfort and anger became more and more noticeable to those seated about him. Cissy McClean dreamily gazed upon the ripples of gossip slowly spreading out from around the Senator as if he were a stone she tossed into the still waters of a calm pond. The next day's society headlines and columnists' copy were still churning in her imagination after dessert when, in excess of even her grandest expectations, a frenzy of photographers' flash bulbs erupted about a small scuffle at Lt. Erp's table between Helen Troyer and her big brother. At his father's behest, Hector Troyer, who also served as his father's Senate aide and shared in his father's unwavering hatred of Admiral Hemmings, forcibly escorted his "frail sister" out of the "lecherous reaches of that Navy Scoundrel" and back to the safety of her father's side. Y.T., Sr. quietly retired from the party under Helen Troyer's watchful eye.

Hector Troyer's harsh words to his sister about loyalty, family honor and plain old, down home common sense during the limousine ride home echoed the Senator's heartfelt sentiments exactly, but fell on deaf ears. Helen Troyer sat pressed against the door of the back seat as far away from her father as possible and stared at passing Washington, D.C. landmarks in a stone-like silence. Once home, she went directly to bed without a word to brother or father. Shaken to the depths of his southern core by the events of the evening and his daughter's icy attitude towards him, Thurman Troyer went to the study with a fifth of Jack Daniel's to brood. He listened to Hector Troyer rant and rave on the subject of revenge for only five minutes before he bluntly ordered him to leave. When Helen Troyer arose the next morning at four-thirty, her father was asleep, slumped over in his favorite chair. The whiskey bottle was nearly empty. She tip-toed past the study and left for the airport to meet Y.T., Sr. The night before, at Cissy McClean's party, the young Naval Aviator had promised to teach her how to fly an airplane. It was a thing she had, inexplicably, always wanted to do, but none of the Army Air Corps pilots her father so favored ever had the nerve to do it, probably out of fear that if she ever got hurt or killed, Senator Troyer, Chairman of the Senate Armed Forces Appropriations Committee, would never forgive—or fund—them ever again.

"What in the hell are we waiting for?" Anna Elise asked the Sugarman impatiently as they stood in the shadows at the far end of the hospital corridor down from Y.T., Jr.'s room.

"Shush woman. We be a tad early."

"You got me drunk enough to come down here to the hospital, now let's get on with it. I want to see my grandson—or I want another drink."

"Hush already, woman. Hush." They waited. After a few minutes the door to Y.T., Jr.'s room opened and Scarlett Angelina Brookings stepped out. The pair fell into a near hypnotic trance, fixated on the clock-like rhythm of her hips and the steady tick-tocking of her high heels on the floor as she walked away from them towards the elevators. The trance broke only when the elevator doors closed upon her. "Sheee-it damn, that is one stone-fine piece of tail."

Anna Elise smacked the Sugarman upside the head and they started down the corridor towards Y.T., Jr.'s room. "Does she come to see him every night?"

"Every blessed night. It must be love, the lucky little bastard."

Anna Elise elbowed the Sugarman in the ribs, but as they walked down the corridor to Y.T., Jr.'s hospital room, she smiled ever so slightly and whispered to herself, "Yes, that's my boy. That's my boy."

They quietly pushed open the door to Y.T., Jr.'s room. The room was dimly lit. At first, Anna Elise could not make out who was at his bedside, but as her eyes adjusted to the light she recognized her brother's progeny, Wilson Cassidy, sitting in a wheelchair beside the bed, with his swing shift bodyguard standing behind him. He leaned forward to look closely at Y.T., Jr's face, placid in sleep, with the expression of a pirate eyeing a treasure he is about to seize for his own.

"Stop right there, you prick," Anna Elise cried out just as Wilson Cassidy was about to reach out and touch her grandson. "You keep your filthy hands off my boy."

The bodyguard instinctively came forward to protect his charge. The Sugarman stepped in front of Anna Elise. With a flick of a switch blade, he arrested the bodyguard's advance and quickly ushered him out of the way with the knife's blade digging into his sternum.

Anna Elise charged directly towards her nephew, who now sat helplessly trapped beside the bed in his wheelchair vainly searching the room for help from his bodyguard. She grabbed the drainage tube the doctors had placed in Wilson Cassidy's chest following his recent heart surgery. She pulled out the slack in the tube and bent down to look him directly in the eye.

"I know what you are up to, you scum bucket, and you are not going to get away with it."

Wilson Cassidy moved only his eyes, alternating between Anna Elise and her grip on the tube coming out of his chest. He gasped for breath.

She slowly pushed him back away from the bed and towards the door as she spoke, "This is war, Wilson. *This is war.* You will not steal my family away, not as long as I have a breath left in these lungs. I don't care what it takes or how long. And if I ever see you near my boy again, I'll not only rip out this tube, I'll reach in and pull out your God damned heart! Now get out!"

She pushed him out the door. His body guard followed sheepishly, persuaded by maliciously grinning Negro in his face and the knife he was holding at his chest.

Anna Elise and the Sugarman stayed through the night to watch over Y.T., Jr. as he slept. In the morning they had him moved to another hospital floor and Anna Elise went home with a renewed sense of purpose to her life.

On the way back to his room, Wilson Cassidy decided he would now need more than just Scarlett Brookings to get the job done.

Wilson Cassidy's father had never forgiven his sister for stealing his brand new Cadillac *El Dorado* and driving it into the Chesapeake Bay.

~~~

Complex 34

The design was both ingenious and eloquent. There was only one minor drawback: it did not work. Vasili Ivanovich divined that conclusion upon his first quick glances through the reams of specifications and blue prints. No question about it. He also knew why it would not work. The immediate problem, though, was Vasili Ivanovich could not even see clearly, let alone think clearly, because of the dense banks of tobacco smoke roiling across the conference table and into his painfully pinched shut eyes. As tensions during the meeting steadily increased, visibility decreased and the team of would-be Thomas Edisons culled from THE CUSTOMER's Engineering Department, each zealously harboring his own particular eccentricity as empirical evidence of inventiveness, became increasingly stubborn in its collective insistence that since each and every component had been specified scrupulously, evaluated excruciatingly and tested tenaciously, the entire system, therefore, must absolutely and without deviation operate precisely as it had been conceived—as if nature could be forced by mere human consensus and bold bureaucratic edict to forfeit her precious secrets.

The longer each of THE CUSTOMER's engineering specialists droned on in painfully minute detail about technically arcane issues during the meeting, the more tunnel-visioned the group became and the more the two observing NASA astronauts pulled at their collars and squirmed uncomfortably in their seats. The problem the group had gathered to resolve in the smoked-filled conference room in Bethpage, New York, was one of simply getting from here to there; of getting accelerometers, gyros and space sextants "talking" to on-board computers in the appropriate language and getting on-board computers to download accurate and correctly formatted command signal information into digital autopilots, so that the digital autopilots could fire rocket engines and hydrazine thrusters at precisely the right times and at exactly the right points in space to achieve the Presidential holy grail of allowing man to navigate to, land upon and return safely from the moon, a goal Vasili Ivanovich saw clouding with Pall Mall smoke and, perhaps, genuine doubt.

Ignoring a very sober, very serious and otherwise very intelligent appearing man speaking on at length on the topic of bonding, *vis-a-vis* rivets, welds and adhesives as if it were at all relevant, Vasili Ivanovich peered through the fog born of burnt Carolina cash crops at the two NASA astronauts at the far end of the conference table. Who were these young men, he asked himself, with the Herculean strength and Odyssean courage to sit atop a three hundred, sixty-four foot tall stack of high explosives; to be hurtled through space at 24,000 miles per hour locked inside what amounted to a high tech artillery shell; to venture over 252,710 miles away from the only known human life in the solar system, in the galaxy or even in the entire universe to stand upon a hostile, barren rock devoid of even an atmosphere to sustain life? And, thinking back to the evening before as Vasili Ivanovich sat in awe observing Y.T., Sr. and these two demigods revel in Bacchian feasting and drinking, swapping tall, lusty tales even he could hardly believe, why did these brave, great men of human history speak and act so much like Frik and Frak? It jarred his sensibilities. Then, after closing all of the bars near the restaurant, the foursome had gone for a drunken stroll on a Long Island beach during which the two astronauts began baying like a pair of hungry wolves at the full moon hung above their heads in the clear night sky. Vasili Ivanovich watched in wonder as Y.T., Sr. joined them. Finally, the mild mannered scientist, without the foggiest notion of why he was doing it yet completely unable to resist, lifted up his proud Russian snout to howl at the earth's ancient satellite. These remarkable men called astronauts were utterly beyond his comprehension. Also beyond his comprehension was how the four of them made it back to the hotel afterward, since no one was sober enough to walk, let alone drive, but there were some mysteries, the answers to which Vasili Ivanovich preferred not to know.

The solution to the problem vexing America's epic quest into outer space lay safely locked away in the middle left hand drawer of Vasili Ivanovich's desk in the Engineering Department at the old O'Reilly Candy Factory building in Meadowlawns, Missouri. It was funny how these things came to pass, he mused during a brief but heated debate there in the conference room about dowel pin materials. Years ago, Arthur Needleman had so casually suggested that the two of them kill an hour or two and catch a few chuckles listening to "the wild ass schemes of those pointy-headed Poindexters" at NASA's Jet Propulsion Laboratory in Pasadena, California. What resulted from that singular afternoon was a hope, a dream, a passion, an obsession, which had possessed Vasili Ivanovich's very soul for the next seven years. Known only to himself, Arthur Needleman and, of course, Y.T., Sr., so as to protect his pet project from the harassment and inevitable volleys of flak fired off by Rolf Guderian, Simon Salisbury, Hugh Betcha,

Dirk Rangely, Mort Mortenstein, *et al,* over wasted resources, wasted time and wasted profits, Vasili Ivanovich secretly developed a revolutionary guidance and control system for NASA's Surveyor series of unmanned space probes, one of which was nestled snugly in its black box, successfully navigating its way to land on the moon even as its inventor sat trapped in the smoky conference room there in New York. If he could only get out of there he could start adapting his system for the Apollo program and get something useful done for THE CUSTOMER, for NASA and for AMERICA.

He looked across the room for Y.T., Sr. to help get the meeting back on track. Incredibly, the Fearless Leader of the company sat blissfully absorbed in working a crossword puzzle. Vasili Ivanovich watched his boss nudge the astronaut sitting beside him, the one who might very well be chosen by destiny to be the first human being ever to set foot on the moon, no doubt to ask him if he knew what a seven letter word for 'angst' would be. Vasili Ivanovich closed his burning eyes and tried to rub that pain out of the center of his forehead with no success whatsoever.

"You damn near bought the farm on that ride, didn't you?" Billy Saul Sawyer finally said as they paced around the scorched, mangled wreckage of Y.T., Jr.'s Harley-Davidson. In reality, though, the two friends were warily circling one another like predators who meet in the jungle as strangers, heads low and hair bristling on the nape of their necks. Despite all the years spent growing up together, the two did not recognize each other. When Billy Saul Sawyer stopped pacing and simply shook his head, Y.T., Jr. stopped directly opposite him and leaned on his cane. Y.T., Jr. looked down at the remnants of his accident of five months before, which his father had retrieved from the San Francisco Police Department impound yard and had ordered flown back to Meadowlawns on the Erp

Industries, Inc., Learjet by Frik and Frak to be there in the Erp garage when his son was released from the hospital. Y.T., Jr. slowly nodded his head as he tried to trace a way out of the maze of twisted tubular steel with his eyes.

Y.T., Jr. had always been the strongest person Billy Saul Sawyer ever knew. It was a strength which transcended raw muscle power. As long as they had known one another, Billy Saul Sawyer could always beat him at arm wrestling, match after match after match, but it had been Y.T., Jr., giving away four and a half inches in height and thirty pounds in weight, who finally vanquished play ground bully Barry Boswagger in the sixth grade. Y.T., Jr. had the strength to stand up even to Vice Principal Snyder in defense of his friend when, as sophomores, the two were caught smoking in the john, mercifully saving Billy Saul Sawyer from a suspension and another beating from his father. It was the strength to simply remain friends with the bumbling farm boy throughout the painful social stratification of Harry S. Truman High School as Meadowlawns evolved from a rural community to an affluent suburb of Kansas City. Now, though, Billy Saul Sawyer was openly taken back at the frail condition of his friend. The accident, the coma and the long months in the hospital had ground him down into a stick man of his former self, leaning on a cane, vacantly gazing at his wrecked motorcycle, pain etched upon his face. Billy Saul Sawyer's heart flooded with pity. He wanted to reach out to help and to protect his friend, just as Y.T., Jr. had done so many times for him, but he did not know what to say. He did not know what to do.

Y.T., Jr. avoided Billy Saul Sawyer's earnest, yearning cow eyes. It was one of the few things the Marine Corps had not changed about him. Boot camp had certainly bulked up his muscles and burned the fat off his lumpy, adolescent body. His doughy facial features were now crisply cut like the creases in his khaki uniform, right down to a cleft in his chin, which the Marines must have chiseled in themselves, because it had never been there before. Instead of habitually pushing unkempt locks of hair back off of his forehead and out of his eyes, Billy Saul Sawyer absently brushed the top of his new crew cut with his fingers. He not only had the appearance of a Doberman Pinscher straining at his leash, the Marines had given him a bark, too. His voice was louder, firmer and coarser, commanding attention by erupting in short clipped sentences like a boxer's body blows.

"Can't help much this time. Not with all the tools in a Sears store," Billy Saul Sawyer barked. "Besides, no time. Got my marching orders."

Y.T., Jr. did not know quite how to talk to this transformed friend of his. He cleared his throat.

"A week. To Asia, clear the other side of the damn world. A place called Da Nang."

"To the war?"

"Not much of a war. But it's the only one we got." Billy Saul Sawyer's new facade suffered a hairline crack, "Least ways, that's what everybody in the Marines says."

Y.T., Jr. started to speak, but stopped. He did not know what to say.

"I'm a good Marine. I found something I do good. Even my dad's proud of me."

Y.T., Jr. nodded. His stomach knotted.

"I wanted to stop by and see you. I heard about the accident. I heard you were in bad shape."

Y.T., Jr. nodded. He looked at his charred Harley.

"Well, looks like you'll be all right." Billy Saul Sawyer said it, but he did not know if he really believed it. They stood in silence, now on opposite sides of the political fault line forming in American society. "Don't know as I could say as much for your Harley."

Y.T., Jr. nodded.

"I just wanted to see you again. Guess I'll go. Send you a postcard from our little war."

Y.T., Jr. nodded.

Billy Saul Sawyer left. Y.T., Jr. heard the familiar cough, belch and growl of Mr. Sawyer's pickup truck back out of the driveway and fade away. He tried to fight off, then simply ignore, another headache. He suffered from them recurrently ever since he woke from the coma, but certainly the confrontation with PFC Sawyer and the ache of viewing his twisted Harley-Davidson might have brought on this particular one. Y.T., Jr. tried to remember the last time he had seen Billy Saul Sawyer, but often the past was difficult to recall. Since the accident, Y.T., Jr. sometimes felt unmoored from time, a mental derelict adrift in a dissonant sea of raw perceptions and sensations, riding the swells and troughs of churning memories.

"Hey. Hey! HEY! WAKE UP!" Marty Keegan yelled at Y.T., Jr. They sat on their usual spots at the Cassidy family grave site, drinking beer and smoking marijuana. "What the fuck is wrong with you, anyway?"

Y.T., Jr. shrugged his shoulders absently, thinking how he had nearly forgotten how good it felt simply to be outside on a warm, clear summer night. There and then, three weeks later, he remembered—finally: the last time he had seen Billy Saul Sawyer was when he came over to tune up his motorcycle for him to take back to Berkeley one last time before he went into the Marines. "Nothing, just thinking."

"Anyway, so I said, 'Circulation? You're telling me I've got to be a God damned paper boy? I didn't come to Columbia University to learn how to be a fucking paper boy. I came to study Journalism.' And so, he said, 'Hey, if you want to learn the newspaper game, you've got to start at the bottom.' So I said, 'What is this? Chutes and fucking Ladders? I came here to be trained as a writer, to learn how to be a reporter, not to play children's fucking board games.' So he said, 'This will put you directly in touch with our readers, *your* audience, a unique and invaluable learning experience.' And so, I said, 'Bullshit, bull fucking shit. I ain't paying hundreds of dollars for six credit hours in Paper Boy 101.' And he said, 'You'll never get into J-School, if you don't.' Fucking bullshit. Fucking Chutes and Ladders."

Y.T., Jr. nodded. He took a drink of beer. He had been listening to the sordid tale of the trials and tribulations of a freshman journalism student being abused by upper classmen for almost an hour now. "So, what finally happened?"

"I'm a fucking paper boy, that's what finally happened—but, I met this other guy, Rudd, Mark Rudd. He's an English major or something. Anyway, he's about the only cool guy on the whole student paper. He took me aside and gave me the usual Big-Brother-Hang-In-There-I've-Been-There-Myself-and-You'll-Make-It-Through-All-This pep talk. *But,* get *this,* he's also like working to be the chapter president of the Students for a Democratic Society. And, he got me a slot on their underground paper, an alternative to the fluff and circumstance of the official Columbia propaganda rag. Instead of doing lap dog stories about Grayson Kirk's latest speech or fart—as if anyone can tell the difference—their paper does real stories about real life. Important stories. I'm working on one about how the University is pushing people out of their homes and trying to rob the people of Harlem of Morningside Park to build, get this, a new gym. Fucking jock pukes think they can have anything they want. But just wait, we'll get the story out. We'll stop them."

"Sounds good…better, at least," Y.T., Jr. said half-heartedly, thinking vaguely of the practical jokes the *Triumvirate* always played on the radicals at Berkeley. They were such easy targets. So earnest. He held little patience for them and hoped that Marty Keegan did not get sucked into their vaporous revolutionary rhetoric.

"So, have you seen Billy Saul lately?" Marty Keegan asked.

Y.T., Jr. nodded. "About three weeks ago."

"I hear he's gone mental, joined the fucking Marines and is marching off to war."

"He's different now. The Marines have done a number on him, that's for sure."

"Sounds like a regular Frankenstein to me."

"I don't know. You know him. Underneath all that new khaki wrapping paper, I think he's still the same old Billy Saul. He just sent me a postcard. He's garrisoned at the Da Nang airport, which he said rhymes with Poon Tang. I guess he finally got laid, in Thailand."

"Long way to go for a piece of muff pie. I feel sorry for whoever was on the receiving end of his pent up wad—she probably had it coming out of her ears by the time he got done."

Y.T., Jr. nodded his head.

"I just can't believe he got sucked into it."

"Sucked into what?"

"Into the Marines. Into the war. Into American Imperialism in southeast Asia. Boy, I tell you, not with *my* fucking life, you don't. No way."

Y.T., Jr. popped another Budweiser and blankly stared at the "Resist" button on Marty Keegan's chest as his friend began ranting and raving his newly found line of radical political thought and theory.

Another hot, sweltering August night and, once again, the air conditioning in the swank Kirke Gardens "Luxury" apartment, rented for Scarlett Angelina Brookings by Wilson Cassidy, had broken down. Their bodies wore a glossy varnish of sweat as they lay naked, side-by-side, head-to-toe. The bed was stripped down to its sheets. A lazy breeze gently billowed the curtains. Y.T., Jr. slept, dreaming of medieval knights on courageous crusades, galloping down the Pacific Coast Highway on motorcycles to storm the Hearst Castle. She idly traced her finger along the crooked scars his accident had carved on his legs as if seeking escape from a maze to some secret, safe destination. She sighed. It was unprecedented. She had never in her life missed any man and now there were two. Somehow, Wilson Cassidy, the Puppet Master, had gotten his strings tangled and Scarlett Brookings savored the sweet irony of his miscalculations. Instead of fulfilling the role of seductress, she herself had been seduced. She bedded Y.T., Sr., in accordance with his evil intents; and, now, she lay naked next to his son, having made passionate love to him in every room in her apartment—including the carport, the elevator, the hallway and her storage closet—on their two-day orgiastic journey to her bedroom.

Scarlett Angelina Brookings was a mysterious gem of colorful beauty in the brutal and ugly world of a beef packing magnet. Owned, but not possessed, she was like a Monet, constantly being arranged and rearranged in the stark white gallery of the Kirke Gardens Apartment for a continuous parade of coveting gawkers. Most of the men Scarlett Brookings had known in her twenty-four short years were on the downhill side of life, selected by Wilson Cassidy for secret Machiavellian purposes he kept closely guarded in the dark, chilled chambers of his flawed heart. Cool and aloof, she had yet turned them all—businessmen, politicians, lawyers, doctors and scientists, alike—into pigs, groveling at her feet as if foraging for scraps of her love, doing ridiculous things they no doubt believed were romantic. No matter how love stricken they became, though, those men always retained a hard kernel of objectivity and rationality, which insured they would know exactly how foolish their behavior really was. Scarlett Brookings found the taste of male angst delicious and relished its infinite varieties and permutations, like a connoisseur delights in the flavors and bouquets of different vineyards.

The Erps, though, had committed the ultimate blasphemy, having touched the *object de art.* What money, gold and diamonds could not buy was acquired with a mere smile and a laugh—*her* smile and *her* laugh, rare commodities in the tightly controlled world Wilson Cassidy allowed her. Father and son made no demands on her and harbored no foolish expectations. Whether it was at a concert or at Dante's eating pizza, whether they sat talking under the stars on the Cassidy family grave sites or making love in the middle of a high school football field somewhere, Y.T., Jr. made her feel like more than canvas and crusted paints. He made her feel alive. And now she would miss him terribly when he left for Berkeley the next morning. The angst she so enjoyed in others now burned in her own heart. Smiling at her uncharacteristic surrender to emotion, Scarlett Angelina Brookings fell asleep beside Y.T., Jr., confused by reawakened feelings of true love and angst over the duplicity orchestrated by Wilson Cassidy.

Less than twelve hours later, Frak coached Y.T., Jr. through an ILS approach into fog-shrouded San Francisco Airport in the Erp Industries, Inc. Learjet, while Frik chomped his cigar and visually mauled glossy images of Playmate bodies back in the cabin. An ex-Navy instructor pilot, Frak noted that Y.T., Jr. was a little heavy on the rudder pedals, but considering his injuries and his layoff from the cockpit, it was to be expected. They both shared the amazement how, after slogging and slogging through stone gray clouds chasing needles on the instrument panel, the airplane broke out of the overcast at two hundred feet above the ground with a windscreen full of runway all decorated as if for Christmas with red, green, blue, amber and white lights. They taxied to the ramp and opened the door to find Arthur Needleman standing behind a brand new, shiny black Harley-Davidson *Electro-Glide*.

"I am nowhere," Arthur Needleman said through his patented, shit-eating grin. He raised his fists up beside his ears. His fingers blossomed out like Fourth of July fireworks. *"I am everywhere."*

Arthur Needleman was a plump, tow-headed, thirty-four year old man who, though always impeccably dressed in a three-piece suit and tie, looked more like Huckleberry Finn than IBM's Thomas Watson. He was a study in perpetual motion, talking and gesturing on endlessly, even when standing all alone in the middle of an airport tarmac. If anyone had been within ear shot, they no doubt would have been convinced that his was a train of thought teetering on the brink of derailment, powered by a speeding, runaway locomotive and that surely somewhere up ahead a bridge was out. Neither Frik nor Frak ever attempted to comprehend what Frik called Arthur Needleman's "Zen Salesman Bullshit," and couldn't really care less whether he was nowhere, everywhere or anywhere. What was of essential importance to them was that they were all together so that now their layover would be covered on Needleman's expense account instead of theirs. Frik hurriedly shuffled into the Fixed Base Operator's office leaving a contrail of cigar smoke in his wake, first to call Fu Loin's, then to make dinner reservations on Fisherman's Wharf, while Frak stabled the Learjet for the night.

Y.T., Jr. did not hear Arthur Needleman. He was transfixed at the sight of the motorcycle. He thought nothing. A cacophony of perceptual memories stormed through his consciousness. By the time the tempest subsided, Arthur Needleman had donned a captured University of Southern California Trojans football helmet and mounted the rear seat of the Harley-Davidson.

"Come on, son. There are treasures to rape, horizons to pillage and women to burn! And I've got the matches to start the conflagration!" Arthur Needleman held out a Diner's Club credit card like a miniature red cape before a reluctant bull. "A man can't spend his whole life sorting coins from kisses."

Y.T. Jr. was mysteriously drawn to the motorcycle despite the knot in his stomach. He stepped slowly towards it.

"You think you got mountains to climb? Hell, just wait till you see me dance this one by Mortenstein on my expense report." But Arthur Needleman already knew that the purchase would have Y.T., Sr.'s approval. With gestures as lively and wild as the contorted expressions impossibly assumed by his doughy face, he exclaimed, "Come on, come on, come on now, boy! It little profits that idle kings among these barren crags rule and dole unequal laws unto a savage race. We cannot rest from travels."

Y.T., Jr. mounted the bike and silently tested the feel of the throttle and the brakes.

"Enjoy greatly! Suffer greatly—both ashore and far, far out upon the dim sea!"

Y.T., Jr. started the bike and revved the engine higher and higher and higher.

"Let us take our hungry hearts and roam!"

In a squeal of rubber burning against asphalt, Y.T., Jr. sped off into the dark and foggy night, heading for the Pacific Coast Highway. Nonplussed in the least, Arthur Needleman maintained an on-going commentary worthy of Lewis Carroll.

Penelope Xing sat on the bed, knitting the quilt she had begun at Y.T., Jr.'s Intensive Care Unit bedside at San Francisco General Hospital, but still had not completed. She wore a bright red teddy with a text book on the history of the Renaissance propped up before her so she could continue her relentless academic march through time between customers. She did not look up from the book when the door to the room opened. She wanted to finish reading the section on the Medici family before she went back to work.

"Good evening, sir," she said wearily. "I'll be with you in just a moment. Please make yourself comfortable."

Suddenly a package of Hostess Twinkies fell in her lap, startling her. She looked up to see a smiling, wind-blown Y.T., Jr. standing before her in the room. Behind him, Fu Loin stood in the doorway beaming—literally beaming with happiness, an odd and very rare sight indeed. Fu Loin did not even scream and swear at her for reading in bed as he usually did.

"Oh my god," Penelope Xing gasped and stuttered.

Y.T., Jr. suddenly realized that the voice narrating all of his dreams about medieval knights on glorious mechanized crusades was Penelope Xing. He was visited by a vision of her faithfully reading her history assignments to him every night at his bedside in the hospital.

"Ah, Little Whitey, so good, so good, so good to have you back again. So good," Fu Loin chattered over and over and over again with tears of joy streaming down his cheeks.

Y.T. Jr. turned to Fu Loin and slipped him a fifty dollar bill. They bowed to one another as Y.T., Jr. slowly closed the door. Before he could turn back to the bed, he found himself locked in Penelope Xing's embrace with her legs around his waist and her arms around his neck, slowly sinking to the floor where they, incongruously, made passionate love to one another in the middle of Fu Loin's whore house.

Still glowing the next morning from the warm, moist welcome of Penelope Xing, Y.T., Jr. unlocked the door to his campus apartment in Berkeley and pushed it open. Taken back by the black hole gaping before him like an unexplored cave, he hesitated and drew a deep breath before slowly and carefully stepping inside. Every wall, window and ceiling had been painted black. Bathed in ultraviolet light, Day-Glo posters hung like square planets in the vastness of outer space. A glowing, white T-shirt writhed in the middle of the living room floor. As his eyes adjusted to the darkness, he saw the T-shirt was Murph, apparently fighting a losing battle to keep from being swallowed and digested by his arch enemy, the bean bag chair. Murph did not notice Y.T., Jr. come in because of the stereo headphones pumping Jefferson Airplane into his ears at excessive sound pressure levels and the fact that the goggles he wore were painted over with the same black paint as the walls, windows and ceilings in the apartment. Y.T., Jr. could barely make out the scratchy sounds of Marty Balin's guitar licks and Grace Slick's voice wailing about the white rabbit of Lewis Carroll's literary trip.

The air hung pungent with the odors of saffron incense, hashish and soiled sweat socks. Y.T., Jr. carefully stepped around Murph to spelunk further into the apartment. As he moved through the room, he experienced a queer sensation of excessive height, as if he were walking at the edge of a cliff. He stopped to steady his balance and noticed that all of the legs had been amputated from the tables and chairs, lowering the level of living in the apartment by two feet. He pressed on, finding Clinton A. Owsley III in the bedroom sitting on the floor facing a corner. Stepping quietly up behind his roommate, he saw that Clinton A. Owsley III stared into a lava lamp, hugging a Judy Garland album and whispering over and over, "Oh Auntie Em, Oh Auntie Em."

Y.T., Jr. gently placed his hands on Clinton A. Owsley III's shoulders. His friend looked back up at him. The neural impulses of recognition slowly registered in his brain and a smile began to bloom on his lean face.

"It's all right now, Oz." Y.T., Jr. smiled reassuringly at him. "Everything's all right now."

His friend had returned. Like Lazarus, Y.T., Jr. had come back from the grave to get him and take him home from his Technicolor dreams to the black and white world of reality—and just in time, too. Clinton A. Owsley III relaxed his sweaty death grip on his ivory handled souvenir from the Red Dog Ranch and slowly slipped the derringer back into his buck skin fringed boot. Still, his road to recovery would be a rocky one: in October the California State Legislature outlawed LSD and, worst of all, a blow came which knocked him back into his internal, psychotic land of Oz for four weeks when, on December 15, 1966, Walt Disney died.

Clinton A. Owsley III, Penelope Xing, Fu Loin, Murph and the collective counterculture of the Bay Area were not the only people glad to see Y.T., Jr. come back. Special Agents Williams and Walters were as ecstatic as F.B.I. Special Agents ever get on that sunny California morning their surveillance cameras framed and photographed Y.T., Jr.'s return to his Telegraph Avenue apartment in Berkeley.

The Bureau, under the ever vigilant eye and approving memos of Director J. Edgar Hoover, had concluded that of all the subversive political groups sprouting up like dandelions to besmirch the Eden of America in 1966, the *Triumvirate* was one of the top ten threats to the security of the United States government. Having difficulty fathoming the humor of the *Triumvirate's* stunts, the Bureau mistook satire for radical nihilism and the inability to discern any ultimate political agenda whatsoever in their actions scared Director Hoover most of all. The Students for a Democratic Society issued manifesto after manifesto. The Black Panthers wore those alarming black berets. But the *Triumvirate* was a complete mystery that played upon the deepest bureaucratic paranoia of Director Hoover and his empire. The Bureau leapt into action: a file was opened; surveillance and wire taps were ordered; and brave foot soldiers were dispatched to a tenuous outpost right in the heart of "injun country"—Berkeley, California. It took Special Agents Williams and Walters less than seventy-two hours to eliminate Clinton A. Owsley III as the revolutionary master mind of the threat to national security. Murph, with his Day-Glo jump suit and his outrageous appearances at every hippie event in San Francisco, kept them fooled for several weeks before they sadly reported back to headquarters that he was "more bark than bite." The return of Y.T., Jr. was their first hot lead in months and they wasted no time burning up the teletype lines to Washington, D.C., with the latest developments in the case, finally thickening the file to respectable proportions.

The mobile house trailer, stuffed full of electronic equipment and parked out in the middle of a scorpion infested stretch of sandy flats, was an unbearable sweat box, so much so that Vasili

Ivanovich and his team of engineers and technicians sat posted at their stations monitoring the telemetry from the launch pad dressed only in boxer shorts and A-frame undershirts. Even so, Vasili Ivanovich pondered seriously whether his profuse perspiration might pose any danger of electrocution from the tangle of wires underfoot. Every so often, the gloved hand of Gus Grissom or Ed White or Roger Chaffee darted across the television monitor in front of him to flip a switch or twist a dial. The endless drills had become so routine that it almost seemed as if NASA was determined to wring every last drop of enthusiasm out of their nation's epic endeavor. Vasili Ivanovich idly contemplated fate, trying to comprehend why his noble pursuit of scientific knowledge always placed him in such ridiculous and demeaning circumstances. Suddenly, his monitor flashed bright white, his headset filled his ears with frantic chatter and he watched in horror as the three brave astronauts of Apollo I died their fiery deaths.

Cape Kennedy was closed completely, sealed off from the world by the military. An armed sentry was posted outside all the trailer doors, including the one housing Vasili Ivanovich and the Erp Industries technical team while the government tried to figure out what exactly had happened on the launch pad of Complex 34. 1967, which had started only twenty-seven days ago with such excitement, hope and promise was now, literally, in ashes. For the rest of the day, Vasili Ivanovich sat quietly in front of his blank television monitor and meditated on the high human price of prideful ambitions.

~~~

In the Black

A Place in the Sun

Practiced now at his grisly craft, he quickly and skillfully bound the legs together and hoisted the body up. He always knew which ones still held a glimmer of life behind those dull, unfocused eyes, now staring directly into eternity. With them, he routinely paused to picture Y.T., Jr. in his mind before he slit their throats to let their black blood flow forth between his legs like the river Styx itself.

The day started just like any other day for the guardian at the gates of that bovine hell called the Cassidy Beef Packing Company, until Barry Boswagger's supervisor pulled him off the line and sent him upstairs. There, a secretary showed him into the waiting room outside Wilson Cassidy's office that all the meat packers sardonically called, "The Bull Pen." Still dressed in his blood-splattered smock, boots and butcher's hat, Barry Boswagger wondered why he was going to be "axed," for Wilson Cassidy relished the act of firing people and handled the discharge of every errant employee personally.

Death had begun to pervade Barry Boswagger's life on that fateful day when Rebecca Sue Simmons tossed her cookies all over the sidelines during the last great game of his football career. *Pregnant.* The word hit home like a sledge hammer to the middle of his forehead. Of course, no one—not even Coach Sox—believed Barry Boswagger when he said it wasn't—it couldn't be his child she was carrying. They hadn't even done it, yet. The honorable thing was still done and their wedding was hastily arranged. They might as well have slit his throat that day, for, ever since, the life flowed out of him and his hopes and dreams began to be dismembered and butchered until, instead of scoring the winning touchdown in the Rose Bowl on his way to glory and wealth as a pro football demigod, he ended up a cutter on the floor of a factory of death. Now, even that small scrap of life would soon be ground up into dog food.

They—Rebecca Sue Simmons and Barry Boswagger—were the very best Meadowlawns had to offer. Both of their lives had been wantonly destroyed and wasted. Barry Boswagger firmly believed someone should have to pay for that tragedy. Just as he began again to plot his revenge, the secretary showed him into Wilson Cassidy's office, directing him to stand in the middle of a sheet of plastic so as not to soil the carpet.

Wilson Cassidy sat behind a massive mahogany desk guarded on either side by nondescript men in gray flannel suits. A nurse in a crisply starched white uniform sat in a far corner watching a machine quietly, but noticeably scribbling traces representing Wilson Cassidy's vital signs. Having been sternly lectured as to the limited scope of her authority, the nurse sat silent, even as Wilson Cassidy, against all medical advice, alternated tokes from one of his beloved Havana cigars with deep draws from a medical oxygen mask.

Barry Boswagger assumed that the distressingly thick file Wilson Cassidy intently paged through was his own personnel file. But how in the world could so many bad things have been written about him in such a short time? He had not even completed his twelve month new employee probation period. Actually, the folder and several additional bound volumes were filled with the crisp, efficient reports of Federal Bureau of Investigation Special Agents

Williams and Walters detailing the activities of the *Triumvirate* and Y.T., Jr. Wilson Cassidy had developed quite a warm relationship with J. Edgar Hoover based upon their mutually held belief in the essential Americanism of eating red meat, as well as the generous discounts accorded the cafeterias at F.B.I. Headquarters and the F.B.I. Training Academy in Quantico, Virginia.

Wilson Cassidy closed the file and pushed it aside. One of the gray flannel valets immediately ushered it off the mahogany desk and out of sight. Wilson Cassidy covered his mouth with the oxygen mask. He scrutinized Barry Boswagger carefully, so carefully that it seemed as if he were counting each splatter of bovine blood on the boy's smock. Barry Boswagger nervously shifted his weight from foot to foot, but met and held Wilson Cassidy's icy stare. *Good,* thought Wilson Cassidy. Though he wished the boy had served another six months slaughtering cattle to sufficiently harden him, his plans had become overtaken by events—especially the surprise defection of affections by Miss Scarlett Angelina Brooking—so he needed to put the boy into play now.

Wilson Cassidy set aside his oxygen mask and crammed his Havana into the corner of his mouth. "I've seen you play ball. You had some kind of moves out there on the grid iron."

Barry Boswagger had braced himself for the worst. Therefore, he didn't know what to say, except, "Er…ah…thanks, I guess."

"No Big Ten ball for you? Big Eight? Or Pac Eight? You've got the talent."

"No one ever came to recruit me. I, ah, had a kind of bad season my senior year. And, you know, my grades—"

"Fools!"

"Yes, sir."

Wilson Cassidy sucked on his oxygen mask. The machine monitoring his vital signs scribbled and scratched in the brief silence.

"Son, business is a lot like football. A good businessman has got to have moves. A college professor didn't teach Gayle Sayers or Jim Brown their moves. A college professor didn't teach me my moves and you don't need any college professor to teach you how to be a success. You've already got the moves. I have confidence in you. You just have to get into the game."

Barry Boswagger struggled to follow Wilson Cassidy's logic. His capacity for comprehending metaphors and philosophy was being sorely tested, but he had a vague impression that what the man was saying was actually good. Maybe he wouldn't be fired after all.

"Uh-huh." He slowly nodded his head.

"So, how about it, Barry?"

"How…about…what?"

"Are you with me?"

"With me?"

"You've got the moves and I want you on my team. I want to give you a route. It's not the top, of course, but it's the first step on the staircase."

"A route?" Barry Boswagger stood dumbfounded.

"In the western suburbs: Raytown, Independence, Meadowlawns. I believe you are already familiar with the area?"

"Yes, sir."

"You'll be selling and servicing our established accounts, like Meadowlawns Memorial Hospital, Dante's Restaurant, and company cafeterias, such as Erp Industries."

"Erp Industries?" Barry Boswagger's eyebrows arched and his eyes lit up.

"One of our best local customers." Wilson smiled a conspiratorial smile.

Barry Boswagger smiled for the first time in a long, long while. Somehow Mr. Cassidy knew. He knew everything. He knew about him, Rebecca Sue Simmons and Y.T., Jr. And he had the power to make things right.

"Are you with me?"

"Yes, sir! All the way."

"Good. You start tomorrow. Get yourself cleaned up and go ahead and take the rest of the day off."

Wilson Cassidy never gave anyone any time off, ever. "Yes, sir. Thank you, sir."

"You'll do just fine, son," Wilson Cassidy said as he watched Barry Boswagger being led out of his presence. He prayed that the dim ex-athlete would not fumble again and let him down, for the stakes were much, much more than a few hundred thousand dollars worth of beef sales. The needles on the machine frantically tried to keep pace with his accelerated cardiac rhythms and breathing, as they did every time he thought of his aunt, her son and the only Cassidy heir left on the face of the earth. "Damn them. Damn them all."

On his way downstairs, Barry Boswagger could feel some of that old spring come back into his steps. The sun would shine down on him again: literally because he would get out of that dark, dank, odoriferous factory of death and out on the road in his own refrigerated delivery truck; and figuratively because Wilson Cassidy, the head of the entire company had plucked him from his ruin to give him a chance to make something of himself again and to avenge the wrongs done him and Rebecca Sue Simmons. He sensed that Wilson Cassidy had big plans for him and, even though he had no idea what they might be, he vowed to do everything in his power not to let him down.

He took a long look at the newspaper clipping from the *Meadowlawns Citizen Journal* pasted to the inside door of his locker. It was an article about Y.T., Jr.'s motorcycle accident, complete with a picture of the mangled and charred Harley-Davidson. He lingered long, gazing on the picture and words that had seen him through the darkest hours of his short life.

"Pay backs are a bitch," he muttered and slammed the locker door shut. He stopped for several mid-afternoon boiler makers at the West End Grill and then went home to tell his ex-cheerleader wife the good news.

~~~

Sgt. Pepper's Band

"Half a million—*ARRRGGGKKK.*" Hugh Betcha belched out a lethal fog of garlic. "It's fan-fucking-tastic."

Salisbury winced visibly and nearly audibly. Precision being his holy grail, his life was a relentless crusade of corrections. "Four hundred thirty-six thousand troops, to be exact, have been deployed to the Southeast Asian Theater of Operations."

"What—*ARGK*—ever."

"And more on the way," Mort Mortenstein giggled, rubbing his hands together fiercely. "How delightful! How marvelous!"

"Fucking choppers are dropping like mallards in autumn," enthused Hugh Betcha.

Simon Salisbury sipped at his second glass of wine and shot a suspicious sneer over the rim of the glass at his obese car pool companion.

"Yes, indeed. Yes, yes, indeed. Dropping like mallards." Mort Mortenstein drew out each word as he wrote them down in his journal. He snapped the book covers shut with a singularly smug, self-approving clap. "Genius. We are the essence of genius."

"Hmmmm. But I would not suppose a genius might warehouse ball bearings in crates stacked in an open cow pasture." Simon Salisbury scraped his fork across his plate in a way he knew was sure to grate on his target's nerves.

Hugh Betcha growled—lowly, but audibly—through a mouthful of Dante's rigatoni lunch special. He dropped his fork and thrust his hands into his sport coat pocket. He fished out a large, full key ring and shook them like trophies from the hunt in front of Simon Salisbury's face, dangerously close to his wire-rimmed glasses.

"Listen, you little shit, I told you it was N-P. No Problem. Under control. Got it? And at the rate I'm churning inventory, we are going to have a problem keeping up with demand. I suggest you and Mortie here, get off your fat arses and get the financing in place so I can start exercising our contract options before they expire. If you don't, then maybe we can just turn our precious prairie warehouses into fucking bowling alleys. And then, we'll be shit out of luck for millions—*God Damned Millions!*" Point made, Hugh Betcha turned his attention back to his rigatoni.

Simon Salisbury smiled slyly behind his Chablis, relishing his role as catalyst. He could never let his Keystone Cop-like companions get overly complacent.

"Boys, boys, boys. Let's not bicker amongst ourselves. We're on a roll." Mort Mortenstein had recently acquired the habit of fondling samples of the source of their new found wealth in the palm of his hand. He reached into his pocket to indulge himself. "With so much at stake, it's understandable that nerves will sometimes fray and tempers might flare in the heat of battle. Staring into oblivion day after day, a man becomes hardened or he is broken." Mort Mortenstein assumed a pale imitation of the infamous two thousand yard stare, peering into the cheap oil painting of Roman ruins hung on the wall of Dante's dining room.

Simon Salisbury frowned at the regular *click-clickety-click* of ball bearings coming from beneath the table in Mort Mortenstein's direction. The utter absurdity and incongruity of a vision of this pudgy accountant in Humphrey Bogart's role as Captain Queeg in *The Caine Mutiny* aggravated him as surely as the timbre of a fork scraped across china fused Hugh Betcha's nerves. It wasn't until later, back at his office, that he noticed the splotches of marinara sauce from Hugh Betcha's rigatoni lunch wounding his memoranda. Doing battle day after day with his oafish compatriots was fatiguing, and he sometimes wondered how much longer he could go on.

Billy Saul Sawyer's unit had been chewing on the Demilitarized Zone between North and South Vietnam for four months now. The latest fire fight had lasted a twelve-minute life time. Lying back against a small hill, he mindlessly shoved a full magazine into his M-16. Looking left, he saw Weasel. Right, he saw Fleck. He relaxed. Closing his eyes, he dropped his head back against the hillside and listened to the fire support base pound out its jungle rhythms in the distance and mentally followed the beads of sweat, like launched artillery shells, as they rolled down his forehead and across his temples inside his helmet. Waiting for the Sarge's signal, he reveled in the pleasure of exhaustion and the adrenalin rush of combat.

They lost another FNG—Fucking New Guy—and Raven had taken a round in the thigh, but it was nothing serious. The Lieutenant needed a body count to radio back, so while they waited for the dust-off chopper to come pick up the battle debris, the platoon pushed through the bush in the area of the enemy's muzzle flashes to count the number of dead Charlie. He worked swiftly and skillfully with his KA-BAR knife, just like the grizzled old short timer had shown him when he had joined the platoon in-country—of course, only after he had survived those first few fire fights and showed that he might be around for a while. You had to do it right or you'd mess them up by tearing them or breaking the loop. Then, they were of little value or use.

In the first few months of his tour, life in-country was such a dissonant kaleidoscope of perceptions, impressions and emotions that events rushed by with little time for contemplation or reflection. Now, though, the patterns of battle emerged just like they had told him at Camp Pendleton. War started making sense in its own crazy way to Billy Saul Sawyer and, having been thoroughly indoctrinated in the sanctity of sacrifice on the field of battle by the Marine Corps, he began to observe carefully how exactly soldiers faced the ultimate glory for their countries. In his mental catalog, he noted that, in general, North Vietnamese soldiers and the Viet Cong died a more hideous death than Americans, more often than not torn to bits by the mammoth fire power of United States artillery and aircraft brought to bear on the situation. It was something of a comfort to know that superior weapons technology was on your side. Oh sure, Eddie got blown to smithereens by a sapper attack and Wild Bill got cut in half by a flying piece of corrugated steel from a blown up utility shack at the fire support base, but, by and large, the American casualties he had seen were usually in a form still recognizable to fellow soldiers and, with a shave and wash, probably even to the dead man's family back home. The question that was ever present in his mind, but never formulated to be asked, contemplated and answered, though, was how Billy Saul Sawyer would face his ultimate glory. Such was the stuff of his fitful dreams at night.

"I counted eight," Billy Saul Sawyer called out merrily as he shook his trophies in front of the Lieutenant's face like Hugh

Betcha had shaken his keys at Simon Salisbury. "Can't wait to get back. I sure could use a cold beer."

The Lieutenant, an FNG himself, reflexively recoiled from the sixteen ears cut from the bodies of dead North Vietnamese soldiers and looped through baling wire. He watched Billy Saul Sawyer trot off happily to join the rest of the platoon, then turned back to face the sergeant with a natural look of disgust.

"What can I say? He's fresh off the farm and don't know you can't make a silk purse out of a Cong's ear." Sgt. Pepper laughed, then called out to his troops, "Come on, Marines, play time's over. Let's go home."

~~~

Failure to Communicate

Is this treason? The prospect was fleetingly titillating, even exhilarating. It was also vaguely frightening. She slowly and methodically traced the perimeter of the report's cover with her finger. The Senator's hideaway was dark. The blinds were drawn. The lights were dimmed. Her father was off on a junket to California. Was this what *he* really wanted from her? *She did not know*—and that uncertainty frightened Helen Troyer more than idle thoughts of treason.

She had never really cared whether or not she ever got a pilot's license, but the idea of her flying in an airplane so absolutely appalled her father that the temptation to flirt with every Army pilot she met in the Senator's office was irresistible. Many were the warriors who had vainly sought to tame the "Senator's little hellion." They would take her out to the airport and walk her around their little airplanes, pointing out the different parts and their functions in hushed tones as if divulging the secrets of a magician's act. Some even let her sit in the cockpit and fiddle with the controls. One and only one Army Air Corps pilot, grounded and manning a lonely outpost at the far end of the Aleutian Islands chain, dared to take her up for a "ride around the patch." Usually some excuse was made about airworthiness or maintenance or weather or safety or paperwork that only proved the G.I.s were more interested in maneuvering Helen Troyer than teaching Helen Troyer to maneuver an airplane.

Helen Troyer recalled that glorious day when Y.T., Sr. instructed her to taxi the Piper Cub to the end of the runway and then, without warning, hopped out. Suddenly, she was all alone in the airplane and he was motioning her to take-off, fly the traffic pattern and land again—*solo!*

Helen Troyer long ago mastered all the rules of the closed and confined world of the Washington social set, like a master mathematician knows the immutable laws of algebra, and she worked people like theorems and proofs, manipulating the figures about her to come to predictable and inevitable outcomes. While the Army Air Corps pilots imagined her to be a wild, desirable spitfire of a woman, civilian suitors knew her to be a cold, calculating Machiavellian, who played them all for her own amusement and her father's aggravation. She had known all along that no sensible Army Air Corps pilot would ever let her break the "surly bonds of earth" in their flying machines, but she loved pushing them to the brink and watching them squirm at the prospect of their military careers falling over the edge into an arctic oblivion. With Y.T., Sr., a *Naval Aviator,* though, she found herself alone and adrift in the currents of uncharted waters.

She was certain that Y.T., Sr. would defy her father and take her for an airplane ride, but she never once imagined that he would actually let her fly the airplane herself. Helen Troyer also never foresaw that their first clandestine meeting at tiny Dead Mule "International" Airport out on Chesapeake Bay, just south of Annapolis, would become a regular weekly event nor that she would catch herself musing during idle moments about the next flight days before hand. She did not realize that Y.T., Sr. was truly teaching her how to be a pilot as he talked her through turns, climbs, dives, slow-flight, stalls and landings, imagining instead the look on the Senator's face "if only daddy could see me now." Slowly and surely, though, under the steady and patient tutelage of Y.T., Sr., she was acquiring piloting skills, as well as aeronautical knowledge served up in small, regular portions during their conversations over the famous all-you-can-eat crab cake dinners served up at Captain Bob's Sea Shanty Restaurant.

Helen Troyer found herself out-calculated and out maneuvered to the brink as she sat alone in the airplane on the runway, listening to the sixty-five horsepower engine shake and rattle the little Piper's tube-frame and fabric-covered fuselage. For the very first time in her life, she experienced sweaty palms, as she nervously gripped and re-gripped the airplane's stick and throttle, staring down the asphalt runway and out across Chesapeake Bay. Y.T., Sr., who failed to fit the tried and true equations of Washington society life, smiled his infectious smile and backed off beyond and slightly forward of the end of the left wing tip.

She knew there could be no turning back for her.

He whirled three fingers in the air over his head.

Helen Troyer held the brakes and advanced the throttle slowly and smoothly. She instinctively reviewed the pre-take off checklist and scanned the instrument panel—engine gauges green and instruments set. She snapped a salute back with her right hand.

Y.T., Sr. turned, kneeled, and lowered his right hand to point toward the imaginary bow of an aircraft carrier, like a Flight Deck Officer launching a pilot off on a mission.

Helen Troyer smiled at his antics and relaxed. She was ready. She released the brakes. Moments later she was airborne on her very first solo flight.

If only the Senator could see her now, thought Y.T, Sr., watching her turn crosswind as she flew around the traffic pattern at Dead Mule "International" Airport.

He sat alone in the cafeteria, looking into a black, steaming cup of Arlotta McGrudy's insult to Columbia coffee bean growers. It was a newly acquired habit. An empty table flanked him at every quarter, while beyond, hourly workers crowded together in their usual pre-work klatches, talking and joking with a little extra volume to emphasize the isolation of the boss's son on his first day back to work for the summer. The scene was not lost on Barry Boswagger, who caught glimpses of Y.T., Jr. from the kitchen as he unloaded boxes of Cassidy ground beef from his truck into Arlotta McGurdy's walk-in freezer. His anger could not be cooled by the regular blasts of arctic air he caught with every hand truck full of cattle flesh. As the instrument of Wilson Cassidy's will, Barry Boswagger would bide his time and await the invitation of fate to see that his will be done.

Scarlett Angelina Brookings slowed at the cafeteria as she hurried to the blue print room with Vasili Ivanovich's early morning request for outline drawings. Only an hour earlier, she had shared a morning cup of coffee with Y.T., Jr. on the balcony of her Kirke Gardens apartment after a long night of celebrating his return from Berkeley for the summer. The din of the cafeteria ebbed at her passing as workers gazed longingly at the apparition of beauty in their industrial midst. Behind her by ten paces, came a hunched Rolf Guderian, shadowing her mission to the blue print room, as he was often wont to do, not only to ogle her curvaceous form, but to keep tabs on Vasili Ivanovich's projects and activities. He could not wait until he had deposed the ridiculous Russian and inherited not only his office, but his red-headed goddess of a secretary he so secretly coveted against all of his Aryan principals of superiority. Rolf Guderian's pleasant contemplation of her shapely calves and firm thighs beneath her tight, bright-red knit dress was interrupted by a glimpse of Y.T., Jr. as he passed the cafeteria door. Y.T., Jr. represented the single greatest threat to his ascendancy to the Big Office and his dreams of establishing a thousand year business Reich.

Scarlett Angelina Brookings turned the corner to the blue print room, while Rolf Guderian absent-mindedly continued straight ahead, forgetting where he was going as the cloud of Y.T., Jr. cast a pall over his corporate vision of *lebensraum*. Finally running into a fire escape door at the far end of the Old O'Reilly Candy Factory Building, he dejectedly sulked back to his desk in the Engineering Department to stew in the cold, dark shadow of nepotism.

In a far corner of the cafeteria, Hugh Betcha shoved donuts into his gaping, crushing garbage truck of a mouth while Mort Mortenstein carefully sipped coffee and Simon Salisbury fussily dunked his tea bag. The Car Pool's morning staff meeting of subterfuge was only briefly interrupted for a round of shaking heads and disparaging remarks when they noted the arrival of the Sugarman who sat down across the table from Y.T., Jr.

"Does Peckerfelt have his tit in the wringer again this year?" Hugh Betcha asked, donut custard oozing out of the corner of his mouth like pus from an infected wound.

Simon Salisbury winced and shook his head. "No, Not this year."

"Rangely's the Old Man's babysitter this summer," said Mort Mortenstein. "After the accident…" He caught himself about to speak the unspeakable. Mort mentally edged himself back from the brink.

"Couldn't have happened to a nicer guy," said Hugh Betcha as he attacked a jelly donut. "Shit, maybe now Marketing will actually get something done."

"You know, someday soon this situation may very well present itself to one of us," noted Simon Salisbury in a cautionary tone. "You fellows would be well advised to make contingency plans for the occasion."

"Contingency plans?" asked Mort Mortenstein nervously. Always alert to potential disasters, the pudgy accountant went so far as to maintain a well-stocked underground bomb shelter in the back yard of his home, ever since the Cuban missile crisis. "What kind of contingency plans?"

"A simple job description, plans for an innocuous assignment and some specially prepared files for the boy to be buried in for the three-month term of his summer labors."

"Hmmm." Mort Mortenstein made a note in his journal.

"Just sit him in the corner and threaten to beat the living daylights out of him if he peeps."

Just as Hugh Betcha expounded upon his own personal management style, Frik and Frak sat down with the Sugarman and Y.T., Jr., prompting another round of wagging Car Pool heads and tongues. Slowly the klatches broke up and dissipated to their labors.

Jo Ann buzzed him, again. He ignored her, again.

"Why…why…why me, Rudyard?" Dirk Rangely asked his closest confidant, the muted Siberian tiger head mounted in mid-snarl on his office wall behind his desk. The VP/Marketing paced with tireless endurance and precision, which might have made his drill sergeant proud had he been able to hold his head up high, but the weight of an uncertain future bowed his back bone like a gulf shrimp. Dirk Rangely knew why: "I broke from the pack too soon, eh my friend? I'm getting too close, too soon and the Old Man had to knock us down a notch or two. You would look good in the big office, but, alas, I am simply yet another victim of my own talents and successes."

But such knowledge brought little comfort. He nodded in agreement with his own Hamlet-esque performance. The heat and humidity of summer began to press hard upon him, even though it was only early June and his office possessed air conditioning, unlike the rest of the Old O'Reilly Candy Factory Building. Sales and Marketing had to keep its cool at all costs, Dirk Rangely had advocated earnestly, then pleaded pathetically. Y.T., Sr. agreed, but only so as to minimize the interference with the productivity of Erp Industries, Inc., workers by outsiders. Visitors rarely lingered long on the sweltering factory floor out beyond the cool oasis of the Marketing Department Conference room, thereby minimizing delays and interruptions in meeting production quotas and shipping commitments with stupid questions and the ever annoying fondling of work-in-process. Dirk Rangely peered out the peep hole camouflaged in the 'G' of the name plate on his office door, at his "troops" as he liked to call them. He fancied himself their Patton and they his Third Army.

"There he is, God damn it, like a turd in my fucking swimming pool."

Y.T., Jr. sat at an empty desk, sipping coffee, aimlessly doodling on a borrowed pad of paper and flipping nonchalantly through a back issue of *TIME Magazine,* just as he had done for the past week and a half since his return to Meadowlawns. The boredom of waiting for Dirk Rangely to decide what to have him do almost made Y.T., Jr. wish he was back in the machine shop in the basement, where, indeed, the work was grueling, but time never dragged as it did there in the bastion of starched white collars and firmly knotted red ties. His marketing "rotation" was proving to be worse than even last summer's subterranean nightmare.

"Damn it! I'm in charge here. Patton would have slapped that damn malingerer silly—but, then again, George S. did not have the Old Man to contend with. I'm just going to have to take hold of the reins here, and…and…and…" Dirk Rangely said, confidently slamming his right fist into the palm of his left hand, but his gut churned his breakfast of a western omelet, home fries and toast like a cement truck preparing to disgorge another new section of Interstate 70. He nervously checked his pulse again for the fortieth or fiftieth time that stressful morning, but he bravely resisted the temptation to dig for a miniature airline Tanqueray bottle from the bottom desk drawer. The thought of a smiling stew with a serving tray filled with a platoon of tiny green, glass soldiers in white screw-top helmets made his wander lusting soul long to be en route to somewhere…*anywhere.*

"What in God's name am I going to do?" Dirk Rangely growled out through his grinding teeth. He pressed his forehead against the door, as if believing a better view through the peep hole might reveal the answer. He hissed through his teeth, "Damn it, Rudyard, help me out here."

Jo Ann instinctively sensed his presence. Even Simon Salisbury admired her efficiency. She noticed the toes of his wingtip oxfords at the bottom of his office door that she had persuaded the Sugarman to cut too short for the doorway. The undercurrents of gossip at Erp Industries, Inc., swept along the notion that Jo Ann's attentiveness to her boss sprang from the deep well of her unrequited love, a notion Dirk Rangely not only did not disabuse, but actively fostered in meeting asides, through the wisps of steam off cafeteria coffee or between gulps at the drinking fountain. To be sure, he was often sorely tempted by his slender, raven-haired secretary who faintly resembled a softer, less melancholy Jacqueline Kennedy. Jo Ann did nothing to quell such rumors as it afforded her some measure of protection from the prowling, sex hungry junior managers of THE CUSTOMER who regularly haunted the halls of Erp Industries, Inc., immune from the edict of corporate celibacy. Her true motives, though, were much more pragmatic.

Jo Ann could read her boss's moods, actions and words like a weatherman reads temperature, dew point and barometric pressure to forecast upcoming stormy weather. She knew the threats—both real and perceived—of Y.T., Jr.'s presence in his department had driven Dirk Rangely into his schizophrenic *Fight or Flight* debate with himself, again—a debate that *"Fight"* never, ever won. Usually, it kept him harmlessly preoccupied and out of her way, but now his agitated pacing threatened to spill out of his office like a dirty river cresting its banks to disrupt the quiet calm Jo Ann enjoyed with the Marketing Department clerks. Jo Ann had to push his "Flight" button, and fast, to get him on a TWA jetliner to somewhere—*anywhere.*

Jo Ann studied the Old Man's son from across the office. Her immediate mission was to keep Dirk Rangely and the youth as far apart as possible. The only way to do that would be to have Y.T., Jr. handle the Marketing Department correspondence. Although memos, letters and TWXs were the red blood cells of the company's circulatory system, the mere sight of them always made Dirk Rangely queasy—just as the sight of real blood made him sick, even though he was obsessed with his pulse, checking its rate twenty or thirty times a day. Handling company correspondence would be a harmless diversion for Y.T., Jr.'s three month internship and would assure the two would stay out of each other's ways.

Knowing she had a cycloptic audience peering through the peep hole in the door, Jo Ann got up from her desk and deliberately made a great show of familiarizing Y.T., Jr. with the TWX machine, the correspondence files, the incoming and outgoing mail bins and explaining his duties as the Marketing Department's newest mail clerk. She sent him off directly to deliver the morning's incoming TWXs throughout the Old O'Reilly Candy Factory Building. She returned to her desk, trying now to think of a way to convince Dirk Rangely that a business trip needed to be made to Europe, so the Marketing Department could settle back into its familiar, relaxed daily routine and Jo Ann could get back to her more important duties that no one else there knew about.

Dirk Rangely pressed his eye hard against the door and observed with amazement the scene of Jo Ann dealing with Y.T., Jr. He glowed with glee. He really did love that woman and if the lessons of P. Peckerfelt's ex-boss's fling were not so odiously strong and clear, he would surely court that comely maiden. With a sigh of relief, Dirk Rangely retreated to his desk chair. This time, he answered Jo Ann when she buzzed his office and welcomed her in to give him a manila folder full of trade magazine clippings about emerging new markets in Europe. He watched closely as she turned smartly and walked back out with a saucy pendulum movement of her hips. Who was this angel that had come to his rescue? He regretted again that circumstance beyond his control prevented him from ever pursuing this Guinevere for his own personal Camelot. Perhaps…just perhaps, when he was the "Old Man."

A shiver ran up his spine and he instinctively looked over his shoulders, left then right, searching for the gangly, gawky private investigator that Y.T., Sr. used to hunt and track down wayward executives who strayed from their wives with the young women so abundant in the Old O'Reilly Candy Factory Building.

All was soon well again in the Marketing Department as Dirk Rangely took out a TWA international route map to plan his own personal *Operation Overlord,* and Jo Ann got back to screening his calls and routing the mail every which way around him. Y.T., Jr., in his boredom with white collar ways, began to actually read the TWXs, memos, letters and reports that passed through his hands daily. Y.T., Jr., caught up in the slurry of corporate communications like cholesterol clogging the arteries of commerce, became fascinated as well as alarmed by the unfolding narrative of "Buying and Dying" as Erp Industries, Inc., supported President Johnson's foreign policy in Southeast Asia being executed with excessive managerial efficiency by the ex-C.E.O. of Ford Motor Company, Robert McNamara, with their enigmatic black boxes sold to the Department of Defense and its contractors.

Clinton A. Owsley III sat in the back seat of the VW Bus next to Squeaky, fuming. Charlie rode shotgun as Tex drove helter-skelter away from the border: North, back to Los Angeles. It had been a bad summer all right, bad enough to bring him to the brink of...what? Rebellion?...Criminality? In the eyes of King George the whatever, Thomas Jefferson, George Washington and Patrick Henry were all criminals, were they not? And what about today's "Red Coats:" the INS, the ATF, the FBI, the DEA, the FAA, the FDA, the IRS...Who else? The DoD...Who else? The CIA! The CIA! The CIA!

He knew they were watching. They were all watching. He knew they were listening—all of them. But it did not matter anymore. In the alphabet soup of oppression, only one set of initials held importance, those of a man with a sagging, jowly, blood-hound mug that looked over the shoulder of every bureaucrat, sitting behind every green Steelcase desk in every blandly suffocating government office Clinton A. Owsley III had been hauled into that summer, courtesy of the covert machinations of Federal Bureau of Investigation Special Agents Williams and Walters. It did not take hallucinogens to see that these men with their stiffly starched white shirts and tightly knotted ties were each but a nameless, faceless pillar for the tyranny that pressed so hard upon him as he sat in his underwear after being strip searched at U.S. Customs coming back from their lab in Mexico, naked against the brute force of his own government, save for pair of boxer shorts.

For mile after mile, Charlie railed against the system. Tex sat oafishly mute. Squeaky giggled continuously. Clinton A. Owsley III felt himself harden like setting concrete, locked in a staring contest with the face of evil, an evil that had to be stopped—and stopped before the full effect of his recent draft reclassification took its toll on his freedom, his hair, his wardrobe and, quite likely, his life.

"There is an evil in the world," Clinton A. Owsley III repeated, first quietly to himself, then louder and louder still.

Squeaky giggled next to him, hallucinating wildly from the test tabs of the latest batch of LSD cooked up in the Mexican lab. They had been able to get it across the border by hiding it in drops on each of the notes of the George M. Cohen song book that Squeaky clutched to her heaving, giggling chest.

"You're damn right there's an evil in this world of ours," Charlie screeched. "You're God damned right about that fact, my friend. I know. I've seen it. I've seen it myself."

Tex groaned and stared out as far as he could down the long, white-dashed line dividing the lanes of Interstate 5, leading back to Los Angeles. "Doesn't he ever stop?" Tex asked himself silently.

Without skipping a beat, Charlie picked up on the theme of evil in the world and seamlessly wove it into the sermon he had been delivering to his flock of one in the front seat of the VW Bus as they hurtled through the California night.

Clinton A. Owsley III's resolve hardened to rid the world of this evil, to rid the world of Lyndon Baines Johnson.

And thus another summer passed quickly—this one too quickly, thought Scarlett Angelina Brookings as she gently stroked Y.T., Jr.'s hair. His head in her lap, they were on the very top bench of the *Fighting Eagle's* stadium at Harry S. Truman High School. Far below, Marty Keegan and Billy Saul Sawyer trotted around the cinder track again and again. It had been the best summer in many years. A cool breeze chilled her spine momentarily, as if to remind her of the shadow Wilson Cassidy still cast over her. It had been many, many years since she had entered a grid iron temple, where she, herself, led the multitudes in the rituals of the great American didactic, the Yin-Yang of punts and touchdowns, of offense and defense. It had been many seasons since her fall from grace into the grip of Wilson Cassidy. Her passion, sensuality and innocence had been her undoing, as the disgraced English teacher exiled from the education system would attest to after knowledge of their mutual love for D.H. Lawrence, coupled with their torrid affair, suddenly became public knowledge at a school board meeting. The airing of the scandal and the ruination of a fine educator had caught the sharp eye of Wilson Cassidy, who took the deflowered, defrocked and de-lettered young cheerleader under his wing for his own dark, evil purposes.

Y.T., Jr. opened his eyes and looked up into the heaven of Scarlett Angelina Brookings's face. She stroked his temples and smiled.

"You sleep?"

He nodded.

"You dream?" she asked, concerned over his increasingly fitful and animated sleep.

He frowned.

She looked down on the running track where Billy Saul Sawyer and Marty Keegan jostled each other like slow motion roller derby opponents. "What's with them?"

Y.T., Jr. scowled as he lifted himself up on his arm and turned to look down on the playing field. He watched his two friends jostle and check one another through the north end of the track coming out of the back stretch. "For as long as I can remember, the Keeg could beat up on Billy Saul Sawyer, even though he gave away four inches in height and fifty pounds. But now that Billy Saul's a Marine, he can't have his way with him and it drives him crazy."

Y.T., Jr. watched Billy Saul Sawyer trot easily ahead of Marty Keegan. After a summer of reading UH-1 Huey helicopter crash and damage reports, bomb damage assessment reports, Erp Industries, Inc., sales forecasts based on Southeast Asia theater troop escalations, and all the rest, he was relieved that Billy Saul Sawyer had come back intact from Da Nang to a safe posting stateside. He closed his eyes and laid his head back down on the soft pillow of Scarlett Angelina Brookings's lap. He savored the gentle stroking of her hand through his hair and tried not to fall asleep again, lest he dream again of losing his balance, of metal scrapping across concrete, of the heat of burning gasoline and the dull pain that stubbornly refused to yield to morphine.

"Head Smashed. Blains smashed. Vely sad. Vely sad." Fu Loin described the death of the infant at the hands of the Japanese soldier in horrifyingly graphic detail. "Eye ball fall out of baby head. Soldier clush it with boot. Vely sad. Mother weep. Soldier shoot her in head. *BANG!* Shoot her dead."

Penelope Xing was startled when Fu Loin nearly shouted out the 'bang' and clapped his hands suddenly to recreate the soldier's rifle shot. Penelope Xing tried to imagine being a mother; tried to imagine watching her own child be brutally murdered; tried to imagine if the soldier's bullet entering her brain might have been a release from her *faux* anguish that surely paled there in Fu Loin's reception room nearly three decades later and half a world away. Maybe it was the American blood in her, but she could not bring herself to weep for the lost child, nor the mother, no matter how hard she tried. And that saddened her more than the human tragedy itself.

She stared at Fu Loin. He stared back into the deep well of his past, an ever so slight tremor on his lips. It was all so different than in the texts of history she read between her appointments. Fu Loin had been there in Nanking the day the Japanese Imperial Army arrived and began to round up the men and women to seal their conquest of the northern provinces bordering Manchuria in the years before World War II. Fu Loin rocked and muttered to himself as if to ward away the memories of those times left behind so long ago, all the while fondling his beads.

Penelope Xing watched closely, as if she were witnessing the ripples from a splash of history reach out through time to rock this frail leaf of a soul. She contemplated her daily routine of classes, studying and evenings at Fu Loin's. She reflected on her own longings that seemed only to come alive with thoughts of Y.T., Jr., and his comings and goings in sync with the tidal rhythms of college semesters. The calling of history to her had been a way of reaching out beyond herself, but her times with Y.T., Jr., challenged that essentially passive, second-hand intellectualized living of life. Y.T., Jr. was real. His life was alive with action—at the Filmore, in the Haight, at Berkeley, at full bore on the Pacific Coastal Highway—in ways that Penelope Xing had never felt in her own life before he came to Fu Loin's with the ex-Colonel and the ex-Navy Commander that first night last January. In fact, until he came, she had never been beyond the San Francisco peninsula in her entire life. She had never broken her routine of classroom lectures and copulation sessions. But now she had a taste for stepping off the shore and wading into the stream of time for human endeavors that she had only known as history. She wanted to be a part of history, to be more than a passive, dispassionate observer of the litter and debris left in the wake of those people fully engaged.

Penelope Xing looked over the coffee table at Fu Loin rocking in anguish over his memories. She briefly felt a chill breeze of apprehension at the terrible costs that human endeavors of such magnitude as governments can affect and reek on individuals, but was still not afraid. The risks of living and dying without having experienced life beyond the Embarcadero became far more fearful for her. She got up and went to sit beside Fu Loin. She put her arm around him and he slowly surrendered his head to the comfort of her shoulder. Fu Loin sometimes asked himself why he kept this one, who was an under achiever in his business, but he talked of the past to no one other than her and none of the other girls were ever allowed to witness this weakness in him. He knew that she did not tell of these conversations and the toll it took on him. It was their secret.

As she comforted Fu Loin, Penelope Xing thought on how to become part of history, part of the history of the present time, her history. She thought of the posters on campus she had seen announcing the national war moratorium in Washington, D.C., in the fall. She contemplated what she had been told about the Free Speech Movement at Berkeley. She thought of the pictures from the war in Vietnam—napalm blooms, phosphorus blossoms, men in black pajamas bound and blind-folded, an American infantryman with an M-16 in one hand and a half-naked crying child in the other—that had never haunted her until she began to listen to Fu Loin's reminiscing. It seemed there was something important happening in her lifetime. It seemed something worth being a part of, if only because it was *her* time and *her* life. She felt the ache of an insignificant life like that of a tightening, cramping muscle.

Penelope Xing sat for a long while, cradling Fu Loin in her arms. In the morning she called Murph to ask for a ride to Washington, D.C., on *The Bus.* She had never left California in her entire life, but she felt the strangely calming touch of destiny sooth and comfort her in this momentous decision.

Yet, when Murph answered the phone, she was silent. The telecommunications line, empty of voices, hissed like a soft rain.

Finally, Murph softly asked Penelope Xing. "Are you on *The Bus?*"

The Bus. Penelope Xing closed her eyes and saw it: It looked like a Jackson Pollack drop cloth. She imagined it crossing the Bay Bridge, a bouquet of youthful mockery floating in the drab currents of rush hour traffic. What she could not imagine was that the Blue Bird school bus was originally painted blue, not yellow, and instead of ferrying suburban school children to and from their daily classes, *The Bus* had hauled sailors to and from the aircraft carriers docked at Alameda Naval Air Station until put out to pasture in a government surplus scrapyard, where Murph, using his share of the *Triumvirate's* LSD profits, purchased it and put it back on the road with the help of twenty gallons of Day-Glow paint. It would soon be going to Washington, D.C., to protest the war it had so faithfully served.

Soft electric rain fell in the telephone handsets.

"It is a great wave," whispered Penelope Xing.

Soft electric rain.

"And we are but small rocks," answered Murph.

It was a force unfelt, like gravity, but irresistible.

"Are you on *The Bus?*"

"Yes," she said. "Yes, I am, Murph."

And when Y.T., Jr. returned to Berkeley for the new school year and visited Fu Loin's, Penelope Xing was gone.

~~~

On the Bus

The cream-colored Cadillac *De Ville* convertible with Illinois license plates cruised south down Interstate 95 with the top down, long strands of hair dancing like crazed Salvador Dali puppets in the slip stream above the heads of the occupants. Marty Keegan rode the hump in the back seat, flanked by two pretty, yet clueless coeds along for the adventure that a weekend in Washington, D.C., promised. Mark drove the borrowed luxury sedan, courtesy of Bill's father, courtesy of the handsome salary paid him by Commonwealth Edison. Mark and Bill were having a loud and animated debate, followed like a tennis match by Diana, who sat between them in the front seat, but which Marty Keegan could not hear in back over Jack Bruce, Ginger Baker and Eric Clapton blasting "I Feel Free" out of the rear stereo speakers.

"Cadillac!" Marty Keegan yelled at passing vehicles, pointing to the occupants in his own car. *"CAD-DIL-LAC!"*

The coeds blew kisses to passing motorists, flashed the peace sign and smothered Marty Keegan in hugs and kisses. He fondled their breasts openly and winked teasingly at commuters imprisoned in their daily routines. The coeds were from his Poli-Sci class. Being a revolutionary had its upside—and Marty Keegan was looking forward to the prospect of getting laid in the nation's capitol.

Marty Keegan's freshman year at Columbia University had been a text book case study in the carnage that results when youthful dreams crash head-on into institutional granite and cultural concrete. His naive vision of emerging from the Ivy League's only journalism school a crusading reporter, then following in his grandfather's footsteps, battling to change the world for the better of all mankind, wound up threshed and winnowed by the undergraduate Core Curriculum and course pre-requisites, until the grains of his aspirations laid bare for the millstone of the American education system to grind them into flour ready for proper societal leavening. But the same hormonally supercharged hubris, the universally youthful aura of immortality, and an embedded sense of familial destiny that propelled his recklessness on the *Fighting Eagles* gridiron and sustained his rebellion in the halls of Harry S. Truman High School could not be contained by the Morningside campus, and it wasn't long before his restlessness spilled over the dikes of academia.

After a thoroughly unsatisfying *Lions'* football season that involved far more running, bench pressing and bench sitting than gridiron playing, Marty Keegan sought quiet refuge at what he called "Butler Beach"—the library stacks where he spent free afternoons and evenings on the fourth floor paging through the bound copies of *TIME, Life, Newsweek* and the *New York Times,* digging back through the decades to wander through the great watershed events of the Twentieth Century captured first hand by the idols of his craft—absorbing the heat of amazing photo journalism and heroic reporting of the ferocious battles of World War II exploding off glossy magazine pages; then back to feel the despair and desperation of that economic dust bowl known as the Great Depression rising from musty newsprint like an Oklahoma dirt devil; and then back again further into the "Roaring" decade that led to that very Black Tuesday in October, 1929, when Y.T., Jr.'s grandfather plummeted to his death at the other end of

Manhattan Island. The "Crazy Years" of Jazz, Flappers, Art Deco, Prohibition, amazing technological advances and seemingly plentiful material excesses gave Marty Keegan a creepy, yet uncomprehended feeling of *déjà vu* as he sat there forty years downstream in American history.

Seeking inspiration and, perhaps, redemption and validation from the acolytes of Walter Lippman and John Dewey, it seemed the more free time Marty Keegan spent at "The Beach" the more doubt gnawed at his faith in journalism like termites feasting on the foundations of a home. How could those reporters and editors of those times have missed a monster like the 1938 *TIME Magazine* "Man of the Year," Adolf Hitler, and the horrors he unleashed on the world? How could they have not seen and understood what would happen? It was all right there in *Mein Kampf*, in Hitler's own words, for crying out loud. How could they have not stopped him? Instead of wasting ink and paper on the "outpouring of birthday greetings" and praise for Benito Mussolini and all he had accomplished "for the good of Italy and humanity," why did they not stop these madmen, stop the suffering, stop the violence and stop the death they reeked on their fellow mankind? Who really cares if he and Hitler made the trains run on time, if those trains ended up running to Auschwitz and Treblinka? As Marty Keegan jogged through Morningside Park or around the Central Park Reservoir, he tried but could not fathom how the supposed watchdogs of the Fourth Estate had so badly missed the realities staring them straight in the face that would later spawn some of the darkest years of modern history. And so he reached back further, back into his own family's past.

Marty Keegan's grandfather spent his entire bright but short newspaper career at the *Kansas City Star*. A.B. Keegan was a fourteen year old paperboy who, family legend had it, followed cub reporter Ernest Hemingway around the office during the six months of his tenure there before he left to drive ambulances in Italy during World War I. Twelve years later, the elder Keegan, by then a reporter for the *Star*, went to Amarillo, Texas, to look into the suspicious death of a lawyer's wife who was blown to smithereens in the family car six blocks from home. After just two days of investigation, he somehow learned what authorities could not or would not: that the husband was having an affair with his secretary. His intrepid investigative reporting resulted in a fifty-four page confession and a newspaper story that won a Pulitzer Prize. Unfortunately, the stellar journalistic career launched by that prize aborted only a few short years later when he was fatally injured covering the 1935 Metal Workers strike violently raging through Kansas, Oklahoma and Missouri. His own father not having the grit or stomach for the kind of danger men like Ernest Hemingway and A.B. Keegan faced in their work became a school teacher, and so it was on an annuity funded by his grandfather's prize money and death benefits that Marty Keegan attended Columbia University. Marty Keegan searched for and found A.B. Keegan's story on microfiche. He read and reread his ancestor's prize winning prose. Somewhere in the intervening years, journalism seemed to have lost the fire that burned in the bellies of Joseph Pulitzer, William Randolph Hearst, Ernest Hemingway and A.B. Keegan. The Columbia freshman felt a heavy ancestral obligation in living up to his grandfather's prize winning legacy; but, here, at the journalistic Mecca founded and funded by Joseph Pulitzer, himself, which had recognized and honored a bud in Keegan family tree, he had become uncharacteristically unmoored and adrift from his own ancestry and ambitions.

Strangely, the thirty year old story of murder in a high plains cattle town written by his grandfather resonated in Marty Keegan, softly at first, then louder and louder still. For a long while he was not sure why, until one day jogging up East Park Drive, out of the blue he recalled a series in the *New Yorker* about murder in Kansas by Truman Capote. Returning to Butler Beach he found the first article in the September, 1965 issue, and then the three following installments. It was a different kind of reporting, a different kind of story telling: a style that seemed to break away from the rigid Who-What-Where-When-How of the journalism of the past that had so obviously failed mankind by missing Hitler, Mussolini, Stalin and Mao and their terrible meanings for civilization, even as those monsters worked their wills right before the supposedly unblinking and objective eyes of the Fourth Estate. He reread the Capote magazine series. He sought out a copy of *In Cold Blood* and wolfed down the novelization of true crime and yet hungered for more of this so-called "New Journalism."

Somehow, moving back and away from a strict factual, photographic rendition of space and time, with a feel more of fiction than current events, these *New Journalists* had, like verbal Dalis, Picassos or Pollocks, captured the essential truths and a more primal reality of the crimes, sports, politics, cars, celebrities and music they wrote about. The chasm between facts and reality, between objective observation and subjectively divining truth, between passive recording of sensory input and journalism as a verb—as a call to action and change—opened before him. In his mind, Marty Keegan always equated a reporter's job with just seeking the truth and faithfully documenting it. He had always understood that was enough. But this new and improved novelized presentation of reality demonstrated that his role needed to be more than a simple gatherer and sower of grains of truth. From his own winter of independent research at Butler Beach, Marty Keegan saw that the "Johnny Appleseed" model of journalism, spreading seeds called facts, had obviously failed in the past to move and protect society. The more that establishment publications, editors and reporters attacked what they called "parajournalists," the more Marty Keegan sought them out and embraced them. Weren't the very giants of Journalism, like Hearst and Pulitzer—the very founder of the Columbia School of Journalism, no less—derided as purveyors of so-called "yellow journalism" by the same kind of establishment types of their era? Didn't his own grandfather do more than just report? Didn't he solve a crime? Didn't he bring a murderer to justice? Didn't he change things for the better? He believed if his grandfather were alive, he would have changed the arc of history far beyond the city limits of Amarillo in the decades that followed. Marty Keegan, too, heard the siren calling to change the world through his words.

And so, Marty Keegan turned away from news locked in history and neatly stacked up in Butler Beach. He turned away from the staid and stale academic hot house vision of journalism and began seeking new news and new news telling and new news to be made. He lost interest in the *Lions* and their endless workouts. He would not return to the team in his sophomore year. Eventually, he went AWOL from the *Columbia Spectator* as well. His jogging ventured further north from Central Park to the upper reaches of West Riverside Park and St. Nicholas Park. The time he spent on the fourth floor at Butler Beach dwindled and he drifted farther and farther afield from Morningside Heights, mainly north towards 125th Street and easterly towards Lenox Avenue, seeking out and exploring new and sometimes unconventional reading rooms—bars, coffee shops, diners, parks—to escape the soft oppression of the Columbia Cabal of students, faculty and administrators, and their worship of establishment values.

By energy or inertia he eventually gravitated to Stella's Diner, a quiet family establishment on the outer fringes of Harlem, where he devoured home-style southern cooking, gallons of coffee, the *Village Voice* articles and anything he could find authored by Truman Capote, Gay Talese, George Plimpton, Norman Mailer, Terry Southern, Thomas Wolfe and Hunter S. Thompson. Shunned at first by the regulars, his persistent, yet quiet presence eroded away the novelty and resentment of having an obvious college student intruder in their midst, and, in time, he became an accepted fixture to be mostly ignored, except by Stella's daughter, Yolanda, who closed the restaurant with her sister, serving customers while Bernice cooked. Polite, functional exchanges between Yolanda and Marty Keegan rooted and grew, until late at night, after all the other patrons had gone, she would sit with him to share a cup of coffee and conversation, usually under the heat lamp glare of Bernice through the server's window to the kitchen. Woven into talk of themselves, their families, their homes, their futures, and their friends, Marty Keegan first learned how the hunger of Columbia University for real estate to expand hurt people and families Yolanda knew in Harlem and Washington Heights, forcing them out of their homes like refugees by swallowing up block after block of rental properties in their quest for campus *lebensraum*. Yolanda doubted the diner could long survive Columbia's academic imperialism as the college was actually Stella's landlord, owning the building where Yolanda's mother founded her business shortly after

World War II.

Any more than Austria and Czechoslovakia had survived Hitler's ambitions, Marty Keegan thought to himself. He perceived malevolence in the University's actions that he laid at the feet of its "Fearless Leader," President Grayson Kirk, and he felt an obligation to do what the journalists of the Twenties and Thirties had not done: stop the evil existing before his own eyes.

Marty Keegan asked if Yolanda would help him to help the friends, family and neighbors wronged by Grayson Kirk. She agreed, so they began to meet sometimes before her shift, sometimes after closing, when she would lead him deeper and deeper into Harlem to tenement buildings, to small family businesses, to minister's offices, to Well's Restaurant to meet with the economic exiles created by Columbia University, seeing and hearing first hand their plight, their frustrations and their pains. Affecting his best Capote-Wolfe-Thompson voice, Marty Keegan strove to capture the cultural clash between the *Haves* and *the Have-Nots* in New Journalism-style stories, profiles and vignettes that he sent to the editors of every alternative press publication he could find. With Yolanda's by-line, some of the stories were published in neighborhood newsletters, church bulletins and civil rights organization pamphlets. When their narrative turned its focus from past individual injustices to the future city-wide impact of the new gymnasium to be built in Morningside Park, an issue that merely simmered began to boil and others began to join Yolanda and Marty Keegan's chorus of protest.

Marty Keegan also brought those stories back to the activists that gathered at the West End Bar on campus, which stoked the fires of their outrage at *"The System"* and its obviously inherent injustices, helping them to feel a little less self-centered in their resistance to the War in Vietnam, which had a rather self-serving purpose in advancing an avoidance of undesirable encounters with the local Selective Service Board. There he was embraced by a group of middle-management radicals who yearned for action and were growing increasingly bored and impatient with the slow and plodding "praxis-axis" leadership of the Columbia chapter of the Students for a Democratic Society, which saw educating and organizing as their role in fundamentally transforming society. Marty Keegan had broken the gravitational pull of academia and smashed the paradigm they strained against in their endless hops-sodden debates by crossing campus boundaries and dealing with real people with real problems. He did not talk. He did not debate. He had gone off on his own to figuratively set a bomb and light the fuse that blew the Columbia gymnasium project off its racist rails.

As the radicals rallied to the cause of an oppressed minority in America, Marty Keegan found himself awash with timid whispers and prodded with inconspicuous nudges from less intrepid and more fearful peers that sent him into the stacks of Columbia's International Law Library on the trail of Grayson Kirk evils that were not merely local to the Eden of academia there on the Upper West Side of Manhattan but were playing out on the world stage. As war raged in Southeast Asia, Grayson Kirk and his minions collected millions upon millions of dollars from the *Institute for Defense Analysis* to research and develop new and improved weapons to more efficiently and effectively kill foreign citizens and subjugate their sovereign nations for exploitation by the corrupt and immoral American capitalist system. Marty Keegan painted Grayson Kirk's hands red with blood in a series of exposes detailing Columbia University's complicity with the Military-Industrial Complex in a conspiracy of international death and destruction. Marty Keegan felt his dogged reporting would have made his grandfather proud. The administration of the University which had once honored A.B. Keegan took a much less favorable view of his role as one of the "IDA Six" radicals and called upon the Pentagon to call upon the Federal Bureau of Investigation to quell what quickly became a public relations nightmare. Instead of a Pulitzer Prize, he was rewarded with an official government investigative file of his very own.

And so, Marty Keegan found himself sandwiched between two coeds in the back seat of the cream-colored Cadillac *De Ville* convertible with Illinois license plates—an automobile that reeked of the very essence of free market economics and American industrial muscle—which transported the vanguard of American student radicalism southbound to the nation's capital to participate in a national Moratorium against the War in Vietnam. With thoughts of getting laid—and maybe ending a war, too—dancing in his head, Marty Keegan had no idea that a Craftsman tool box in the trunk held dynamite, blasting caps and timers.

Wilson Cassidy surveyed the family graves. He could literally feel his blood pressure rise, so he swapped his cigar for a medical mask and took a series of deep breaths from the oxygen tank that followed him as his ever faithful companion. Each Budweiser beer can, each Steak and Shake wrapper, each cigarette butt represented repeated acts of injury for the brave and industrious Cassidy men who labored to build and sacrificed to protect the greatest nation on God's green earth. This place was sacred, not some "Boot Hill" filled with outlaws, cowboys and criminals shot dead or hung by the neck, then planted in plain pine boxes in unmarked graves, rightfully discarded by even the crudest and primitive of frontier societies. As he stoked his cigar again and contemplated his family's pivotal role in the unfolding history of the United States of America, a distant rumbling of diesel cylinders slowly percolated up through the night. A grinding of gears drew Wilson Cassidy's eye to the narrow roadway leading to the top of Cassidy Mount. He made a mental note to have his lawyers finally purchase the cemetery and see to it with all the force of law available that, once and for all, the Wilson legacy be maintained and respected in proper fashion. Then he waited.

A Cassidy Meat Packing Company refrigerated delivery truck slowed at the crest in the road and jerked to a stop. Inside, Barry Boswagger stared through the windshield at the man who owned and ran the company he worked for—who owned his job and could take it back as quickly and unexpectedly as he had given it to him. Barry Boswagger had no idea why his supervisor had ordered him to come to "Boot Hill"—as they all called it—after sundown, when his shift was finished. He feared this or any meeting with the owner of the company. Feared for his job. Feared for his future. Even feared, somewhat vaguely, for his life. But not to come was unthinkable.

The two men, separated by decades and generations—not to mention genetics, upbringing, tradition, and perspective—regarded one another through the misty night in the cemetery. Wilson Cassidy was unsure of this, his second choice to be the instrument of his will, but he was slowly being stripped of time, options and patience.

Barry Boswagger dismounted the delivery truck cab and slowly walked towards the old man in the light colored suit and Stetson Open Road Hat. Had he paid more attention in history class, Barry Boswagger might have recognized the sartorial homage to the man

Wilson Cassidy's father, Wiley Cassidy, and political boss Tom Pendergast had picked and placed in the U.S. Senate, later to become President, Harry S. Truman. He walked slower than normal, arms held slightly away from his sides with his hands clearly visible, not wanting to alarm Wilson Cassidy nor his two armed body guards who lurked in the shadows. Barry Boswagger stopped fifteen feet from the beef monarch of America.

The stroke he had suffered, induced by the stress of preserving his family lineage and the surprisingly stout resistance of his Aunt Anna Elise, had not impaired his thinking, but verbally expressing his thoughts became increasingly difficult for Wilson Cassidy. A stuttered, stammered and slurred delivery did not faithfully reflect the clarity of thought that still guided his business decisions and now his assessment of the critical juncture at which the Wilson family heritage found itself and the dramatic actions that needed to be taken.

"Wank ooooooo fa yoming."

Barry Boswagger's face twisted in uncomprehending contortion. In the soft moonlight, he saw how Wilson Cassidy's face drooped as if gravity exerted greater force on the left side of his body than the right, pulling down the left side of his mouth in a queer cartoon expression.

"Thank you for coming," a voice translated from the shadows behind Wilson Cassidy. It belonged to Travis Marbling, Wilson Cassidy's aide-de-camp who had become fluent in his boss's unique, stroke-induced dialect.

Wilson Cassidy waved off Travis Marbling and motioned Barry Boswagger over, launching into an impassioned monologue that Barry Boswagger struggled earnestly to follow without success. Wilson Cassidy explained how his plans to use Scarlett Angelina

Brookings to bring Y.T., Jr. into the Cassidy fold had been frustrated and foiled by the weakness of human emotions.

On his deliveries, Barry Boswagger had seen Y.T., Jr. with a strikingly beautiful red-head. He listened as Arlotta McGurdy sermonized on the blasphemous nature of their carnal relations, as she understood them from the rumors which floated so freely in her cafeteria.

Wilson Cassidy implored his route salesman-cum-conspirator to understand the calamitous nature of the current state of family affairs between the Cassidies and the Erps and the dangers for the future of his clan, his company and America.

Barry Boswagger understood all too well the dangers Y.T., Jr. represented to young beautiful women like Scarlett Brookings and his auburn-haired wife, Rebecca Sue Simmons.

Wilson Cassidy explained his plan for bringing Y.T., Jr. home to the fold of the Cassidy clan to insure the perpetuation of the most successful and profitable lineage in the history of the meat packing industry.

Barry Boswagger comprehended not one word being said to him, but clearly misunderstood that destiny once again embraced him with warm rays of sunshine, offering a sanctioned opportunity to avenge—avenge with "extreme prejudice" as if he were the Cassidy Meat Packing Company's very own top secret Phoenix assassin program—some unknown sins apparently perpetrated by Y.T., Jr. on his boss, and in the process, exact personal revenge for the wrongs done to Rebecca Sue Simmons and to the best quarterback who ever played for the Harry S. Truman High School *Fighting Eagles*.

"Unnerschtandt?" Wilson Cassidy asked, poking Barry Boswagger in the sternum and staring him directly eye to eye—at least with his undrooping right eye.

The fact that they met in a cemetery cemented his confusion. Barry Boswagger slowly nodded and began dimly formulating his vengeful plan, completely contrary to his boss's desires.

Wilson Cassidy turned and, as one of his bodyguards held open the suicide door on his Lincoln *Continental*, climbed into the back seat. The Cassidy family had reluctantly abandoned the Cadillac brand after his father's *El Dorado* sank into Chesapeake Bay. In an unfortunate gesture that cemented Barry Boswagger's murderous misperceptions, Wilson Cassidy pulled the trigger on a craggy gun formed by his contorted hand and pointed at his route delivery salesman-cum-assassin.

"We expect results," Travis Marbling warned Barry Boswagger as he handed him an envelope containing five thousand dollars in cash. He then joined Wilson Cassidy in the Lincoln *Continental*.

Barry Boswagger watched them drive off into the night. He pulled the money out of the envelope. He had never before held even a single one hundred dollar bill in his hands—not even when he was still being pursued by college recruiters—let alone fifty. He pledged to Wilson Cassidy, to Rebecca Sue Simmons and to himself, to fulfill his destiny and do what that peach truck in downtown San Francisco failed to do: kill Y.T., Jr.

Penelope Xing woke suddenly in the middle of the night. Her text book on American history slid from her lap and fell to the floor of *The Bus* with a thud, startling her. She had lost all notion of time and space in the days or, maybe weeks, since they left San Francisco. Not having ever been outside the state of California—and at most only a hundred miles or so from San Francisco on Y.T., Jr.'s Harley-Davidson—travel was an unfamiliar and strange experience for her to begin with and the possibility of Murph following an efficient and readily measurable straight-line track from San Francisco to Washington, D.C., was as hallucinatory as Penelope Xing flapping her arms and flying across the country. What Murph lacked in direction, though, he made up for in stamina. *The Bus* had been in constant motion, stopping only for diesel fuel, groceries and rest stops since they had embarked on their odyssey.

It took a few foggy moments for Penelope Xing to orient herself to the inside of *The Bus*. It was dark both inside and out. There was only the soft halo around Murph in the driver's seat from the glow of the dashboard lights. Headlights speared into the night, goring it as they bored into the heart of America along a vein of blue highway. Avoiding the Dwight D. Eisenhower National System of Interstate and Defense Highways only added to Penelope Xing's disorientation. The two-lane road signs were small, labeling towns that she had no idea even existed. Outside the metal cocoon of *The Bus*, she had no idea where they were relative to a Rand McNally road map. Various human forms and shapes were scattered haphazardly, sleeping on the bench seats. She knew none of them. They seemed to follow in Murph's wake squawking for tabs of LSD, like seagulls flock behind a fishing boat. Even when conscious, most of them were so stoned that reality seemed but a deep, distorted dream and conversation as logical as Lewis Carroll dialog, so it would be pointless to even ask any of them where they were. Penelope Xing felt alone and frozen in time, yet also moving relentlessly through space. She bent over to pick up her text book. She watched Murph carefully, not sure if he was even still awake as he drove them, hopefully, eastward through the darkness.

Penelope Xing got up and slowly walked to the front of the bus, feeling their motion through the night more acutely and supporting herself by grabbing the back of each seat as she shuffled forward, hoping not to fall and wake any of her fellow travelers.

She sat down on the empty bench seat behind Murph and whispered his name.

Murph's stare bored into the night, like a shell-shocked Marine.

"Murph," she said a bit louder.

He hummed and nodded his head. A shudder and a quick S-turn spasm momentarily roused a couple of sleepers behind them. They quickly settled back into their slumbers.

"Oh, man," he moaned.

"You okay?"

"Mmmmm. Oh, yeah. Oh yeah."

"Where are we?"

"Half again as far again as time and space allows." They sat, staring down the rail-like headlight beams, which went off a cliff of darkness. "Arkansas? I don't know, maybe Missouri. Not Texas. Anymore."

They meandered cross-country like a slow motion ricochet: Donner Pass, Promontory Summit, Hoover Dam, Alamogordo, Central City, Little Big Horn, Dodge City, the Alamo. Penelope Xing's impatience to embrace real-time history slowly evaporated. She spent the days paging back and forth through her history book, reading about the places they passed, times they had missed in history. So much death. So much suffering. In the constant motion of *The Bus,* she felt like she was falling, falling sideways.

"Murph. When we get there…"

"One never knows. We can only move. We can only do."

"I cannot understand how these things…how events…how what we do…Will it make a difference?"

"Will it make a difference to you?"

Penelope Xing pondered. "I think so."

"Then it will."

"But is that even important?"

"Is this important to you?"

"It is, but I don't know why."

"Neither will they, but it will be."

"Who is *they?*"

"*They* don't even know who they are. But it will be important to them."

Penelope Xing rested her head on the chrome bar between her and Murph, confused and falling sideways through the night towards St. Louis, then Harper's Ferry, then Gettysburg, then Washington, D.C.

J. Edgar Hoover sat at his pathologically tidy desk staring at the three files Clyde Tolson had placed on his ink blotter: Senator Thurman Troyer, Wilson Cassidy, and an unfamiliar one—Y.T. Erp.

J. Edgar Hoover did not think in terms of friends and foes. He always considered those around him as either allies or adversaries. 'Friend' and 'foe' were too permanent and as a bureaucrat who had survived five different Presidential bosses, he understood that today's allies are tomorrow's adversaries—and it really didn't matter what political party was in power—Robert Kennedy might as well have been a Communist for as much compatibility as there was between the two men.

The question before J. Edgar Hoover was—actually, what is the question before him? With his agency being solicited by both a retired, adversarial United States Senator and an allied successful businessman, the F.B.I. Director's curiosity heightened to learn how two polar opposites could come to have a common interest in the third file about this Y.T., Erp fellow, which carried a respectable heft for as new as it was—though nothing compared to those files which had lived and breathed for decades in the file cabinets of the Bureau. If J. Edgar Hoover was nothing else, he was a curious man who did not believe in coincidences. This outlook sustained him and, ultimately, protected him during a bureaucratic career that was, just that year, entering its sixth decade. No one survives that long in an organization like government without knowing things, and curious people are the ones who go out of their way to know things. Now, J. Edgar Hoover hungered to know even more about Y.T. Erp, Sr., his company, his business with the government, and how this nobody from the heartland became such a threat to a Senator from Georgia and the company who supplied his agents with U.S. Prime beef to insure his army stayed at the top of their form.

As he methodically reviewed Y.T. Erp, Sr.'s F.B.I. file, J. Edgar Hoover began to literally squirm in his office chair as he highlighted red flag after red flag after red flag that jumped up from the pages. His company was deeply involved in classified military projects and yet seemed to have an inordinate number of employees who were foreign born—including Nazis and Communists! His ex-Red Army Chief Scientist was meeting with America's Apollo astronauts. His alcoholic Marketing Director seemed to travel around the world with no apparent business purpose. His Purchasing Department seemed to be hording mission critical commodities. His Manufacturing Manager was a suspected pedophile. His mother had blackmailed a United States Senator and his son attended the University of California at Berkeley. Y.T. Erp, Sr. secretly traveled around the country on his own private jet.

J. Edgar Hoover pondered a moment, then scribbled a quick note for Clyde Tolson to have the Erp file labeled a *Top Priority,* to be assigned to a tiger team of crack Special Agents who specialized in counter espionage. J. Edgar Hoover watched Clyde take away the file to see to it that his commands were carried out, oddly unsettled at the unfamiliar feeling of compassion he felt as he observed the slight slur as Clyde spoke, the slight slowing and unsteadiness in his gait, the uncharacteristic weary drooping of the shoulders. Clyde Tolson's stroke had taken a physiological toll and J. Edgar Hoover saw a biological adversary he was powerless to apprehend and arrest. The unfamiliar feelings of compassion, concern and fear, as stunted as they were within the character of the F.B.I. Director, passed quickly and he moved on to a review of the next file on a well-known Hollywood actor. Deeper in the stack of files and reports for the Director's review were the ones for Marty Keegan and the *Triumvirate*.

Clinton A. Owsley III gripped and re-gripped the pistol beneath his jacket, fighting the urge to shoot Charlie in the back of the head. The monologue never, ever ended and after being encapsulated in the VW bus for nearly a full day's worth of hours, he could barely contain himself from doing bodily harm to his traveling companion.

How in the world did Tex absorb so much crap and not blow a gasket? Twenty-four straight hours of it? The drive to DC seemed interminable, but that was where his target lay and only that focus, that goal kept his violent urge in check. They had hundreds of miles yet to go and if he didn't keep his frustrations bottled, his world would surely find a bloody end there on the dry prairie just west of Abilene, Texas. What would Tex do if he put a bullet through the back of Charlie's head right there and then? Clinton A. Owsley III imagined that he would just glance over casually from the highway centerline and with a barely uttered "huh," then turn back to the highway to keep on wordlessly driving to Dallas, to Nashville, to Washington, D.C., in a state of blissful disengagement.

Clinton A. Owsley III had been in need of transportation and did not want to deal with the government at the airport, nor try hopelessly to look inconspicuous on a terribly long Greyhound Bus ride across the country. So, he enlisted Tex and Charlie to journey to the October Moratorium, funding their gas, food and fun by spreading pink and purple Owsleys along Interstates 10 & 20 on the way from Los Angeles to Dallas. It was only the greater evil of the government that held his rage in check. Once he got to the nation's capital, he could ditch the Spahn Ranch extras and pursue his mission of revenge against the alphabet soup of agencies which had made his life a living hell.

It was actually quite surprising that Clinton A. Owsley III had not been apprehended already, since it had been over a year since California declared LSD-25 an illegal substance. With all the talk of revolution, he had his own cause, his own revolt to handle, which had nothing to do with the coming storm over the war in Vietnam. His mission was intensely personal and deadly serious. Whether it stopped the war or not was not his concern. He only wanted to stop the nightmares. He could only do that by stopping the leader of the "free" world.

Finally, exhausted from being up for three straight days, Clinton A. Owsley III, against his will and better judgment, fell into a deep sleep and dreamed of cars kissing parking meters and unseen horses screaming in the background, while Tex slowly and silently cruised the streets of Copeville, Texas, and Charlie rambled on and on, and on, and on, and on.

Eventually, Tex found his way back to Interstate 30 and headed on again towards Washington, D.C., turning his back on his hometown, his childhood, his family and his upbringing, leaving a void which Charlie filled with hatred.

By habit, Y.T., Jr. would find his way to Fu Loin's on Saturday nights. The apartment on Telegraph Avenue was empty. Penelope Xing's room on the fifth floor was empty. Y.T., Jr. and Fu Loin sat in silence, sipping green tea, as suitors came and went. With every visit, Y.T. Jr. noticed the growing splotch of postcards Penelope Xing sent to Fu Loin taped to the wall behind the cash register. One day in October he brought in a map of the country and mapped the route of *The Bus* across the United States, ending in St. Louis, Missouri, with an image of the Gateway Arch and a quote from Thomas Jefferson: "The earth belongs to the living, not to the dead."

Y.T., Jr. decided then to follow in the skewed and scattered wake of Penelope Xing's pilgrimage with Murph. He left that night on his Harley-Davidson to cross the country to Washington, D.C. By the time he reached the Wyoming basin, any doubts of what he was doing and why he was chasing one of Fu Loin's employees across the country had dissipated and nothing in the flat corn fields of Nebraska, Iowa or Illinois stirred any reflection on the rationale for his journey. He just knew there was a reason for him to be heading east. Not for the war. Not for peace. Not for Billy Saul Sawyer's fate or, even, Penelope Xing's fate either. But there was a reason he was going. A reason he felt but did not comprehend. And so he drove on, followed by F.B.I. Special Agents Williams and Walters, whose investigation of the *Triumvirate* had recently been granted Director-level priority.

"There once was a time..." Y.T., Sr. thought out loud, remembering the smile, the toss of her golden locks, the curious tilt of her head as he bounded out of the Piper Cub cockpit at the end of the runway at the Dead Mule International Airport and stepped away to let Helen Troyer solo for the very first time. He slowly squeezed his chin between his thumb and index finger to create a Kirk Douglas-like cleft as he savored the memory. It was a moment in time that changed everything for a Senator's daughter and a lowly Navy lieutenant. He lifted his gaze from her grave to the horizon, east, as if he could peer back through the relentless revolutions of the earth to earlier, rosy-fingered dawns.

Far up on the knoll above him, on the path that led back to the Troyer family plantation, Frik and Frak stood their usual vigil: The ex-Colonel, smoked intently and stared relentlessly into the mist rising over the rugged Georgia landscape; the ex-Navy Commander looked up at the contrails high overhead, arms crossed and clearly uncomfortable on the ground. The ex-Navy Commander could not fathom how deep this ritual's taproot bored into the soul of Y.T., Sr. He knew only of the airways in and out of Georgia that brought them to and from the tiny sod runway willed by Helen Troyer's grandmother to be built and meticulously mowed for the past eighteen years, specifically for these visits by Y.T., Sr. to the grave of the true love of his life. It was a dying wish of a saddened elderly woman that Senator Troyer respected and honored, even though it enraged him to this very day.

Y.T., Sr. walked back up the hill and soon the Cessna 185 climbed out and away from the Troyer family plantation into the deep blue of a crisp, clear October sky. Y.T., Sr. sat in the left seat flying. The ex-Navy Commander worked the radios to contact Atlanta Center to get their clearance to Washington's National Airport. The ex-Colonel sat in the back savoring a brand new copy of the latest issue of *Playboy*. He would nearly be finished by the time they touched down in the nation's capitol.

~~~

Ignorant Armies

Finally! After pinballing endlessly—recklessly across the North American continent, *The Bus* found its way into the nation's capital. As Murph crossed the Potomac River and began to snake aimlessly around the entrails of avenues and streets in Washington, D.C., Penelope Xing felt at once overwhelmed with the bold and enormous monuments erected to the familiar icons of the history of the United States of America and the endless Acropolis-like buildings that seemed to have sprouted up everywhere as citadels for civil servants too numerous to contemplate. The initial effect of the Olympian government presence was exactly as intended: to belittle the being of this common citizen and to trivialize her cares. And yet, as they drove on and on and on, with Murph narrating incoherently like a hallucinating amateur tour guide—which, in fact, he was—she was struck by the obsession with white sandstone, white marble, and, evidently, endless buckets of white paint. They passed the White House and then the Capitol Building for what seemed like the fifth or sixth time, and a smile cracked on Penelope Xing's face that reflected a crack she perceived in the facade of an empire's vanity as she began to appreciate how the practitioners of the second oldest profession endeavored to separate and cleanse themselves from the first oldest profession by proclaiming their virtue in the color chosen for their architecture, as if the purity of a bride could be guaranteed by an ornate, white wedding gown.

Suddenly, Penelope Xing felt a fellowship—if not, indeed, a kinship—with the legislators and office holders who would prostitute themselves, their principles and their beliefs so nakedly for their own material and political gain. Time and again, she witnessed in her studies history lay bare the manipulations, machinations and, ultimately, the failings of the ruling classes of all colors, creeds and geographies. She felt oddly at home here on the opposite side of the country, three thousand miles from where she had spent her entire life. She no longer felt so small and so insignificant. She looked forward to Friday's protest with heightened anticipation, ready to embrace the opportunity—*finally!*—to live, to breath, to *be* a part of history.

Then, Penelope Xing made a mental note to send Fu Loin a post card and wondered which tourist attraction would please him most to see.

The cream-colored Cadillac *De Ville* convertible with Illinois license plates prowled Constitution, Independence and Pennsylvania Avenues with a hungry purpose: hunting for a home for the explosives in the trunk. Marty Keegan and the girls dozed in the back after partying and driving through the night down the Atlantic Coast from New York. Bill, Mark and Diana spoke in hushed whispers masked by an eight track tape's endless looping of Jim Morrison and The Doors. They pointed to the very same sites Penelope Xing was absorbing, but occasionally they commented and nodded, then Bill scribbled in a spiral notebook. The cream-colored Cadillac *De Ville* convertible slowly circled the Tidal Basin. They went to Foggy Bottom, to the Supreme Court, to the Department of Justice, where inside, even as they passed by, J. Edgar Hoover sat at his desk reviewing files and the plans for his agency's response to the upcoming Moratorium to End the War in

Vietnam protest demonstration scheduled for the next day. They crossed the Fourteenth Street Bridge and warily took measure of the Pentagon and the government's preparations to gird itself against the voice of its citizens.

"They think of everything, don't they," Diana said, pointing to rows and rows of green portable restrooms beyond a line of barricades.

"Let's hope not," said Bill, writing in his notebook.

"If they did, they'd be tying down the building to stop the levitation," said Mark.

"Levitation?" asked Diana.

"Yeah, Abbey Hoffman, Jerry Rubin and Allan Ginsberg say they are going to do an exorcism on the Pentagon with a bunch of burnt out Beat-types," said Mark.

"Those guys are Bozos," scoffed Bill. "Let's go over to Langley."

"You don't want to check out Arlington?" asked Mark.

"Why—those guys are already dead," said Bill.

Clinton A. Owsley III did not know what happened to Charlie and Tex—and frankly did not really care. He figured maybe they turned around and headed back to California, though Charlie had prattled on and on about Cincinnati and going there to open a can of whoop ass on some character he called "The Colonel," who might have been his father or his step-father or the director of an orphanage where he once lived—it was often hard to follow and to make sense of Charlie's ramblings. After two thousand miles trapped in the VW bus listening to Charlie's chaotic, disorderly and, apparently, endless monologue on injustice, intolerance, racism, paranoia, violence and society's meltdown in an apocalyptic holocaust that would make the Civil War look like a day at the beach, Clinton A. Owsley III reached a breaking point and could not take another angry incoherent word of it, so he had Tex drop him off at the West End Market in Dyersburg, Tennessee, to catch a Greyhound Bus the rest of the way to Washington, D.C., As he waited, he contemplated the irony of joining his namesake product in this mode of transport. Clinton A. Owsley III had avoided arrest after LSD had been outlawed the previous year by hiding the inventory of his trademark Pink Owsleys, Purple Owsleys and Owsley Blue Dots in a steamer trunk that was continuously being shipped to different cities on Greyhound Buses in an evidentiary shell game played out across the entire state of California.

When the bus sighed to a diesel-exhaling stop in the market parking lot, Clinton A. Owsley III boarded and found a seat in an empty aisle as far back as he could and settled in for the final legs of his journey to confront and vanquish his squint-eyed, slack-jowled nemesis. He kept his knapsack on his lap the entire time, taking comfort in the weight of the Colt Model 1911A1 semi-automatic pistol, the extra magazines and the two hundred rounds of forty-five caliber ammunition it contained. He used the quiet time from Ripley to Covington to Millington to Memphis to Nashville to Knoxville to Morristown to Johnson City to Kingsport to Bristol to Marion to Wytheville to Roanoke to Lynchburg to Charlottesville to Fredericksburg to Springfield to Washington, D.C., focusing his ire and steeling his resolve to assassinate the President of the United States of America.

When Clinton A. Owsley III disembarked at the Greyhound bus station in the nation's capital in the dark hours of Friday morning, after yet another twenty-four hours without sleep, the first thing he did was find a tourist map. He studied it carefully, then headed down Louisiana Avenue with grim determination to find Pennsylvania Avenue, the Red Dog Ranch derringer in his boot and the Colt M1911A1 pistol and ammunition on his back.

Lance Corporal Billy Saul Sawyer was posted on top of the Treasury Department Building. From his sniper's hide he watched the crowds start to slowly assemble in front of the Lincoln Memorial on that crisp, clear Friday morning in October to protest a war none of them had likely ever seen. He had seen it, up close and personal, and he vaguely resented their arrogance in being so insistent about something they knew so little about.

He saw signs that said, "SUPPORT OUR GIs. BRING THEM HOME NOW!"

Home? Home where, he wondered. Here? The United States? Washington, D.C.? Meadowlawns? Pendleton? Quantico? Da Nang?

Billy Saul Sawyer wasn't really sure where exactly home was for him anymore. He was also not sure exactly why he had been transported from Quantico and ordered, without explanation, to report to the top of that particular government building, but he found himself there with a Winchester Model 70 sniper rifle and as much ammunition as he had ever been issued in Viet Nam. He did not know the spotter, who was spending the downtime reading a book appropriately called *The Stranger* by Albert Camus, while they waited.

But waiting for what, he wondered.

Bored, Billy Saul Sawyer paced the rooftop of the Treasury Department Building with a pair of binoculars, taking in the sights of the city: the White House, Lafayette Park, the Ellipse, the Washington Monument, the Capitol Building, the Reflecting Pool and the Lincoln Memorial, as well as carefully observing the crowd growing in the Mall like a colorful paint-spill of humanity—hundreds at first, then thousands, then tens of thousands, even hundreds of thousands as some would later claim.

Eventually, an uneasy feeling overcame Billy Saul Sawyer. He sensed a danger in the sheer number of people he saw gathered below and began to understand why he might have been positioned there with a rifle if, somehow, for some reason, the situation got out of control. He assumed the Gunny would give him his rules of engagement soon enough and wondered how many others like him were out there in the city.

Y.T., Erp, Sr. never scheduled meetings, except when circumstances allowed no alternative. To make an appointment generally required giving a purpose for the meeting. In business, stating your purpose was tantamount to giving the enemy your battle plan—*Hey, look everybody, we're on our way to Pearl Harbor now and we'll see you on the seventh, Yours truly Admiral Yamamoto.* Surprise being the essence of a winning strategy, revealing what you wanted up front invariably put you in a position of weakness, because it gave time for THE CUSTOMER to think about the upcoming meeting, to ponder the subject at hand and to prepare lists of questions, accusations and, most inconveniently, demands to be made of Erp Industries, Inc. Most people naively thought negotiations represented the last stage of the sales process to determine a final selling price to close an order. Y.T., Sr. knew business was one continuous negotiation that began long before any phone call or meeting occurred and continued long after the contracts were signed, the purchase orders were issued and product was shipped.

Without a calendar filled with scheduled meetings, Y.T., Sr. was free to roam at will about the familiar seventeen and a half miles of corridors that had literally been built up around him during his service in the Navy as the very first occupant of the Pentagon during World War II. To the casual observer, he might appear to be aimlessly wandering from desk-to-desk, doorway-to-doorway, cubicle-to-cubicle, coffee urn-to-coffee urn with no evident intent or purpose in mind, joking, laughing and generally socializing, certainly not demonstrating any business-like demeanor or intent, and that was precisely how he wanted it to appear. In the largest office building in the world with the greatest number of secrets to hide from the rest of civilized society outside its five walls, scrutiny and curiosity were the last things he wanted aimed in his direction when he was trying to conduct business.

Y.T., Sr. hardly ever sat for meetings. If any meeting actually required a conference table, chairs and an overhead projector, he surrounded himself with Erp Industries, Inc. minions to speak and listen on his behalf, allowing himself to appear to be absorbed in working a crossword puzzle or even, in extreme circumstances, to doze off now and again, all the while paying close attention to every word said in the room. On his "rounds," Y.T., Sr. always seemed to be "just dropping by to say hi", to check on a wife, child, mother, golf game or bowling league or, like a crafty Dutchman trading trinkets with North American Indians, to barter logo-ed key rings, Swiss army pocket knives, or Sheaffer pen and pencil sets in exchange for a heads up, an insight or some nugget of information about recent events or hidden machinations within the military-industrial complex. Sometimes he ended up hunched over a drawing or paging through design specifications, test reports or bid solicitations. But most often he simply conversed for as long or as short a time as the person he had selected and sought out wanted before moving on to the next desk, doorway, cubicle or coffee urn on the mental target list he had prepared over his morning coffee.

Y.T., Sr. spent much of his time in steno pools, drafting departments and operational support groups, because that is where the real work got done which was merely set into motion by the appointees and brass parked at the top of the political and military command food chain. And while the stenographers, engineers, planners and administrators gladly accepted his trinkets, what they really appreciated was simply that Y.T., Erp, Sr. spent time with them and showed interest in their lives, their work, their observations and their opinions. Since he never took notes, people were more at ease and prone to dropping their guard, often revealing much more information than they might normally do if they knew what they said was being documented. They felt like they were just catching up with a familiar friend. Blessed with a large capacity memory, Y.T., Sr. waited until later, when he was alone, to write down the information gleaned from his conversations in a spiral bound note pad to be typed up later by Wanda W. Willet and placed in his files.

On this particular Friday in October, Y.T., Sr. found most of the folks he stopped by to see inattentive and ill-at-ease. There was clear concern for the storm of protest gathering that morning at the Lincoln Memorial, which, according to the threats of the protest leaders, would soon enough be headed their way later in the day. Whether on console color TVs in the offices of Secretaries, Under Secretaries, Generals and Admirals or on black and white portable models at the desks of Colonels, Captains, Majors, Commanders and GS-12 through 15s or on radio sets of Lieutenants, Sergeants and GS-5 through-11s or on the sometimes hidden transistor radios of the steno, motor and janitorial pools, the entire population of the Pentagon was obsessively tracking the strength and direction of the Moratorium mob like Gulf Coast residents warily follow every twist, turn and wind reading of a hurricane as it plows across the Caribbean.

With the United States Department of Defense establishment totally distracted by the autumnal expression of dissatisfaction by so many students, professors and activists, Y.T., Sr. abandoned his futile rounds and found a stairway to the roof of the Pentagon where he could stare directly into the face of the political gale blowing their way.

After burning at least another forty gallons of diesel fuel, Murph parked *The Bus* on the campus of George Washington University at four o'clock Friday morning. Penelope Xing and the transplanted hippies, Diggers and Red Dog Ranchers from the Haight spilled into the faculty parking lot with a sense of wonder and disorientation, partly from the hallucinogens, partly from the total cessation of motion beneath them as they planted their feet on *terra firma,* and partly from the electric tingle from an energy which was tangible on the campus and on the streets of the nation's capital. They had arrived, finally, for the making of history and, though it was still the middle of the night, the campus was alive with motion and noise, crackling with excitement and anticipation.

Like a pied piper, Murph, in his Day-Glo green jumpsuit adorned with sewn-on patches and tin foil, organized his minions of pranksters and, somehow, without the aid of a map and without ever before setting foot within the District of Columbia, led his band of protesters down Twenty-first Street to the National Mall to help end the war in Vietnam, more like a kindergarten teacher might lead a class on a field trip than a sergeant would lead his platoon into a firefight. Penelope Xing trailed along at the end of the line, sure that she would never lose sight of such a cartoonish cast of characters. She thought for sure that, arriving so early, they would be the first ones on the Mall, but, as they crossed Constitution Avenue, small clots and tumorous growths of people had already begun to attach themselves to the sides of the Reflecting Pool and even seemed to be metastasizing right before her eyes. Intense and purposeful activity occurred at the steps of the Lincoln Memorial, setting up platforms, signs, banners, speakers, and microphones. Some people were already handing out pamphlets and giving speeches. Others were serving coffee, pastries and, probably drugs. Street musicians were scattered about playing guitars and singing. Small clusters of people gathered to chant, meditate and pray. Photographers snapped pictures and, here or there, an oddly well-dressed individual seemed to linger a bit too long and watch a bit too intensely the pre-dawn activities.

Penelope Xing watched Murph lead his charges into West Potomac Park. Looking east, she saw the Washington Monument. Looking back one last time at Murph and deciding that she would surely be able to find them again later in the morning, she turned east and walked to the Washington Monument, then up Madison Drive past the Museums and National Gallery until she stood across from the home of Congress and gazed on the very seat of the government's power, from which all the laws of the land spewed forth and toward which the will of the citizens—her will, too—would be focused that day. As the sun rose, white buildings all around began to glow and Penelope Xing smiled at the inside joke she shared with her government. By the time she had walked back down Jefferson Drive past the Smithsonian, Penelope Xing saw that the crowd had grown exponentially and realized that finding and joining Murph would now be an impossible task. She suddenly felt terribly alone amidst a hundred thousand people and began to reflexively second guess the wisdom of coming across the country to be jostled, mauled and, perhaps, even crushed by history in the making as it bore down on her like avalanche of humanity. As if she were working at Fu Loin's, she abandoned herself to the crowd as it pressed her forward toward the Lincoln Memorial until the protesters packed together so tightly they could no longer move. Penelope Xing listened to the speeches, the cheers, the songs and the chants filling the clear October air. The Lincoln Memorial and the Capitol Building disappeared behind the shoulders of the men and women surrounding her. Her only anchor to a world beyond the crowd was the top of the Washington Monument, erect against the deep blue sky behind her.

And when, on cue, the Moratorium began to drain from the National Mall and flow like lava towards the Fourteenth Street Bridge to take their anger and their rage directly to the war makers at the Pentagon, Penelope Xing drifted along like a leaf riding the ebb and flow of a tide. Thinning out some now that it was in motion, the mass of humanity relaxed its tight grasp on her and she began to think a bit more clearly to wonder, what really had they accomplished that morning with their speeches and their cheers and their songs and their chants? Had they made history? What was different now? Would future Penelope Xings read of this day and yearn to have been part of it all? She looked to the faces of those around her and saw no answers, only purposeful intent as they surged towards the Pentagon.

As they marched across the Potomac River, she wondered what they would accomplish when they got there. Getting closer, she caught a glimpse of the grave markers in Arlington National Cemetery to her right. Getting closer yet, her doubts and apprehension turned to abject fear as she saw the orderly line of soldiers in real army uniforms with real guns—soldiers just like the ones Fu Loin described in his firsthand account of the rape of Nanking—lined up to meet the Moratorium protesters and protect the Department of Defense.

F.B.I. Special Agents Walters and Williams had not spoken at all for the last hundred miles along Interstate 70. It had been a grueling trek following Y.T., Jr. across the country on his Harley-Davidson. He had only made stops which were absolutely necessary for gas and food in a race against time to reach Washington, D.C., and find Penelope Xing before the Moratorium protest scheduled for Friday, October 21 began. The last substantive conversation between the Bureau partners occurred hundreds of miles behind them in Indiana, as they speculated on the use of amphetamines by their quarry to stay awake mile after boring mile, hour after empty hour. Special Agent Williams athlete's foot had begun to itch horribly and fill the car with the bouquet of dirty sweat socks. Special Agent Walters had run out of breath mints to mask his chronic halitosis. Both men's shirts were stained with condiments from a myriad of fast food restaurant entrées consumed en route. With their F.B.I. issued hypoallergenic appearance soiled and their organizationally homogenized dispositions fraying, Special Agents Walters and Williams were greatly relieved to finally cross the Potomac River and turn on to Constitution Avenue. And yet, Y.T., Jr. kept driving and driving and driving around the city.

The Moratorium turned out to be bigger than anyone—Y.T., Jr., Special Agents Walters and Williams, the Park Police, Penelope Xing, even the organizers—expected—everyone except Director J. Edgar Hoover, of course—and following Y.T., Jr. in the mess which had been made of downtown traffic became such a challenge that Special Agents Walters and Williams called for backup, a request which was immediately approved despite the heavy burden on law enforcement resources caused by the protest against the war in Vietnam, an approval which had come straight from the top. The suspicions of the Special Agents were confirmed when Y.T., Jr. finally found *The Bus* in the faculty parking lot at George Washington University. Seeing it empty, he realized Murph and Penelope Xing were on foot, so Y.T., Jr. mounted his Harley-Davidson and found Pennsylvania Avenue, then worked his way back to the Moratorium to find them with four teams of F.B.I. Special Agents now tracking his every move.

As Billy Saul Sawyer watched the crowds grow steadily during the morning from hundreds to thousands to tens of thousands, his gut churned in reaction to a well-honed sense of danger acquired in boot camp and sharpened in the jungles of Southeast Asia. He looked over at the EE-8 field telephone that had remained silent since he and the spotter stationed themselves on the roof, as if he could will it to ring. They still had not received any orders. The unknown always intensified gut churnings.

The spotter finally set aside *The Stranger* and took an interest in the events of the day. The National Mall was packed with protesters. The two Marines heard the sound of speeches being made, but could not make out the words. They heard music, but it sounded like a neighbor playing a scratchy old seventy-eight RPM record. Every once in a while a cheer would rise from the crowd that sounded like the faint roar of F-4 Phantoms somewhere overhead.

The spotter started scanning the crowd with his M49 telescope and after a few minutes called out a target for Billy Saul Sawyer. He picked up his Winchester Model 70 and aimed in the general direction indicated by the spotter. Guiding him in from landmark to landmark, the spotter brought his cross hairs to bear on the intended target.

"Blond, shoulder-length. Tight blue halter top packing thirty-eights. Nice round ass. 'Stop the Bombing' sign—now ain't that sweet," said the spotter. "I'd give her a seven-point-two. And what does my friend, the judge from East Germany, say?"

Billy Saul Sawyer looked over at his spotter and laughed. "Eight. Definitely an eight."

"You've been in the field too long my friend," said the spotter as he went back on the scope. "Of course, you are from East Germany. There is that."

Billy Saul Sawyer looked again at the blond in his cross-hairs. He thought she really was an eight, maybe even an eight and a half, but he did not say so out loud.

So, in the absence of any other orders from the Marine Corps, Billy Saul Sawyer and his spotter spent the next few hours girl watching through their sniper scopes.

Marty Keegan had not yet gotten laid and the co-eds had wandered off to explore the Georgetown University campus, but the day was young and the entire weekend lay before them still. Marty Keegan was not sure what they were doing there parked in the shadows of the *Hoyas* stadium bleachers, instead of joining the Moratorium activities on the National Mall. Curious as to what was going on at the back end of the cream-colored Cadillac *De Ville* convertible behind the open trunk lid he hopped out and wandered back to see what Mark, Bill and Diana were doing. As he rounded the rear quarter panel, he saw Bill just about to pound a blasting cap into the end of a stick of dynamite with a hunk of two-by-four. He reacted instinctively, immediately putting his shoulder into Bill's ribs just like Coach Sox taught him over and over and over again in practice in order to punish the opposing team's kick returners. Bill was forced to release the board, the blasting cap and the stick of dynamite harmlessly back onto the floor of the trunk.

"What the fuck are you doing?" cried Marty Keegan, who lay piled on top of Bill. He was no demolitions expert, but Marty Keegan had blown up plenty enough stuff on Billy Saul Sawyer's father's farm—not to mention a toilet, locker and chemistry lab or two at Harry S. Truman High School—to know how to handle dynamite.

Mark and Diana stood frozen in shock at the sudden eruption of violence against one of their own.

"Man, I think you broke my ribs," moaned Bill.

"You are damn lucky you have ribs left to break," said Marty Keegan. "What the hell?"

"You didn't have to hurt him," whined Diana.

"Actually, yeah, I did. He would have blown us all to smithereens."

Diana looked down at Bill.

Bill looked up at Mark.

Mark shrugged his shoulders and looked at Marty Keegan.

"Yeah, well, maybe, maybe not," admitted Mark.

"What the fuck is going on?" asked Marty Keegan, getting off Bill and standing up.

"We need to bring a little bit of the war home to them," said Diana, "right to the government's own war mongers."

"At Georgetown?"

"We're hoping we can find the ROTC building," wheezed Bill.

"What? And blow up some innocent college kids like us?"

asked Marty Keegan. "Why not the Pentagon—those guys are the real culprits."

"We checked it out earlier and the place is locked down like Ft. Knox," said Mark. "There's MPs and soldiers everywhere."

"The only place without soldiers guarding it is where they set up the portable johns," said Bill.

"Johns?" asked Marty Keegan. "What if…"

"What if what?" asked Mark.

"What if we blew up the johns?" asked Marty Keegan, thinking back to one of the more successful high school pranks he had pulled off with Y.T., Jr. and Billy Saul Sawyer.

"You mean, like, splattering all those soldiers with piss and shit?" asked Bill.

"Yeah," said Marty Keegan. "I've done it before. It kind of makes a statement. And they really, really hate it."

"I like it," said Mark. "I definitely like it. Like, it's time the shit really hit the fan."

Diana giggled at the thought of it.

"You know what to do with any of this?" asked Bill pointing into the trunk.

Marty Keegan looked over the explosive paraphernalia in the back of the cream-colored Cadillac *De Ville* and nodded.

"I think I can work with this stuff."

They piled into the cream-colored Cadillac *De Ville* and headed back over the Potomac River, leaving behind the co-eds.

The EE-8 field telephone rang on top of the Treasury Department building startling both Billy Saul Sawyer and his spotter, as they battled their boredom by ogling and grading protesting co-eds through their sniper scopes. The spotter answered and after a moment of listening pointed away from the

Lincoln Memorial toward Lafayette Square in front of the White House. Billy Saul Sawyer turned and quickly got on the scope of his Winchester Model 70. The spotter kept his ear to the field telephone and put his eye to the M49 telescope to scan the area across the street from the White House. Without their target identified, unsure of their mission and unclear of the danger, the soldiers could feel the adrenalin surge into their bloodstreams as their breathing and heartbeats accelerated.

"Coming through Lafayette. West side. Towards Pennsylvania. White male," the spotter exhaled in sharp, whispered barks out of habit, even though the two Marines were alone on the roof. "Blue jeans. Orange and blue T-shirt. Tie-died. Shoulder-length brown hair. Red tennis shoes. Armed with a pistol. Off Jackson heading towards the White House."

Billy Saul Sawyer chambered a round and scanned the west side of Lafayette Square.

"If he starts to cross Pennsylvania, take him."

"Red tennis shoes…red tennis shoes," whispered Billy Saul Sawyer, half to his spotter and half to himself.

As he drove his Harley-Davidson down Jackson Place looking for Penelope Xing, Y.T., Jr. spotted Clinton A. Owsley III mere moments after F.B.I. Special Agents Williams and Walters. The surveillance distance of the two Special Agents did not assure they could intervene with the armed suspect approaching the White House, so Special Agent Walters radioed their field commander to have them alert the closest sniper team, while Special Agent Williams photographed the felony unfolding before their very eyes with a Bureau issued Nikon equipped with a telephoto lens.

Y.T., Jr., seeing Clinton A. Owsley III with the pistol in his hand, peeled off, jumped the curb and arced around the walkway, until he was S-turning slowly beside his friend as he walked through the Park.

It took Clinton A. Owsley III a moment to rouse from his trance-like state and notice the motorcycle and rider beside him. "Slinger?"

"Hey, Oz. What's up, man?" asked Y.T., Jr. nonchalantly as the speed winder whirred on Special Agent Williams Nikon. "Out for a walk in the park?"

"I-I-I gotta, I gotta…" Clinton A. Owsley III stuttered. "He's gotta be stopped. I gotta…"

"Yeah, I suppose," agreed Y.T., Jr., as they slowly made their way through the trees to the center walkways that lead to Pennsylvania Avenue and the White House. "Hungry? I am. Pancakes sound kind of good, don't ya think?"

Clinton A. Owsley III slowed to a stop as if his train of thought had been catastrophically derailed. He wondered how long it had been since he had eaten. He did not know.

Y.T., Jr. circled him once and stopped beside Clinton A. Owsley III. "Yeah, pancakes. Buttermilk. Just like back home at Sears."

Clinton A. Owsley III stared curiously at Y.T., Jr. The would-be Presidential assassin had a soft spot for pancakes, which Y.T., Jr. was well aware of having shared many, many meals with him at the iconic restaurant off Union Square in San Francisco.

"With real maple syrup. *Real. Maple. Syrup.*"

Clinton A. Owsley III's shoulders slumped a bit. His head nodded slightly.

"Come on. Get on."

Clinton A. Owsley III got on the Harley-Davidson behind

Y.T., Jr. and they slowly rolled towards Pennsylvania Avenue.

"Got him? *Got him yet?*" queried Billy Saul Sawyer's spotter urgently. "Long hair. Red tennis shoes. Pistol. He's got a pistol, man."

Billy Saul Sawyer sited his cross-hairs on Clinton A. Owsley III as the target came out from behind a row of trees, but he did not respond to the spotter.

"Take the shot if he goes to cross Pennsylvania. Hear me? That's the order. Take it."

Billy Saul Sawyer did not recognize his intended target, but when he moved his aim to the motorcycle rider next to him, he immediately recognized his friend from Meadowlawns. He went into brain lock, passively watching the two talk through his sniper rifle's scope.

"He's there. There in the park," the spotter said. "Got a motorcycle? There's two, now. Come on, they're moving. They are moving to Pennsylvania. You gotta have them. Take the shot. *Take the shot!*"

Billy Saul Sawyer did have his target, but simply watched as Y.T., Jr. and Clinton A. Owsley III drove out of Lafayette Square on to Pennsylvania Avenue and disappeared into traffic.

Special Agents Williams and Walters tried to speed around the square to catch their quarry, but lost contact with their target. Y.T., Jr. had known all along he was being followed the entire way from San Francisco, so after he cut through Lafayette Park with Clinton A. Owsley III behind him on the bike he purposely and methodically serpentined back through the streets of Washington, D.C., to lose them.

Special Agents Williams and Walters frantically radioed their surveillance tag teams, but they had lost the motorcycle, too. They radioed for more assistance, but the Moratorium protesters were on the move to the Pentagon and the quarry they trailed for three thousand miles vanished into thin air. Special Agents Williams and Walters reluctantly turned back towards F.B.I. headquarters at the Justice Department Building to explain the serious lapse in their field skills to their Supervisor and to process the incriminating evidence in the Nikon to add to the *Triumvirate's* growing file folder.

Billy Saul Sawyer took his eye off the scope and rested his forehead on his forearm.

"What the fuck, man?" asked his spotter. "We could've took him, easy."

Billy Saul Sawyer did not answer. Instead, he decided, then and there, to volunteer for another tour of duty in Vietnam. He no longer felt at home in the country he had taken an oath to serve and defend.

Penelope Xing slowed, then stopped completely, allowing the river of bodies heading towards the Pentagon parking lot to flow around her like a rock in the middle of a stream. After all the hours driving and thinking, after all of the platitudes and outrage expressed at the Lincoln Memorial in word and song, she found herself faced, not with speeches, music or the black and white typeset of a history text, but with men in uniform armed with rifles. In the face of raw government power, she suddenly felt every bit as small and insignificant as the government wanted her to feel. Frightened and despairing at her vanity of being part of history—of making history—Penelope Xing felt acutely homesick, wishing she were back in her fifth floor room at Fu Loin's looking forward to Saturday night and Y.T., Jr. coming by later to hold her and, in the morning, to take her away to somewhere, anywhere to be free for a few precious hours on a Sunday afternoon.

"You look lost."

In the Black

The voice from right beside her literally made Penelope Xing jump and step back.

"I'm sorry, I didn't mean to startle you," the young, clean-cut man oozed in a southern-country-hillbilly accent that Penelope Xing could not place geographically. "I feel a bit out of place, myself. I just came over to see what was going on. Pretty crazy, huh?"

Penelope Xing suddenly felt put at ease at the natural charm of the stranger.

"My name is Bill," the stranger held out his hand.

"Penelope." She extended her hand and felt Bill's grip slowly, erotically embrace her hand, squeezing like a blood pressure cuff, in what was certainly the most sensual handshake she had ever experienced.

"I'm a Senior over at Georgetown. Majoring in Foreign Service," Bill said, lingering in their handshake, well beyond the norm for strangers or family. "I just came down to see this Moratorium thing firsthand and I noticed you looking a bit confused or overwhelmed and thought maybe I could help out."

"Uh, er, thanks?" Penelope Xing mumbled.

"It's okay. Don't worry. I mean, I work for Senator Fulbright—or I mean I did over the summer."

"Oh."

Bill smiled and gazed dreamily down into Penelope Xing's eyes. Slowly, very slowly he released her hand from his embrace.

Penelope Xing melted and smiled back.

Y.T., Sr. stood on the Pentagon roof with binoculars scanning the crowd that spilled over the Fourteenth Street Bridge and onto the Pentagon grounds. Frik and Frak joined him to silently watch the events, images of which surely would fill the network news broadcasts that evening and newspapers the next morning.

He smiled as he saw the protesters confront the MPs with flowers, planting them in the muzzles of their rifles. He was amused by the group splintered off from the main crowd meditating and chanting to exorcise the evils out of the Pentagon. *Little do they know,* he mused. His binoculars settled on a lone female who seemed to have been left behind by the mob of protesters marching intently on towards the steps of the Pentagon guarded by soldiers and U.S. Marshals six stories below. He recognized the pretty, young woman from his son's hospital room after the motorcycle accident. She had spent days there knitting and reading aloud, left at night then returned in the morning. He knew who she was. Fu Loin had briefed Y.T, Sr. thoroughly on Penelope Xing.

His eye was suddenly drawn to a clean-cut young man making a bee-line across the grounds towards the banks of portable johns, who, like a predator, spying the easy pickings of a vulnerable prey separated from the herd, quickly turned his focus and suddenly veered towards Penelope Xing. He watched the young man stalk his way to her side, then press himself on the young woman. He watched Penelope Xing let down her guard and succumb to the charms that were evident even to Y.T., Sr. six stories above. He watched until his attention was drawn to a growing ripple of activity near the Pentagon steps. Soldiers and Marshals seemed to be slowly stirring and preparing for some kind of activity.

Y.T., Sr. turned to the ex-Navy Commander, pointed towards Penelope Xing, and made his intentions clear. Moments later, Frik and Frak headed downstairs and outside towards Penelope Xing and the unknown stalkeer.

Scanning the crowd and the increasing activity on the Pentagon steps, Y.T., Sr. missed Marty Keegan and Mark quickly making their way through the crowd to the portable johns carrying a duffel bag filled with explosives. They dropped the duffel bag on the floor of an empty john in the middle of the rows and began running away from the Pentagon and the johns as fast as they could to meet Bill and Diana in the cream-colored Cadillac *De Ville* convertible for their getaway.

Their sudden movement caught Y.T., Sr.'s eye. He followed them for a hundred yards, then caught sight of Frik and Frak parting the sea of protesters with their mere bearing and demeanor, as they headed directly for Penelope Xing and Bill. A burst of activity back on the Pentagon steps drew his attention again as a line of soldiers waded into the crowd of protesters, using their rifles as clubs to break up the protest. In their wake, U.S. Marshals began arresting protesters who stood their ground, whether intentionally or inadvertently after being dazed by a rifle butt to the head.

As soldiers engaged citizens, a bomb blast from the middle of the rows of portable johns rocked the grounds and shifted the battle between the protesters and soldiers into high gear. Panicked protesters stampeded away from the Pentagon steps. Soldiers gave chase and seemed to hurry their efforts to get as many licks in on the protesters while they had the chance, before they retreated completely.

Penelope Xing and Bill, only a few hundred yards away from the portable johns were thrown to the ground before Frik and Frak reached them. Panicked, Bill quickly got to his feet and fled the scene, leaving Penelope Xing on the ground shaking her head to clear her thoughts and comprehend what had just happened. In truth, she had, indeed, become, not just part of history, but had changed the history of the country by saving the life of a future president of the United States, who would have been in the blast zone, had he continued to follow nature's urges until spying Penelope Xing.

Frik and Frak reached Penelope Xing and protectively escorted her back through the line of soldiers into the safety of the government's defensive perimeter.

Later that evening, after the violence and the arrests abated, Frik and Frak escorted Penelope Xing to National Airport and assisted her aboard the Erp Industries Inc. Learjet. Y.T., Sr. was already in the back cabin. Within twenty minutes they were climbing out of the nation's capital away from the violent pandemonium as ignorant armies clashed by night.

Y.T., Sr. and Penelope Xing had a long, rather pleasant conversation about war, government, history, life, liberty, and family as they flew to Kansas City, where Y.T., Sr. disembarked.

After refueling, Frik and Frak flew Penelope Xing back to Fu Loin's where she yearned to see Y.T., Jr. the next night, not knowing he was still back in Washington, D.C., the object of an intensifying F.B.I. manhunt.

~~

IN THE BLACK

1968

Nowhere Man

It was a shock to the nervous system of Erp Industries Inc. Over the Christmas to New Year's shut down, the conference room at the front of the building—across from the "Old Man's" office door guarded so diligently by Wanda W. Willet—simply disappeared. In its place was a brand new executive office that became the focal point of speculation and whispered gossip for all the would-be pretenders to the helm of the company.

The Old O'Reilly Candy Factory Building woke at five am every weekday with the jangling of the Sugarman's keys in the lock on the employee's entrance door. It was a ritual he had repeated every day for over forty years, save for a four year period when he lied about his age to join the Army Air Corps to become a crew chief in the 332nd Fighter Group, commonly known as the Tuskegee Airmen. No one—not even the United States government—knew the Sugarman's real age, though it was widely accepted that, like the Old O'Reilly Candy Factory Building, he had come into this world sometime before the turn of the Twentieth Century. So, unlike the majority of the patriotic citizens in the days, weeks and months following Pearl Harbor who lied about their age to join the military because they were too young, he had been too old to join the Army. And thus he rightfully earned the moniker "Pops", because he truly could have been father to not only the teenage enlistees but to many of the veteran officers as well.

As the building blinked to life with the flickering of aroused florescent lights, Homer McKinley Morganfield performed a careful pre-dawn walk around inspection as attentively as those he had done countless times on the red-tailed P-51 Mustangs he tended in Italy during World War II. Lives depended on it then and lives might just depend on it now, whether averting an industrial accident from a machine tool in need of maintenance or in the skies over a faraway battlefield from the failure of an Erp Industries, Inc. black box due to a soldering mistake made under faulty lighting or an erroneous quality control reading from uncalibrated test equipment.

By the time all the lights came on, all the manufacturing equipment was powered up, all the thermostats were set for the day, and he returned to his workshop, a cup of coffee steamed on his workbench. Arlotta McGurdy was always the second person to arrive at work and never failed to show her appreciation for a kitchen that was in the best working order of any she had endured in her cafeteria culinary career. The Sugarman sat with his coffee to compile his "To Do" list and log his observations in the latest volume of a journal that dated back to the administration of President Calvin Coolidge.

The Sugarman came to the Old O'Reilly Candy Factory Building in the Roaring Twenties, when he realized, after a brief stint on the road with the Blue Devils territory band, that he did not have the roaming bone needed to make a living on the road playing his tenor saxophone. Nor did he want to leave Kansas City for New York, New Orleans or Chicago to seek jazz fame and show business fortune. He never said so, but gossip in the clubs between Twelfth Street and Eighteenth Street held that only a woman could have derailed his monstrous talent from its inevitable success, though the Sugarman never did marry or have any children of his own. So he settled into a regular job as janitor at the Old O'Reilly Candy Factory Building, where he applied the same self-discipline and focus as he had on his rigorous saxophone practice routine. And though he abandoned music as a career, he harbored safe his passion for jazz and regularly made the stage at the Sunset, the Subway and the Reno nightclubs for their legendary all night cutting sessions, trading riffs with the likes of Lester Young, Coleman Hawkins, Ben Webster, Herschel Evans, Chu Berry, Budd Johnson, and Buddy Tate and holding his own. It was a passion that burned throughout his life.

The O'Reilly Candy Company was a regional enterprise whose chocolate confections were a favorite in ranching and farming communities throughout the Great Plains states. The family run business, founded in the wake of the 1893 World's Columbian Exhibition in Chicago, had survived World War I and the Great Depression. It was an unsung hero of World War II when much of its production capacity was commandeered to support Hershey's output of D Rations for the troops. What the company could not survive was its own sales success with a candy bar consisting of nougat, peanuts and caramel covered with a chocolate coating, which noticeably eroded the sales figures of the Mars *Snickers* bar in the Wichita, Oklahoma City, Omaha, Sioux City, and Denver markets in the years of the post war baby boom. The O'Reilly family finally received an offer they simply could not refuse and after nearly seventy years in business, confection production ceased. It was just at that time an upstart defense contractor was in desperate need of more space as it rapidly outgrew the second floor of a shoppette above a Rexall Drug Store, Lucky Pierre's Beauty Salon and Vernon's Bait and Tackle Shop, in Raytown, Missouri.

It was no accident that Y.T., Sr. acquired the Old O'Reilly Candy Factory Building and kept on one and only one employee: Homer McKinley Morganfield. After her husband's suicide and New York state probate court's thorough picking of the carrion of his estate, Anna Elise Erp returned to Meadowlawns penniless and exiled from the Cassidy family fortune, thanks to her brother's spiteful nature, so she was forced to find gainful employment boxing confections eight, sometimes ten or twelve hours a day. During those overtime sessions, inevitably in the weeks leading up to Valentine's Day, Easter, Halloween and Christmas, Y.T., Sr. sat in the Sugarman's workshop doing his homework or followed the janitor through the building learning more about metalworking, woodworking, electronics, pneumatics, hydraulics and engine mechanics than he ever would in high school shop class or a college engineering program. Not many realized it or even gave it much thought, but Y.T., Sr., was second only to the Sugarman in intimate knowledge of the building that once sheltered him and his mother from the Great Depression and was now home to his business. Even more important than an apprenticeship in the practical arts, the time the Sugarman spent with Y.T., Sr. helped to fill that paternal void left by the stock market crash of 1929.

The sudden appearance of a new executive office, the construction of which the Sugarman supervised personally each day between Christmas and New Year's, sent a shudder through those who aspired to become the "Old Man" and filled them with alarm that, perhaps, an unfamiliar interloper had somehow unfairly leap-frogged over them all to become the heir apparent to Y.T., Sr.

But the person who was always third to arrive at the Old O'Reilly Candy Factory Building, P. Peckerfelt, remained totally unaware of the newly constructed executive office, because he always stealthily entered the building through the loading dock man door. He scurried as hurriedly as he exited the Junior Misses Department at Sears, Roebuck and Company to his cramped and cluttered office at the very center of the manufacturing floor, where unfamiliar noises, noxious odors and imminent dangers usually discouraged all but the most recalcitrant visitors. There in the hours before the avalanche of distractions began with the start of the workday for the hourly employees, P. Peckerfelt reviewed sales orders, work orders, inventories, work-in-process and finished goods waiting to ship to chart the metamorphosis of United States government policies into private sector bank deposits. P. Peckerfelt knew, like a steamboat pilot on the Mississippi, that every day the river channel of commerce, changes and today's journey is always different from the day before, as will be tomorrow's. It was his special talent to be able to successfully triage the sometimes hourly manufacturing emergencies and crises to navigate product out the door in order to move greenbacks into the Erp Industries, Inc. bank account. Living a life totally "overcome by events" left little time for aspirations to greater glory, like, for example, becoming the "Old Man." P. Peckerfelt's constant wish was only to be like Custer's horse, getting out of that day's battle alive to fight another day. Therefore, he took little if any notice of the remodeling that was as far removed from his world as the moon from Cape Kennedy.

Simon Salisbury prided himself on being the first Erp Industries employee through the front door—at least on those days that either he or Mort Mortenstein piloted the car pool from their suburban sanctuaries to the Old O'Reilly Candy Factory Building.

"One out of three gets you into Cooperstown," consoled Mort Mortenstein on those days that Hugh Betcha inevitably delivered them to their labors sometime between eight and eight-thirty, after stopping at The Donut Hut for a pre-breakfast snack to hold him over until he was able to get to Arlotta McGurdy's cafeteria line for an "Early Bird" special to take back to his office to consume, all the while distributing bits and pieces of it onto the paperwork that passed across his desk that morning, much to the aggravation of the supplier salesmen who received his food and coffee stained purchase orders.

On January 2, 1968, though, Simon Salisbury delivered the Car Pool to the Erp Industries parking lot precisely at seven AM. He glided easily into his reserved spot strategically located in between Mort Mortenstein's and Hugh Betcha's posts, which assured that the doors on his ivory-colored Buick *Riviera* remained ding-free. As usual, Mort Mortenstein, not really caring who got there first, held the front door open for his vain partner and followed him into the front lobby. As they passed the reception desk and entered into the Erp Industries inner sanctum, they were brought up short by the sight of the new executive office. Suddenly, the promise of empty resolutions made so recently evaporated as they stood confronted with a direct threat to their career ambitions on the very first working day of the new year.

Hugh Betcha, oblivious to all but the aromas emanating from Arlotta McGurdy's steam table, pushed between the pudgy accountant and prissy personnel director, in that stiff-legged, middle-aged lumbering gate which was the legacy a high school and college grid iron career left on his knees and plowed on towards the cafeteria line.

Simon Salisbury noted that the office was well-appointed, though in a generic fashion. The huge mahogany desk was completely devoid of any wood pulp products, save for an in-box with a single solitary sheet of paper in it—no doubt, Y.T., Sr.'s Memo for 1968. Family pictures decorated the credenza, though the faces of the woman and two children were so extremely nondescript, it was impossible to determine if the photo actually came from the store with the frame. Pictures hung on the wall that betrayed an interest in outdoor activities—pursuits completely foreign to Simon Salisbury—fishing or hunting, perhaps, but in no place in particular for no quarry specifically that he could discern. The lights were already on, ready for the work day, yet the overstuffed desk chair remained pushed completely beneath the desk. The phone was silent. The shades were open to view the long rolling hills in front of the Old O'Reilly Candy Factory Building, leading down to the containment pond near Meadowlawns Road, which was formerly known as County Road M. It was a view that all envied and despaired of ever having until their ascension to the "Old Man's" office.

The name plate on the door said "Melvin W. Vapors." Outside was a secretary desk, which would be manned every day of the week from 8 am to 5 pm by a different Kelly Girl, who, of course, had never met or even seen Melvin W. Vapors and had no idea what his position was within the organization nor how his responsibilities contributed to the bottom line of the business. But certainly, the proximity of this new office to the front door and the flag pole out front flying *Old Glory* portended a vested power that stoked the embers of envy throughout the executive ranks of Erp Industries, Inc.

Simon Salisbury had never met Melvin W. Vapors and had no idea who he was, even though that name had mysteriously just appeared on *The Memo's* distribution list the previous year and on the Erp Industries, Inc., payroll reports. One day, a razor thin personnel file on Melvin W. Vapors had been delivered to his desk in an inner-company envelope without any sender information on it by Y.T., Jr. during his job rotation in Dirk Rangely's Marketing Department the past summer. The manila folder contained neither a resume nor job application—only a social security number and a post office box address—but Simon Salisbury knew better than to attempt to interrogate Y.T., Jr. about it, and promptly filed it away.

Simon Salisbury and Mort Mortenstein skulked directly back to their own smaller and less lavishly appointed offices to start the New Year under an overcast of doubt and insecurity. Mort Mortenstein searched the Accounting Department in vain for the existence of any expense report ever filed by Melvin W. Vapors. Simon Salisbury retrieved the thin manila folder that had been delivered by Y.T., Jr. from the file cabinet and stared at its meager contents as if they held the key to the corporate management power play evidently unfolding around them.

Rolf Guderian looked up from the floor plans of the Old O'Reilly Candy Factory Building spread out on his desk with dripping contempt at Vasili Ivanovich, who was absorbed in some ridiculous engineering exercise at his horrifically cluttered table that was not even a proper office desk. Rolf Guderian was correct in assuming that the mad Russian was completely unaware of the not-so-subtle shift in the winds of corporate war that had just occurred even though he had spent nearly every day at work over the Christmas holiday shutdown sliding his slide rules and scribbling out his calculations as the noise of saws and hammers could be heard coming from up the hallway leading towards the Big Office. Just as he had during World War II, Vasili Ivanovich would be swept away by the ambitions of greater men. Of course, Rolf Guderian had been there every day during the shutdown, too, as the ingrained habits of a loyal Nazi prison guard die hard. Besides, he could never let Vasili Ivanovich out of his sight, lest his "meal ticket" somehow escape his clutches.

Whoever this Melvin W. Vapors person was, he had executed what appeared to be a brilliant tactical move, much like Operation Market Garden, parachuting into the heart of Erp Industries, Inc., to take and hold a strategic position. Rolf Guderian was determined to thwart it, though, just as the Wehrmacht had done to Bernard Montgomery's plans during the closing days of World War II in the Battle of Arnhem when the British general reached for a "bridge too far." But how? That was the question nagging the noggin of the greasy little Nazi as he poured over the floor plans of the theater of battle. He considered a panzer blitz through the "lowlands" of the Accounting Department; but, numbers and mathematics not being Rolf Guderian's strong suit, he despaired that without an alliance with Vasili Ivanovich he could never prevail over Mort Mortenstein—and, unfortunately, the mad Russian cared not a whit for any calculations which involved dollar signs. The big office remained as remote and tempting a target as was the United States to Adolf Hitler, separated as they were by the Atlantic Ocean.

As Rolf Guderian snidely wondered what in the world could have been so important—even more important than the sudden appearance of Melvin W. Vapors or his new office—to Vasili Ivanovich that he had not only spent precious days off working through the holidays, but would be even more distracted and more disconnected from the empirical world around him than usual, the Russian mad scientist poured through the drawings and schematics of the inner workings of Grumman's Lunar Excursion Module in quiet desperation to insure that the Erp Industries, Inc. black boxes contained deep within its guts would operate precisely as he had designed them during the vehicle's first test flight in low earth orbit when the Saturn 1B rocket launched NASA's Apollo 5 mission into space in less than three weeks. At precisely eight o'clock, Rolf Guderian shook his head in disdain and rolled up the floor plans of the great battle to come.

As the trickle of workers into the Old O'Reilly Candy Factory Building grew into a stream, the building came alive with sights seen, sounds heard, smells sniffed and vibrations felt since the dawn of the Industrial Revolution. Individual thoughts, feelings and aspirations became suppressed as the engine of commerce accelerated and workers settled into their normal daily routines. When Vasili Ivanovich's secretary excused herself from her post for the usual morning coffee break, Rolf Guderian, like a Pavlovian dog, rose and followed her to the cafeteria, finding a seat at a remote table that afforded him an unobstructed view of the beautiful redhead, where he stoked his fantasies until joined by Adolf Himmlerlicht and Herman Eichmanhoff to hold their council of war.

Scarlett Angelina Brookings sat alone on the first day back at work with a cup of coffee, remembering the summer mornings with Y.T., Jr. at her Kirke Gardens apartment that seemed so long ago and far away after only four months, wondering vaguely what was happening. He had not returned to Meadowlawns from the University of California for the Christmas holidays and she had not seen him since he left for the fall semester last September. She had written him without reply and, while his lack of response was not unusual, the strange emptiness she felt at his absence was new and unprecedented for her. She had spent many holidays alone and actually preferred it that way rather than endure the company of men chosen for her by Wilson Cassidy. Now, though, an unfamiliar loneliness haunted her. She felt a vague, unsettling premonition that Y.T., Jr. somehow warranted her worry. And, for the first time since high school, she wondered what the future might hold for her and if she could dare to dream of a new and different life for herself.

In the hallway outside the cafeteria, Scarlett Brookings noticed Y.T., Sr. charging by, followed by Frik and Frak, no doubt on their way to the airport to fly off to an important business meeting. Their eyes met. Y.T., Sr., slowed his pace ever so slightly, but enough that the ex-Navy Commander noticed the narrowing gap between them, as well as the warm smile of the gorgeous redhead as she followed them with her eyes.

Barry Boswagger scanned the Erp Industries workers like a predator as they herded themselves into the cafeteria for the morning coffee break. He waited patiently for Arlotta McGurdy to verify the contents of his delivery of Cassidy beef cuts and ground chuck for the week's planned menu. He searched for Y.T., Jr., but knew it was futile. Arlotta McGurdy told him that the boss's son had not come back from college for the Christmas break, and so Barry Boswagger would have to bide his time to do what he misinterpreted was Wilson Cassidy's will. Arlotta McGurdy was nothing if she was not thorough, careful and conscientious, especially when it involved spending Y.T., Sr.'s money. Barry Boswagger did not mind, though, because it gave him repeated opportunities to linger, to surveil and to plot, without being noticed, except by the keen eye of a seasoned Ozark backwoods hunter and moonshiner, Orley Bovine, who sensed danger in the hungry look of the Cassidy Beef Packing Company's route man. As Barry Boswagger scanned the cafeteria, his gaze landed upon

Scarlett Angelina Brookings, sitting alone, peering down into the steam rising from a cup of coffee. Something about her expression reminded Barry Boswagger of his sad, chronically depressed wife, Rebecca Sue Simmons, whose psyche had been weighted down and broken by the shame of her "involvement" with Y.T., Jr. and subsequent miscarriage. It steeled his resolve to exact his—and Wilson Cassidy's—revenge.

Scarlett Angelina Brookings was not the only one wondering about Y.T., Jr. In the days, weeks and months following the surprisingly and alarmingly huge Moratorium war protest on the Washington Mall that past October, J. Edgar Hoover sprang into action, assigning teams of technical analysts to pour over every photo taken and every frame of news reel film footage shot of the event to figure out exactly what was going on and exactly who was involved. No one was going to get away with attacking the United States and destroying government property on his watch—even if it was just portable shit houses. A bomb was serious business to the Federal Bureau of Investigation, whether in the hands of Russian KGB agents or college students, so as forensic scientists examined every sliver of wood and fleck of feces from the blast zone near the Pentagon, surveillance teams were dispatched from their field offices to college campuses across the fruited plains, from sea to shining sea, especially places like Columbia University, Michigan University and the University of California at Berkeley, which seemed to be the spawning grounds for the latest existential threat to the security and welfare of the greatest nation on earth.

While the piles of file folders and field reports at F.B.I. headquarters grew exponentially to the Director's great satisfaction, the Secret Service was spinning its wheels trying to identify and locate two suspected assassins who had approached the White

House on a motorcycle, brandishing weapons in what could only have been a daring, but ultimately futile daylight attempt on the life of President Lyndon Baines Johnson. Of course, J. Edgar Hoover already knew it was, in fact, Y.T., Jr. and Clinton A. Owsley III in Lafayette Park on a Harley-Davidson that day. But knowledge being power and the Director being a man loath to share not only his Congressionally authorized, but clandestine extra-Constitutionally acquired power, J. Edgar Hoover kept that information to himself and let his fellow federal colleagues flounder in their ignorance, pursuing false leads and imaginary conspiracies in a law enforcement snipe hunt. Well-timed sharing of disingenuous excerpts from select reports would be enough to keep them out of the way of the F.B.I.'s own, more critical investigation, the results of which, of course, would redound to the Director's own credit, legend and, of course, power.

Within twenty-four hours of the events of October 21, 1967, the F.B.I.'s sensitive spider web of agents, informants and co-opted local law enforcement officers located Y.T., Jr. and Clinton A. Owsley III crossing the Delaware River near Wilmington, heading north. Special Agents Williams and Walters were dispatched immediately and raced north bound in their nondescript Plymouth sedan, willfully violating all speed limits, to resume their surveillance of the *Triumvirate* brain trust, authorized and prepared to affect an arrest if the pair came too close to the Canadian border. They caught up with Y.T., Jr. and Clinton A. Owsley III just as they entered Bear Mountain State Park north of New York City and assumed an all too familiar position in trail of the Harley-Davidson, which they had grown weary of over the thousands of miles traveled, logged and accounted for on their Bureau expense reports. The beauty of Bear Mountain Park was lost completely on

Special Agent Williams who drove that shift, attentive only to the need for maintaining contact with the target vehicle without revealing their presence to the driver and passenger. Special Agent Walters took in the scenery, though only in search of further clues to the conspiracy or threats to the investigation thereof.

The report of Special Agents Walters and Williams detailed the visit of Y.T., Jr. and Clinton A. Owsley III to an estate in Millbrook, New York, owned by the heirs to the fortune of the former Treasury Secretary for Presidents Warren G. Harding, Calvin Coolidge and Herbert Hoover: Andrew Mellon. The mansion was very familiar to local, state and federal law enforcement, thanks to the diligent work of a former Bureau Supervisor, now an assistant district attorney, G. Gordon Liddy, who had broken up Timothy Leary's so-called "League of Spiritual Awareness", which was deemed a flimsy cover for endless LSD fueled parties, epiphanies, breakdowns and emotional dramas of all sizes, shapes and noise levels. What Walters and Williams missed in their observations and their report failed to detail was that Y.T., Jr. had brought his friend to Millbrook to help him re-establish some measure of mental balance and ultimately banish any thoughts of presidential assassination from his addled mind with the help of the Harvard psychologist who had become the media ordained psychedelic guru for the "tune in, turn on and drop out" generation. Unfortunately, Timothy Leary had fled Millbrook to escape the harassment of G. Gordon Liddy and was just then in Hollywood to prepare for his upcoming nuptials. So Y.T., Jr. and Clinton A. Owsley III mounted up and pointed the Harley-Davidson west towards California.

Special Agents Walters and Williams dogged the two students back to the University of California at Berkeley, faithfully reporting their progress back to Washington, D.C., every night via the teletype machine at the local F.B.I. field offices along the way, detailing the address, arrival time and departure time at each college campus where the duo overnighted, trading Clinton A. Owsley III's laboratory grade LSD to indigenous students for a meal and a place to sleep for the night. Local field agents would later follow up on profiling those generous campus natives and investigating their tribal rituals at the addresses provided, but for now information on those impromptu way stations at Penn State, Antioch College, Washington University, the University of Kansas, and University of Colorado, where Y.T., Jr. and Clinton A. Owsley III stopped to rest on their way back to Berkeley waited patiently in manila folders in Washington, D.C., awaiting assignment for further bureaucratic action.

While numbingly mundane in a narrative sense, the overwhelming number of factual dots added to the official file of the *Triumvirate* by Special Agents Walters and Williams was a rich fodder for the analysts and profilers back at Headquarters, who tirelessly connected, disconnected, then reconnected the dots between Timothy Leary and Purple Owsleys, between the Free Speech Movement in Berkeley and Marty Keegan at Columbia, between a San Francisco massage parlor operation and government defense contracts, between a Kansas City meat company and America's race for the moon, between Learjets and Harley-Davidsons, between a red-headed courtesan and a Chinese-American prostitute, between a former Navy Lieutenant and the former Senator of Georgia, between a high school cheerleader and the leader of a radical group bent on the destruction of the United States of America.

"Hello?" Penelope Xing queried hesitantly into the darkness of her room on the fifth floor of Fu Loin's emporium. A heavy breathing answered. "Hello? Who's there?"

There was no ticket for her when she had gotten back to Fu Loin's signifying a waiting client to service. There should not have been anyone there in the room, but the heavy breathing was unmistakable. She had no weapon, just history text books, spiral notebooks and several Bic pens. She backed out of the room to scan the hallway for assistance from a co-worker, but the fifth floor hall was quiet and empty. The lamp was deep in the room, so she slowly opened the door to allow the dim light of the hallway to spill into her room. She could not see anyone, but there on the dresser was a box of Twinkies, the sight of which made her sigh with relief, then smile to herself.

Penelope Xing entered the room and, without turning on the lights, undressed and slipped between the sheets to slide next to Y.T., Jr., who, exhausted from his transcontinental journey, barely stirred. Pressed together, the warmth of his body radiated to embrace her and for the first time in many months, Penelope Xing felt happy and safe, though completely unaware she was just then under the ever watchful eyes of J. Edgar Hoover's minions.

Dirk Rangely returned to work in mid-January after rolling the Christmas break into a personal vacation, followed by an overseas business trip, timed to bring him back to the Old O'Reilly Candy Factory Building well after the dust from the Old Man's annual Memo had settled and corporate life had, hopefully, gotten back to normal. He breezed through the lobby and came face-to-face with Melvin Vapors's empty new office and a clueless Kelly Girl who did not know who Melvin Vapors was, nor even who Dirk Rangely was. He looked past the Kelly Girl to absorb the alarming splendor of Melvin Vapors's office, then shuffled back to the Marketing Department to lock himself in his office to stew. Finally, he buzzed Jo Ann to bring him a tape measure to determine once and for all whose desk was larger: his or Melvin Vapors's.

In Dirk Rangely's in-box was *The Memo.* Of course, like all the others, the image of that corporate correspondence would never stain his retinas.

M E M O R A N D U M

January 2, 1968

TO: ALL DEPARTMENT HEADS
FM: Y.T. ERP, SR.

"Set your course by the stars, not by the lights of every passing ship."

~Omar N. Bradley, General of the Army

Sincerely,

Y.T. ERP, SR., PRESIDENT
ERP INDUSTRIES, INC.

YTE/www

~~~

The Cruelest Month

"Hey—*Hey! Wake up,*" Poncho whispered urgently through his gritted teeth.

Billy Saul Sawyer roused himself and popped his eyes open to see Poncho's camouflaged-painted face nose-to-nose with him.

"Quiet, man. Quiet," Poncho hissed. "Be cool. Be cool, man."

"Yeah...yeah," Billy Saul Sawyer exhaled. He closed his eyes again and listened to the jungle. "What time is it?"

"Zero Dark thirty."

"Duh."

"A couple of hours till dawn."

Billy Saul Sawyer nodded. He opened his eyes and Poncho was still nose-to-nose with him.

"Again?" Billy Saul Sawyer's spotter had seen it before. Sometimes the nightmares were even worse. Back in the bunker on base, it didn't matter with all the noise from bombs, artillery shells and aircraft arriving and departing, so he usually let his fellow Marine thrash it out in the hope that, like a fever, the shakes and sweats would purge his partner of the demons infecting his soul—whatever they were. There in the jungle, though, staring across the border into Laos, waiting for enemy movement on a pathetic dirt path which was a capillary in the Ho

Chi Minh Trail, it could mean an untimely end to their tour of duty.

"Yeah, you know," Billy Saul Sawyer said with a shrug of the shoulders. "Catch a nap?"

"Sure. Okay." Poncho backed off as Billy Saul Sawyer sat up. He smiled and patted him quietly on the shoulder. Poncho laid back and pulled his jungle hat over his eyes.

"Sleep tight. Don't let the jungle bugs bite," whispered Billy Saul Sawyer, echoing the words his mother so often whispered in his ear at night when she put him to bed as a child. He rubbed his eyes, then peered through the Starlite scope. The near full moon helped make the view of the dirt path amazingly clear through the scope. The trail was empty. He closed his eyes and listened, but all he heard was "injun country" without any injuns. Yet. So, he waited patiently watching for his prey and working hard not to think about his nightmares.

As the Continental Airlines jet had descended through ten thousand feet on approach to Saigon's Tan Son Nhut airport, the humidity of Southeast Asia reached up from below to smother Billy Saul Sawyer in a warm embrace that welcomed him back to the war. Having slept fitfully since October, haunted by the memories of his sniper rifle's cross-hairs marking center mass of his best friend's body and a stranger in his ear urging him frantically to pull the trigger, the familiarly uncomfortable swelter of Vietnam had a somewhat soothing effect. Here, the lines between friends and enemies were more clearly drawn and there would be few, if any, moral dilemmas like the one on top of the Treasury Department Building in Washington, D.C., to face, having to decide between duty and friendship, love and orders. Feeling, ironically, as if he were back home again, though ten thousand miles from his family's farm, Billy Saul Sawyer was finally able to relax and napped on the Southern Air Transport flight to the Marine base at Da Nang, where he was processed in-country, armed, then waited for the weather to clear so he could board a CH-46 *Phrog* helicopter which would take him even further north to join the Third Marine Amphibious Force at the Khe Sanh Combat Base.

At Khe Sanh he met Poncho, his spotter, who was not Latino, but a short, stocky, red-haired corporal from Boston who had gotten his nickname from a wrestling match he lost with his rain gear during boot camp. Poncho might as well have been Puerto Rican, though, as Billy Saul Sawyer could still barely understand his New England accent after five months together. The Mutt-and-Jeff couple blindly accepted the wisdom of the Marine Corps pairing them up and began attaching themselves to regular patrols to get Billy Saul Sawyer oriented to the geography beyond the protective berms and barbed wire surrounding the base. Poncho's previous sniper partner had notched his short-timer's stick one last time eight months before Poncho's tour was up, so he accepted his new teammate and helped speed the FNG through his orientation. It wasn't long before Poncho and Billy Saul Sawyer were separating themselves from the outgoing patrols to get themselves in position to guard against and disrupt the routine night-time infiltration attempts by the North Vietnamese Army and the Viet Cong. The sudden crack of his Winchester Model 70 rifle, occasionally heard on quiet nights, would bring comfort to his fellow Marines, who tried to rest and sleep, all the while dreading the next enemy sapper attack on the base during the siege by the North Vietnamese Army.

Billy Saul Sawyer preferred the sniper's way of war to the carpet bombing of the Air Force from twenty thousand feet or mob style air assaults in a gaggle of UH-1 Huey helicopters like in his first tour. Although it was just him and Poncho out there in injun country on their own with little practical chance for the cavalry or the Air Force to ride to their rescue if they were ever discovered and surrounded, it afforded a more personal touch to the anonymity of war. Engagements involving hundreds or even thousands of troops spread out over acres and acres of land inevitably meant that a soldier's victory or death were surrendered to the group dynamic. Casualties were less the result of deliberate individual action than random occurrences of fate incidental to the battle—mostly soldiers getting caught in the wrong place at the wrong time in fields of fire laid out by officers at planning tables far removed from the smell of gunpowder.

After only two months, Billy Saul Sawyer, like other snipers, had come to have a bounty put on his head by the North Vietnamese. These bounties only grew in size as the weeks dragged on and he ranged further and further beyond the perimeter, moving more from defense to offense and racking up higher value kills of enemy officers, rather than just low level recruits trying to place bombs around the camp. The sniper team ranged further and further west, setting up their long range ambushes closer and closer to the Ho Chi Minh trail to harass and disrupt the flow of war matériel into South Vietnam. It was a morale buster for the NVA when the Charlie in front or behind you, pushing a bicycle stacked full of rifle cartridges or mortar shells silently crumpled into a heap, dead from Billy Saul Sawyer's 30-06 bullet expertly placed from hundreds of yards away. If an officer fell, then so much the better.

Billy Saul Sawyer and Poncho preferred the time they spent outside the wire. Although dangerous and sometimes nerve-racking, it was still much calmer than the beehive of activity at the base, with helicopters and C-130 transports coming and going amidst the inbound and outbound artillery shells and, at night, sudden explosions and eruptions of small arms fire from enemy patrols probing the perimeter. Khe Sanh did have hot food and sometimes cold beer—depending on the state of generators, refrigeration space and the ingenuity of supply sergeants—as well as bedding in covered bunkers, though that sheet of corrugated metal forming the roof to keep the rain off could suddenly be launched airborne from a randomly placed mortar shell and cut a man's body clean in half. Billy Saul Sawyer had seen that happen. So, while rest and sleep were technically possible, the Khe Sanh Combat Base was not a very relaxing place, especially as the North Vietnamese siege of the Marines intensified during the Tet Offensive of 1968.

In the jungle, it was quieter. It had its own noises and its own tempos, much less frantic than that of the war machine of the most powerful country on earth shifted into high gear. During downtimes when they camped off-base, Billy Saul Sawyer had quiet time to think and reflect. He and Poncho traded whispers about Boston and Kansas City, about the *Red Sox* and the *Chiefs*, about the trials and tribulations of high school, about the relative intelligence of the chain of command from Washington, D.C., on down to General Westmoreland and his minions, and about girls, love, sex and getting back home—though on the last subject Billy Saul Sawyer listened more than he talked as Poncho spoke of his hopes and dreams for the future with his girlfriend, Anna. The time in the jungle with Poncho made Billy Saul Sawyer remember those nights on Boot Hill, when he, Y.T., Jr. and Marty Keegan merrily desecrated the graves of the Wilson family's dearly departed in the middle of the night.

Billy Saul Sawyer put his concentration on their mission on pause for a moment to listen to his fellow Marine breathe softly in slumber beside him and absorbed the comfortable familiarity of friendship there in the jungle with Poncho. He savored the rare moment of personal connection and human intimacy as he waited to kill the enemy.

Although minutes could seem interminably long, time never did stop and daylight always came. It was their fourth day out. Billy Saul Sawyer and Poncho took turns watching a trail in Laos from an anonymous hilltop in South Vietnam, waiting for any signs of movement on one of the innumerable footpaths which comprised the Ho Chi Minh Trail. The humid air seemed to blanket the jungle. Morning drifted into afternoon and Billy Saul Sawyer lay on his back, peering into the sky, wishing they did not have to return to Khe Sanh that night. What was the point? There would not be any mail waiting for him, just debrief interviews and paperwork. He wondered where Y.T., Jr. was at that very moment. The last time he had seen his friend was through his rifle scope, driving away on his Harley. But then Billy Saul Sawyer realized he wasn't sure exactly what day of the week it was and what time it might be halfway around the earth, "back in the world." He looked over at Poncho, awake, fed and alert, staring at the dirt scar on the hillside a thousand yards away, made by millions of determined footsteps over the years, decades, perhaps centuries. Funny, how you can know a person, without having to know them at all. He closed his eyes and fought back the memories from the top of the Treasury Department Building in Washington, D.C.

Poncho wordlessly nudged Billy Saul Sawyer, who rolled and got back on his rifle scope for a shot. There was a barely perceptible change in the jungle sounds. Billy Saul Sawyer saw the glint flash in the far away jungle and reflexively fired before it disappeared. He was sure it was a reflection off the scope of the NVA sniper that had been hunting them for the past few weeks as they patrolled the border area.

"Whaddaya think?" asked Billy Saul Sawyer of his spotter. "Maybe I at least got close enough to scare him and shit his pajamas."

Poncho did not answer.

Billy Saul Sawyer looked over at his spotter, expecting a smart ass reply, but he was dead, shot in the head through his spotter's scope by the enemy sniper. Billy Saul Sawyer had not heard the enemy sniper's rifle fire.

Billy Saul Sawyer pressed his forehead against his Winchester's stock and tearlessly wept for a moment. Then he got a line of sight through his scope to where he had fired on the enemy sniper and plotted the location on his map. It took him nearly two hours to find that spot and when he did, he found the enemy sniper who killed his friend dead with a bullet hole in his neck, piercing the carotid artery, causing him to bleed to death. Billy Saul Sawyer spat on the enemy, hefted his pack, looked back towards Khe Sanh, then turned and moved deeper into Laos. He had no interest in returning to the chaos of the combat base. He had lost all interest in making war for Washington politicians—the ones who wanted him to kill Y.T., Jr. and now, through all their planning and scheming, had gotten Poncho shot dead. He would exact his own revenge for the death of this friend. He would write his own rules of engagement. He would create his own target list. He would wage war within his own borders, boundaries and theaters of war.

Though officially listed as Missing in Action, Billy Saul Sawyer had not gone AWOL from the war.

Anna Elise Erp sat on the back patio in her over-sized wicker chair with the over-stuffed cushions gazing upon the bursts of color blooming in her carefully cultivated garden. She sipped coffee, soaking in the welcome warmth of spring, as she waited for the Sugarman to deliver bags of mulch for splitting her bellflowers and astors, as well as some new annual plantings she had planned.

The modest flower beds that decorated the fringes of her son's house, like colorful frosting on the edges of a cake, began to spread into a maternal void left when Y.T., Jr. entered his teen years and increasingly exerted his independence. By her grandson's junior year at Harry S. Truman High School, much of the backyard expanse of Kentucky bluegrass had yielded to a cottage garden with an *ad hoc* collection of horticultural scenes and rooms connected by narrow pathways and accented with field boulders, rock walls, and landscaping timbers hefted or wheelbarrowed into place by the Sugarman, most often with the help of Y.T., Jr. and his friends, though sometimes with his father, when he was home from his business travels.

Such a garden would have been a decadent indulgence during those years when she worked at the O'Reilly Candy Factory struggling just to make ends meet. Though she dreamed of just having even a modest house again with a yard where her son could play, no doubt like her nephew Wilson Cassidy enjoyed, it did not happen until Y.T., Sr. moved his business to Meadowlawns and built his luxurious home with a mother-in-law suite, so she could help her son raise a motherless child.

Her eyes were drawn to a solitary Japanese cherry tree that stood isolated in a far back corner of the property. It was the only planting that Y.T., Sr. had ever contributed to the landscaping at his home. She never touched or tended to that one tree and, though her son studiously avoided its glorious annual blossoming, he often gazed in deep contemplation upon its dark green leaves or empty branches throughout the rest of the year. It had grown from a cutting off a tree on the edge of the Tidal Basin in Washington, D.C., that had been originally planted in 1912, a gift from the mayor of Tokyo to people of the United States. The tree had matured to flower beautifully every spring in his Meadowlawns backyard as a reminder to Y.T., Sr. of a long ago April cruelty, when Senator Thurman Troyer had his daughter forcibly returned to Ilium, Georgia, to put an end to her scandalous affair with a scoundrel masquerading as an officer and supposed gentleman in the United States Navy before there was any permanent damage to his daughter or his political career. Unbeknownst to all but Helen Troyer, her father was too late, as she had recently become pregnant with Y.T., Jr.

"Cherry blossom time," said the Sugarman as he watched Anna Elise gaze upon the cherry tree. He dropped the bag of mulch from his shoulder.

"Yes, Homer," sighed Anna Elise. "The maiden returns."

The Sugarman removed his work gloves as he moved behind Anna Elise in her wicker chair. He gently placed his hands on her shoulders.

Anna Elise looked up behind her at her friend, lightly patted his hand, then looked back to the cherry tree.

"And a new generation of leaves comes forth," he whispered.

Anna Elise and the Sugarman had never seen Washington, D.C., adorned in the April blossoms of thousands of Sakura. By the time of their one and only visit to the nation's capital together, to confront the senior Senator from the state of Georgia, the petals had long since fallen to the ground and withered.

"Cuba, *SI!* Columbia, *NO!* Cuba, *SI!* Columbia, *NO!* Cuba, *SI!* Columbia, *NO!*" Marty Keegan chanted between puffs as he passed out the Cuban cigars he had pillaged from the office of the President of Columbia University to his fellow protesters. "Hey, David—*Catch!*"

He tossed a cigar across Grayson Kirk's desk to the young radical poet in sunglasses sitting in his office chair behind it.

"Much obliged," said David.

"You look good there on the throne," said Marty Keegan.

David patted himself down for a match. "Got a light?"

"Let me get that for you, comrade."

Marty Keegan walked around the desk and sat on the corner, flipping open and spinning the wheel on the Zippo lighter handed down to him from his grandfather that family tradition mistakenly held was given to A.B. Keegan by Ernest Hemingway before he left the *Kansas City Star* to drive ambulances in Italy. He offered the flame to David, who leaned in to light the cigar.

"Thank you, comrade," said David around a mouthful of cigar as he drew hard on the stogie. "Kind of a soft seat for such a hard ass."

"I'm telling you, it's you. It's really you—maybe you should be in charge of the university."

"Not in a New York minute, pal."

"Yeah, me neither," Marty Keegan sneered, looking back over his shoulder at Mark, J.J. and the other Students for a Democratic Society leaders caucusing behind him to come up with some kind of coherent plan of action, now that they had seized the Low Library administration offices after being evicted from Hamilton

Hall by the Columbia University Student Afro Society who, ironically, didn't want any help from white students and demanded that their protest be properly segregated from the SDS.

"How many are left?" asked Marty Keegan.

"Only about twenty or so. We started with over a hundred."

"Now what?"

"That, my dear sir, is an excellent question." David blew a long, stream of smoke and asked, "I wonder what Fidel would do?"

They puffed on their cigars and pondered on the situation for a moment.

"This cigar sucks," exhaled David.

"Well, mom always said to be careful what you wish for," said Marty Keegan, "'cause you just might get it."

"They seem to be just making shit up as they go along," David said, pointing his cigar at the Steering Committee circle on the other side of the office.

"Yeah. Been there. Done that," said Marty Keegan, recalling the improvised plan to blow up portable bathrooms in Washington, D.C., last fall. "Hell of a way to run a railroad."

"Don't go all Ayn Rand on me, now."

"Perish the thought, my friend." Marty Keegan stood up and waved a fist full of cigars. "If you will excuse me, I've got revolution to spread and, fortunately, it looks like my History class is canceled."

"Thanks for the smoke."

"Cuba, *SI!* Columbia, *NO!* Cuba, *SI!* Columbia, *NO!* Cuba, *SI!* Columbia, *NO!*" Marty Keegan chanted as he went to explore activity in the rest of the executive office suite.

Marty Keegan's participation in the student demonstration quickly devolved into more a matter of curiosity than commitment, a schizoid split between revolutionary and writer. He had joined the protests at the construction site of the Morningside gym that he had proselytized against to the community. When police pushed back on protesters storming the fences to stop construction, he followed the radicals' ricochet back to the campus Sundial, where Mark stood on the granite podium to issue demands and a call for action. Somewhere between clinging to chain link, yelling at the cops, and getting absorbed into a growing crowd that morphed into a riotous mob storming Hamilton Hall like Mongols invading Europe, he began seeing the unfolding events through a journalistic third eye, floating above the scene from within it, gaining the perspective of a sportscaster to the action on the gridiron, watching the plays unfold, offense and defense colliding in a choreographed chaos incomprehensible from the view behind a face mask. He heard himself chant with the others. He saw himself breech the doors of Grayson Kirk's office suite and ransack the file cabinets and desk drawers, seizing a bottle of sherry, some soft core pornography and, of course, Cuban cigars, all the while mentally narrating the play-by-play on the field into the folds and recesses of his gray matter for future use.

The rush of action had been exhilarating like a football game kick off. Afterward, all the SDS committee work of talking, planning and drawing X's and O's on the political chalkboard became downright stupefying, like a post game film session with Coach Sox. The plot line ground to a halt, and endless exposition spewed forth from the protest leaders, so Marty Keegan was left with only a cast of characters to study and amuse himself with their antics, which he did as he wandered through occupied territory, observing, wondering and taking notes, both mental and written, on the collegiate confetti strewn through the offices and hallways, like the letters and memos from Grayson Kirk's correspondence files.

Marty Keegan took Grayson Kirk's bottle of sherry and his cigars, climbed through an open window to the ledge outside the university president's office and sat to smoke, drink and observe the activity on the grounds around Low Library. He pondered the day's events, impressed that the scruffy band of a few hundred radicals had actually brought higher education to a grinding halt in the most powerful country in the world. He made notes to himself in a spiral pad he had liberated from Grayson Kirk's secretary's desk and wondered what the outcome would be.

"Hey! Hey, you up there," came a shout from below.

Marty Keegan looked up from his scribbling, then down to the ground below.

"Yeah, you. On the ledge."

Marty Keegan did not recognize the individual, but was instantly aware he was being accosted by a member of the news media. He furrowed his brow as if in a hall of journalistic mirrors at having tables turned on him, becoming the subject of reporting as he himself pondered the subjects of his own future reporting.

"WABC News." The TV reporter reached up with a microphone. "What's your name?"

"You know," Marty Keegan, shouted back down at the report. "I'm not really —"

"Are you a student at Columbia?"

"Yeah." He nodded and noticed the camera man filming the encounter from several paces behind the reporter.

"What's your name?"

Wary, Marty Keegan answered, "Umm, Luke. Luke Jackson."

"What are you studying?"

"Ah…Evolution, I guess. It seems to be breaking out all around us."

"What do you want?"

"Want?"

"What do you hope to accomplish? Why are you doing this?"

"To win."

"To win what?"

The question totally stumped Marty Keegan. Back at Harry S. Truman High School, Coach Sox had drilled an ethos of winning into his players, but had never spelled out what it really meant to end up with the most points after sixty minutes of highly regulated sports violence. As he pondered that void, Marty Keegan noticed a New York City policeman loitering on a nearby walkway behind the news crew, mindlessly twirling his nightstick like a malevolent yo-yo, propellering it clockwise, catching it, then reversing the motion. The cop's face remained stonily impassive, but his eyes hungrily hunted the scene around Low Library as if for prey. Noticing the interview for the nightly news, the patrolman followed the camera angle up and locked into a stare down with Marty Keegan, cracking a half smile and twirling his nightstick a little bit faster.

"I don't know. Gotta go," Marty Keegan finally answered. He scrambled back inside from the ledge, chased by a vague premonition of mayhem and pain.

Y.T., Sr. leaned on a wall at the shoreline in front of the Jefferson Memorial facing north, looking out over the water. He was confronted with hundreds and hundreds of Japanese cherry trees in full bloom, ringing the Tidal Basin. He hated April in Washington,

D.C., and took great pains to avoid it if at all possible, but based on a brief and cryptic phone call from someone he trusted intimately, he came and now waited. He studied the Washington Monument, just a little less than two hundred feet taller than the Saturn V rocket he had watched earlier that month blast off from Cape Kennedy. The next launch later in the year would carry astronauts for the very first time and Y.T., Sr. momentarily abated in his hatred for cherry blossoms and all they represented to him personally, as he pondered the next step forward in mankind's epic reach for the moon.

Over his shoulder, Y.T., Sr. noticed a naval officer descend the steps of the Jefferson Memorial and pass behind him heading along the path around the Tidal Basin. Y.T., Sr. looked again at the cherry blossoms and reflexively gritted his teeth, then turned to follow the officer.

Admiral Hemmings's son served in the PT Boat service during World War II, a career path that led John F. Kennedy to the Oval Office and the younger Hemmings to a Presidential appointment to Rear Admiral by the former skipper of PT-109. Y.T., Sr. finally met him after VJ Day and their paths casually crossed every so often during their respective careers on opposite sides of the fault line of the Military-Industrial Complex. It had not been hard for Y.T., Sr. to see a trimmer, fitter though somewhat taller version of his former Bureau of Aeronautics commander's squat, stocky, no-neck physique as well as a hereditary echo of the hard-chiseled glare of youthful determination which would weather into his craggy, squint-eyed visage. While Admiral Hemmings the Elder never mentioned the accomplishments of his son, Y.T., Sr. was well aware of and impressed by his service record, as was the U.S. Navy command structure, which consistently filled his personnel jacket with well-earned recommendations for promotion. Admiral Hemmings the Younger understood the invaluable assistance and support Y.T., Sr. provided as his father's right-hand man based in Washington, D.C., during the dark years of World War II, but far beyond respect for that call of duty, there was a brotherly love for the fellow officer turned businessman, who, over the past two decades since World War II, never, ever abandoned the Hemmings ship. Long after his discharge from the Navy and long after Admiral Hemmings the Elder's retirement—far beyond any possible usefulness in furthering the business interests of Erp Industries, Inc.—Y.T., Sr. continued to stay in close contact with his former commander. In letters and the rare phone calls back to Annapolis during his many deployments through the years, Admiral Hemmings the Younger learned of Y.T., Sr.'s visits with his father for lunch, for dinner, for drinks, for golf, for sailing his father's cruising yacht on the Chesapeake Bay, or joy riding in whatever Erp Industries corporate aircraft Y.T., Sr. was piloting at the time. It was much more than the love and respect for a fellow service member. Both Admirals understood and accepted the sacrifices demanded by a Navy career and fully accepted Y.T., Sr. as a full-fledged family member. Admiral Hemmings the Younger never resented Y.T., Sr.'s role as surrogate son, as he brought such great joy to his father and yet never once diminished the love for his natural born son.

Y.T., Sr. unhurriedly closed the gap with the son of his former commander and casually fell into stride beside him as he led the way around the perimeter of the Tidal Basin towards the Potomac River. They walked in a silent element formation.

"Lieutenant," said Rear Admiral Hemmings. "I am glad you came."

"Of course, Admiral. It's good to see you again."

"How long has it been?"

"A few years. I lose track."

They maintained a steady pace around the Tidal Basin.

"I know I do not have to tell you how this town works," Rear Admiral Hemmings said curtly, scanning the horizon to his right.

"No, sir. No, you don't." Y.T., Sr. pushed his hands into his pants pockets. He checked the tops of his shoes, then looked forward down the trail, squinting away sight of the cherry trees.

"It can be a very hazy line between paranoia and security," said Rear Admiral Hemmings. "And in my experience, many bureaucrats do not need a war to get themselves lost in the fog."

They walked twenty yards in silence.

"Is there something I need to be concerned about?" asked Y.T., Sr.

"They seem compelled by their very nature to write reports and generate official paperwork," said Rear Admiral Hemmings. "Most times it ends up being civil service nesting material. But sometimes it can cause people with agendas to start asking questions. And questions tend to make individuals uncomfortable. Uncomfortable individuals are unpredictable."

"Questions?"

"A rather large tributary of paperwork flows through my office covering a rather wide range of subject matter of concern to the Navy, which is generated by a full ladle out of the pot of organizational alphabet soup. A great deal of it is classified. Surprisingly, much of it has some relevance and import to operations, though it might not be all that interesting to the uninitiated. Sometimes, there in the flotsam and jetsam, an item catches your eye."

Y.T., Sr. listened.

"You understand my position here."

"Yes, sir."

"How is your boy doing?"

Rear Admiral Hemmings turned to look at Y.T., Sr. without breaking stride. The only change in his expression was a slight squinting of his right eye.

Y.T., Sr. met his gaze. "He is well, thank you. Going to school in California."

"Yes, Berkeley, isn't it?"

Y.T., Sr. wondered how and why Rear Admiral Hemmings, who he had not seen in several years would know that information, but answered only, "Yes, sir."

"He has a friend in the service, correct?"

"Yes. In the Marines."

"William Sawyer."

Again, Y.T., Sr. wondered about the Admiral's knowledge.

"Were you aware he went M.I.A. in I Corps?"

"No, I had not heard."

The Admiral led Y.T., Sr. onto a trail branching off their path to loop back towards the Jefferson Memorial. They walked a bit in silence.

"What do you think about that nasty business up at Columbia University?" asked Rear Admiral Hemmings nonchalantly.

Another curious change of topic, thought Y.T., Sr. "Frankly, sir, I don't really understand it."

"Nor I. Once the authorities got around to dealing with the situation, though, quite a few heads got cracked."

"I saw pictures in the newspapers. It did seem to get a bit bloody."

"I believe one of them was a friend of your boy."

Y.T., Sr. had to think for a minute. "Keegan? Marty Keegan."

"Yes. Ended up on the business end of a policeman's billy club. It can get nasty if you get sideways with one of New York's finest. Is he all right?"

Y.T., Sr. shrugged his shoulders, unsettled by the direction of their conversation.

"Those in the business of hazy paranoia might take an interest in such things." Rear Admiral Hemmings looked across the Tidal Pool towards Capitol Hill.

Y.T., Sr. slowly nodded his head. "Thank you, sir."

"You have friends in town?"

"Yes."

"Good." They walked a few paces and Rear Admiral Hemmings looked Y.T., Sr. directly in the eye again. "Sadly, it is all too often true that there are some in the organizations we lead who are not on our side."

Y.T., Sr. checked the tops of his shoes again and absorbed that thought.

They had circled back to the Jefferson Memorial. Rear Admiral Hemmings stopped, turned towards Y.T., Sr. and reached out his hand. "I will be leaving here soon for a fleet command in the Pacific."

"Congratulations," said Y.T., Sr., shaking the Admiral's hand.

"You were a very good friend to my father." Rear Admiral Hemmings squeezed Y.T., Sr.'s hand a little tighter.

"He was a great man. I was honored to know him."

"He was quite fond of you."

"Thank you."

"Best of luck to you," said Rear Admiral Hemmings. He abruptly turned and marched towards a government car that suddenly appeared behind him to return to the Pentagon.

Y.T., Sr. watched the Admiral drive away, then slowly turned and walked to the Jefferson Memorial, where Frik studiously ignored the inscriptions of the third President of the United States in favor of the glossy photographs in the latest issue of *Playboy* and Frak stood with arms crossed watching jets jump off the National Airport runways.

An hour later, the Erp Industries, Inc. Learjet leapt off runway one-eight and climbed to flight level two-eight-zero, bound for Meadowlawns, with Y.T., Sr. in the back cabin, lost in thought.

~~~

Subterranean Homesick Blues

All of his carefully laid plans had, somehow, tragically gone awry. He could not figure it out. He believed he had covered all of his bases. He thought he had thought of everything to think of and, yet, here he was: face-to-face with Y.T., Jr., who had miraculously finished his summertime work assignment to reorganize the file cabinets in the Accounting Department in a mere week and a half, instead of the intended three months.

Mort Mortenstein sat behind his desk drumming his fingers nervously on top of his leather-bound journal. He had taken heed of Simon Salisbury's warnings. He had prepared. He had put contingency plans in place. He had done *everything* his Car Pool partner recommended. It should have worked, but Y.T., Jr. had not milked his assignment as any normal employee would have. The Accounting Department had any number of clerks who would have been lucky to complete the assignment by Christmas, let alone Flag Day. It was as if the young man had no notion whatsoever of how to be a normal company employee. Instead, he had just done the work diligently and completed the project in a timely fashion. So, now what?

Y.T., Jr. sat across the desk surveying the office walls, shelves, and assorted furniture tops of the Erp Industries, Inc. Chief Financial Officer. Mort Mortenstein's office was a pathetically impersonal place. Besides the obligatory family photo on the credenza, which unflatteringly documented the diminished stature, expansive waistline, barn door ears and extreme hyperopia encoded in the Mortenstein DNA, there was precious little collectible evidence which would assure any kind of conviction in a court of law, unless the charges were theft of decor from a Holiday Inn. Besides a pipe caddy, a medallion of St. Matthew, a dusty abacus, and a statuette of a caduceus with a winged helmet, a bat and snakes, the only items that reflected on Mort Mortenstein's personality as a unique individual were a walnut plaque on which was mounted one of the Marman clamps used to secure the Fat Man atom bomb in transit before it had been loaded into Frik's Boeing B-29 Superfortress and dropped on Nagasaki to end World War II, and, next to it, a framed, black-and-white publicity photograph autographed by the man who manufactured it, Herbert "Zeppo" Marx, neither of which Y.T., Jr. recognized.

Mort Mortenstein drummed the cover of his journal.

Y.T., Jr. wondered if the contents of Mort Mortenstein's journal recorded all the extracurricular profiteering activities of the Car Pool he was learning about from perusing the Accounting Department invoices, inventory reports and correspondence while moving them from one file cabinet to another. He sighed heavily, wishing he were back home in Berkeley.

They sat that way until eleven-thirty, when Mort Mortenstein deferentially dismissed the Old Man's son for lunch, then carefully recorded this latest corporate misadventure in that day's journal entry. Afterward, he fled to Dante's to meet his Car Pool partners, dreading Simon Salisbury's puckered scowl and Hugh Betcha's garlic laden stream of invective, when they learned of his incompetence.

In the Black

Peering over the seat back through the rear window as he slouched awkwardly down and across the front seat of his 1960 Plymouth *Valiant* parked in the rear lot of Erp Industries, Inc., patiently waiting for his quarry, P. Peckerfelt, to leave for lunch, P.I. Parmakianski observed and duly noted in his spiral flip notebook Scarlett Angelina Brookings idling in her midnight blue MGB *Roadster* at the rear employee entrance. He carefully documented in his childlike block-style printing the date, the time, the weather, the make and model of her car, the car's color, the approximate direction in which the sports car was pointed, the down position of the convertible top and swept up style of Scarlett Angelina Brookings' hairdo—then quickly scratched out all that incriminating information when Y.T., Jr. emerged from the Old O'Reilly Candy Factory Building and climbed into the passenger seat without opening the door. He noticed but, as a professional courtesy, ignored the bland government sedan pulling out and following the *Roadster* as it drove away. He did not notice the canary yellow Chevy *Chevelle* station wagon pull out and follow the bland government sedan following the MGB.

Being Thursday, P.I. Parmakianski was not surprised to see Anna Elise Erp pull in and execute a nine-point three-point turn to reverse direction in her white Cadillac *El Dorado* before the Sugarman emerged from the employee entrance and joined her for their regular weekly lunch at Dante's.

As he waited, he saw Leon Debs with Doug and Ike, his Czechoslovakian charges, loitering on the loading dock. They seemed to be waiting for someone. Leon Debs impatiently paced back and forth, predictably stopping every third circuit to verbally abuse his ever present, over-sized companions, who merely bobbed their heads and smiled moronically. It made P.I.

Parmakianski think of that Warner Brother's cartoon with the big dog and the little dog, until his eye was drawn back to the employee entrance as Dirk Rangely's secretary, Jo Ann, emerged from the Old O'Reilly Candy Factory Building, a bulging, over-sized purse hanging from the crook in her left arm. She coolly scanned the parking lot from behind black Francois Pinton Jackie 1 sunglasses, then walked like a Pan Am stewardess directly over to yet another idling bland government sedan, got in and drove off.

P.I. Parmakianski perked up when Prunella Spoons came out, got into her red Ford *Thunderbird,* a perk courtesy of her settlement from the Missouri State Department of Transportation in honor of her late husband's untimely demise beneath a steam roller, and drove off. It would not be long now, so he started his car. Predictably, P. Peckerfelt came out shortly thereafter and drove off in his two-tone green and white Rambler *American.* P.I. Parmakianski slipped the *Valiant* into gear and followed from a safe distance. He knew they would not be heading to Dante's.

After P.I. Parmakianski pulled away, a black Cadillac pulled up to the Erp Industries, Inc, loading dock and disgorged a long-haired, blue jean-wearing college student, a squat, round man in a nylon AFL-CIO windbreaker and a dark man in a trench coat and fedora who spoke to Doug and Ike in their native Slovak tongue. Leon Debs looked on with incomprehension pooling in his black beady eyes, until a fatted envelope appeared from beneath the trench coat, which he intercepted as it was passed to his comrades. What now passed for a smile after his career as a professional punching bag flashed across his jab deformed face as he pocketed the money, spun on his heels and went back into the

Old O'Reilly Candy Factory Building. After a few concluding instructions from the man in the fedora, Doug and Ike followed after him and the black Cadillac drove off.

Orley Bovine, hidden behind a stack of pallets with a mason jar of moonshine, contemplated the anti-capitalist transaction he had just witnessed and spat.

Secretly, she wished he had come. If only he had come to Chicago on his motorcycle to rescue her and take her away. But he didn't. It took a long time to even admit her own feelings to herself—too long and now the path of her life was setting up like a long, barren stretch of concrete highway through the stark Kansas prairie. It wasn't turning out to be the absolute disaster she had initially resigned herself to, but it certainly wasn't the fun and carefree college life she had expected as the logical and inevitable sequel to a successful social and academic career at Harry S. Truman High School. Instead, she found herself rattling around in a little bungalow in "Birdtown," the older and decidedly downscale residential section of Meadowlawns, where all of the streets were ironically named after American songbirds that could never be heard over the mechanized agony of the nearby scrap yard operation. Barry Boswagger's unexpected promotion at the Cassidy Meat Packing Company had allowed them to escape a roach infested apartment and buy their own little piece of the American dream, but glory, acclaim, social status and future wealth were naught but faded memories for the former homecoming queen and the star quarterback of Harry S. Truman High School *Fighting Eagles.*

Rebecca Sue Simmons and Barry Boswagger settled into the routine of a working class life. Barry Boswagger was up and out of the house at four-thirty in the morning to get his refrigerated truck loaded up to make deliveries of U.S. Standard grade beef products to institutional cafeterias. It was physically demanding work that kept arm and leg muscles previously honed for the grid iron strong, while allowing his formerly trim midsection to begin swelling with unburned calories. After a late afternoon nap and early dinner, he retired to a cramped workshop in the back of the one-car garage where he cared for a growing collection of guns, knives and melee weapons. Some nights he joined his wife on the sofa to lapse into slumber midway through prime time. Other nights he went out, telling Rebecca Sue Simmons he was meeting the boys from work at the Longhorn Tavern for beers, but more often than not, he wandered the night trying to figure out how to faithfully fulfill the misinterpreted expectations of Wilson Cassidy, for which Travis Marbling had handed him the envelope stuffed with so much cash.

Rebecca Sue Simmons' day was sprinkled with household chores, errands and soap opera story lines that never quite filled the long, creeping hours between five o'clock in the morning and three-thirty in the afternoon, when Barry Boswagger usually shuffled through the back door to park his weary bones in the recliner and nod off. This summer had become especially empty as her former *Fighting Eagles* cheerleading squad mates Mindy Covers and Suzie Meanderdil stopped calling and dropping by when they came home for summer vacation, rather herding together elsewhere at unknown watering holes with other Harry S. High alumni, based on the "greener pastures" pursuits they now shared through higher education. There were no social committees, pep rallies and after school clubs for Rebecca Sue Simmons in Birdtown, so she had lately found herself aimlessly driving their used, canary yellow Chevy *Chevelle* station wagon around town. It was during those drives that her long buried feelings about motorcycles, Steak & Shake French fries, and Y.T., Jr., percolated up to her consciousness. As Barry Boswagger snored beside her on the sofa, basked in the glow of the television set, she dwelled more and more on her pre-Chicago life and times and her daytime driving excursions became less and less aimless as Rebecca Sue Simmons began to haunt the places of her past—like the Meadowlawns Steak and Shake and the Harry S. Truman *Fighting Eagles* stadium—and began to stalk Y.T., Jr. home on summer vacation at the Old O'Reilly Candy Factory Building, at Y.T., Sr.'s large, luxury home in the quiet upscale part of Meadowlawns far from the noisy scrap yard and at Scarlett Angelina Brookings's Kirke Gardens apartment.

And so, Rebecca Sue Simmons found herself parked near the crest of Boot Hill one sweltering August night, while Barry Boswagger was at the Meadowlawns Bowl-O-Rama for league night, watching Y.T., Jr. and Marty Keegan drink Budweisers, perched on the grave markers of the Wilson family progenitors.

"The postcards and letters just stopped," said Y.T., Jr. "The last one was like March, I think, so I went by the farm and his dad said that the Navy said he was Missing In Action."

"Fucking war," growled Marty Keegan.

"Yeah," Y.T., Jr. agreed softly, contemplating his father's company's role in supplying black boxes for the American war-making machinery he had learned about last year in the Marketing Department and the blood money profiteering of the Car Pool he had learned about that summer working in Accounting. "His mom's taking it pretty hard."

"Fucking government."

"Yeah."

Y.T., Jr. finished his beer, shook the can to hear the metallic rattle confirming it was empty, then tossed it over his shoulder. He offered another Budweiser to Marty Keegan, studying a new, unfamiliar asymmetry in his friend's face. He opened a fresh beer for himself and dropped the pull tab into the can.

"So, what happened—there?" asked Y.T., Jr., pointing to the left side of his own face, mirroring Marty Keegan's right eye, which appeared half-closed beneath a now drooping eyebrow.

"Fucking pigs."

"What?"

"When they cleared us out and took back the campus."

"You were part of that?"

"Till the bitter end, when they turned loose the bullies in blue with their billy clubs." Marty Keegan traced the scar that ran across the right side of his forehead and down the side of his eye, weighing down his countenance physically and mentally, remembering the slight smile that cracked the stonily impassive glare of the patrolman who rained blows down on him. "It was a righteous beat down."

"You get arrested?"

"Oh, yeah. It was a zoo at the precinct. Yolanda bailed me out the next morning."

"And…"

"Yeah, suspended, too."

"So, now what?"

"Coach Sox always told us that everything is fun and games until you get hurt—then you know it's a real fight," said Marty Keegan.

"Yeah, and?"

"I'm going to Chicago for the Democratic National Convention."

"What for?"

"They have to be stopped. The war has to end. No more Billy Sauls." Marty Keegan's voice trailed off. "No more Billy Sauls."

"How are you going to do that?"

"Hey, LBJ gave it up, didn't he?"

"But—"

"And we brought Kirk to his knees at Columbia. Sometimes blood has to run, to run out the tyrants."

"Yeah, I guess."

"You should come."

Y.T., Jr. took a long drink of his Budweiser.

"Could have been you or me instead of Billy Saul," said Marty Keegan. "We could be next. They're gonna get us. It's got to stop."

"And this is going to stop it?"

"Oh, there's going to be more than just a couple hundred of us this time and this time we'll be ready for them," said Marty Keegan bitterly. He had vowed never to be beaten like an animal again. "Don't need a weatherman to know which way the wind is blowing—and it's blowing towards the windy city."

Y.T., Jr. shook his head.

The conversation between Y.T., Jr. and Marty Keegan was observed by Special Agents Williams and Walters who were parked on the other side of Boot Hill, watching through their binoculars and documenting the undoubtedly nefarious meeting of radicals in the deserted cemetery through their Nikon's telephoto lens. They also dutifully logged the license plate number of a canary yellow *Chevelle* station wagon to be included in the report which would be transmitted back to F.B.I headquarters in Washington, D.C., in the morning, where the fingerprint card of Marty Keegan from his April arrest in New York City was slowly and methodically making its way to the top of the pile for analysts to compare with prints found on pieces of a door from a portable john and what were believed to be fragments of the bomb that exploded near the Pentagon the previous October.

While his wife was stalking Y.T., Jr. on Boot Hill, Barry Boswagger was at the Meadowlawns Bowl-O-Rama for league night, but he was not competing. Instead, he sat sipping bourbon and watching the Ladies Industrial League, as the Erp Industries, Inc. team took on the steno pool from the local Ralston Purina cat food plant. In the long absences of his quarry from Meadowlawns while he was away at the University of California at Berkeley, Barry Boswagger latched his focus onto the stunning red-head he had so often observed to be in the company of Y.T., Jr. in the Erp Industries, Inc. cafeteria, as he delivered slaughtered cattle flesh and bone to Arlotta McGurdy. In his concussion addled mind, courtesy of an aggressive quarterbacking style encouraged by Coach Sox, he had come to believe through hours of sometimes silent, sometimes out loud dialog with himself during his long days of driving, that he could save this young, innocent beauty from destruction at the hands of Y.T., Jr., to, somehow, make up for failing to save Rebecca Sue Simmons in her hour of need. And so, he had begun to stalk Scarlett Angelina Brookings, convincing himself that this, too, was part of Wilson Cassidy's grand scheme, even though, as F.B.I. reports documented, it had been weeks since Y.T., Jr. had been seen at the Kirke Gardens Apartment complex or observed in her company.

"I am very sorry to have troubled you, sir," said P.I. Parmakianski in a hushed tone, as he bent over the chicken paprikash lunch special he had ordered at the West End Grill, dunking the shorter end of his narrow black tie, which was always knotted askew, into the sauce.

"No problem, Julius," said Y.T., Sr., though it was highly unusual for the private detective to initiate contact with him. He drank only coffee. "Eat. Please, before your meal gets cold."

"I didn't know what else to do." P.I. Parmakianski ignored his meal.

"You know you can always come to me," Y.T., Sr. said, knowing that he never had before and normally never would, "when necessary."

"I—I do think, yeah, I think so,"

"Is this about Mr. Peckerfelt?"

"No, sir."

Y.T., Sr. was intrigued. "Who, then?"

"Jo Ann, Mr. Rangely's secretary—"

"Dirk talks a good game, but he would never step over the line."

"Oh, no sir. Mr. Rangely is not involved. No, sir."

"Who, then?"

"I'm not quite sure. But I don't think it is about any kind of, you know, the usual hanky-panky."

"What then?"

"Blackmail."

"Who?"

"You, sir."

Y.T., Sr. and P.I. Parmakianski spent the next ninety minutes reviewing excerpts from his greasy, grimy notebook, blurry black-and-white photographs and photocopied Erp Industries corporate documents as the untouched chicken paprikash coagulated.

"Bullshit," Marty Keegan told himself out loud, walking south towards the Conrad Hilton hotel and thinking of Lord Lytton's adage that "the pen is mightier than the sword," as he and thousands of fellow protesters were chased out of Grant Park with tear gas.

He was ready this time. Like Coach Sox always said, he knew now he was in a real fight, courtesy of the New York City police department that past April, not some polite academic war of words to settle a philosophical or political policy debate—and he literally had the physical scars to prove it. So he had prepared himself—and not by attending the college professor's blackboard planning session for the upper echelon elites of the equality obsessed SDS or by participating in lame revolutionary boot camp activities in Grant's Park, charging back and forth across the greens in half-assed rugby scrums, as if that would be effective in confronting Mayor Daley's thugs. He had armed himself with an improvised black jack made of lead weights, a sweat sock and duct tape, small enough to conceal beneath his jacket, but heavy enough to be lethal.

He already carried the badge of honor of being arrested at a protest—been there, done that—and he had grown impatient with the plodding pronouncements delivered all afternoon, amplified with bull horns that theirs was a peaceful protest. Bullshit. People were dying—for real—and now it was time for real action. He was done writing articles and penning pamphlets. He was done organizing, demonstrating and protesting. No more posing for the cameras, headlines and mugshots. He was done just play-acting to make a point. It was time to effect real change with real action.

The Greyhound bus dropped him off in Chicago late Monday afternoon and he spent all day Tuesday walking the streets of downtown to learn the lay of the land, planning attack and escape routes. Wednesday afternoon, he wandered the inside perimeters of the protesters in Grant Park, ignoring the tinny megaphone *tête à tête* between organizers and police officials, instead carefully studying the formations of Chicago police officers and Illinois National Guardsmen deployed for the defense of Democrat party delegates, who were there to coronate their pick for the next Commander-In-Chief to send more young men off to die in Southeast Asia. Though it was August, Marty Keegan was dressed in layers to help absorb the blows of billy clubs and carried an industrial mask in his coat pocket to help protect against tear gas and mace. Besides his black jack, he carried a small Mason jar of gasoline and his grandfather's Zippo lighter. A.B. Keegan changed the world one way and Marty Keegan would do it his own way. He was just biding his time.

No one really knew what happened, but policemen rushed the statue of General John A. Logan to clear away the protesters perched there like flag waving pigeons. It did not really matter why they did it. Marty Keegan knew the battle had begun and he braced himself for action. Not long after, tear gas canisters were fired into the crowd and the protesters began spilling out of Grant Park and into downtown Chicago.

Marty Keegan flowed along with the crowd, carefully positioning himself two or three people deep into the crowd as a buffer to protect himself, like working his blockers on the grid iron. Ten thousand strong, the protesters collected in front of the Conrad Hilton Hotel, where Democrat party officials, including their eventual Presidential nominee, Vice-President Hubert Humphrey, were staying. He watched and waited patiently for his opportunity.

"The whole world is watching!" the sea of protesters began to chant as Mayor Daley's police force waded into the crowd like a charging line of Napoleonic soldiers later that evening, their billy clubs and mace filling the air. "The whole world is watching."

I hope not, Marty Keegan thought to himself, as he sliced through to the far flank of the crowd, watching the police line loosen and fray as it violently engaged the protesters. Then he saw his prey. A cop had separated himself from the thin blue line to chase a smaller group of protesters with a spray can of mace. Marty Keegan had done it dozens of times on the football field. He exploded out from the crowd. Instinctively angling to stay in the opponent's blind side, he barreled into his target, driving his shoulder underneath the outstretched left arm delivering the stream of mace. At the same time, he swung his black jack as hard as he could into the officer's knee, hearing a satisfying crack as the cop crumpled to the curb. Body blows brought the policeman's arms down to protect his ribs, then Marty Keegan delivered a series of upper cuts to the underside of the pale blue helmet, driving him into a coma from which he never recovered.

By the time fellow officers noticed the assault and ran to the rescue, Marty Keegan was already heading up the alley he had scouted the day before. He tossed the Mason jar Molotov cocktail into their path and disappeared into the night.

It would take several weeks before the pictures a *Chicago Sun-Times* photographer took of Marty Keegan's attack found their way into the hands of law enforcement authorities. By that time, the F.B.I. had identified him as one of the Pentagon bombers.

Travis Marbling sat behind Wilson Cassidy, watching him running the bottom corner of the pages of the latest F.B.I. report delivered by special messenger across his thumb and sensing the beef magnate's growing impatience with the droning recitation of the latest quarterly sales figures for the company, a topic he normally obsessed over. He knew what was on his mind. Travis Marbling subtly twirled his fingers at the presenter to quicken the meeting's pace towards an end.

In the Black

"God damn it," Wilson Cassidy blurted out with only a slight residual slur from his stroke, when his executive staff retired to their offices. Much to all the doctors' surprise, he had rehabilitated his speech to near normal, not through any medical treatment or therapy, but the same sheer individual will power that had built the Cassidy beef packing empire. Travis Marbling pushed him from the conference table back to his desk. The weakness on the left side of his body persisted. Though he could walk slowly with a cane, in the privacy of his office, he conserved his strength as much as possible with a wheel chair. "They were supposed to watch over him. Guard against exactly this kind of thing. God damned government paper pushers."

"A minor setback," said Travis Marbling calmly.

"A God damned cluster fuck."

"We can manage this."

"God damned right we can."

"What should I do first?"

"You have a 'come to Jesus' meeting with that two-bit pigskin pusher and get his ass in gear."

"Yes sir."

After Y.T., Jr. boarded the Erp Industries, Inc. Learjet and returned to Berkeley for the fall semester, Rebecca Sue Simmons, like her husband, continued to stalk him by proxy. Following Scarlett Angelina Brookings during the day, while Barry Boswagger followed her at night, husband and wife remained completely clueless that they shared at least this one common interest. As the weeks passed, the former head cheerleader knew before anyone else did—even before Scarlett Angelina Brookings herself knew—why the strain of the red-head's form-fitting dresses against her taut body became ever so slightly more strained as autumn stripped the leaves from trees, including the cherry tree in the back yard of Y.T., Sr.'s home. Cooling temperatures made a more layered wardrobe seem natural while hiding the same news Rebecca Sue Simmons had learned on her own follow up visit to the gynecologist: the rabbit had died and Scarlett Angelina Brookings was pregnant.

~~~

Nothing to Fear, But Fear

Y.T., Sr. knew exactly where to find Arthur Needleman: at the shoe shine stand. It was where he had first met his West Coast sales manager seven years earlier, clear across the country at the St. Francis Hotel on Union Square in San Francisco. Arthur Needleman was drawn to hot dog carts, coffee shops, newsstands, bakeries, barber shops and, of course, shoe shine stands, like bees are drawn to nectar, craving the human interaction and banter with proprietors and personal service providers and feeding off of those interactions, absorbing energy like a psychological flywheel to propel his manic pace through the day.

Arthur Needleman was the son of one of the most respected and revered men in the cloistered world of Madison Avenue. His father was the man who single-handedly doubled Proctor and Gamble shampoo sales with a solitary word: Lather, Rinse, *Repeat.* Wilfred Gustave Needleman was an avid student of the human herd and the most effective methodologies for corralling their disposable income into the coffers of corporations who paid handsomely for his propaganda wrangling. Throughout his career, "W.G." prided himself on taking a strict scientific approach to the understanding of human behavior, but despaired at the disdainful whispers, both real and imagined, for his profession—in spite of the millions upon millions of dollars of tangible results his "pseudo-science" produced. The overt lack of respect from all but his peers and his clients pierced the adman's pride deeply, the wounds of which he sought to heal by sending his son to the Massachusetts Institute of Technology to become a "real" scientist.

Arthur Needleman was enrolled in the Aeronautical Engineering program with a minor in Astronomy, which interested him immensely more than his major. Although he excelled in his studies, his heart was not in becoming a scientist or an engineer. He saw the undergraduate program through, though, receiving a Bachelor of Science degree *magnum cum laude* only for his father's sake. While W.G.'s approach to his fellow human beings, including his family, was coldly clinical and remotely statistical, his son preferred to deal with folks belly-to-belly, on an equal footing, learning from them and enjoying their company, rather than analyzing how to make them jump through hoops or chase through mazes towards some dubious reward, like a B.F. Skinner experiment. After graduation, Arthur Needleman sought to get as far away as possible from the laboratory-like sterility of the Needleman household in New York City as soon as possible. His escape path led to a drafting board at the Lockheed Advanced Development Division in Burbank, California, where he spent long days drawing excruciatingly intricate details of the landing gears of top secret aircraft. The unbroken hours in the company of templates, t-squares and mechanical pencils quickly began killing his spirit. He literally felt his soul slowly drowning in the increasing quantities of alcohol he consumed after work in the company of fellow "Skunk Works" worker bees, until one Tuesday afternoon he walked over to his supervisor's desk under the watchful eye of forty disbelieving engineers in his section and tendered his resignation. Due to the classified nature of the work done there for Kelly Johnson, Arthur Needleman was escorted out of the Lockheed facility immediately by security and collected his last paycheck that Friday.

On the way home from his last day at work, Arthur Needleman stopped at a bookstore and stocked up on fiction, verse, history and philosophy tomes. He consumed these voraciously on Venice Beach, until the day he finished Jack Kerouac's *On the Road,* after which he impulsively jumped into the gift he received from his father upon graduating from M.I.T., a Porsche *Spyder,* and headed north up California Highway 1. Along the way he stopped at every coffee shop, diner, bowling alley, driving range and tavern between Los Angeles and San Francisco, until he crossed paths with Y.T., Sr. at the St. Francis Hotel. After a wide ranging conversation, ricocheting from sports cars to the "Buttoned-Down Mind" of Bob Newhart to the validity of Roger Maris breaking Babe Ruth's record of sixty home runs in a 162 game season to Dylan Thomas's "Do Not Go Gentle into that Good Night" to Fred McMurray's invention of Flubber in *The Absent Minded Professor* to Eisenhower's dire warnings about the "Military-Industrial Complex" to Soviet Cosmonaut Yuri Gagarin becoming the first human to journey into outer space, Y.T., Sr. told Arthur Needleman to call him after he got home from his Pacific coastal odyssey to go to work for Erp Industries, Inc.

Y.T., Sr. climbed up on the shoe shine stand in the lobby of the Parker House Hotel in downtown Boston. Arthur Needleman was already sitting there, scanning the *Boston Globe* obituaries and analyzing the upcoming World Series pitching match-up between *Tiger* Denny McClain and *Cardinal* Bob Gibson with Aldo as he buffed Arthur Needleman's Florsheims to a high gloss. Without looking, he handed Y.T., Sr. the Lifestyle section of the paper.

"I have to go with St. Louis, of course," said Y.T., Sr., pulling out his pen to work the crossword puzzle.

"I hate to break this to you, but it's going to be Detroit," answered Arthur Needleman. "I hope you don't have a lot riding on the Series."

"Hmmm." Y.T., Sr. filled in six down. "Aldo, your thoughts?"

"This is Boston," said the shoe shine man as he dabbed polish on Y.T., Sr.'s Oxfords. "I gotta go American League, so I agree with Artie on this."

"We'll see. We'll see," said Y.T., Sr. "So, anyone we know kick off?"

"Looks like Patrick O'Hurley crossed the bar."

"We know him?"

"No, but he'll do."

"How's our buddy, Peckerfelt, making out these days?"

"He's dealing with it. That Leon Debs guy is a real piece of work, though."

"Anyone listening to him?"

"Oh, there are always a few malcontents who are just looking for any excuse to make trouble and stir the pot."

"I don't need any union problems in the shop."

"Nothing to fear, my good man, but fear itself. Orley's pitching in, too. Boy, he sure hates Debs's guts."

"We're at a critical juncture with negotiations right now. Let me know what I can do to help."

"Oh, I think everything is good-to-go right now. You won't need to worry about manufacturing."

"Okay." Y.T., Sr. filled in twenty-three across. "And how are he and Prunella getting on?"

"Never seen him happier."

"Good. Good for him."

"Front desk," Arthur Needleman whispered as he nudged Y.T., Sr.'s arm with his elbow. Without lifting their heads from their newspapers, both men caught a glimpse of Vasili Ivanovich pacing near the front desk, alternating between checking his wrist watch, then furtively glancing in their direction, then contemplating the scuffed condition of his cheap brown shoes, then rubbing the center of his forehead, then repeating the ritual again and again.

They would be late if they didn't get going, Vasili Ivanovich fretted to himself, Y.T., Sr.'s long ago lesson in tardiness ever fresh in his mind. What was taking so long?

"You gentlemen are all set," said Aldo.

"I shall retrieve our carriage," said Arthur Needleman hopping down from the stand and heading toward the front entrance under the watchful eye of Vasili Ivanovich.

Y.T., Sr. paid Aldo and tipped him generously. *"Tigers,* huh? You *Red Sox* fans are all alike."

Aldo shrugged. "Thank you, sir."

Vasili Ivanovich met Y.T., Sr. halfway and walked with him to the hotel entrance. "I've checked and double checked everything—absolutely everything and—and the design is good. It is good. I swear it."

"I'm sure it is," said Y.T., Sr.

"But you've read the memos. They are *all* blaming us—Grumman, Raytheon, Bell, Marquardt, Rocketdyne, the government, *Von Braun."* Delays in getting the Lunar Excursion Module flight ready had forced NASA to completely change the mission profile for Apollo 8, which was originally planned as a second Lunar Module/Command Module test in an elliptical medium Earth orbit in early 1969. "And this Raytheon fellow, Mc-Mc-Mc—"

"McCarthy."

Vasili Ivanovich shuddered at the mere mention of the surname of the Senator from Wisconsin whose subcommittee hearings precipitated his relocation from Washington, D.C., to Kansas City so many years ago.

A porter held the door for them. They stepped to the curb to wait for Arthur Needleman.

"Everything is going to be just fine," Y.T., Sr. said, putting his hand on Vasili Ivanovich's shoulder. "Trust me."

Vasili Ivanovich bowed his head and shook it slowly. He had seen it all before: the finger pointing, the accusations, the burying of facts and the inevitable purging of the innocents.

Arthur Needleman pulled up in a red four-door Ford *Torino* from Hertz and rolled down the window. "Need a lift?"

Y.T., Sr. read the question in Vasili Ivanovich's painfully pinched expression at the sight of Arthur Needleman. "You know, he went to school here in Boston."

Vasili Ivanovich just shook his head dejectedly and acquiesced to Y.T., Sr.'s gestures to get in the front seat, wondering if he might have the Colt .45 caliber semi-automatic pistol with him and what it would feel like pressed against the back of his head.

"A clean windshield. Powerful gasoline. And a shoe shine," said Arthur Needleman as he squealed the tires pulling away from the Parker House Hotel and raced his way out of downtown Boston in a way that only compounded Vasili Ivanovich's anxiety and terror.

In the back seat, Y.T., Sr. worked on the *Boston Globe* crossword puzzle.

"So, I hear old 'Fuzzy' McCarthy has done pretty good for himself at Raytheon," said Arthur Needleman.

In the Black

"Assistant Chief Engineer," said Y.T., Sr., from the back seat.

"You know, Vasya," Arthur Needleman said, winking at Vasili Ivanovich, "Fuzzy and I were classmates back at M.I.T."

Vasili Ivanovich's worry-furrowed brow suddenly smoothed out. He looked back at Y.T., Sr. who was filling in the answer for forty-six down and finally understood.

Arthur Needleman arrived at St. Anthony Catholic Church just as Patrick O'Hurley's funeral procession departed for Westview Cemetery. He turned on the *Torino's* headlights and fell in at the end of the long line of cars. Y.T., Sr. finished the crossword puzzle as they drove non-stop to Raytheon headquarters in Lexington, arriving on time for their meeting, after which the rabid hounds of bureaucratic reprisal turned their hunt to find others to blame besides Erp Industries, Inc.

Billy Saul Sawyer heard the O-1E *Bird Dog* before he saw it and hurriedly finished the last of the hog badger he had hunted and killed a few days before. Since April, Billy Saul Sawyer had slowly and steadily migrated northwest, deeper and deeper into Laos, living off the land as he put nearly four hundred miles between himself and Khe Sanh during the summer months. He continued to hunt the enemy as he had before being officially declared M.I.A., only now there were no after action reports to be filed nor captains, lieutenants and sergeants to answer to for his actions. He had planned to move to the western slope of the valley in a couple of hours to keep the sun behind him, but decided to take advantage of the overhead activity and started moving right away. The C.I.A.'s Ravens, the forward air controllers operating covertly in officially neutral Laos, were unwitting allies in the private war he waged since Poncho had gotten killed. The North Vietnamese soldiers—who were not supposed to be in Laos either—could not help themselves from shooting at the unarmed Cessnas and once they started firing, thereby revealing their positions, Charlie became easy prey for Billy Saul Sawyer—so easy, in fact, the North Vietnamese had placed a very large bounty on the life of the one they called *"Ma Trang,"* the White Ghost. The added benefit the Ravens offered was that the F-4 *Phantom* and F-105 *Thunderchief* air strikes they called in always created more than enough noise and havoc to completely cover his escape.

The Cessna crested the ridge and began trolling up the valley towards him, flying at tree top level. Billy Saul Sawyer quickly found a spot that gave him a panoramic view of the valley, knowing that the pilot would soon enough flush out the enemy unit he had most recently been tracking. The familiar cracks of AK-47s soon echoed in the valley. Billy Saul Sawyer scanned the valley floor for muzzle flashes as the *Bird Dog* chandelled to reverse direction and gain altitude to mark their position with a smoke rocket. Billy Saul Sawyer wanted to get off a few rounds before the fighters showed up on the scene with their bombs, but suddenly the Cessna's engine sputtered and black smoke began to trail the plane as the pilot dove back to tree top level to make it harder for the AK-47s to find their mark. He glided just above the outstretched jungle branches, slowly and steadily bleeding off his airspeed until he was able to slip and careen into a small clearing. Black smoke marked the crash site and the race was on.

Billy Saul Sawyer moved quickly across the hillside, rushing to get in place before the North Vietnamese soldiers reached the downed pilot. As he moved beyond the crash site, he saw that the pilot, though injured, had pulled himself from the cockpit and taken cover, armed with a pistol. Billy Saul anticipated the direction from which the enemy would approach and positioned himself with a clear view back over the hiding pilot towards the spot where they would most likely emerge from the jungle.

"Hang on, pal," Billy Saul Sawyer said softly, dividing his attention between the pilot and the edge of the clearing. As much as he wanted to hurry to the aid of a fellow soldier, he knew if he did, neither of them would make it out of the ass end of the day alive. "Just hang on, pal."

In his scope he saw the movement at the edge of the jungle. The enemy carefully scouted the clearing. They fired randomly into wreckage.

"Don't do it," Billy Saul whispered to the pilot. "Don't give yourself away."

The pilot held his fire.

They waited.

More shots. Then, an enemy soldier stepped hesitantly to the edge of the brush. He paused, then took another step. His pith helmet, centered in Billy Saul Sawyer's cross-hairs made an easy target, but he did not take the shot.

The soldier took another step, then another, slowly crossing the clearing to the burning plane.

"Just hunker down," Billy Saul Sawyer said, checking quickly on the pilot.

The soldier looked back and waved his unit forward.

Billy Saul Sawyer watched three more soldiers, one-by-one, slowly slip the cover of the jungle into the clearing. They stayed close together, just as he hoped they would, and started chattering in Vietnamese. Billy Saul Sawyer planned to take them Sergeant

York style—last to first—and slowly counted down as they approached the first soldier.

He shot and killed the last soldier out of the jungle. Believing the ambush came from behind, the other three reflexively turned and started firing their AK-47s back into the jungle they had just come out of and Billy Saul Sawyer was able to finish them off with three more quick shots they never heard or saw. If there had been any more soldiers behind them, they probably had just gotten fragged by the undisciplined firing.

Just to be sure, Billy Saul Sawyer waited where he was a long five minutes watching the jungle intently. After a pair of *Thunderchiefs* screamed overhead, shaking the jungle floor, without dropping their bombs, he looked back at the pilot and called out, "Marco."

No reply.

"Marco."

Finally, weakly, came the reply, "Polo."

"Hang on. I'm coming."

First, Billy Saul Sawyer checked the enemy soldiers, making sure they were all dead by stabbing them all in their hearts, then he went to the pilot, who had been shot in the leg and looked to have broken his arm and maybe his collar bone in the crash landing along with collecting a face full of cuts and bruises.

"Hey, you're Casper, right?" the pilot asked weakly, surprised to see a Caucasian tending to his wounds. *"Ma Trang."*

"Yeah, the friendly ghost," Billy Saul Sawyer chuckled.

"I'm Doug."

"Good to meet you, sir." Billy Saul Sawyer very gently hugged the pilot, trying not pressure his broken arm. "You are the first American—hell, you're the first person I've talked to in over six months."

"Thank you."

"No problem. It's all in a day's work," said Billy Saul Sawyer. "Let's get you home."

It was over thirty clicks back to Lima Site 20 Alternate where Doug had come from, but fortunately they met a C.I.A. Hmong team halfway that had been dispatched to recover Doug's body, which helped them back to Long Tieng. At the air base Doug's fellow Ravens were amazed to see him alive. Doug was taken to the infirmary, while a scruffy collection of civilians took Billy Saul Sawyer to the base bar for round after round of free beers. It was a good thing that they had introduced him to the three Himalayan Black Bears in the cage beneath the bar before he got drunk or he would have thought he had been hallucinating.

Three days later, severely hung over, but with a belly full of the first real food he had eaten since Khe Sanh, Billy Saul Sawyer found himself across a desk from a C.I.A. officer dressed in khakis and a buttoned down short sleeve shirt with thick rimmed glasses and short slicked back hair. He reminded Billy Saul Sawyer of one of those Freedom Rider college students who went down south to help the Negroes in Alabama or Mississippi, only with a hauntingly malevolent air about him. The case officer shuffled through papers in an open manila file folder, smoking a cigarette with his left hand, while nonchalantly winding, unwinding and rewinding a set of dog tags around the fingers of his right hand.

Billy Saul Sawyer clutched at his chest, but the dog tags were his.

"Been a while, huh?" the case officer said.

He moaned and rubbed his temples. "Yes sir."

"Do you know who we are?"

Billy Saul Sawyer had a vague idea, but said, "No sir. Not really."

"We are not here."

"Okay." Billy Saul Sawyer slowly nodded.

"Those out-of-uniform Air Force pilots and their little planes without any insignias?"

"Uh-huh?"

"Not here."

"Doug?"

"Yeah?"

The case officer shook his head. "The Geneva Accords say so. And the United States government always keeps its promises."

"Okay…"

"We do appreciate what you did for Doug and, on behalf of the Company, I want to thank you."

Billy Saul Sawyer shrugged. "You know…all in a day's—"

"So, what do you want, Mr. Sawyer?"

The question confused him. Besides, no one had ever addressed him as 'mister' before.

"Would you want to go home?"

Billy Saul Sawyer sat stone faced. After Washington, D.C., Khe Sanh and nearly eight months alone in the jungle, 'home' had become as abstract a concept for Billy Saul Sawyer as microbiological creatures.

"You could stay here—we can always use another gun around, especially one as skilled as you—but there's always the off chance some regular Air Force Joe or State Department weasel might start asking too many questions and make your— shall we say—*situation* somewhat difficult." The case officer tapped the contents of the manila file folder, toppling the ash from the end of his cigarette. He leaned back in his office chair. "Or, you could go back into the jungle, but I wouldn't think that to be a good long term career plan.

Did you know the gooks have a twenty thousand dollar bounty on your head?"

Billy Saul Sawyer shook his head.

"They must really hate you."

"I guess I understand that, sir."

"Nearly eight months on your own."

"Yes sir."

"You are a pretty resourceful fellow. The Company is always looking for resourceful types. Would you be interested?"

What choice do I have, Billy Saul Sawyer asked himself. "Yes, sir."

"Good then. Let's get you back home."

Billy Saul Sawyer began the long covert journey from the secret air base south of the Plain of Jars in Laos to a safe house in San Francisco that the Central Intelligence Agency, through an exceedingly convoluted chain of fronts and holding companies, leased from Fu Loin.

The Sugarman sat waiting for Senator Thurman Troyer to return to his office on Capitol Hill, collecting looks of all kinds from passing Congressional staffers, elected officials and lobbyists—quick curious glances, patronizing gazes and red hot glares—largely depending upon the region of the country they represented. He calmly turned a worn fedora around and around in his hands by the brim between his splayed out knees, in time with the first and third beats of Ella Fitzgerald's "Love for Sale" as it ran through his head over and over again. Anna Elise Erp sat to one side of him. On his other side sat the woman he had spent the better part of seven months trying to find ever since Senator Troyer had forced his daughter into exile from Washington, D.C., to the family plantation in Ilium, Georgia, abandoning Y.T., Sr.

The Sugarman had worked his old Kansas City jazz connections hard. He knew that from their perches up on stages and bandstands, musicians see everything and on their breaks collect the same kind of gossip that pervades every kind of workplace, including the comings and goings of the clients of the clubs they played as well as the company those clients kept. He sought out the sidemen who had worked the U-Street corridor in Washington, D.C., as they passed back through the Sunset, the Subway and the Reno nightclubs in Kansas city until he got the lead he needed. Then he and Anna Elise drove to the nation's capital in her brother's borrowed Cadillac *El Dorado*. It took three days of scouting Logan Circle in the afternoons and camping out at the Bohemian Caverns at night until they found Dahlia Feathers and convinced her to come with them to the Senator's office.

Coming off a procedural vote on the Senate floor, Senator Troyer was brought up short by the three visitors parked in the reception area of his office. While he did not recognize the black man with the fedora and the white woman looked only vaguely familiar, he knew Dahlia Feathers well.

"They are not even constituents," whispered his secretary who sidled discretely up to his side, "but we cannot get them to leave."

Senator Troyer waved her off.

Anna Elise Erp stood up and calmly asked, "May we speak privately, sir?"

Senator Troyer slowly nodded and motioned for her to enter his office.

"Sir, you are scheduled to meet with General—"

"Thank you, Grace," Senator Troyer politely, but abruptly cut her off. "I will not want to be disturbed."

Standing at the door to his office he swept his hand towards the sitting area where a pair of sofas faced each other, separated by a coffee table. As Anna Elise Erp sat down, Senator Troyer took a long look at the beautiful woman sitting next to the Sugarman who had sung her way out of the Murder Bay slums, who reminded him so much of Lena Horne and who surely could bring about the end of his political career, should the unforgiving electorate of Georgia ever find out about their relationship. His mistress turned and met his gaze with a hard look in her eyes. The Sugarman had explained to her all he had done to his own daughter. The Senator exhaled deeply and closed the door.

Senator Troyer sat down across from Anna Elise and studied her face carefully, until he recognized the resemblance to the young Navy Lieutenant whose path of destruction through his legislative agenda, his life and his family, like Sherman's march to Savannah, evidently knew no limits nor the bounds of common decency.

As they sat without speaking, Anna Elise watched one of the most powerful men in the nation wither before her eyes. She, frankly, had not expected that; but, then again, she did not yet know the full magnitude of the Troyer family tragedy: Helen Troyer was not only dishonorably pregnant, upon returning home to Georgia, she had been diagnosed with cancer and refused all medical treatment in order to protect the health of her unborn child. A great wave of fatigue suddenly swept over the Senator as he finally accepted the cold, hard fact, sitting there across from the plain looking woman who had spawned his nemesis, that all of the government prestige and power he had accumulated over the decades of public service could not save his daughter's life or repair his fractured family relationships and now he, uncharacteristically, did not know what to do anymore.

Senator Troyer missed several scheduled meetings and another vote on the Senate floor that day as he and Anna Elise Erp spoke intimately at length, person-to-person, parent-to-parent, and, finally, as grandparents-in-waiting, until the Chairman of the Senate Armed Services Committee excused himself and stepped into his hideaway to make a call to the Pentagon on his private line. The next day, a Douglas C-54 *Skymaster* flew Helen Troyer from Robins Air Force Base to Andrews Field. An ambulance took her to a VIP suite at the Bethesda Naval Hospital, arranged by Admiral Hemmings, where the diagnosis of the doctors in Georgia was confirmed.

Helen Troyer's face lit up when she was reunited with Y.T., Sr. While the cancer was eating away at her from the inside, her beauty was still unmarred and shown through the weariness brought on by disease and the final weeks of her pregnancy. As Anna Elise and Senator Troyer agreed, a Navy Chaplain conducted the wedding ceremony in the hospital room with the Sugarman as Y.T., Sr.'s best man. This was the first and only time Senator Troyer ever spoke with Y.T., Sr., when he and the newlyweds exchanged a brief private conversation after the Chaplain finished.

The doctors were confounded. None thought she would make it, but Helen Troyer's will and strength saw her through the full term of her pregnancy and the delivery of a healthy baby boy. After the birth of Y.T., Jr., she quickly succumbed to the cancer with Y.T., Sr. by her side at the end. While he accompanied her body back to Georgia to be buried in the Troyer family plot, the Sugarman drove Anna Elise Erp and Y.T., Jr. back to Kansas City where she would care for him until his father could make all the necessary arrangements to move his business back to his boyhood home. Before leaving Washington, D.C., though, Anna Elise Erp insisted on visiting the office of Missouri Senator Forest C. Donnell, who graciously invited his colleague from Georgia to come down the hall to meet his grandson. When they left Capitol Hill, Anna Elise Erp was struck by the barren branches of the cherry trees surrounding the Tidal Basin as they drove by on Independence Avenue, then crossed the Potomac River, bound for home.

The day after Y.T., Sr.'s return from Boston, Scarlett Angelina Brookings was waiting outside of his office to see him, undeterred by the glaring glances and impatient exhales of Wanda W. Willet as she noisily shuffled papers back and forth across her desk. He took Scarlett into his office, closing the door behind them much to the chagrin of his secretary. Scarlett Angelina Brookings confessed to her unsavory arrangement with Wilson Cassidy. Y.T., Sr. assured her that he had known all along about her "relationship" with his meddling maternal cousin since the day he instructed Simon Salisbury to hire her to be Vasili Ivanovich's secretary. She apologized for the duplicitous things she had been forced to do the past two summers. He told her he was well aware of the beef magnate's machinations and, as of that day, her long ordeal of enduring his manipulations was over. She told him she was pregnant. He promised he would take care of her always.

There had been many women since Helen Troyer, but Y.T., Sr. had never again fallen in love, until he met and hired Scarlett Angelina Brookings.

~~~

In the Black

1969

Riders on the Earth

Y.T., Jr. sat on the fifth floor fire escape. His legs dangled over the edge. He looked at the moon which would officially be full in just two more days. Dropping his Marlboro over the edge, he watched the butt fall to the alley below and just as it seemed to hit the pavement, firecrackers started popping in the streets of Chinatown below to celebrate the New Year. Fireworks began to explode somewhere over the waterfront, reflected off the bay waters near the Embarcadero.

Awakened by the reveling, Penelope Xing climbed out on the fire escape, sleepily munching on a saltine cracker. She knelt down behind Y.T., Jr. and rubbed his shoulders gently, "Sorry I fell asleep."

"That's okay. It's not really your time, yet, is it?"

"It's Fu who has another month to go, not me. But if it means he can make a buck, he'll go along. With two New Year's celebrations he can sell twice as many fireworks."

"Which one will it be?"

"Ah, the year of the Rooster, I think."

"What's that mean?"

"I dunno. It's astrology. And it's Chinese astrology to boot. Not my thing."

They listened to the celebrations in the streets.

"I think he's right," said Y.T., Jr.

"Who?"

"Oz. He says they're everywhere. He says he can feel the eyes of *The Man* pushing on him. He says it's so bad, sometimes it's hard to even breathe."

"He's paranoid. And he drops too much acid."

"No. I think he's right."

"Murph says that too, but he's just crazy. Are you crazy?"

"Sometimes."

"Well, it fits with the times."

"Okay, Miss History, you're the expert. Just how crazy are our times?"

Penelope Xing thought for a moment. "I don't know. It depends on where we end up."

"You mean in history?"

"Yeah."

"So, we'll all be dead by then."

"I suppose."

"So, who cares, then?"

Y.T., Jr. turned and pulled Penelope Xing's head gently towards him to kiss her.

Suddenly there was a fierce pounding on the door and Fu Loin screeched in a high-pitched voice. Penelope Xing went to the window and answered him in Chinese. Y.T., Jr. listened to their conversation.

"What is it?"

"He says you must leave right away."

"Why?"

"Because they are coming for you in the morning."

"Who?"

"I don't know."

Penelope Xing and Y.T., Jr. went back into her room and opened the door. Fu Loin stood pacing in place and frantically fondling his prayer beads.

"He come," said Fu Loin, pointing down the hall to a bearded and scruffy Marty Keegan, who had been a fugitive on the run since the Democratic National Convention in Chicago. "And now they come for you. I know. I hear. I know. Please, you must go."

"Who comes?" Penelope Xing asked Fu Loin calmly, quietly in Chinese. She rarely saw him this upset, except when he spoke of Nanking. "Who is coming in the morning?"

"Zhanshi! Zhanshi!" Fu Loin uttered frantically. *"Zhanshi* come."

"Soldiers?"

He shook his head and rubbed his temples with his hands. *"Jingcha. Jingcha."*

"Police?" interpreted Penelope Xing.

"Jingcha. Police. Yes, they come," nodded Fu Loin. "Please, little Whitey, you must escape. Flee now please."

"They are after me," said Marty Keegan from down the hall. "There's a warrant. Because of Chicago."

"No! No!," Fu Loin insisted, pointing at Y.T., Jr.'s heart. "They come for you, too. *Jingcha* come for you. I know. I hear. I know."

"I don't want to cause you any problems," Y.T., Jr. said to Fu Loin.

"No. No problem for me. Problem for you." Fu Loin looked up and down the hallway. "They watch you. Now they come for you."

"I guess Oz was right," Y.T., Jr. said to Penelope Xing.

"Him, too. They come for all," said Fu Loin. "Please, my friend, save yourself."

Y.T., Jr. grabbed his jacket, wallet and keys from Penelope Xing's room and followed Fu Loin down the hall towards Marty Keegan.

"Hey, man, I didn't mean to bring this down on you," said Marty Keegan.

"Chicago?"

"Yeah, I—"

"No time. No time," Fu Loin shooed them on down the stairway.

Before Penelope Xing even realized it, Y.T., Jr. was gone. Tears welled up in her eyes.

"No. No. No," Fu Loin stopped Y.T., Jr. and Marty Keegan from leaving through the front door. "They know. They watch. This way."

He led them into the back office and down another stairway into the basement of the building, then through a series of secret passageways and tunnels connecting neighboring buildings and blocks until they came up a stairway into a small warehouse three streets over. Fu Loin hustled down an aisle of shelves and returned with jackets and baseball hats for Y.T., Jr. and Marty Keegan to help hide their identities. He hustled down another aisle and returned pushing a Vespa scooter.

"You leave here. No go home. They watch there, too. They watch everywhere. No train. No bus. They watch," said Fu Loin, giving Y.T., Jr. the keys to the scooter. "Go Oakland. I call Sonny. Angels will help you."

"Angels?" asked Marty Keegan.

Y.T., Jr. nodded. "Hell's Angels."

"Sonny will help."

"But what does he want."

"No problem. I have done it. I have done it. He owes me."

Y.T., Jr. got on the scooter. Marty Keegan got on behind him.

Fu Loin went to the doors that opened up into an alley in back of the building. He motioned for them to wait, then slipped out to check that the alley was clear. When he swung the doors open, Y.T., Jr. and Marty Keegan sped out and headed for Oakland.

In an apartment above, Billy Saul Sawyer heard the commotion in the warehouse downstairs and instinctively grabbed his pistol. When the doors to the alley creaked open and the scooter engine started up, he went to the back window of the C.I.A. safe house and looked out. As the scooter emerged and scurried down the alley, he grabbed the sniper scope that was dismounted from his Winchester and followed the scooter down the alley. He shuddered with an eerie sense of *déjà vu* as his cross-hairs again caught his friend making an escape. The Company had told him to stay put, but this time he would help. He could not let it happen again, so he broke down his Winchester rifle and began to pack his things to slip away into the concrete jungle.

Penelope Xing stood in the hallway outside her room weeping long after Fu Loin led Y.T., Jr. away, trying to absorb the seismic shift in events in those first moments of the New Year. She tried and failed to stem the aftershocks of worry and anxiety. Then she remembered about Oz.

Penelope Xing hurriedly dressed and called a cab to take her to the Vogue Theater, where she knew Clinton A. Owsley III would be, as the regular midnight showing of *2001, A Space Odyssey* had become a weekly religious ritual for him and an acid dropping cult from the Haight. Murph would likely be there with them. She only hoped that they would not be too tripped out to understand. The movie was only half over when the cab dropped her off. Since it was New Year's Eve, the theater was less crowded than usual and Clinton A. Owsley III and Murph were easy to see in their usual seats far down front in the middle of the tenth row. She sat down between them and explained what had happened at Fu Loin's that night and how the police were going to be at their apartment in the morning. She did not listen as Murph convinced Clinton A. Owsley III that they had to leave right away.

"You've seen it, man. You know how it ends."

Clinton A. Owsley III nodded his head, not thinking about the movie, but the plot of his own life. Reluctantly, he rose and followed Murph to the emergency exit at the front of the theater, which opened to a back alley. Sneaking out through the exit door, they disappeared into the night and vanished from the San Francisco peninsula.

Penelope Xing's eyes absently absorbed Stanley Kubrick's images of outer space for the next hour, but her mind dwelled on more earthly concerns.

"You *dolt,*" Travis Marbling hissed at Barry Boswagger. "Unbelievable."

The former quarterback wasn't quite sure what exactly it meant, but the tone of the insult was certainly delivered with the same venom as when Coach Sox berated him whenever he threw an interception, so now, as then on the sidelines, he kept his mouth shut and just took it. The New Year had not started off so well for the Cassidy Beef Packing Company employee.

"The father, not *the son,*" Travis Marbling emphasized his point by poking his index finger into Barry Boswagger's chest—just like Coach Sox. "Jesus, where is your head at?"

Barry Boswagger shook his head. He mumbled, "Sorry, coach."

"What?"

"Nothing, sir."

"Just make it happen," Travis Marbling turned away and left Barry Boswagger to finish loading his truck for the day's run, muttering under his breath, *"Idiot."*

Barry Boswagger sighed and hoped the rest of the year went better than the first work day of 1969; but on his delivery stop at Erp Industries, Inc., scanning the cafeteria for a glimpse of Scarlett Angelina Brookings, he was shocked to see his wife there in the red head's usual place, sipping coffee with the other secretaries and smiling in a way he had not seen in a long, long time. He realized again, as if for the first time, how pretty she was, now in a new dress he did not remember buying her, and with make up on and her hair done up. The shock was so great, he took the signed receiving sheet from Arlotta McGurdy and slipped away without a word. Barry Boswagger's fears were confirmed later that day when Rebecca Sue Simmons was not home after he got off work at three-thirty that afternoon.

In the days between Christmas and New Year's Day, Y.T., Sr. had paid a visit to a small bungalow in Birdtown and shared a cup of coffee with a former Harry S. Truman High School cheerleader, after which a razor thin file folder for a new employee appeared on Simon Salisbury's desk. The prissy Personnel Director did his imposed duties and at eight o'clock Thursday morning, January second, Rebecca Sue Simmons took her place as Vasili Ivanovich's new secretary.

Barry Boswagger was not the only one unsettled by the sudden personnel change in the Engineering Department. Besides inducing a severe case of bunker mentality in Rolf Guderian, who locked himself in his office with Himmlerlicht and Eichmanhoff, an unsettling sense of passing drifted among all the employees, whose whispers seemed like a collective sigh at the loss of beauty from their industrial midst. Even more than the mysterious vanishing of Scarlett Angelina Brookings, the executive crust of management at Erp Industries, Inc. was further confounded by the fact that *The Memo* for 1969 was missing from their inboxes. In its place, each and every employee received from Y.T., Sr. an eight by ten color reproduction of *Earthrise,* the photograph taken by astronaut William Anders from lunar orbit on December 24, 1968 during the Apollo 8 mission, the first manned voyage to orbit the moon.

Magnificent Desolation

For J. Edgar Hoover there was only one stage of bureaucratic grief: *Anger.* And, in the Director's opinion, when it came to grief, it was far better to give than to receive, so his anger flowed like a lava field down from the top, scorching those in the organization who were not prescient enough to have covered their ass or nimble enough to deflect the molten flow of blame to others. As he read the field reports delivered to his desk on the first Monday morning of the New Year, a volcanic pressure built beneath the dome of his high forehead. If J. Edgar Hoover had been a cartoon character, Clyde Tolson surely would have seen steam venting from his ears.

The Director read that on the very first day of 1969, his agents came up empty handed when they went to serve search and arrest warrants on the subjects of at least twenty pounds of file folders filled with twenty pound weight paper filled with nearly four years of Bureau observations collected at a great expense funded by the taxpayers of the United States of America. In a mere two weeks, a new President would be inaugurated—and Dick Nixon was no slouch. He could play hardball with the best of them and J. Edgar Hoover was certain his new boss would not be impressed by the fact that his Bureau had let a terrorist bomber, a would-be presidential assassin and the two kingpins of the illicit hallucinogenic drug trade in California—which was destroying the moral fiber of the youth of the greatest nation on earth—slip through their hands in one fell swoop. Somehow, the *Triumvirate* triumphed—at least for the moment. But, J. Edgar Hoover had not stayed Director for nearly a half a century by letting others triumph.

Before they even felt the heat of their boss's rage on the other side of the continent, Special Agents Williams and Walters had already begun bending, breaking and scorching any and all of the Constitutional protections guaranteed to all citizens in the Bill of Rights necessary to locate and apprehend Y.T., Jr. and his known associates.

The government and Wilson Cassidy were not the only ones hunting Y.T., Jr. Safely camouflaged in a crowd which gathered to witness the early morning commotion on the streets of Chinatown New Year's Day, Billy Saul Sawyer had watched the F.B.I. raid Fu Loin's Emporium, accompanied by a contingent of the San Francisco Police Department, which participated reluctantly, because they knew that some of their names and the names of the command structure above could possibly come to light as clients of Fu Loin. The small Chinaman Billy Saul Sawyer had seen aid his friend's escape at the warehouse below the C.I.A. safe house was questioned by two agents who looked equal parts angry, frustrated and worried at coming up empty handed. Fu Loin's broken English and shrugging shoulders yielded no useful and actionable information, so Special Agents Williams and Walters moved on to stoke their frustration further by interviewing a gaggle of scantily clad women who exhibited an uncommon familiarity with local law enforcement officers gathered at the scene and a command of the agent's native language no better than Fu Loin's. When it became clear that the raid was a total bust, the federal government and the S.F.P.D. quickly retreated before the news media caught wind of their epic failure and broadcast it to the world.

In the Black

Billy Saul Sawyer thought he knew who would know Y.T., Jr.'s whereabouts and headed towards the Greyhound Bus station as the crowd dispersed. With the few belongings he owned in the duffel bag hefted over his shoulder, including his broken down sniper rifle and ammunition, he serpentined his way across the western states to evade detection, like he had done in the jungle of Southeast Asia, buying a series of one-way tickets to Boise, then to Salt Lake City, then to Albuquerque, then to Cheyenne, then to Bismark, then to Omaha then, finally, to Kansas City, where he checked into a cheap hotel in Raytown, Missouri, and began searching for Scarlett Angelina Brookings.

Vasili Ivanovich started to sweat profusely as soon as the elevator began its ascent to the Service Module Umbilical with Y.T., Sr., the Sugarman, and a push cart full of test equipment and tools. They passed in silent awe the three stacked stages of Wehrner Von Braun's Saturn V monstrosity, which would hold nearly a million gallons of kerosene, liquid hydrogen and liquid oxygen required to lift less than a thousand pounds of mankind from the surface of the earth and tear them from its gravitational pull to journey to the moon. When the elevator stopped, nearly three hundred feet above the floor of the cavernous Vertical Assembly Building, they were met by NASA and Grumman engineers and technicians who led them slowly and carefully out to the Lunar Module Adapter. It was the final opportunity to check the Erp Industries black boxes buried deep within the LM-5 *Eagle* before Apollo 11 was rolled out to Launch Pad 39A at Cape Kennedy.

"Ho-ly sheee-it," the Sugarman said to Y.T., Sr., drawing out all the syllables, as he took in all that American technological brain power had imagined, that American industrial muscle power had built and that American will power had caused to be created.

Y.T., Sr. put his arm around the Sugarman's shoulders and drew him close. "I'm glad you got to see this."

"And is that why you brought the ole Sugarman along here?"

"That and the fact that if by any chance anything needs fixing, you have the best pair of hands in the company."

The Sugarman shrugged his shoulders and smiled, then nodded towards Vasili Ivanovich, who, now absorbed totally in the task at hand, had stopped sweating. "He's a good man."

"Yeah. I'm not worried."

The Sugarman smiled and moved to the edge of the gantry. He looked up to the ceiling, then down the fifty stories to the floor of the single largest room on the face of the planet. Arthur Needleman, P. Peckerfelt and Orley Bovine waited and watched far below. "Damn, I'd sure like to meet the janitor that takes care of this place. Fo' sho'."

Y.T., Sr. laughed aloud. They patiently waited for the better part of an hour, until Vasili Ivanovich backed away from the spacecraft and nodded, signaling that everything was satisfactory with the black boxes which would navigate the *Eagle* to its landing in Tranquility Bay, then guide it back to dock with the *Columbia* command module to return Neil Armstrong, Buzz Aldrin, and Michael Collins—who by coincidence, were just then on the next gantry above checking their Apollo capsule—safely back to earth. Y.T., Sr. pointed the astronauts out to the Sugarman and Vasili Ivanovich, who recalled them from the smoke filled meeting room at Grumman and their late evening together on a Long Island beach several years ago.

The Erp Industries, Inc., team returned the following day to the Kennedy Space Center to watch Apollo 11 make the three-and-a-half mile journey over the marshy Florida flatlands from the

Vertical Assembly Building to the launch pad. Little was said during those six hours, as they sipped Orley Bovine's moonshine, watched the crawler crawl, imagined the history that would be made in just two months and contemplated their role in it. The following morning, they gathered at the Ti-Co Airport to return to Kansas City. Before being allowed to board the Erp Industries, Inc., Learjet, Y.T., Sr. sat privately with each employee and had them sign a non-disclosure agreement in the presence of a local notary of the public. When, at last, P. Peckerfelt signed and climbed the stair steps into the Learjet cabin, he was brought up short by Frak, who smiled *That Smile!* and handed him an airsickness bag. The two men stared at one another.

"Don't worry," said the smiling ex-Navy Commander around his ever present toothpick. "You won't need it this time."

P. Peckerfelt just nodded warily and took his seat.

Y.T., Sr. finally boarded, but turned left into the cockpit, followed by Frik who turned right and parked himself in the first passenger seat usually reserved for Y.T., Sr. He opened the June issue of *Playboy*.

"You know where the door is, now everybody buckle up," ordered Frak. He stared down at the rumpled ex-Air Force Colonel who studiously ignored the co-pilot's curt preflight briefing. *"Right."*

Frak went into the cockpit with the alarmed stares of all but Arthur Needleman fixed on the door he closed firmly behind him. Arthur Needleman pulled out Thomas Berger's *Little Big Man* and resumed reading where he had left off after the flight down to Florida.

When the Learjet reached flight level three-six-zero, Y.T., Sr. came out of the cockpit and Frik went in. He stood at the front of the cabin and read the alarm on P. Peckerfelt's face.

"It's an F.A.R.—Federal Aviation Regulation—that he has to wear an oxygen mask above thirty-five thousand feet if the other pilot leaves the controls."

The explanation did little to calm P. Peckerfelt, who looked as if he were anticipating being thrown out of the speeding jet seven miles above the surface of the earth without a parachute.

Y.T., Sr. reminded them all of the non-disclosure agreement they had just signed, then proceeded to explain to the men how soon they all were going to become very, very wealthy. He answered all of their questions openly and honestly, until Frik came back out of the cockpit and told him they were ready to begin their descent into Kansas City. Then, Y.T., Sr. went back to the controls to shoot the ILS to Runway 18 at Wheeler Downtown airport, leaving the passenger cabin in silence for the remainder of the flight.

Once the Learjet was parked at the fixed base operator and the cabin door opened, Y.T., Sr. stood and shook hands with each man as he deplaned, thanking them and reminding them again of the agreement they had signed in Florida. Arthur Needleman was the last one out and stayed behind to stand with Y.T., Sr. on the tarmac, watching as the fuel truck refilled the tanks with Jet-A. Frik and Frak went inside to check the weather and file a flight plan to Las Vegas.

A tall figure, dressed in a pinstripe suit, white shirt and red tie emerged from the fixed based operator and strode confidently towards the pair carrying a brief case.

"Mel, baby, glad you could join us," Arthur Needleman called out, reaching out his hand to shake.

"Excuse me, but it is Melvin W. Vapors, *Esquire,* to you, sir," replied the man as he stepped up and looked disdainfully down at the West Coast Sales Manager.

In the Black

"Wow." Arthur Needleman turned and said to Y.T., Sr., "Typical Harvard Law Asshole."

"Yeah, but he's my asshole," said Y.T., Sr.

"And, as your attorney, sir, I advise you to begin drinking heavily."

The three laughed and Y.T., Sr. listened as Arthur Needleman and Melvin Vapors shared tall tales from their college days in Boston.

Frik and Frak emerged from the fixed based operator. Frik motioned the men aboard and followed, seating himself in the left side pilot seat. Frak watched the fuel truck pull away and did a quick walk-around inspection of the aircraft. When he got back to the cabin door, he boarded and pulled it shut, then took his place beside Frik in the cockpit. Within ten minutes they were climbing out over the prairie west of the Missouri River to the final round of negotiations.

As the Erp Industries Learjet streaked west across Kansas, Y.T., Jr. and Marty Keegan rumbled east through the Badlands of South Dakota on State Highway 44 in a 1959 Ford F-100 pickup truck that they had gotten from the Hell's Angels in exchange for the keys to Y.T., Jr.'s Harley-Davidson. The two were now clean shaved and had their hair cut short, more like Marines than radical college students from Berkeley and Columbia. In the bed of the pickup was one of Clinton A. Owsley III's steamer trunks filled with cash and LSD that Y.T., Jr. remembered was parked at the Sacramento Greyhound Bus Terminal, the contents of which funded their fugitive lifestyle.

"But I haven't done anything wrong," said Y.T., Jr., who could not believe they were having the same conversation yet again.

"It doesn't matter," said Marty Keegan. "It just doesn't matter."

"Yeah, it does. It does matter. It matters to me."

"Don't you get it? You're a wanted man. You've got the F.B.I. coming after your ass now, like I do."

"You know, you never did say why they're after you. 'Cause of the Columbia take over thing?"

"I think that's how they ID'ed me—when I got arrested—but it's more because of Chicago and maybe the bomb in DC."

"Bomb? What bomb?"

"We blew up some shitters at the Pentagon, you know, for shits and giggles." Marty Keegan chuckled.

Y.T., Jr. did not. "And Chicago?"

"Well, I kind of assaulted a police officer."

"Kind of?"

"I don't know if he was the one that died or not."

"Died? Holy crap, you murdered a cop?"

"Yeah, I mean maybe. I don't know—I could have. It was crazy." Marty Keegan turned and looked out the passenger window.

Y.T., Jr. drove on in silence through hunting grounds that had long ago been wrested away from the Lakota Sioux by the United States government.

"I don't think you've got any other options, except to join in and fight," said Marty Keegan. "In their eyes, you're one of us now anyway and good luck getting the feds to change their minds about that."

"But I haven't done anything wrong."

"It just doesn't matter." Marty Keegan shook his head. "Except, I'll tell you this: I don't know about you, but I'm not going to let them put me in a cage like an animal. No way."

"What do you mean?" Y.T., Jr. looked over at his friend.

"It just doesn't matter anymore. It just doesn't matter."

In the Black

They paralleled Interstate 90 on the blue highways through South Dakota and Minnesota until they reached Madison. They found the rented house in the student slums of the Mansion Hill neighborhood, where members of the University of Wisconsin chapter of the Students for a Democratic Society sheltered and fed them, then sent them on their way east.

Penelope Xing walked to the Post Office on Stockton Street to check her box for mail. Inside, nestled amidst the junk mail, bills and magazines was a postcard from the Devil's Tower National Monument in Wyoming. She went across the street and found an empty, unshaded bench in Washington Square and sat, absorbing the warmth of a sunny June day and feeling the fragile and tenuous connection with Y.T., Jr. maintained courtesy of the United States Postal Service. The message was cryptic and nonsensical, as usual, to obscure his identity, but the greeting was the same as always—"Hi Twink,"—and so was the sign off—"Love, Dave & Harley."

Penelope Xing read the postcard over and over, gently rubbing her slightly bulging belly, grateful that Fu Loin let her stay and help manage the Emporium. It was an indulgence she readily accepted, but did not understand. They never spoke of it. She would not display the postcard on the wall behind the counter, like Fu Loin had done with the ones she had sent him when she traveled cross country with Murph to Washington, D.C. Instead, she would keep it hidden safely away with the others, as far as possible from prying and dangerous eyes.

Little did Penelope Xing know, though, that each and every postcard from Y.T., Jr. had been examined, photographed and cataloged by Special Agents Williams and Walters before it was ever even placed in her post office box. And though Y.T., Jr. was always careful to mail the souvenir cards at least two states away from where they were bought, he had forgotten about the postmark. As the F.B.I. watched through the lenses of their cameras and binoculars while Penelope Xing enjoyed a few moments bathed in the warmth of a summer day before she went back to work at Fu Loin's, the government knew that the father of her child was most recently in Madison, Wisconsin.

The television sets, inexplicably, just started showing up at the Old O'Reilly Candy Factory Building in mid June—ten brand new color TVs were delivered to Orley Bovine's loading dock each week, which he and the Sugarman delivered and set up throughout the building in every department and manufacturing unit, being careful to position the sets to maximize reception and minimize radio frequency and electro-magnetic interference from test equipment, machine tools, typewriters and copy machines. The object of much conjecture and some worry, the television screens stayed dark for weeks and weeks.

When the day came to turn them all on, Sunday, July Twentieth, Dirk Rangely paced his office rehearsing the fiery speech he had been working on all week—ever since Y.T., Sr. informed him he would have to be in charge for the mandatory Erp Industries company picnic scheduled for that day, which, as far as Dirk Rangely could see from the preparations during the week, was going to be more like a banquet or a wedding reception than a traditional picnic. And then, who in his right mind has a picnic in a factory? Be that as it may, though, he saw this opportunity as his big chance. He felt it. He knew it in his heart and he had repeatedly told the stuffed Siberian tiger head that this day would make or break his chances of becoming the "Old Man."

In the Black

Dirk Rangely checked his watch, then his pulse, then his watch again. The Old O'Reilly Candy Factory Building had been slowly filling with employees and their families since noon, most of whom begrudged the fact that they were forced to come to work on a Sunday afternoon. So Dirk Rangely, anticipating a hostile crowd, reflexively reached for the white-capped Tanqueray gin bottle in his desk drawer. He stopped himself—this was *too* important. This was *too* big. He collapsed into his desk chair with the burden of making history bearing down upon him.

He was supposed to start his speech at two o'clock, but waited to make his entrance six minutes late, as was his habit. He paused to primp and pump himself up at the door to his office, then confidently strode from the Marketing Department to the company cafeteria and bounded up onto the dais, where tables were set up for the executive management of Erp Industries, Inc. and overlooked the cafeteria now filled with employees and their families waiting for an explanation of exactly what the hell kind of company picnic this was going to be. He shook hands with P. Peckerfelt, Simon Salisbury and Rolf Guderian on his way to the speaker's podium in the center of the dais. Fellow executives stabbed him with the envy in their eyes, feeling he had somehow stolen from them this opportunity to stand in for Y.T., Sr. Dirk Rangely's palm felt so greasy after shaking with Rolf Guderian, he had to grab a napkin and wipe it off. As he did, he looked to his right and noticed the empty chairs where Y.T., Sr., Vasili Ivanovich and Arthur Needleman should have been sitting. He tamped his stack of index cards containing a speech he was certain would go down in history with the Gettysburg Address and the Pearl Harbor Declaration of War against the podium. He took a deep breath to ready himself before plunging into the oration he had been boring

Rudyard with all week long, but as he looked out over the sea of faces scowling in his direction, the occasion of this particular "picnic" and the reality of what it was all about sank in and made the self-aggrandizing words on the index cards suddenly meaningless.

"You know," Dirk Rangely began with uncharacteristic hesitancy, "Well, um, first let me thank you all for coming—"

"As if we had any damn choice," heckled Leon Debs from the back of the room.

Murmurs of ascent rippled the assemblage.

Dirk Rangely, tossed aside his index cards. He stood up ramrod straight and scanned the crowd left-to-right, then back again. For the first time in a long, long time spoke from his heart.

"We are here today to witness together the history that we as a company, as a team, as a group of regular folks out here in the middle of the country will have had a part in making. While you may know that in a little over an hour, two of our nation's astronauts will land on the moon, what you may not know is that they will be guided there by the hands of those of us in this room. The hands of people we know in engineering who calculated, invented and drafted. The hands of people we work beside at our desks who bought and paid for the parts that other hands of those we see here every day received, inspected and inventoried for the hands of those we pass by in the halls and out on the floor who would assemble those parts into something bigger and better. The hands of friends, acquaintances and, yes maybe rivals here, tested and retested those critical guidance systems, then other hands packaged them carefully and took them through the doors on the back of this building to load on trucks to be delivered, finally, ultimately, to the top of a rocket in Florida, so a man—mere flesh and bone just like you and me—on this very afternoon—could reach the moon."

The Erp Industries Inc. cafeteria was as silent as a cathedral.

"Please take your families to your desks, to your work benches, to your machine tools and show them where you work. At three o'clock we will turn on the televisions which you have no doubt been curious about and together we will watch history being made, *by your hand.*"

"Let us then break bread together. Miss McGurdy and her staff have been working extremely hard since terribly early this morning to prepare a sumptuous prime rib feast for us all. After dinner, you are welcome to leave or stay as you wish." Dirk Rangely paused to scan across the faces in the hushed audience. "But after dinner I would invite you to join me to watch a man set foot on the moon…*by your hand.*

"Thank you," Dirk Rangely said softly and sat down in his seat next to the podium.

The workers of Erp Industries, Inc., slowly filed out of cafeteria and quietly made their ways to their work areas. At three o'clock, the fifty-plus color televisions scattered throughout the Old O'Reilly Candy Factory Building were turned on. At ten after three, Walter Cronkite's voice echoed through the factory as he began to narrate the final fulfillment of President John F. Kennedy's challenge to the nation issued eight years before of "landing a man on the Moon and returning him safely to the Earth."

"Damn it. It's the radar. No-no-no. Switch the radar—" Vasili Ivanovich urged into his microphone as he interpreted the stream of data on the screen of his console in the Lunar Excursion Module support trailer at Cape Kennedy.

Beside him sat Y.T., Sr, and Arthur Needleman silently watching an unexpected twist in the dramatic events of a Sunday afternoon in July. Behind them sat Frik and Frak, watching the video feeds intently. The LEM support trailer was filled with consoles and the hushed, intense chatter of technicians and engineers monitoring telemetry feeds from two hundred thirty-eight thousand miles away and updating Gene Kranz's White Team on their assessments of system performance and mission success or failure.

"The twelve oh-one and twelve oh-two errors are okay," Vasili Ivanovich advised the chain of command at the Houston Mission Control Center. "It's okay. It is okay. No problem. No problem. Just task prioritizing."

The LEM descended from six thousand feet above the surface of the moon when guidance and navigation alarms went off distracting Neil Armstrong and Buzz Aldrin. Vasili Ivanovich repeatedly advised the guidance team that the situation was okay.

When he saw from the data on his console that Neil Armstrong had taken manual control of the LEM to avoid boulders strewn about the originally plotted landing site, Vasili Ivanovich looked up at the video monitor as the clinical dialog of two astronauts—sounding so damn much like Frik and Frak in the Learjet cockpit—floated dreamily through his consciousness.

"Contact light!" said Buzz Aldrin

"Shutdown," said Neil Armstrong.

"Okay, engine stop. ACA—out of detent."

"Out of detent. Auto"

"Mode control—both auto. Descent engine command override off. Engine arm—off. 413 is in."

"We copy you down, *Eagle,*" acknowledged CAPCOM from Houston.

In the Black

"Engine arm is off," Neil Armstrong confirmed to Buzz Aldrin. He then responded to CAPCOM, "Houston, Tranquility Base here. The *Eagle* has landed."

Vasili Ivanovich sat in stunned silence, staring at his console. They made it, he thought. Then before the full realization hit him, the crowded trailer erupted as technicians and engineers leaped up, cheering and hugging one another. Without realizing it, Vasili Ivanovich was on his feet cheering, too. To his right he saw Arthur Needleman and wrapped his arms around the man who had set this entire adventure in motion for him with a sales call they made on the Jet Propulsion Laboratory years and years ago and lifted him up off his feet. When their embrace broke, Vasili Ivanovich turned left and saw Y.T., Sr., still staring at the video monitor. He hesitated, then grabbed the man who had saved him from a life of quiet desperation in a Washington, D.C., radio repair shop after World War II in a bear hug.

"Spacibo, spacibo, spacibo," the Russian whispered into Y.T., Sr.'s ear.

The ex-Navy Commander smiled *That Smile!* hearing his former VF-51 squadron mate announce he had "caught the wire" on the surface of the moon. The ex-Colonel, who himself had made history in a B-29 over Nagasaki, teared up witnessing a fellow Air Force pilot make a very different—and a very much better kind of history in outer space.

For Erp Industries, Inc., the mission was only half over. The five men stayed at the console in the LEM support trailer the entire night, watching Neil Armstrong and Buzz Aldrin walk on the surface of the moon a few hours later, then, the next day monitoring their blast off from the surface of the moon to rejoin Command Module Pilot Michael Collins for the return trip to earth.

Once the LEM ascent stage was released to lunar orbit, Vasili Ivanovich, shut down his console and they finally left the Kennedy Space Center. Their celebration Monday night ended with driving their rental car out on the beach where Y.T., Sr., Vasili Ivanovich and Arthur Needleman toasted the success of Apollo 11 with vodka and howled at the moon—around which the Erp Industries, Inc. black boxes that Vasili Ivanovich had dreamed up and created continued to orbit.

Y.T., Sr. walked off alone down the deserted beach and tried to imagine the "magnificent desolation" Buzz Aldrin and Neil Armstrong had witnessed firsthand.

Far out to sea, lightning from passing storms arced across the horizon.

~~~

Woodstock Nation

That Sunday, every shop, every gas station, every fast food restaurant, every bar—every business open to the public seemed to have a television tuned to news coverage of the Apollo 11 moon landing. Y.T., Jr. and Marty Keegan watched Neil Armstrong set foot on the surface of the moon at a noisy Irish bar called Fagan's on the east bank of the Cuyahoga River in the Flats of Cleveland, Ohio. Y.T., Jr. knew what the event meant to his father, so while everyone else used it as an excuse to celebrate wildly and drink excessively, he told Marty Keegan he was going out for air and would be back in an hour or so.

Y.T., Jr. drove the Ford F-100 pickup truck down to the beach at nearby Edgewater Park, which they had passed on their way into town. As he sat in the sand, staring into the darkness, across Lake Erie towards Canada, a plan came to mind. He doubted that Marty Keegan would go along with it, but Y.T., Jr. did not care. It was a way out and he was going to take it. He went back to Fagan's and picked up Marty Keegan to go meet up with members of the Jesse James Gang at Kent State University, who put them up for the next few days. When they got back on the road, headed towards upstate New York, Y.T., Jr. decided not to share his plan.

Rebecca Sue Simmons attended the Erp Industries, Inc. company "picnic" alone. Barry Boswagger refused to come on principal—that principal being the five thousand dollars Travis

Marbling had paid him for services as yet unrendered. She was awestruck that the whole *rocket-Apollo-outer-space-moon-landing thing* she watched on the *CBS News Special Report* with everyone else in the Engineering Department was in any way connected to what went on in the building where she now worked. She had no idea that this was what Y.T., Jr.'s father did at his company. She stayed after dinner to watch Neil Armstrong and Buzz Aldrin walk on the moon, then celebrated with her co-workers, drinking from a glass of champagne that never seemed to be empty.

It was after midnight when Rebecca Sue Simmons piloted the canary yellow *Chevelle* station wagon back to Birdtown, followed by Billy Saul Sawyer. Since returning to Meadowlawns, he had been unable to locate Scarlett Angelina Brookings. He had observed Barry Boswagger staking out her Kirke Gardens apartment, though, and learned that Rebecca Sue Simmons had taken her job at Erp Industries, Inc., so he started following them, hoping they would lead him to the only person he thought could help him find Y.T., Jr.

He parked up the street and walked towards the bungalow as Rebecca Sue Simmons crookedly pulled the station wagon into the driveway and left it askew, thanks to all the champagne. Birdtown was unusually quiet without the scrap yard operating. Billy Saul Sawyer noticed that all windows on the bungalow glowed with light. Every jungle instinct that had kept him alive in Southeast Asia warned him of danger.

As Rebecca Sue Simmons fumbled with her keys at the front door, Barry Boswagger flung it open, pulled her inside by her hair and slammed the door shut.

Billy Saul Sawyer ran around the back of their house. He had already scouted the workshop in the garage and knew what the former Harry S. Truman *Fighting Eagles* quarterback was capable of doing and what weapons he had to do it. As the drunken marital quarrel rose in volume, the former Marine slipped into the kitchen through the unlocked back door. Unfortunately, loud domestic disturbances were an all too common occurrence in Birdtown, so the screaming voices, the crashing of furniture and the shattering of breakable decor items raised no alarm with neighbors. Billy Saul Sawyer grabbed a knife off the counter and pressed himself against the wall beside the doorway between the kitchen and the living room.

A gunshot went off in the living room and Rebecca Sue Simmons came stumbling frantically into the kitchen. She tripped and fell to the floor, then desperately clawed her way to shelter beneath the kitchen table.

Barry Boswagger appeared in the doorway and got only one more wildly drunken shot off, shattering an empty Jack Daniels bottle on the counter before Billy Saul Sawyer plunged the butcher knife into his chest. The former cutter looked in shock at the knife in his heart and recognized it as the kind he had used on the killing floor at the Cassidy Beef Packing plant. Billy Saul Sawyer held it in place and pulled Barry Boswagger's face nose-to-nose with his own, until he no longer felt breath from his victim's mouth and saw the dull glaze of death film over his eyes. He dropped the dead man to the floor to bleed out on the linoleum, a Smith and Wesson revolver still clenched in his hand.

The ex-cheerleader panted in panic on the floor beneath the kitchen table, until her breathing began to slow. She looked back at Billy Saul Sawyer standing over her dead husband.

At best, it was a fifty-fifty chance that, hearing gunshots, someone in Birdtown would think to call the police, but it was a risk Billy Saul Sawyer could not take.

She suddenly crawled through Barry Boswagger's blood to kneel in front of Billy Saul Sawyer and hug his legs tightly, burying her face in his thighs. All she could think was that, finally, someone had come to rescue her. Finally, he had come. And she was rescued. *Finally.*

Billy Saul Sawyer knelt down and took Rebecca Sue Simmons into his arms.

"Thank you…thank you," she wept over and over again.

He stroked her auburn hair gently.

"Thank you," she whispered.

"I have to go."

"No. No, you can't. You can't leave." She wrapped her arms around his neck and held him tightly.

"I will come back. I will. But for now I have to go."

She held him even tighter.

"If the police don't show up in ten minutes, call them yourself," Billy Saul Sawyer told her softly, still caressing her hair. "I was never here. You did this. You had to. He was going to kill you. The gun is still in his hand."

She nodded.

"I'll come back after."

"After what?"

"After they decide it was self-defense. Don't worry, they will. As long as that is what you tell them."

She nodded.

"Then I'll come back."

"Promise?"

"I do."

And she believed him

"But I have to go now."

"Go where?"

Billy Saul Sawyer thought for a moment, then answered, "Boston."

"Why"

"To make things right for a friend."

"Who?"

"Poncho."

"Who's that?"

"I'll explain when I come back."

"You will come back, won't you?"

"Yes. Yes, I will. I promise."

Rebecca Sue Simmons believed him and after he left, she did exactly what Billy Saul Sawyer said to do.

"I'm sorry, but Mr. Erp had to leave suddenly in the middle of the night," the hotel clerk at the front desk told Arthur Needleman and Vasili Ivanovich when they went to check out Tuesday morning.

"What? But how are we going to get home?" whined Vasili Ivanovich quietly, nursing a headache from the copious amounts of vodka consumed the night before. "He just left us? How are we going to get home?"

"Vasya, Vasya, Vasya." Arthur Needleman folded his arms on the counter and bent over to rest his throbbing forehead on his arms. He slowly shook his head.

"What?"

Arthur Needleman rolled his head and looked up sideways, "Seriously?"

"What?"

"Just two days ago, my friend, you put a man on the moon," Arthur Needleman said standing up straight and poking Vasili

Ivanovich in the chest for emphasis. "I think we can figure out how to get from here to Kansas City."

The Russian erupted in a spasm of laughter that brought tears to his eyes.

The laugh was infectious and Arthur Needleman began giggling hysterically.

"Excuse me, but would one of you be a Mr. Dahoogerzilla," asked the hotel clerk, butchering the pronunciation of the surname.

"Yes, yes. It is I," said Vasili Ivanovich, wiping the tears from his cheek. "It is I."

"Mr. Erp left this for you." The clerk handed him an envelope with a valet parking ticket inside.

"What's this?" asked Vasili Ivanovich.

"I don't know," Arthur Needleman just shrugged. "Why don't we go see."

As they waited at the curb, the parking valet returned with a brand new red Mercedes 280 SL *Roadster*. He gave another envelope to Vasili Ivanovich. Inside was a note from Y.T., Sr. that said, "In profound gratitude for a job well done."

"Well?" asked Arthur Needleman.

"I think we found our way home," said Vasili Ivanovich, smiling broadly as he anticipated the look on Rolf Guderian's face when he parked his brand new Mercedes Benz next to the ex-Luftwaffe Corporal's decade old Volkswagen *Beetle* in the Erp Industries, Inc. parking lot. "You drive. And, please, can we put the top down?"

"It's your car," said Arthur Needleman as he slid into the driver's seat. "We can do whatever you want."

"Yes, please."

"Powerful gasoline. A clean windshield," said Arthur Needleman as he put the convertible top down.

"And a shoe shine," Vasili Ivanovich finished with a smile.

They sped away from the hotel onto Florida Highway A1A, north towards home.

Anna Elise's call had come at two-fifteen Tuesday morning. Y.T., Sr. called Frik and Frak and by three AM they were en route to Kansas City. The Sugarman met him at the Wheeler Downtown airport in Anna Elise's Cadillac *El Dorado* and drove him directly to Hospital Hill where Scarlett Angelina Brookings was still in labor. Y.T., Sr., Anna Elise and the Sugarman sat together in the waiting room. Nothing was said, but they all privately recalled their terrible waits together years before at Bethesda Naval Hospital.

Late Tuesday night, Scarlett Angelina Brookings gave birth to a healthy baby girl. It was after midnight by the time Y.T., Sr. was able to visit with them in her room. When Scarlett Angelina Brookings fell asleep after the nurse took the baby back to the nursery, Y.T., Sr. had the Sugarman drive him to the Old O'Reilly Candy Factory Building. He had one last thing to do.

The Sugarman let them in through the employee entrance. They walked through the dark and quiet factory to the front and sat down in the "Big Office." Y.T., Sr. reached into his credenza and retrieved a bottle of Hennessy Cognac. He poured two glasses and handed one to the Sugarman.

They clinked their glasses together in a silent toast and drank.

"You've had a hell of a few days, son," said the Sugarman.

Y.T., Sr. nodded. "I am beat."

"I believe it. I believe it, sho' 'nough. How long has it been since you got a full night's sleep?"

"V-J Day…Maybe?"

"For real now."

"Friday? Saturday? Who knows. Time flies when you're having fun."

"You should go home, now, boy.""

"You know I have one last thing I have to get done." He looked around his office and sipped the cognac. "And I'm out of time."

"I can do it," said the Sugarman.

"I can't ask you to—"

"I can do it. And I will, sho' 'nough. End of discussion."

Y.T., Sr. refilled their glasses. They drank in silence.

"But—"

"Go," the Sugarman said cutting Y.T., Sr. off. He tossed him the keys to his mother's Cadillac. "Now."

"But how will you get—"

"Orley will bring me by with all the stuff in the morning. We'll be out of this joint before anybody knows."

Y.T., Sr. nodded. He stood up wearily.

"Congratulations, son."

Y.T., Sr. hugged the Sugarman and went home to sleep.

The Sugarman spent the rest of the night packing up the things in Y.T., Sr.'s office and moving all of the boxes to the loading dock. When Orley Bovine arrived at work Wednesday morning, he helped the Sugarman load everything into the bed of his pickup truck. They drove to Y.T.,Sr.'s house and moved all the boxes into the garage. Orley Bovine went back to work. The Sugarman drove Anna Elise's *El Dorado* to Hospital Hill.

Y.T., Sr. would never again be seen inside the Old O'Reilly Candy Factory Building.

Anna Elise was standing outside Scarlett Angelina Brookings's private hospital room, when Special Agents Williams and Walters got off the elevator and approached with a Missouri State Highway

Patrol Trooper following at their heels. She felt the hairs on the back of her neck bristle and her spine reflexively stiffen.

"May I help you," Anna Elise asked in her most polite, most kindly grandmother voice, as the two F.B.I. agents walked up to her.

"Please stand aside, ma'am," commanded the State Trooper, whose imposing stature, felt drill sergeant's hat, side arm and brusque, barking manner directed towards an elderly woman, quickly began drawing stares from patients, staff and visitors, like metal filings to a magnet.

The growing commotion on the maternity ward made Special Agents Williams and Walters quickly regret having brought the trooper. They whispered a request that he wait for them by the elevators.

"We need to speak with this patient, ma'am," said Special Agent Walters politely.

"But you can't go in there," said Anna Elise weakly.

"We are with the Federal Bureau of Investigation," said Special Agent Williams a bit more firmly, flipping the wallet with his badge and identification card in Anna Elise's face. "We are here on official business."

The noise level on the floor continued to rise as spectators began to gather to watch the confrontation.

"Official business?" Anna Elise echoed.

"Yes ma'am, official bus—"

"Pray tell what possible business could you have with my daughter-in-law and granddaughter?" she asked, knowing exactly why the two federal law enforcement officers were there and what they wanted.

Something in Anna Elise's firmer, sharper tone caught the two men off guard and they took a hesitant step back. Just as the two

Special Agents began to feel the cognitive dissonance blossom in their brains from the contradictions between their official field reports and the familial information just uttered by Anna Elise, the door to Scarlett Angelina Brookings's opened and Dr. Theodore McCleary, her obstetrician, came out, closing the door behind him. He stopped beside Anna Elise and immediately sensed the tension between her and the two imposing men confronting her.

"Are these men bothering you, Mrs. Erp?" he asked Anna Elise.

"Why, I am not sure." She gave Special Agents Walters and Williams the same calm, steely-eyed look she had once given Thurman Troyer in his Senate office. "Are you bothering me?"

The doctor looked down the hall at the deliberate lingering of bystanders. Beyond them, he saw the State Highway Patrol Trooper loitering by the elevator.

"Gentlemen," Dr. McCleary quietly addressed the two F.B.I. agents in his most authoritative medical expert manner, "I do not know what is going on here, but unless you have a warrant or a court order, I would strongly suggest that your presence here is unwelcome and that this is neither the time nor the place for whatever it is you have in mind."

The four stood in a silent stand-off in front of the door to Scarlett Angelina Brookings's room.

"We will just be leaving, then," said Special Agent Walters as the two men backed slowly away, knowing the breast pockets of their suit jackets held no written authorization from a court to enter the hospital room.

Anna Elise smiled.

"We did not mean to trouble you," said Special Agent Williams.

"Oh, I am sure you just don't know any better," Anna Elise said sweetly.

The two F.B.I. agents left, collecting the waiting State Trooper on their way out.

"Thank you so much, doctor," Anna Elise said. "How is she?"

"The girls are doing just fine," answered Dr. McCleary. "They should be able to go home by Friday."

"Thank you again."

Anna Elise watched the man who had delivered her granddaughter stop at the nurse's station to update Scarlett Angelina Brookings's chart. As he did, the Sugarman got off the elevator and came down the hall towards her.

"Homer, please stay here beside the door and do not let anyone in, except the nurses or the doctor," Anna Elise asked the Sugarman. "There is something I need to do, and I will explain when I get back—it will only take a few minutes."

The Sugarman nodded and stood by the door.

Anna Elise Erp went downstairs to a pay phone in the hospital's main lobby and made a collect phone call to Georgia.

As Melvin W. Vapors sat in his office at the Old O'Reilly Candy Factory Building for the very first time ever, he watched the *CBS News Special Report* coverage of the return of Apollo 11 with the door closed. That day, Thursday, July 24, 1969, at 11:51 AM Central Daylight Savings time, the *Columbia* Command Module Capsule splashed down in the Pacific Ocean near Hawaii. Once Neil Armstrong, Buzz Aldrin and Michael Collins were safely aboard the aircraft carrier *Hornet,* the final contractual contingency was satisfied and he sprang into action. In the waiting area outside his office sat two paralegals and an armed Brinks security guard with two push carts, one empty and one with mail trays filled with envelopes. In his own brief case were five large envelopes he guarded personally.

The lawyer, the two paralegals and the armed Brinks security guard began to move quickly through the building, as time was of the essence. They visited each department and gathered all of its employees together. The unusual activity caused panic and alarm at first, until word quickly spread that each envelope the paralegals handed out contained a five thousand dollar bonus check for each and every employee with a personal note of thanks from Y.T., Erp, Sr.

For some, though, the arrival of Melvin W. Vapors and his team at their office was cause for anxiety and fear. He ordered Hugh Betcha to turn over all the keys for the clandestine warehouses in Lee's Summit to the armed Brinks security guard. Simon Salisbury was ordered to turn over the correspondence files containing each and every memo he had written to himself, including any replies. Mort Mortenstein was ordered to turn over the personal journal he kept which documented the entire history and all the financial activities of the Car Pool. In the Marketing Department, Melvin W. Vapors asked Dirk Rangely to vacate his office for a few minutes. He led his secretary, Jo Ann, in and closed the door for a private conference, after which, she turned over all of the company confidential documents she collected right under Dirk Rangely's nose in the bottom file cabinet drawer to smuggle out of the building and sell to the highest bidders among Erp Industries, Inc., competitors. When, finally, they had visited all of the departments, distributed all of the bonus checks, and filled the Brinks security guard's cart with most of the items on Melvin W. Vapors's checklist, they made one last stop by the Sugarman's workshop to fill the now empty cart which had carried the bonus checks with the all of the To-Do lists, work records and journals, as well as the his complete collection of *Playboy* magazines, the janitor had kept there since being hired by the O'Reilly family in 1925.

Melvin W. Vapors escorted the Brinksman and the confiscated items to the loading dock, where they were placed in the back of an armored car. In the parking lot, P.I. Parmakianski's 1960 Dodge *Valiant* idled. Melvin W. Vapors went over to take the box of grimy notebooks he had filled over the years with his sparse, almost Hemingway-like narratives of the extramarital activities of Erp Industries, Inc. employees and to give the gangly, gawky private investigator a personal check from Y.T., Sr. for one hundred thousand dollars. Once that last box was loaded, the Brinks truck drove away, followed by the Dodge *Valiant*.

Melvin W. Vapors checked his watch. He would make it.

He dismissed the paralegals and went to the executive conference room, where P. Peckerfelt, Vasili Ivanovich, Orley Bovine, Arthur Needleman and the Sugarman gathered around the mahogany table.

"It will be done," Melvin Vapors announced.

He then passed out the five large envelopes he had been carrying with him containing the checks and stock option contracts that would make them all millionaires, just as Y.T., Sr. had promised on the Learjet coming home from Cape Kennedy in May.

At the close of business that day in Las Vegas, Nevada, the Hughes Tool Company took possession of Erp Industries, Inc.

When they got back to the Kansas City F.B.I. Field Office, embarrassed that an elderly grandmother had called their bluff and forced them to fold their hand, Special Agents Walters and Williams worked through the weekend pouring over their notes and their reports trying to figure out how in the world they had gotten things so wrong. The gambit of pressuring vulnerable family members to get information was usually foolproof—but, in this case, only if Y.T., Jr. was the father of the child. As they sat dejected in the conference room in the downtown federal building Monday morning, drowning in their own paperwork and fearing the Director's wrath at their chronically continuing failures, a Bureau secretary delivered an urgent teletype message that Y.T., Jr. and Marty Keegan had been positively identified on the campus of Kent State University. The agents quickly arranged for a charter flight to Cleveland, Ohio, and left Kansas City that afternoon.

As Special Agents Walters and Williams drove to the airport that Monday morning, Anna Elise and Y.T., Sr. sat outside on the back patio, drinking coffee and enjoying the view of her garden. After leaving the Sugarman at the Old O'Reilly Candy Factory Building early Thursday morning, Y.T., Sr. went home and slept for nearly the entire day. He sat up all night Thursday, until it was time Friday morning to go to Hospital Hill and bring home Scarlett Angelina Brookings and their child. Anna Elise let her son have a peaceful weekend, helping his new family settle into the house in Meadowlawns. As they drank their coffee Monday morning, she told Y.T., Sr. about the F.B.I. visit and her call to Senator Thurman Troyer. Afterward, Y.T., Sr. meditated on the cherry tree in the backyard. When the pot of coffee was empty, Y.T., Sr. called Frik and Frak to ready what was now his personal Learjet to go to Washington, D.C., where he would speak with those friends he had in the nation's capital that Rear Admiral Hemmings once asked about.

Y.T., Jr. and Marty Keegan rarely stayed more than three or four days at any one place before moving on to make sure they stayed ahead of their pursuers. By the time Special Agents Walters and Williams arrived in Kent, Ohio, the pair of fugitives had already continued on their journey east, first to State College, Pennsylvania, then north to the Finger Lakes region in upstate New York. While the F.B.I. searched in vain for them at colleges and universities in Buffalo, then Rochester, and then Syracuse, they hid out in a remote vacation cabin on Seneca Lake, which was owned by the father of one of Marty Keegan's fellow Columbia University radicals he had met during the occupation of Grayson Kirk's office.

As they waited, Y.T., Jr. finally shared his plan with Marty Keegan, whose stamina and will had noticeably weakened under the constant grind of being on the run. It was simple: that weekend a music concert was going to be held in the Catskill Mountains. From the posters plastered on all the college campuses they had visited traveling across the country, Y.T., Jr. knew many of his friends from San Francisco—Janis, Jimi, Jerry, Country Joe, Carlos, Jack, Marty and Grace—would be there. If they could just get to Woodstock and hook up with them, backstage security would keep them safe while they got connected with the right people who could help them get north across the border and safely into Canada, under the convenient cover of fifty thousand rock and roll fans leaving when the festival ended on Monday.

Marty Keegan wearily agreed and Friday morning they set out for Bethel, New York, unaware that the influx of far more music lovers than anyone—promoters, fans, musicians, city councilmen, the governor and the media—ever expected into the rural concert site created massive traffic jams, putting law enforcement all across New York state on heightened alert. Passing through Ithaca, a conscientious Tompkins County Sheriff's Deputy recognized the black Ford F-100 pickup truck mentioned in his morning briefing and immediately notified dispatch, who notified the F.B.I. office in Syracuse who notified Special Agents Walters and Williams who quickly organized a posse of federal agents who sped down Interstate 81, then east on State Route 206, while the two agents flew ahead in a Bell Helicopter *JetRanger* commandeered from the State Police.

Along all the routes to the Woodstock Music and Art Fair, word passed through every official and unofficial law enforcement channel to be on the lookout for Y.T., Jr. and Marty Keegan in the black Ford F-100 pickup truck.

The closer Y.T., Jr. and Marty Keegan got to the festival the heavier traffic became. Somewhere near Hancock, heading south on Route 97, an unmarked police car began following them, which Y.T., Jr. readily spotted from the years of towing two dedicated and determined F.B.I. agents around the Bay area. He expected them to pounce at any moment, but for miles and miles, the tail hung back and Y.T., Jr. realized that they were there just to keep tabs on them until the rest of the F.B.I. team could catch up. It was not long before the position reports from the unmarked police car reached the *JetRanger*, which immediately changed course to join the pursuit.

Traffic became thicker and thicker and the forward progress of the Ford F-100 pickup became slower and slower. The single unmarked car was joined by another and then in a few miles down the road a third. Soon a helicopter loitered overhead.

Coming into Callicoon, traffic slowed to a crawl. Frustrated, people were parking their cars on the side of the road and the growing number of pedestrians seemed to be making faster forward progress than the motor vehicles. A Highway Patrol checkpoint ahead tried to turn away traffic from Route 17B leading into Bethel.

"We're not going to make it," said Y.T., Jr. "You've got to get out."

"Get out? What do you mean?"

"They're behind us now and we're not going to make it to the festival."

"Who's behind us?"

"The cops. You've got to get out and get lost in the crowd."

"But what about you?"

"I haven't done anything wrong."

"I told you, it doesn't matter to—"

"I haven't murdered a cop. You have and that matters." Y.T., Jr. stared down his friend. "Look there's a checkpoint up ahead and the feds are behind us."

"But—"

"I'll pull into that gas station over there. You get out to go to the bathroom and leave out around back. Get into the crowd, hike, hitchhike, get a ride—whatever. Just get to the festival, find them and get to Canada."

"Are you sure?"

"Yeah, I'm sure. I didn't kill a cop. I didn't bomb the Pentagon. I'll be all right."

Marty Keegan slowly nodded.

"When I pull in, take the backpack with the rest of the acid and the money and get the hell away as fast as you can."

Marty Keegan peered out the windshield at the growing traffic jam ahead. "Thanks."

Y.T., Jr. turned down Olympia Circle and into the gas station in the small town. He pulled up to the pumps and got out to fill the tank.

Marty Keegan got out, grabbed the backpack out of the truck bed and headed towards the service station's restroom. He passed by the door and quickly slipped around behind the station. He ran down to the Delaware River and along its banks to get around the police checkpoint, then joined the stream of people heading towards Woodstock on foot down Highway 17B. When he looked back, the black pickup truck was surrounded by police cruisers. A helicopter landed in the street in front of the gas station. Three men got out and approached Y.T., Jr. who stood with his hands in the air. Two of the men handcuffed his friend and put him into the back of a New York State Highway Patrol cruiser. It was obvious from his expensive suit, his casual gait and his bossy demeanor that the third man, Travis Marbling, was a civilian.

Marty Keegan walked and walked and walked. As he got closer and closer and closer to Max Yasgur's dairy farm, more and more cars and vans sat abandoned on the side of the road and the line of pedestrians grew into streams, then rivers then a tidal wave that drained into a natural bowl which steadily filled with four hundred thousand people gathering together for "Three Days of Peace and Music." There were no ticket takers. There were no policemen. Once over the hill, he kept constantly on the move through the crowd, until the next day, Saturday afternoon, when he came across a small encampment near the stage which flew the flag that Y.T., Jr. had described to him with the emblem of an eyeball inside a triangle inside a circle—the flag of the *Triumvirate*. He hung back and watched the steady parade of people—some of them familiar and famous—come over from the stage to visit the tent, which was guarded by a large, loud and highly animated individual in ski goggles and a Day-Glo green jump suit, specially modified with aluminum foil, plastic wrap and a *Triumvirate* emblem patch over his heart—like a psychedelic strip club bouncer—then return to the huge platform flanked by monstrously tall sound towers where, just then, Carlos Santana was performing.

In the Black

During a lull in the foot traffic to and from the makeshift dispensary, Marty Keegan went over and introduced himself to the man in the Day-Glo green jump suit. Murph took him inside the tent to meet Clinton A. Owsley III. Marty Keegan explained to them what happened to Y.T., Jr. and what their plan had been. Monday morning, as Jimi Hendrix finished "The Star Spangled Banner" and launched into "Purple Haze," the three joined the Woodstock exodus and were never seen or heard from again.

Billy Saul Sawyer went to Boston, where he found Poncho's family and his fiancé. He met with Anna at a local coffee shop and explained to her what happened to the man she loved on that unnamed hill in South Vietnam near the Laotian border. He gave her Poncho's dog tags, which he had carried with him ever since he deserted the Marines. At least Poncho would no longer be M.I.A. to his loved ones.

In a carefully orchestrated legal process, through which Rebecca Sue Simmons was closely shepherded by her attorney, Melvin W. Vapors, the former Harry S. Truman High School cheerleader was absolved of any and all criminal liability in the death of her husband, Barry Boswagger. Afterwards, the lawyer handled the sale of the Birdtown bungalow and negotiated a severance package far more generous than normally would be expected for a mere secretary of the Hughes Tool Company.

Billy Saul Sawyer returned to Meadowlawns, as promised, and took Rebecca Sue Simmons to live with him in Langely, Virginia, for a year, after which they would be stationed somewhere overseas.

J. Edgar Hoover grew increasingly annoyed as John Mitchell prattled on over the phone with empty platitudes about "greater goods," "higher justices," and "legacies." The Attorney General really did not have to keep going on and on and on. The Director knew what the Oval Office expected him to do and, though it galled him to do so, he would do it.

He responded to the apparently never ending monologue with an irregular series of empty syllables: “Uh-huh.” “I see.” “Yes.” “Hmmm.” “Of course.”

He did not really care what any of these people had done for the nation; the arrest should have been a feather in the Director’s cap, not a black eye. But J. Edgar Hoover had not remained at the top of the heap for five decades by ignoring one of the most important bureaucratic rules of engagement necessary to assure survival: knowing which battles to fight. This one was not one of them. Then he saw his opening.

“Just to be clear, we are talking about the Erp boy, correct?” he asked the Attorney General of the United States.

He listened.

“And the West Wing?”

He listened again.

“I understand completely. The situation will be handled as you wish.” He listened again, then said, “Of course. Good-bye.”

The Director of the F.B.I. verbally instructed Clyde Tolson to verbally instruct the Executive Assistant Director of the Criminal Investigative Division to verbally instruct the Deputy Assistant Director to verbally instruct the Section Chief to verbally instruct the Special Agent in Charge of the San Francisco Division to verbally instruct Special Agents Walters and Williams to execute the Nixon Administration’s wishes, washing his hands of the affair in a way that would leave no breadcrumbs to track back to his office.

“Oh, and Clyde, please pull the tape of Mitchell’s call, catalog it and put it in the safe,” J. Edgar Hoover asked his assistant as he took the next file from the top of the stack in his in box. "And make an off-site copy."

Just in case hell did freeze over and future events defied the laws of gravity by rolling shit back uphill to his doorstep, J. Edgar Hoover, as always, would be prepared.

Y.T., Sr. stood alone next to Helen Troyer's grave. The sharp blue September sky was empty, except for the ghostly white waxing moon, around which the *Eagle* ascent stage continued to circle in a steadily decaying orbit, which would ultimately end with its crash into an unknown location on the lunar surface. Far up the hill behind him, a tall figure dressed in a three piece suit waited. He was flanked by two other men in suits. Behind them stood two Georgia State Highway Patrol Troopers.

The black Ford *Crown Victoria Police Interceptor* with government license plates made its way across the plantation, kicking up clouds of red dust from the dirt road cutting through the peanut fields, under a dozen watchful eyes.

Y.T., Sr. did not look up the hill until he heard the sound of the *Crown Vic* slide to a stop and the engine was turned off . Two car doors opened in quick succession, then slammed shut. He watched as the driver's side rear door was opened by the driver and a figure emerged from the back seat. The rear door was slammed shut. He was too far away to hear what was said.

"What's going on? Where are we?" asked Y.T., Jr., emerging into the sunshine from the back seat of the black *Crown Vic*. "And who are you?"

The tall man in the three piece suit came over to Y.T. Jr., whose wrists were handcuffed together in front of him. He leaned in and whispered into his ear, "As your attorney, I advise you to keep your mouth shut. Your father sent me. Do not—I repeat—*do not* say another word."

Melvin W. Vapors stepped back and turned to Special Agents Walters and Williams, who stood on each side of Y.T., Jr.

The two G-men stared hostilely back at the attorney. The irony of the presence of the Georgia State Highway Patrol Troopers was not lost on them.

"You have your instructions, correct?"

Special Agent Walters nodded once.

"Then, release him. *Now.*"

Special Agent Williams took a set of keys out of his coat pocket, stepped forward and took off Y.T., Jr.'s handcuffs.

"And?"

Special Agent Williams then went to the trunk of the *Crown Vic* and opened it. He took out five banker's boxes filled with F.B.I. files and stacked them on the ground in front of Melvin W. Vapors.

"It is all of them, correct?" the lawyer asked

The Special Agents nodded.

"Good."

One of the junior associates behind Melvin W. Vapors handed him three copies of a document he pulled out from his brief case.

Melvin W. Vapors set the documents on the roof of the *Police Interceptor.* He pointed to the bottom of the pages with a pen. "Sign here. In triplicate."

Special Agent Walters hesitated.

"You have your instructions, correct?"

J. Edgar Hoover's minion nodded.

"Then, sign. *Now.*"

Special Agent Walters took the pen, signed each of the documents and returned it to Melvin W. Vapors.

"Now, then, I believe our business here is concluded." The attorney handed the signed documents back to his junior associate, then stepped over, took his client by the arm and moved him away from the black *Crown Vic.* Together they watched the two F.B.I. Special Agents first take a long, lingering look at the five boxes filled with paper that represented the sum total of their efforts over the past four and a half years of their government service—so many late night stakeouts, so many miles traveled, so many reports filed—then get into their car and drive off in a cloud of red dust. As the junior associates loaded the five banker's boxes into the rental car and the Georgia State Troopers relaxed and lit up cigarettes, Melvin W. Vapors led Y.T., Jr. down the hill to where Y.T., Sr. had witnessed the release of his son from federal custody.

"Of course, I will have my guys go through the boxes to verify the contents," Melvin W. Vapors said to Y.T., Sr.

"Of course," Y.T., Sr. nodded. He reached out to shake hands with his attorney.

"I would imagine you two might have quite a bit to discuss, so we'll load up and be off."

"Thank you for everything. *Everything.*"

"It was a pleasure to have helped you, son," Melvin W. Vapors said to Y.T., Jr. "I look forward to meeting again under less stressful circumstances."

"Thank you," Y.T., Jr. said softly, shaking Melvin W. Vapors's hand.

As the attorney returned to the top of the hill to verify the loading of the banker's boxes and leave, Y.T., Sr. turned back towards the gravestone he had been standing next to.

Y.T., Jr. stepped over and read the inscription. "My mother?"

"Yes."

They stood in silence.

"What was she like?"

"Beautiful. Smart," Y.T., Sr. said softly, sadly. "Beautiful."

Silence.

"But what was she like?"

Y.T., Sr. gazed up at the moon and thought for a moment. "Do you want to know what she really loved?"

"Yes, please."

Y.T., Sr. touched the gravestone and silently said goodbye. "Come with me."

He led his son down the path from the Troyer family cemetery plot to the end of the sod runway where the Champion American *Citabria* was parked. A friend of the ex-Air Force Colonel had lent it to him for the day. He motioned Y.T., Jr. into the passenger seat.

"She loved to go flying together," said Y.T., Sr. "Her father, on the other hand, absolutely hated that she did."

"Did she—could she?"

"Yes. I taught her," said Y.T., Sr., smiling at the fleeting memories of the day Helen Troyer soloed at the Dead Mule International Airport on Chesapeake Bay. He noticed his son rubbing the wrists around which the steel restraints of government had so recently been locked.

Y.T., Jr. noticed and looked down at his wrists, too.

"Your mother always said she never felt freer."

Y.T., Sr. got into the pilot seat and started the engine. They took off and remained over the Troyer family cemetery plot, doing loops, rolls, hammerheads, split-Ss, and barrel rolls.

Father and son had never before flown together.

When Y.T., Sr. finished his aerobatics, he flew low across the peanut fields over to the large plantation manor, where Senator

In the Black

Thurman Troyer sat on his porch, first watching his grandson's release, which he had helped arrange, and then the private air show over his daughter's grave.

Y.T., Sr. slowed the plane and flew fifty feet off the ground across the front of the plantation house. He held the wings level as he flew in front of the man who had been his father-in-law for only a few days.

The Senator stood up and stepped to the edge of the porch.

Y.T., Sr. circled around the house again. When he passed the front porch for the last time, he deliberately dipped his wings in thanks, then flew to the Columbus, Georgia, airport to return the *Citabria* to its owner and rejoin Frik and Frak for the flight back to Kansas City on the Learjet with his son.

When Frik and Frak reached their assigned cruising altitude and engaged the autopilot, Y.T., Sr. unbuckled and got the bottle of Hennessey Cognac he had shared with the Sugarman the last time he ever sat at his desk in the Old O'Reilly Candy Factory Building. He poured two glasses and handed one to Y.T., Jr.

"It's good to see you, son," Y.T., Sr. said as they clinked glasses. "Your grandmother will be very happy to see you."

"Thank you," his son replied.

"For what?"

"Getting me out of jail."

"You're going to stay out, right?" Y.T., Sr. winked.

"Yeah. For sure."

They laughed and drank.

Y.T., Sr. took a business check out of his shirt pocket and passed it to his son. "I've been waiting to show you this."

"What the—Is this for real?"

"You bet. All forty million dollars' worth. And look at who signed the damn thing."

"Howard Hughes?"

"You know people sometimes think I'm crazy, but, I'll tell you what, that guy is just certifiably fucking nuts."

"But—You sold it? The company?" The son sat back in shock. "What are you going to do, now?"

"Ah, I don't know. Something will come up. It usually does." Y.T., Sr. took back the check. "I'm going to cash it when we get home. I just wanted you to see it, first."

"But—"

"You know, you left behind some unfinished business."

Y.T., Jr. looked over at his father. "What? Scarlett? No. No unfinished business there. She told me everything and it was over. A while ago."

"Everything?"

Y.T., Jr. looked at his father. "Yes, everything. Even about you."

"A real flaming asshole, that Cassidy cousin of mine is."

"But how can he just get away with —"

"You know, son, men are capable of such incredibly astounding achievements and at the same time such colossally ugly pettiness. We human beings are a messy lot to deal with—especially when you are trying to get something useful done."

They sat and drank in silence for a few moments.

"So, now what?" asked Y.T., Jr.

"Well, at some point you should meet your sister."

He had caught his son mid-sip and Y.T., Jr. coughed and gagged on a mouthful of cognac that went down the wrong pipe.

"Sister?" Y.T., Jr. asked hoarsely, clearing his throat.

"Yeah. Helena Ann."

"Wow."

"Yeah, I guess it will make for some interesting Thanksgiving Day dinners, huh?"

Frak stuck his head out the cockpit door and announced they were getting ready to descend and they would be on the ground in twenty minutes.

Parked at the fixed based operator, father and son deplaned and stood on the tarmac as the Learjet was being refueled.

"It's good to be home," said Y.T., Jr.

"Well, actually, you *do* have some unfinished business. Out west."

As Frak walked back to the plane from the fixed based operator, he said to Y.T., Jr., "We'll be ready to go in five minutes."

"And I have some banking to do," Y.T., Sr. said tapping the forty million dollar check in his pocket.

They stood a moment, then embraced.

"I love you, son."

"You, too, dad."

They stepped apart.

"Have a good flight."

Y.T., Sr. watched as his son boarded the plane and Frak closed the cabin door. His eyes followed the Learjet as it taxied out, then jumped off Runway 18. After it was swallowed up by sky, he went home to his new family.

It was just about the time that Y.T., Jr. was crossing the Continental Divide in the Rocky Mountains at over five hundred miles per hour nearly seven miles above the surface of the earth when a car bomb exploded beneath a Lincoln *Continental* at Jess and Jim's Steakhouse on East 135th Street in Kansas City, killing Wilson Cassidy and Travis Marbling, and sending shock waves through the agriculture and the institutional food service industries.

Local law enforcement called in the Bureau of Alcohol, Tobacco and Firearms and the F.B.I. to assist in the investigation, while the local media speculated wildly on motives ranging from a mob hit to infidelity vengeance to out of control competitive capitalism.

When the F.B.I. lab results came back, the bomber's signature was determined to be identical to an open case from 1967 involving the explosive destruction of portable johns outside the Pentagon. When the Special Agents in charge of the investigation in the Kansas City field office asked to get the files on that case, word came down from F.B.I. headquarters in Washington, D.C., that the materials being requested appeared to have been "misplaced." Everyone knew that nothing was ever really *inadvertently* "misplaced" in J. Edgar Hoover's organization, so the murder of Wilson Cassidy and Travis Marbling went unsolved, as it was not one of those battles worth fighting, and the Cassidy family tree withered and died.

Y.T., Jr. was met at the airport by Arthur Needleman, who wove and sped through the streets like a Formula One driver to San Francisco General Hospital in his cherished Porsche *Spyder,* but by the time they got there, Penelope Xing had already given birth and was back in her room.

"Whitey Two, Whitey Three. Whitey Two, Whitey Three," Fu Loin exclaimed excitedly, pointing to Y.T., Jr., then to the baby again and again, as happy as even a biological grandfather could be.

Y.T., Jr. rushed to Penelope Xing's side, kissed her, then held his son for the very first time.

~~~

Epilogue

"The earth belongs always to the living generation."
~Thomas Jefferson
September 6, 1789
Paris, France

"That's one small step for [a] man, one giant leap for mankind."
~ Neil Armstrong
July 20, 1969
Tranquility Base, Lunar Surface

"The end of a fucking era."
~Marty Keegan
August 6, 1965
Boot Hill, Meadowlawns, Missouri

November 14-24, 1969 — Apollo 12 landed a man on the moon and returned him safely to earth.

December 6, 1969 — Meridith Hunter was stabbed to death by Hell's Angel Alan Passaro at "Woodstock West" — The Altamont Speedway Free Concert during the performance by the Rolling Stones.

1970 — Max Yasgur refused to rent out his farm for a revival of the Woodstock festival, saying, "As far as I know, I'm going back to running a dairy farm."

January 21, 1970 — Timothy Leary was sentenced to 20 years in prison for possession of marijuana.

February 18, 1970 — The Chicago Seven — Abbie Hoffman, Jerry Rubin, David Dellinger, Tom Hayden, Rennie Davis, John Froines, and Lee Weiner — were acquitted of conspiring to incite riots at the 1968 Democratic National Convention in Chicago.

March 6, 1970 — Weather Underground members Diana Oughton, Terry Robbins and Ted Gold were killed in an explosion in a Greenwich Village safe house when the nail bomb being constructed prematurely detonated for unknown reasons.

March 7, 1970 — Columbia University SDS Leader Mark Rudd went "underground."

March 17, 1970 — The United States Army charged 14 officers with suppressing information related to the My Lai Massacre.

April 11-17, 1970 — The Apollo 13 mission to land a man on the moon and return him safely to earth was aborted when, en route to the Moon, approximately 200,000 miles from Earth, the number two liquid oxygen tank in the Service Module exploded.

May 1, 1970 — United States armed forces invaded Cambodia.

May 4, 1970 — Four students were shot dead by Ohio National Guard Troops on the Kent State University Campus.

May 21, 1970 — Bernardine Dohrn read a "Declaration of War" by the Weather Underground against the United States government.

June 9, 1970 — Weather Underground member Bill Ayers participated in the bombing of the New York City Police headquarters.

June 15, 1970 — Charlie Manson went on trial for the murders of Sharon Tate, Steven Parent, Abigail Folger, Wojciech Frykowski, Jay Sebring, and Leno and Rosemary LaBianca.

September 18, 1970 — Jimi Hendrix died.

October 4, 1970 — Janis Joplin died.

November 3, 1970 — Ronald Reagan was reelected Governor of California; Jimmy Carter was elected Governor of Georgia.

December 31, 1970 — Paul McCartney filed suit for the dissolution of the Beatles' contractual partnership.

During 1970 — 448 colleges and universities were either closed or on strike.

January 31- February 9, 1971 — Apollo 14 landed a man on the moon and returned him safely to earth.

March 1, 1971 — Weather Underground member Bill Ayers participated in the bombing of The United States Capitol.

April 19, 1971 — Charlie Manson was sentenced to death on all counts.

July 3, 1971 — Jim Morrison died.

July 26-August 7, 1971 — Apollo 15 landed a man on the moon and returned him safely to earth.

August 2, 1971 — Tex Watson went on trial for the murders of Sharon Tate, Steven Parent, Abigail Folger, Wojciech Frykowski, Jay Sebring, and Leno and Rosemary LaBianca.

October 12, 1971 — Tex Watson was sentenced to death on seven counts of first degree murder.

1972 — Howard Hughes sold the Hughes Tool Company.

April 16-27, 1972 — Apollo 16 landed a man on the moon and returned him safely to earth.

May 2, 1972 — J. Edgar Hoover died. He was Director of the Federal Bureau of Investigation and its predecessor, the Bureau of Investigation, for 48 years.

May 19, 1972 — Weather Underground member Bill Ayers participated in the bombing of The Pentagon.

In the Black

June 17, 1972 — Five men were arrested breaking into the Democratic National Committee Headquarters at the Watergate office complex.

November 7, 1972 — Richard Nixon was re-elected President of the United States of America.

December 7-19, 1972 — Apollo 17 landed a man on the moon and returned him safely to earth. To date, Gene Cernan and Harrison Schmidt are the last men to walk on the surface of the moon.

January 30, 1973 — Former F.B.I. agent and general counsel to the Committee for the Re-Election of the President, G. Gordon Liddy, began serving a twenty year sentence in prison after his conviction for conspiracy, burglary, and illegal wiretapping in connection with the Watergate break-in.

February 9, 1973 — Max Yasgur died.

August 9, 1974 — President Richard Nixon resigned.

April 30, 1975 — In the early morning hours, the last Marines evacuated the United States embassy by helicopter, as Vietnamese People's Army troops entered the city of Saigon.

September 5, 1975 — Lynette "Squeaky" Fromme attempted to assassinate President Gerald Ford.

April 5, 1976 — Howard Hughes died.

November 2, 1976 — Jimmy Carter was elected President of the United States.

June 16, 1977 — Wernher Von Braun, the "Father of Rocket Science" and Director of NASA's Marshall Space Flight Center, which developed the Saturn V rocket used for all the Apollo missions to the moon, died.

September 7, 1977 — G. Gordon Liddy was released from prison after President Jimmy Carter commuted his sentence to eight years.

November 7, 1978 — Bill Clinton, former intern for Senator William Fulbright, was elected Governor of Arkansas.

November 4, 1980 — Ronald Reagan was elected President of the United States.

November 3, 1992 — Bill Clinton was elected President of the United States.

1995 — Weather Underground members Bill Ayers and Bernardine Dohrn host a coffee in their Chicago 4th Ward Kenwood townhouse to launch the political career of Barack Obama.

August 9, 1995 — Jerry Garcia died.

May 31, 1996 — Timothy Leary died.

February 12, 1999 — The United States Senate acquitted President Bill Clinton of impeachment charges for perjury and obstruction of justice, stemming from the Monica Lewinsky scandal and the Paula Jones lawsuit.

November 10, 2001 — Ken Kesey died.

November 4, 2008 — Barack Obama was elected President of the United States of America.

January 5, 2012 — My father died.

August 25, 2012 — Neil Armstrong, the first man to step on the moon's surface, died. My father would have been 81 that day.

*****~~~***

Character List

Y.T. Erp, Sr. — Harvard Graduate; ex-Navy Officer and Naval Aviator; Founder, Owner and President of Erp Industries, Inc. in Meadowlawns, Missouri, a Suburb of Kansas City

Y.T. Erp, Jr. — Part Time/Seasonal Employee at Erp Industries, Inc., and heir apparent to the "Big Office"; Graduate of Harry S. Truman High School; Full Time Student at the University of California at Berkeley; Founding Member of the *Triumvirate*

Anna Elise Erp — Daughter of Wiley Cassidy; Mother of Y.T. Erp, Sr.; Estranged Heir to the Cassidy Beef Packing Empire

Wilson Cassidy — Nephew of Anna Elise Erp; President & CEO of the Cassidy Beef Packing Company

Hector Troyer — Son of Thurmon Troyer; Chief of Staff for his Father's Senate Office

Helen Troyer — Daughter of Thurmon Troyer; Wife of Y.T. Erp, Sr.; Mother of Y.T. Erp, Jr.

Jefferson Davis Troyer — Father of Thurmon Troyer; Georgia Peanut Farmer; Unsuccessful candidate for Governor of Georgia

Thurmon Troyer — Father of Helen Troyer; U.S. Senator from Georgia

~~~

Neil Armstrong — ex-Navy Commander and Naval Aviator; Civilian Test Pilot; NASA Astronaut; Commander of Apollo 11; First Man to Walk on the Moon

Hugh Betcha — Vice President/Materiel, Erp Industries, Inc.

Bill — Student at the University of Michigan; Member of the Students for a Democratic Society; Weather Underground founder; Boyfriend of Diana

Barry Boswagger — Harry S. Truman High School *Fighting Eagles* Quarterback; Deliveryman for Cassidy Beef Packing Company; Husband of Rebecca Sue Simmons

Orley Bovine — Shipping Supervisor at Erp Industries, Inc.; Self-employed Distributor for Independent Moonshine Distillers

Scarlett Angelina Brookings — Secretary to Vasili Ivanovich Dzhugashili at Erp Industries, Inc.

William Jefferson Clinton — Governor of Arkansas; Forty-Second President of the United States of America

Horace Cooley — Supervisor/Drafting Department, Erp Industries, Inc.

In the Black

Leon Debs — Former Middleweight Boxer (0-32-2); Warehouse Supervisor, Erp Industries, Inc.

Diana — Student at Bryn Mawr College; Member of the Students for a Democratic Society; Weather Underground Member; Girlfriend of Bill

Doug — Warehouseman at Erp Industries, Inc.; Immigrant from Czechoslovakia

Vasili Ivanovich Dzhugashili — ex-Soviet Army Private; Vice-President/Research & Development, Erp Industries, Inc.; Officially, the First Employee Hired by Y.T., Sr.

Herman Eichmanhoff — Engineering Program Manager, Erp Industries, Inc.

Dahlia Feathers — Torch singer in Washington, D.C.; Mistress of Senator Thurman Troyer

Norman Fellows — Student at the University of California at Berkeley; Roommate of Y.T., Jr.

Frak — ex-Navy Commander and Naval Aviator; Erp Industries Corporate Pilot & Learjet First Officer

Frik — Retired Air Force Colonel; Co-pilot of the B-29 *Bockscar,* which dropped the plutonium bomb on Nagasaki; Erp Industries Corporate Pilot & Learjet Captain

Nelson Fullman — Student at the University of California at Berkeley; Roommate of Y.T., Jr.

Rolf Guderian — ex-Luftwaffe Corporal; Chief Engineer, Erp Industries, Inc.; Second Employee Hired by Y.T., Sr.

Admiral Hemmings (Ret.) — Former head of the Navy Bureau of Aeronautics; Y.T., Sr.'s Commanding Officer During World War II

Rear Admiral Hemmings — Former P.T. Boat Skipper; Son of Admiral Hemmings

Adolf Himmlerlicht — Engineering Program Manager, Erp Industries, Inc.

J. Edgar Hoover — Director of the Federal Bureau of Investigation

Ike — Warehouseman at Erp Industries, Inc.; Immigrant from Czechoslovakia

Jo Ann — Secretary to Dirk Rangely at Erp Industries, Inc.

Marty Keegan — Harry S. Truman High School Graduate; Columbia University Student; Member of the Students for a Democratic Society and Weather Underground; Friend of Y.T., Jr.

Fu Loin — Former Buddist Monk; Proprietor of Fu Loin's Curio Emporium in San Francisco

Travis Marbling — Assistant to Wilson Cassidy at the Cassidy Beef Packing Company

Mark — English Major at Columbia University; President of Columbia Chapter of the Students for a Democratic Society; Leader of the Revolutionary Youth Movement; Weather Underground Founder

Katherine "Cissy" McClean — Washington, D.C. Socialite during World War II

Arlotta McGurdy — Food Service Manager at the Erp Industries, Inc., Cafeteria

Homer McKinnley Morganfield ("The Sugarman") — ex-Army Air Corps Sergeant; Tenor Saxophonist; Maintenance Man at Erp Industries, Inc.

Mort Mortenstein — Vice-President/Accounting, Erp Industries, Inc.

Murph — Red Dog Ranch Leader; Founding Member of the *Triumvirate;* Bus Driver; Friend and Roommate of Y.T., Jr.

Arthur Needleman — M.I.T. Graduate; West Coast Regional Sales Manager for Erp Industries, Inc.

Clinton A. Owsley III — Chemistry Major at University of California at Berkeley; Founding Member of the *Triumvirate;* Friend and Roommate of Y.T., Jr.

Julius Parmakianski — Private Investigator

P. Peckerfelt — Vice President/Manufacturing, Erp Industries, Inc.

Dirk Rangly — Vice-President/Marketing, Erp Industries, Inc.

Simon Salisbury — Vice-President/Personnel, Erp Industries, Inc.

Billy Saul Sawyer — Harry S. Truman High School Graduate; U.S. Marine; Friend of Y.T., Erp, Jr.

Rebecca Sue Simmons — Head Cheerleader at Harry S. Truman High School; Wife of Barry Boswagger

Prunella Spoons — Assembly Line Worker at Erp Industries, Inc.

Wanda W. Willet — Former School Teacher; Secretary to Y.T. Erp, Sr. at Erp Industries, Inc.

Special Agents Williams & Walters — Field Agents of the Federal Bureau of Investigation assigned to the *Triumverate Case*

Melvin Vapors — Harvard Law School Graduate; Friend of Arthur Needleman; Attorney for Y.T., Sr.

Penelope Xing — Employee of Fu Loin's Curio Emporium; History Major at San Francisco State University

~~~

About M.T. Bass

M.T. Bass escaped the Sixties with just a flesh wound and survived a career as a splotch of grease (not even a cog, a nut or a screw) in the Military-Industrial Complex. He lives, writes, flics and plays music in Mudcat Falls, USA.

www.MTBass.net

Coming Soon

Anchorage, 1976 — Albert and Waxy flunk their Intro to Philosophy midterm and decide to drop out of OSU and go to Alaska to "strike it rich" working on the Trans Alaska Pipeline. After Albert's father cuts off his credit card they get bartending & dishwashing jobs at an Anchorage bar, where Albert becomes involved with the bar owner's girlfriend, CiCi, who is also the lead singer in the house band. Albert "acquires" a union card to get a pipeline job for himself, but then learns that Waxy has gotten involved in an unlikely scheme to find and recover a government payroll from an Air Force cargo plane that crashed in the Alaska Mountain Range decades ago.

Available in eBook

Cleveland, 1977 — Grappling with a foreign policy crisis, the U.S. Government targets a hapless rock-'n'-roller as a Russian spy in a classic case of mistaken identity for an innocent, 'Wrong Man' hero…or *is he?* Think of an unholy fictional union between the Rolling Stones and Alfred Hitchcock's *North by Northwest.* Unlike any novel you have ever read, this one has a soundtrack. After all, a story whose characters are musicians should have…well…*music.* Right?

www.MTBass.net

Available in Paperback & eBook

Hollywood, 1950 — Former P-51 fighter pilot A. Gavin Byrd is on location for a movie shoot, when he gets a call from the police that his older brother, a prominent Beverly Hills plastic surgeon, has been found dead on his boat. The Lieutenant in charge of the investigation is ready to close the case as a suicide from the start, but "Hawk" doesn't buy it and decides to find out what really happened for himself.

With help from a former starlet ex-girl friend, a friendly police sergeant whose life was saved in the war by his brother and a nosy Los Angeles Times reporter, Hawk's search for the truth takes him through cross-fire, dog fights and mine fields in Hollywood, Beverly Hills, Burbank and Las Vegas, and leads him into some of the darker corners of his brother's patient files and private life that he never knew existed.

www.MTBass.net

Thank you for reading my story.

CPSIA information can be obtained
at www.ICGtesting.com
Printed in the USA
FFOW03n1225280915
17256FF